For Dara, Callan and Jonah.

"We don't fight because we hate the ones in front of us,

We fight because we love the ones behind us."

Prologue

Frustration drove the warrior on. Fatigue disappeared as rage fuelled his muscles. He ran, not caring what was behind him. Hours seemed to pass although there were no landmarks by which to judge his progress. The horizon still offered no sign of yielding a destination.

Slowing to a stop, he took one deep breath and raged against his frustration. His roar did not echo. Close to despair he sought the answers to questions that should so readily be available.

Where am I? What am I doing here?

The void did not answer.

Scanning the bleak landscape he could discern no obvious mark. There were no mountains to disrupt the horizon, no clouds in the sky and no sign of life. No noise, no wind. It was neither hot nor cold. The barren, grey land was devoid of character. Only the track along which he had been travelling showed any sign that another might have passed here before him yet the only footprints were his own.

He breathed easily. The exertion of the running, that had not winded him, had drained him. He had the unworldly sensation of being in a dream the like of which he had not experienced before. Bending to one knee he picked up some of the gravely dirt and rubbed it between his fingers. It was all very real. Focusing on his strong, callused hands he wondered again who he was.

No memories rushed to fill his mind.

He could not recall coming to such a place or what might have possessed him to come here. It was unsettling. With nowhere to go, but feeling the need to make haste, he began to walk slowly along the path again, his eyes roaming the land for any sign that might give him direction.

The sense of futility at even continuing to walk was a feeling he knew he accustomed to.

Giving up so easily? A rich voice enquired.

Dropping to a crouch the warrior looked around him but could make out no one that might have uttered the words. No movement betrayed the location of the voice.

Remaining in his relaxed crouch he slowly circled and still could detect no vantage point from which someone might remain hidden. Though he felt no fear, his mind raced, seeking to gain advantage.

'Who are you?' he asked.

That is not important yet but you may consider me a friend, came the reply.

The melodic voice seemed to come from everywhere and nowhere at once. It was important to retain some sort of control. He resisted the urge to spin in meaningless circles.

'If you were a friend you would not be afraid to show yourself,' warrior said, standing straight, although his body was tense and ready. He knew he was able, and ready, to fight but could not recall how he had gained this ability.

I have no fear of you but I will show myself if that would make you feel better, the voice reassured, close this time.

The warrior spun to see a tall, well-tailored man with flowing dark hair and long charcoal robes. The stranger stood with his hands clasped behind his broad back. There was no weapon in sight yet warrior was aware of his own lack of armament.

I have no need of a weapon.

'No?' warrior asked, as he sized up the newcomer. The athletic build and stance gave the impression of shocking speed and power. The dark man moved with grace and balance as he walked towards the warrior, always in a position of readiness, his eyes locked on the man before him.

The warrior had summed this faster than words could describe the scene.

You are not very welcoming, my friend, the dark man observed. *It does not do to appraise the ability of one's allies to fight.*

'We are not allies, stranger, nor are we acquainted,' the warrior replied.

We are all too well acquainted, warrior, I think….

'I think not.' The warrior finished the conversation abruptly and glared at the stranger.

Come now. You are not being very friendly. I merely wish to help. Help you have need of I think.

'What do you know of my needs?' the warrior asked.

It is my … gift. I understand the needs of men and sometimes I am able to help them with those needs.

'I have no need of your help,' the warrior replied.

Ha! Really? You do not know who you are nor where you are. You have no idea how you got here or where you are going. You are lost in more ways than you can imagine but you have no need of my help?

'I will survive,' the warrior replied coolly.

Yes, I suppose you would, the stranger eyed him thoughtfully. *That is partly why I am here. Join me for a drink, warrior. Rest for a while.*

'I have no need for either, stranger. State your business and let me be about mine.'

Truly this is not how I intended for this meeting to go, warrior. The stranger sighed and gestured behind the warrior who turned to see a simple table with sliced meats, breads, and a jug of water. *If not amicable I had expected us to at least be courteous.*

'It is easy when you hold all the cards,' warrior observed, coldly.

Perhaps, the stranger smiled, his eyes glistening with dark humour. *Eat.*

The warrior's mouth grew moist at the sight of the food before him. He could feel no hunger nor thirst but a small memory reminded him that a warrior must always make the most of an opportunity to re-supply.

Now, we can be civil at least. The stranger suggested as the warrior sat cross-legged, heaping the meat and water into his mouth. He did not miss the insignificant amounts that the warrior secreted about his person and smiled at the sight. Truly, this was the sort of man he was looking for. *The food is satisfactory?*

'Where am I?' the warrior asked not acknowledging the question. 'How is it that you know me?'

Straight to business, warrior? So distrustful of me still, yet you gorge on the food I have freely provided? The stranger asked.

The warrior looked at him for a moment then swallowed a mouthful of bread before speaking.

'Any man that has the power to make a table of food appear amid this…nothingness is to be treated warily. I think that if you chose to, you would find easier ways to kill me than to go to the trouble of creating this meal merely to poison me.

Perhaps, but do not be too complacent, warrior.

'Nor you stranger,' the warrior chided. 'I notice the meat and bread were sliced already. With all your power are you so afraid to give me a knife?'

The stranger smiled. This could well be the man he sought. His perception of his surroundings pertaining to his own survival was staggering. The stranger had not even considered what the absence of the knife might signify.

No, warrior, he said, *still smiling. I do not fear you at all.*

Mist swirled around the table as though fashioned by a breeze the warrior could not feel. It cleared quickly to leave a real enough looking broadsword.

You may arm yourself as you see fit, warrior.

'Who are you?' the warrior asked, ignoring the blade.

Just a friend.

'I will ask you one more time, stranger, who are you?' authority resonated in the warrior's voice.

I am many things to many people, he said simply.

The warrior looked hard at the stranger before rising and beginning to walk along the path again. The stranger stood with his mouth open, then smiled. It was not often that he was surprised these days. He enjoyed the sensation.

Where are you going? He demanded. *Stop!*

The warrior did not hesitate and kept walking. The stranger laughed.

Very well. You win. I will answer your questions as best I can. In return you will hear me out.

'Who are you?' he stopped but did not turn round.

I am a warrior, the stranger replied, *like you.*

'Not like me. Not like any I have seen before,' the warrior replied walking back to the table and looking again at the only company he could ever remember having.

It is a strange kind of war, the stranger admitted, shrugging.

'I asked who you were, not what you were,' he challenged.

I have many names, not all of them known to you. Who I am is not as important as what I am. A warrior.

'What sort of a war are you fighting?'

It is the war between good and evil. A war that has gone on for eternity.

'And on whose side do you fight, stranger?'

The right side.

'State your business and be on your way then,' the warrior said. 'A warrior of the light would not need to veil his answers with deceit and trickery, therefore you are of the dark and an enemy of mine.'

Well spoken. As I would expect of a fellow warrior.

'I am nothing like you. What manner of creature fights for the dark Lord? Are you a daemon?' the warrior demanded.

With a capital D, he said with a curt bow.

'Are you trying to be funny…Daemon?' the warrior asked, his temper growing.

No. These situations are never funny. They are ludicrous, and I get carried away with the moment. I am merely here to see you.

'Do you know me?'

In a way. I know who you were and I have an inkling of who you will become, the stranger sat back on a large grey rock that seemed to have impossibly been there all along.

'Who am I?' The warrior asked.

You are a warrior.

'What is my name?' He sought some small detail, some truth to hold to so that he might recover the rest of his memories.

What is in a name? A rose by any other and all that, Daemon folded his arms, the thick, corded muscles tightening.

'Do not seek to fill me with riddles, Daemon.'

I do not, warrior. I said I would answer you as best I could, but even I am bound by rules. It serves no purpose for you to know the name of your past life. Not yet anyway.

'Where am I?' he asked, once more surveying the landscape and knowing that it did not belong. "Past life" did not sound too damn healthy.

Would that I could explain, my friend. I am afraid you will just have to accept that for a time you are not in your own world.

'Indulge me, Daemon,' the warrior replied, his pale eyes bristling with anger.

Some things are beyond the comprehension of mortal man.

'Then this is going to be a difficult conversation, Daemon, for I will tolerate no patronising egotistical man, daemon or other.'

Everything is not as it seems and while it does me good to see pride driving you, it is getting in the way. Do you think I look like this? This face, these clothes, this entire landscape and journey are things that you have created from your subconscious.

The warrior did not move again nor challenge the statement so Daemon continued.

Do you think that a peasant from the lands to the east who has never seen a round eye would perceive this journey to the afterlife in such a manner?

'I am dead then?' the warrior asked. The answer did not seem to bother him.

Yes, you are dead. This is your journey, your individual atonement for your deeds in life.

'Do I need to atone?' The warrior could recall nothing.

You do. None pass here who do not. Those that do not wish to or cannot atone, pass into the realm of the dark Lord. Life attracts like.

'This is purgatory?'

Purgatory, limbo, the void. It has many names. You will eventually reach the end of this road and enter whichever realm you serve.

'I serve the light.'

How do you know? Daemon asked. *You cannot remember a damn thing.*

'I know that I am a warrior,' he replied.

It suits me to allow you that part of your memory.

The warrior thought on what the daemon had said but could discern neither honesty nor deceit on his face. 'What would you have of me, daemon?' he demanded.

I have a task to set you, my brave friend.

'I will not serve the dark. I will not become one of you,' the warrior said flatly.

You speak of things you do not understand. What do you think to know about God and the Devil?

'I know that I did not serve the Dark in my life and that I will not serve it in my death.' The warrior's tone was hard.

You cannot even begin to understand the conflict of Good and Evil. I offer you another way to atone other than this wilderness.

'I do not pretend to understand. I will not serve the dark.'

I cannot make you do anything you do not wish to do. All I offer is free will. I will give you back your life; in return I want you to return the favour.

'I will make no deal.'

No deal then. I must ask though. It is my job…so to speak.

'And your job. Warrior of the Dark Lord?'

Emissary, ambassador, messenger, warrior, assassin. I am all these things.

'If I choose to listen to your request, you will return me to life, whether I agree to perform your task or not?' the warrior asked.

I will return you to life.

'What is your task?' The warrior accepted the terms confident that if the daemon changed them, as he surely must, then the warrior would still pursue his own agenda. What could the daemon do? Kill him again?

I want you to save a life, Daemon smiled. *That is all.*

'Whose life?'

That is not important, warrior. All you must do is fight. That is what you are good at anyway, isn't it?

'It is, Daemon, and you would do well to remember that should you consider any action against me,' the warrior said as agony began to rack his body, making him cry out. 'What are you doing?'

That is the pain of your life, warrior. Your body summons you. You will live but the recovery will be a trying one.

'What is my name?' the warrior asked desperately as his vision blurred and pain seared across his skin.

You will be named in your new life.

The daemon motioned with his hand as though lazily granting a wish. The warrior vanished from the grey land.

Genesis

Chapter One

Lauren raced as fast as her five year old legs could carry her. Branches and twigs stung her cheeks and scraped her arms as she plummeted blindly through the brush, the thick undergrowth threatening to break her fragile ankle.

Little sandaled feet crashed through the brambles and her clothing was torn as her small leg muscles pumped frantically. Her dagger was clutched tightly in her right fist.

Feinting left, Lauren jumped to the right and came up behind a tree facing the direction she had come, one hand on the tree the other pointing the dagger. She had to relax her grip slightly and it took all her control to do so. Too tight and she would not be able to manoeuvre it in a fight. The whiteness eased from her knuckles as blood flowed again. Taking a deep breath she listened for pursuit and her eyes strained against the shadows thrown by the strong sunlight.

Nothing.

Perhaps it was just stealthy.

She could hear her own heart pounding in her ears.

Lauren took a deep gulp of air and launched herself once more into the forest.

Mama would be annoyed with her for tearing her clothes but surely she would understand when she explained about the monster. Racing by instinct alone, Lauren flew through the trees towards the spot where Papa was waiting. Big, strong, invincible Papa. Sworn to protect her.

He would kill the monster with his mighty axe, just like in the stories he cooed her to sleep with at night.

She could hear the beast closing on her, crashing through branches and felling trees in its wake, the throaty groan gaining with every step. Why did Mama lie to her? She had always been told there were no such things as real monsters. There was nothing under the bed and no grotesque figure skulking at the window, waiting to tear her to shreds with rows of sharp teeth. Glowing eyes and teeth like knives were the stuff of stories to frighten the smaller children into behaving. Lauren had felt so grown up when she was allowed in on that secret.

Now she knew different.

The black creature would devour her soul.

Lauren half fell, half ran into the clearing where Father was stacking roots and berries into the huge backpack he had brought with him. His axe was buried in a tree stump to keep the blade keen.

The axe was too far away. She was going to die. The scream cut from her lungs, tearing through Ben, striking him with the fear that he had had since his beautiful daughter come to live with him. He would not be there when she needed him.

Ben spun, pulled the skinning knife from the sheath at his belt and ran to his daughter who lay with her knees drawn up to her chest, eyes tight shut. Ben crouched slightly, knife high and ready and peered into the trees.

Nothing moved. The thumping of his heart obliterated the silence. He could hear nothing.

He remained in position forever, aware that his daughter was at his feet in need of him. Training overcame the need for personal contact. Ben did not reach for Lauren and she did not reach for him lest she interfere with his defence of her. His old eyes were still keen as they scanned the trees and undergrowth for any sign of the danger that had terrified his daughter so. He could see the blood on her dress and her skin. His heart ached to reach down to her. The lump in his throat threatened to suffocate him.

The birds started singing again, flitting from branch to branch. They had probably been as startled by Lauren's racing than by any animal in the forest. If there were a bear or mountain cat out there it would seem to have moved off. The sun was warm on the back of his neck and he could feel it through his shirt. The heat seemed to the lift the pressure from him. He could resist the need to grab his daughter no longer.

Ben rolled her on to her back, whispering gently that she was safe. Lauren opened her eyes and seeing her papa she leapt into his strong arms. Everything was right in her world again. Easing her off him Ben checked her for wounds, gratified to see that there were no claw marks merely scratches that had broken the skin. Clutching her to him he could feel the tears of relief well in his eyes. Lauren hugged him back, her tiny arms wrapped tight around his thick neck.

'What happened, my princess? Tell papa what scared you,' Ben tried to keep the urgency from his voice. His eyes flicked every now and again to the forest but he could detect no cause for alarm.

'I saw a daemon, Papa,' she blurted innocently, as she watched her father tend to her scrapes with a moist cloth. 'He was awful.'

'Where did you see him?' Ben asked, eyes flicking to the forest every so often. He knew the forest held plenty of mountain lions and bears. Lauren was not one given to flights of fantasy. She had nodded sagely when she heard the story of the boy who cried wolf one time too many and what had happened to him.

'Over by the stream, the monster was lying in wait to catch me at my secret place,' Lauren referred to the glade where she went to play at her breathing exercises while her father was gathering roots and herbs.

Ben knew exactly where she meant. It would not do for his little treasure to have a secret place when she was so young. Later it would be expected but not now. He had followed her there on several occasions to make sure she was safe.

'What did the monster look like?' Ben asked.

'Oh, he was ugly and scary and really big. He was lying in the water and growled at me when I approached. He tried to grab me. His eyes were so scary. Red and glowing. He looked like one of those crocodiles,' Lauren paused as she made sure she had pronounced it correctly. 'He had claws and scales and everything. I ran as fast as I could back to you papa. I knew you would kill him with your axe.'

Ben had drawn pictures of crocodiles for Lauren. She knew roughly what they would look like. He sat back in the grass. It seemed unlikely that there was a crocodile in the river. It was not hot enough in Ellistrin for one to survive. Still, stranger things had happened. There was definitely something there that he could not leave to roam about the forest. Before he could come back and continue with gathering or hunting he would have to deal with it.

'Come on then, my brave little princess, let's go and tell Mama all about your huge adventure.'

'She will be pleased,' Lauren squealed clapping her hands and skipping, already forgetting her ordeal as only a child can. Ben saw that she had her dagger sheathed but at the open position, should she need to draw it in a hurry.

'Yes, she will,' Ben smiled, dreading the telling of the tale. The tears from Isela and the shouting that would follow at how he wasn't looking after their baby. He knew she would only be upset at the close call but it did not make the prospect any more appealing.

Leaving the backpack where it lay he swept Lauren up on to his shoulders, hefted his axe and bow, and marched off home.

The only eyes following them leave the clearing were of an anxious squirrel who wanted the berries which had tipped out of the packs.

*

Ben left early the following morning. He brought a small parcel of food looped under his arm, wrapped round his other shoulder by a leather strap so that there would be no noise. Isela had carefully prepared it for him while he still slept.

He smiled at the thought. Ever since he had been a young boy he had shown great aptitude in misunderstanding every woman he had ever known. At an early age he had made this confession to friends and been ridiculed for it, only to have them confess later that they had no more of an idea than he as to the mysterious workings of a woman's mind.

It had not improved with time.

Isela had hugged her adopted child dearly during the story and rocked her in her arms. Leading Ben by the hand she had taken him to their sleeping area where they held each other softly. Even at sixty-five Benjad was still capable of appreciating a beautiful woman and his Isela was indeed beautiful. A full ten years his junior Isela was more than a match for him.

She had applied the salves and bandages to his, now arthritic, shoulder and knee to support them as she had done many times in the past before battle. As always, she had been solemn during these times. She had told him once that she used these times to pray. Not that he might fight valiantly in the name of the Lord God as was expected, but that the same God would return him safely to her.

Time to put his mind back on the task at hand. Checking the positions and securing the knife and hatchet on his belt he notched an arrow to his longbow. It was not a good bow but then he was not a great archer. Ben hoped a monster that was not quick enough to catch a five-year-old girl would not mind standing still long enough for him to place a well-aimed arrow into its heart.

If he was lucky, it would sit still long enough for him to walk right up, spit in its eye and chop its ugly head off with one stroke from the double-headed battle-axe now slung to his back. Ben had re-oiled the leather and made sure the blade was keen before securing it to his pack. It had served him in the Legion Wars for forty years and would serve him again this day. It was a friend who had never let him down.

He moved slowly forward, his toes checking the ground before setting his foot down. He paused after every step to check for any change. It was hard progress from lessons hard learned. An impatient Legionnaire did not live to see sixty-five.

Ben's eyes moved constantly not focusing on anything in particular. In the forest, with so many shapes and colours, movement registered faster than anything else. To stare at something was to develop tunnelled vision.

Ben was drawn back to all the times in his past when he had hunted his quarry through forests. Continents away at times. Two-legged prey were the hardest. Feeling his mouth go dry he remembered that more than enough he had been the one who was hunted.

Ben paused at the edge of the clearing, settling on one knee and easing the bow forward but not drawing back. The packs were still in place and a few smaller forest animals were lunching noisily. He made sure he was downwind of the clearing. They were unaware of his presence. The squirrels were in no rush, a good sign that there was no predator about. 'No predator that they could detect,' he corrected himself.

Reminding himself to move cautiously he stepped into the clearing. The squirrels vanished up the nearest trees chittering their angry challenges. The packs were roughly where they had been left. Dragged for only a couple of inches. Badger and the occasional fox print were in abundance but no bear or large cat tracks. Ben took a long draught of cool water and rinsed his mouth. Satisfied, he headed off towards the stream.

*

It was hard to judge the wind the closer he got. It whipped haphazardly off the river current and channelled through the trees. He could smell nothing except for the strong scented flowers of every colour growing on the banks of the river. Butterflies swarmed and danced in the midmorning sunlight. Mini rainbows lanced skyward thrown up by the gentle spray of the fast-moving stream. The frost was lifting already and hung in a simmering mist low to the ground.

No wonder Lauren had chosen this place. She would sit in the stunning beauty of it, ignore it totally, and perform her daily rituals of breathing and knife practice.

Ben smiled at the thought, then froze as he saw a shape in the stream.

Controlling the burst of adrenaline, he corrected his stance to allow for his bad knee.

Slowly he raised the bow. With iron discipline he did not draw back on the heavy cord that would load the explosive strain to release the fatal arrow. A wary enemy had once heard the strain as the wood had overcome its own inertia and signalled the imminent danger.

Although he was only ten yards away it took him two full minutes to move to cover behind a tree from which he could examine the shape fully. Reaching behind him he unfastened the heavy battle axe, ready to draw it at a moment's notice. Although confident that his burly musculature could still swing the lethal implement better than many of the children he saw in the Legion, he was a canny warrior and would rather fight a monster with an arrow sticking out of it than not.

The dark shape hulked in the middle of the stream, mostly submerged. Fast moving water cascaded over its back and, what he presumed was its head, rested on a branch out of the water. The gnarled and scaly black skin certainly gave the impression of being a crocodile but it was not large enough. It had no tail but that could be submerged also. The light reflecting off the water and mist made it hard to see.

Ben moved further up the bank to be sure of a heart or head shot.

Taking aim he prepared to loose the shaft. His shoulders bunched as he drew back on the bow. It was not a war bow but the massive impact from the hunting bow could punch through heavy hide of most animals. He was now only fifteen feet from the animal. The head of the shaft moved up and down unevenly as Ben's heart raced and his lungs were close to hyperventilating. He was almost at the point of dizziness when he realised the shape in the water was human.

*

'First Minister,' the clerk's hands were trembling slightly as he explained the situation, 'we are moving as fast as we can. I cannot get the shipments any quicker. Surely you understand the need to take care in the handling of these goods.'

Wilk could not even bring himself to look at the Knight beside the throne, yet he was aware of the intense stare the black garbed warrior held levelly on him. The clerk knew of Temple Knight Brood's fearsome reputation, as did the whole Empire.

'Do not seek to lecture me on such mundane matters,' Altai snapped at the petty bureaucrat in clipped tones. 'I am well aware of the delicate handling involved in transporting artefacts. I am also well aware of the stench of lies and excuses. There are no excuses for slacking.'

First Minister Altai was a strangely imposing figure for someone so slight. His yellow skin and almond eyes only added to the sense of danger.

'Not even a pure blood,' was the phrase heard repeatedly around the palace, but none dared say it within earshot. The Holy Father had obviously chosen him for a reason, and it would not do to be found second guessing the Holy Father.

Wilk had seen First Minister Altai many times as he was the minister to the Emperor and Holy Father, Saladin the Great, but this was his first, and hopefully last, meeting with him. Altai was of medium height and weight; he dressed in neutral clothes and his hair was neither long nor short. The clerk, who followed fashion as far as his salary allowed him, thought to himself that perhaps it was an effect Altai deliberately sought to achieve. Better to move unnoticed in the corridors of power. Wilk felt the man's eyes bore into him.

'I do not mean to lecture, I know that the Holy Father has matters of greater importance to deal with than waste his time on me. I was merely explaining why we were experiencing difficulties with transport.'

Saladin remained silent throughout the exchange and did not look at the clerk. He handled every artefact with care that was set before him. Trophies from the outlying regions. His Empire. Weapons, religious talismans, and icons all came under his scrutiny and were quickly discarded. Gems and gold were of no interest to him.

'The Emperor Saladin is not in the mood for excuses and failure,' Altai said softly, out of respect for the Emperor who sat listening to the exchange. 'Where are the Ellistrin artefacts? Where are the stores from Alcudia?'

'The Alcudian treasures will arrive within the month. The Ellistrin goods, well, they are still in Ellistrin, Minister,' Wilk stammered.

'Still?' Altai's voice was misleadingly warm.

'Yes, Minister, they have been in one of our storage facilities for some time.'

'And why is that?'

'As the Minister knows,' Wilk explained carefully, it would cost him his life to be seen to patronise the minister, 'Ellistrin is our frontier of the Empire, and we are at war with the Coalition. It is difficult to arrange transport when troops are constantly redirected for supplies and fighting.'

Altai did not speak. He stroked his chin looking at the little man.

'We currently have the old museum curate carrying out identification and inventory for us,' Wilk added.

'One old man?' Altai asked.

'Yes, Minister, he is the only remaining survivor of the occupation who retains this information. You will find some of it quite remarkable and to your liking.' The clerk handed over a list of items.

'Yes, yes,' Altai pored over the sheets. 'It is all remarkably interesting. These religious items from the list. I do not want it on paper. I want them here. I believe your agents are not working diligently enough. I think they could do with more appropriate motivation.'

'Of course,' Wilk said brightly. 'A word from you would certainly lift their spirits.'

'You are not in the presence of the Emperor for a pep talk. I do not think you appreciate your predicament, clerk,' Altai said slyly stepping to the side of the Emperor, giving him the floor.

The clerk was aware that the Emperor had now focused all his attention on him. His gaze held a weight all its own that pressed on the administrator and slouched his shoulders. The artefacts and jewellery were set to the side.

'I was thinking more of a visit from one of the Temple Knights,' Saladin spoke at last. 'I am sure they would be able to assert the need for more haste on the situation. What do you think?'

'Oh, Holy Father, that is a splendid idea,' Wilk spluttered. 'But I don't think there is any need to despatch one of the illustrious Knights to solve a simple supply problem. I will take the matter in hand personally.'

'Good. I like that. If you do not have the matter in hand and have all the items from Alcudia here in two weeks from today, I will see you answer for it. Personally.'

Wilk's face drained of colour.

'Of course, Holy Father, it will be as you saw,' he eventually managed to whimper.

'Good. Now, what of Ellistrin?' Saladin asked.

The clerk began to stammer an answer before Altai cut him off with a whisper.

'If the next words out of your mouth are the form of another excuse,' Altai began. 'I will have one of the guards' attack dogs brought in here to tear your tongue from your miserable mouth.'

Saladin slammed his hand on the edge of the throne as a reprimand to his Minister. Altai snapped his mouth shut but continued to glare at the now terrified clerk.

'The heretics are disrupting the supply routes in the north,' Brood stated. 'I have despatched some of my brothers to oversee it.'

Saladin nodded and allowed his gaze to settle on the clerk.

'You are dismissed, clerk, and see to it that the items are delivered,' Altai spoke to Wilk like a close friend, a warm smile on his face. 'You will be issued fresh directives for the goods from Ellistrin.'

Saladin waited for the clerk to leave before he spoke to the Knight.

'Walk with me, my son. What news of your missing brothers?' the Emperor said rising from the simple throne and taking the Knight by the elbow. Not to lead him, nor for support. It was a sign of their intimate bond.

Saladin escorted the Knight through the gently billowing curtains onto the veranda. It was dusk in the city and the streetlamps lit the landscape for as far as the eye could see. Even from this high vantage point the lights seemed to stretch to the horizon.

'It was as you suspected, my Lord.' Saladin was "Holy Father" or "Emperor," but he was also their general in the holy war. 'I too felt their passing. Joshua fell in the East, short of the front lines in Ellistrin. Killed in battle.'

'Joshua?' Saladin was surprised 'I would never have thought it possible.'

'Nor I, my Lord,' Brood agreed. 'I have prayed much on the matter, but God has not deemed me worthy to show the truth of it. Grapas and Punti were lost on the front lines during our latest advances. The lines are stable again. The last, brother Talan, took his own life.'

'Suicide? Talan?' Saladin asked, seeking to insulate himself against conspiracy and assassination at every turn. Four Knights lost in as many days. Four of the existing Twelve. Unprecedented.

'Yes,' Brood replied. 'Brother Talan.'

'You are certain that it was suicide?' Saladin asked. Talan had been one of the most steady and devout of Knights.

'Yes, my Lord, he had expressed misgivings recently in Knights' council and privately to one of his brothers.' Brood did not add that he was the brother Talan had spoken to. Their bond went beyond being merely fellow Knights.

'And what were his misgivings?' Saladin demanded, not wanting to hear the answer.

'Brother Talan had expressed a fear that he was not performing the role that God had marked out for him, my Lord. He did not believe that God had intended him to use his abilities for war and conquest.'

'I am the Voice of God, Temple Knight Brood. Your brothers do not need to question their faith. I do that for them every day. I spare them the damnation that doubt will bring for I accept the burden of all acts carried out in His name. You will make this clear to your brothers!' Saladin was all but frothing from the outburst.

'I have already addressed the situation, my Lord. The Knights loyalty to the Lord God is not in question,' Brood bowed.

'What of their loyalty to me, Brood?' Saladin did not miss the implications of Brood's statement.

'Their loyalty to you is as unwavering as my own, Holy Father,' Brood said simply. 'And that is without question.'

Saladin reined in his berating of the Knight. He knew those who zealously followed their path could only be pushed so far.

'What of brother Talan then?' Saladin asked squeezing the Knight's hand, more to reassure himself than Brood.

'He could not reconcile his actions to his beliefs, my Lord,' Brood replied.

'He was weak,' Saladin confirmed.

Brood bristled.

'No, my Lord, he was strong. He decided that since he could not give of himself totally to you and his brothers he should go and ask God himself. He took the most painful poison and took forty-six hours of agony to die. It was his way of apologising to you for failing you, I believe. As I have failed you for not averting this incident.'

'You are too hard on yourself, Brood,' Saladin offered, graciously placated by the Knights words. 'You and your brothers provide this Empire with an indispensable service. Your loyalty is above question, your devotion unparalleled. Talan's death was a blessing and I praise him for his courage, as should you all. Bring the bodies of you fallen brothers home for mourning. Bring me word of Joshua when you have recovered his body. The truth will be made known to you when the time is right.'

'Yes, my Lord,' Brood bowed slightly, the black armour writhing around his muscled form.

Saladin smiled warmly in reply. He held a fear of the Knights as many in the Empire did. He understood them for he had created them. He would never be found wanting in their puritanical eyes for he was more zealous than even they. Their impassioned pursuit of the higher power was legendary, but spiritual, never materialistic. Inquisitors, assassins, priests, whatever their role demanded. Anything was allowed because it was sanctioned by God.

But controlled by Saladin.

'I want you to despatch some of your brothers to Ellistrin. They will take control of the deteriorating situation there. We have consolidated our position in the rest of the troubled regions and the last of the heretics are under control. We must once more look to the East.'

'An Empire that does not expand dies,' Brood said, looking out over the city.

'Quite,' Saladin remarked, annoyed at the perceptiveness of the Knight. 'But God's work is never done, and we should never be remiss in spreading his word to the heathens.'

'No, my Lord. I meant no disrespect,' Brood recovered.

'I would like you to oversee the situation in Ellistrin, Brood. Use whatever assets as you see fit. I want it resolved and soon. I expect your usual positive results and the front line to be pushed back and dissolved.'

'When can we expect the troops from the other nations?' Brood enquired of the occupying forces that were garrisoned around the vast Empire. With the nations under control as Saladin had said, it would free many more troops for the front lines.

'The main force will be amassed within the year. I have already sent troops forward. Over one hundred thousand including many of our finest regiments. They are holding the mid-country. The generals are sending the mercenary and auxiliary troops into the lines. They are enough to hold the line but lack the discipline to push forward. We will continue to sacrifice them. It is no cost to us. There is no point in sacrificing the Chosen People in these skirmishes.'

'No, my Lord,' Brood was well aware of Puritan military strategy. Saladin was speaking freely to confirm his own thoughts and not seeking to inform Brood.

'Within a year we will be ready to wipe out the existing line and roll straight across the rabble allied thrown against us. Their coalition of forces will crumble. Each nation's army will be either wiped out or retreat to its own frontier. They can barely hold that precarious line against us now. They will not be able to defend their borders individually against our massed armies.'

The Puritans currently had a million men ranged against a similar number and had held that status quo for ten years.

'And what of the accommodating agreement between the nations and the Empire?' Brood asked of the diplomatic envoys that had been dispatched to each of the enemy capital cities.

'It has worked for us in the past, but I believe they will allow us to garrison their major towns and move our armies freely across their borders. They are aware of what we did in Ellistrin.'

'Yes,' Saladin smiled.

'I will make sure matters are in hand, my Lord,' Brood said.

'Good, I have utmost faith in you. You are dismissed, my Knight,' Saladin said walking back into the main chamber. Saladin had other, more pressing matters to address, as he watched a young girl arrive in the courtroom to serve drinks.

'Ask Altai to come back in on your way out,' Saladin ordered.

*

Isela set down the sodden garments for a moment and pushed a wisp of greying blond hair back behind her ear. She smiled softly as she watched her adopted child run and skip.

Lauren was running about the clearing behind the cabin. The enthusiasm of the child seemed to tire the adults more than it did the child. Isela smiled as she watched Lauren twist and turn, dancing in the sun, the knife and sword flashing in the drills she herself had learned as a child. She smiled at the memory though she could not remember ever having had that much energy. Was she really that old?

Hitching her skirt up Isela dismissed such feelings of age, gathered the washing and headed to the hanging line to dry them. She could want for little more in her life. The years she had spent with Benjad had been the happiest time she had known. Ben was her second husband, the first having died when she was still young in the Outland wars. He was a hero, as was Ben. She had served faithfully and had met Ben while they had been serving together as an auxiliary force to the south. Benjad, a sergeant then, had been a powerful figure, a veteran even back then at the age of twenty-five. He had retired, forcibly discharged, before the invasion of their homeland. His age had eliminated him from combat duty despite his protestations.

Now, instead, they served the Legion by gathering information on troop movements and providing shelter for the Legionnaires as they travelled south to raid the supply lines.

The Legionnaires regularly came through and it was always good to see them. She had known many of them for most of their young lives. Ben had occasionally been taken for forays against the enemy but, for the most part, stayed at home. The enemy rarely troubled them, thinking that such an old couple could have no part in the war. Lauren was always hidden during their visits. Isela had not been molested. Too old and undesirable she supposed. Age had its blessings.

Ben would open a bottle of ale, or something stronger if he had it, which he always tried to have handy even though the price in market was too high. The Legionnaires would tell how the war was going and Ben would give any information he had gleaned from the market. Isela heard the same stories repeatedly from different faces. 'It is going well,' 'We are pushing them back', 'We are holding', 'Won this battle', 'Won that battle'. She had heard that for years but would never douse their enthusiasm with a touch of realism. The invasion had happened ten years ago, and the once seemingly unstoppable Ellistrin Legions had been all but exterminated.

For now, she had to contend with the beast he was away to hunt this day. Though anxious about his well-being she knew he was sensible and would not risk himself foolishly to catch the bear or whatever it was.

At least Lauren was safe.

The relief she had felt had developed into a night of intimate lovemaking. Smiling at the thought she looked over from her work to see Lauren talking to a strange man. Jumping to her feet she produced a knife from beneath her gown. The worry evaporated when she recognised the priest. Smiling she waved to him.

Edom returned the gesture as he walked across with Lauren swinging from his hand, her little voice regaling him with the great stories in her young life. They centred, of course, on her brush with the daemon.

'Greetings Isela. May God smile on you and your home,' Edom said bowing his head slightly.

'Thank you, Father. You are always welcome at our hearth,' Isela curtsied and offered the priest a cup of cold water.

'Thank you, child. How are things with you? Lauren has been telling me about the monster that roams the forest. Her brave father has gone to seek it out, she tells me,' Edom raised an eyebrow to Isela, asking in the secret language of adults so that Lauren would not understand.

'Yes, Father,' she indicated a seat for him, aware that his old frame must be tired after the journey. The nearest settlement was a full day and a night away. 'The good Lord blessed her and kept her safe once more for us, though at times I think she tempts him on purpose.'

Lauren was kneeling dutifully beside the priest, her head bowed, and tiny fingers clasped mimicking prayer. Edom stroked her hair.

'Ben has gone in search of whatever it was gave her such a fright,' Isela said.

'Alone?' Edom asked.

'Yes.' She looked at the priest, the seeds of doubt growing in her heart. 'He did not want to risk leaving us here for three days to go in search of help from town, in case the beast attacked the cabin.'

'I am sorry, Isela, it was not my intention to worry you unduly. Ben is many things, but he is not a stupid man and is wise to the ways of the forest. It is usual to hunt in pairs though, for safety. He must not consider it a great threat. He will be back soon no doubt.'

'Yes. I expect him back tonight. He left at dawn. If the creature, whatever it is, has moved out of the area he will simply leave it and come home. We will alert the town on our next visit.'

'Excellent,' said Edom smiling. 'Nothing to concern ourselves with then. May I impose on you for a night or two, I am travelling north to the mountain camps.'

'Of course, you may stay. It is never an imposition, we love to see you,' she said, imagining Ben rolling his eyes. 'Especially Lauren. She will be waiting for your stories again.'

Lauren was squeezing the priest's hand and smiling at him. She loved his little stories about how God was always so kind and caring and won over the bad people.

'Would you mind looking after Lauren while I finish up here, Father? Perhaps you would be so good as to pray for the safe delivery of my brave man.'

'Of course, Isela,' Edom said reassuringly laying his old hand on hers and thought of his old friend in the forest. 'In harm's way again, you old bastard,' he thought to himself.

'Ben will be returned to us safely,' he assured them both.

Chapter Two

Opening his eyes, but only a crack, the warrior could make out a moving blur, splashing toward him. Big hands reached down to pull him from the water and lay him on the bank of the stream. A man's face came into focus his lips moving. He could not make out the words but could understand the movement of the silent lips. The man with the wrinkled face was explaining that he was severely burned and to lie still. He managed to lift his hand in front of his face and saw that it was black and broken like the clay on a dry riverbed. He could not feel any pain. Somehow, he knew this was not a good sign.

He knew he had been burned so deeply that his nerves had been severely damaged and were not transmitting any information. After a flash of worry about it for the future he was glad of the reprieve from the agony he was granted in the present. His tongue was still moist in his mouth, if slightly swollen. He had not been subjected to a desert heat then. Lightning? Memory did not come to him. Extraordinarily little was coming to him.

He remembered talking to a daemon. Insanity then? Brought on by the pain?

He closed his eyes against the sunlight as it threatened to burn through his skull. The pain in his head was throbbing, growing like a living being, feeding off the trauma caused by the tremendous damage inflicted on his body.

The man helping him stared down at the broken body before him.

'Help me,' he managed to croak through his destroyed lips.

'What?' Ben was sure the man had spoken. 'What did you say?'

The broken, rasping sound came again. Putting his ear beside the man's face he heard him repeat, 'Help me.'

'It's ok, sonny. I have seen worse,' Ben said, truthfully.

Ben tried his best to move him gently, but this was causing more discomfort than it was worth. After only a moment's hesitation he picked him up in one sharp movement and carried him to the shade of a large tree, setting him down on the dewy grass that he hoped would soothe the skin.

'What am I supposed to do with you?' Ben enquired of no one in particular, jumping when the voice beside him rasped again.

'Help me.' Though barely audible, the desperate pleading was clear.

'Of course, I will help you. Rest my friend. I will tend to you.' Ben spoke with the same confident tones that he had used to reassure the younger men when they marched into battle.

'It's ok.' 'It's alright.' 'You will fight bravely and get home,' when in fact many of the young men never came home from the battlefield. Such was the way of war.

Leaving the man where he lay, Ben took his hatchet and headed a short way in the forest to collect long branches. Having collected the necessaries for a stretcher he ate his food and filled his hide canteen from the stream. Splitting the leather food wrap into strips he was able to bind the two poles in a triangle and fasten his jerkin, river reed and weed vines across it to support the body. Setting the man on it he prepared to leave for the longer route home. South, along the riverbank, then north again, through the plains. He could not negotiate the thick forest with the stretcher on his own. Carrying on his shoulder would be quicker but given his current condition Ben doubted the man would survive.

As an afterthought he covered the naked man in soft moss and lichen making sure it was soaked. What made him think to do this, he did not know. The man did not need cover for modesty. He was barely discernible as a human being, never mind a man.

'Sleep tight, we will be safe at home when you wake. There you will get all the care you need,' Ben said, his voice strong and confident. Pulling the brace on his knee tighter, he shouldered the weight and headed off.

*

'Hello, the cabin!'

Isela was already on her feet and moving for the door when she heard Ben's voice. He had been gone for the entire day and the sun had set hours ago. Worry propelled her out the door, her eyes scanning the dark forest for a sign of her husband.

'Ben?' she shouted.

'Over here,' he returned, and Isela took off in the direction of his voice, scrambling through the undergrowth.

Edom woke at the commotion of Isela's passing and tended to the fire. The broth that she had made that evening would not take long to heat. Lauren was thankfully asleep.

'Wait where you are,' Ben called as he heard Isela coming for him. 'You will hurt yourself running through the forest at night.'

The weight hit him in the chest as Isela raced into him flinging her arms around his neck and kissing him.

'You had best not be ordering me around, husband of mine, not if you know what is good for you,' she said, kissing him again.

'Never, my love. Never.' Ben remembered the last time she had gone into a temper. Women were not supposed to be able to punch that hard. She must have inherited the strength from her father who had also been a fine warrior.

'Good,' she smiled. 'What have you brought home with you? Dinner?'

'Hardly,' Ben said, as he re-shouldered the weight. 'I found Lauren's monster.'

'What?' Isela was concerned and touched Ben in the night for signs of wounds. His face held no new scars, only the deep furrows that battle had left.

'Don't worry.' Ben began to move forward again, the dark shape trailing behind. 'It is just an injured man. He was burned but he is still alive. Barely though. He needs help.'

'I suppose you could not have left him,' she said. It was not a question.

'No,' he could see the lights in the cabin as the lamps were lit.

'Father Edom is here,' Isela explained, taking some of the strain.

'That is fortunate,' Ben said without sarcasm. 'His skills will be needed.'

Ben and Isela moved the gurney into the clearing and dragged it the last few feet to the front of the cabin. Edom was already waiting for them. Releasing the straps Ben picked up the wounded man and carried him, placing him beside the fire.

'Hello, Ben. What have you brought back?' Edom asked amiably as he moved to tend the man.

'I found him in the river and brought him here.'

'Do you know him?' The priest asked as he moved the blanket Ben had over him. Testing the moss, he found it dry and added more water. To pull it off now may cause more damage than good. Best to wet it and let it soften.

'I could do but I do not think so. It is impossible to tell with the extent of the burning,' Ben replied.

Edom brought a lamp close and examined the man's face. The burning was extensive and had covered the entire head, face and neck, shoulders, chest, right arm, and leg.

'He must have been caught in a fire to have received these wounds. Have there been any villages cleared recently?' Edom asked. The Puritans often burned villages for harbouring Legionnaire raiding parties.

'There have been a few. I often see the smoke rising far in the distance from the mountain slopes,' Ben replied, accepting a bowl of broth from Isela with a smile. 'Wherever he came from he has travelled some distance.'

'What about clothing?' Edom asked.

'Burnt off him or to him. It was unrecognisable. He has an arrow imbedded in his shoulder. The shaft has been broken. I do not know if it is one of ours or one of theirs but he spoke to me with a local accent so he must come from a village that has been attacked.'

'Is the arrow deep?' Edom asked.

'Impossible to know with the shaft gone but the fire closed the wound, so he is losing no blood.'

Edom probed through the moss to where Ben directed him and found the end of the shaft. Exposing the wounds, he found little infection.

'I think it would do little good to pull it out now. We will have to wait until he is a little stronger,' Edom announced.

'He will live then?' Isela asked.

'That is for God to decide, but we will certainly try to help him. I will begin at sunrise. I would be grateful if you could make sure the moss remains sodden and that his lips are kept moist throughout the night.'

'I will do it, Father,' Isela replied. 'You'd best get some sleep Ben, if you are to be of use to anyone in the morning.'

Ben nodded and kissed her lightly on the forehead before moving to the bedroom.

'It is good to see you again, old friend,' Ben smiled at the priest and extended his hand.

'And you, old dog,' Edom smiled warmly.

'I hope I did the right thing,' he said, searching the priest's eyes.

'It would have been the wrong thing to leave him there, Ben,' Edom smiled.

'I sense trouble,' Ben scratched the rough beard that had grown.

'You have been around it enough to know the signs,' Edom nodded.

'As have you,' Ben looked his friend in the eye. 'What do you think?'

'In our experience, Ben, trouble has no difficulty in finding places to go. If it wants us, it will not have to look too hard.'

Ben smiled again. Warmly this time.

'Being in trouble helps keep us young,' he said winking at Isela and walking slowly to the bedroom, favouring his now inflamed knee. 'If only it kept arthritis at bay.'

Chapter Three

Brood's childhood had been one of pain. Taking it or giving it, but pain, nonetheless. Any memory that might once have existed of his parents was long extinguished by the day of his sixth birthday. The day he was trying to find his way out of the desert.

The day he met his brothers.

'Off!' Appias had shouted kicking one of the young boys savagely in the small of his back 'Get off my cart! Any one of you miserable little bastards not off my cart in one second will be strung out and left for the vultures.'

The children rushed. They knew he meant it.

Some of the soldiers laughed but many more simply turned away. Veterans of many campaigns they had seen much cruelty visited on their enemy and saw no reason to inflict it upon any more children. Especially their own.

Brood could remember that the chief instructor rarely smiled. His face formed a strange grimace only when he was inflicting pain on his wards. The boys he was sworn to protect. Appias would have taken pleasure in gutting any of the twenty boys who were frantically trying to avoid eye contact, lest they feel the cutting wrath of the drillmaster.

The whip lashed out nonetheless and Brood winced, waiting for the pain, strangely thankful when the thick bullwhip cut down the boy beside him. The boy fell without a sound, his shaven head barely bristling as the sun broke the horizon.

'What's wrong boy? Lost your tongue?' Appias beamed for the benefit of the other guards. They watched closely as he marched towards the fallen boy, kicking him into the sand as he struggled to one knee. Three more swift kicks brought a sharp snap as a rib broke. Still he did not elicit a response.

Brood glanced down to see blood ooze slowly from the side of the boy's mouth and received a backhand blow for his trouble.

'Eyes front!' Appias shouted, wiping Brood's blood from his knuckles.

Frowning, the drillmaster stared at the boy who lay at his feet.

'Still not feeling like screaming, you little shit?' he said, lifting his boot to deliver another blow.

'What are you doing?' Rissel screamed at him, freezing Appias to the spot.

'Sir,' Appias snapped to attention before answering. 'The recruit was receiving punishment for moving too slow from the cart as instructed by the chief instructor, sir. He was insubordinate in front of the other recruits, sir.'

'Get the others ready! Leave the boy next to him,' Rissel ordered, waving the hulking form of Appias away. The boy slowly picked himself up. Sand clung to his sweat drenched brow and face and had mixed morbidly with the blood on his chin. The boy's gaze swung lazily around until he saw Brood watching him. Brood was surprised when the boy winked, only to have the mask of pained docility drop back onto his features.

Brood had watched as the drillmaster stormed off shouting orders and gathering the guards and boys together. His small body remained at close attention, and he dared not even wipe the fresh blood from his face.

'Well, recruit. Straighten your back when you are addressing an officer,' Rissel said, waiting for the boy to gather himself. A slow process given the severe beating he had received. 'What is your name?'

The boy did not answer immediately. He coughed once and leaned to one side to hawk a huge gob of blood into the sand.

Brood realised that the boy had remained silent by biting his tongue.

'Joshua, sir,' the voice was even smaller than the boy.

'Were you insubordinate, recruit?' Rissel demanded.

'Yes, sir,' Joshua hung his head.

'Did you deserve the punishment as administered by the chief instructor?' Rissel asked.

'Yes, sir,' Joshua had managed, though blood was now frothing at his lips. A punctured lung?

Joshua resisted the urge to nurse the rib, which was clearly interfering with his lungs. His blood was bubbling. It was leaking into his airway.

'Good,' Rissel observed, ignoring the blood and the implications of it. 'And how do you feel?'

'I am full of joy, sir,' Joshua said smiling.

'Excellent!' the captain beamed and shouted to the rest. 'Watch this recruit lads! He is a fine example of what you can all become.'

Joshua placed his palms together in front of him in solemn salute to the wisdom of an elder.

'Thank you, sir,' he said, softly.

'Drill master,' Rissel shouted, summoning Appias. 'Six lashes for the recruits.'

Appias smiled as he drew his short cane. He was nicknamed among the guards as 'Can I have another' for his reputation for breaking the canes over the backs of the smallest children. He would always need another cane to continue the punishment.

The boys bowed forward and pulled up their undershirts. Appias took to them with a frenzy, the cane making a small whine as it whipped through the air and shredded the skin of the two boys. Joshua was driven to his knees by the second blow as the cane contacted his rib.

'Up, boy,' Rissel ordered through clenched teeth. 'Take your punishment.'

'I will take it for him,' Brood said finally, when he saw that Joshua was going to be unable to get up. Death would have been his only reward.

'You will?' Rissel pondered the suggestion and laughed. This was just the sort of thing that Minister Saladin had wanted reported back to him. 'Excellent. Drillmaster. His six, plus the boy's remaining four. Plus another three for breach of protocol.'

Appias was sweating now and unable to smile through the effort of swinging the cane. On the tenth the cane snapped. On the eleventh, Brood was on his knees. By the thirteenth he was barely conscious. He too did not make a sound.

'Excellent,' Rissel said, mostly to himself. 'Get them sorted Sergeant.'

The sergeant shouted in Appias' stead as the drillmaster gathered himself and wiped the sweat from his brow.

'When you next think about being disobedient,' Rissel instructed them, as Saladin had ordered, 'you will be punished as will the boy next to you.'

Brood held the now grasping Joshua upright in line.

'You are too badly injured to continue,' the boy to Joshua's right whispered, eyes straight ahead. 'You must withdraw.'

'To quit is failure…' Joshua replied, through gritted teeth.

'…and failure is death,' Brood finished for him.

'I am Talan,' the boy to the right said. 'Whatever they have planned for us, stay close to me. I will help you as best I can.'

'You may pay the price for that offer,' Joshua seethed in pain.

'Nevertheless, my offer stands,' Talan replied. Brood looked at him through a swelling eye and saw that Talan seemed to be older and bigger than the rest. He was seven. Maybe eight.

'I am Joshua,' he said, feeling that he somehow knew the boy.

'And I am Brood,' was all the broken child could manage as his chin fell forward against his chest.

'Well met, my brothers,' Talan whispered.

Joshua groaned and finally pitched forward, vomiting blood. Brood and Talan caught him and lowered him to the ground.

'Let him go! Let that recruit go!' Appias shouted and the whip cracked in the air. The lash struck Brood above his good eye and drew a thick gash of blood. Brood and Talan let Joshua go but did not stand to attention.

Appias loomed over Brood as his small figure shook with anger and he adopted a fighting stance in front of his downed comrade. The drillmaster's smile became as menacing grimace, and the cane was replaced by a thicker stick.

'I am really going to enjoy this,' Appias said, pausing as the captain walked behind him.

'You are in the middle of one of the most unforgiving regions on this sorry continent,' Rissel's voice boomed out. 'You are to find your way back to barracks by any means possible. It is one hundred and fifty leagues over open desert. I do not expect many, if any, of you to survive. Those that do will move on to the next stage of your preparation as Warriors of the Lord. May God go with you.'

The boys kept their heads bowed, in reverence to the words, but few were lifted by them.

'Move out!' Appias shouted on cue, and the boys ran for the supply wagon where a guard provided them all with a small blunt knife, some stale bread and a hide of valuable water. Their only aid for the journey.

A few of the younger boys began to weep and one of them ran towards the wagon. An arrow took him high in the shoulder, lifting the frail body and spinning him to the ground. A soldier quickly despatched the boy as he opened his mouth for a final scream. Brood had seen him in training. He had been big for a four-year-old.

Brood had remained in position with his hands before him, ready to battle the drillmaster. Talan crouched in the sand beside the kneeling Joshua.

They were under strict orders not to travel as a group, but he considered waiting for the injured boy.

'You must not have been listening,' Rissel said slowly. 'There will be consequences. For all of you now.'

Brood did not take his eyes from the drillmaster.

'Put that away,' Rissel ordered Appias, and the thick cane vanished. 'Get them on their way. No rations. We will see how the desert punishes them.'

Appias stepped back from the boys and in a magnanimous gesture indicated the open desert dunes.

Brood and Talan lifted Joshua and began their slow march into the rising sun.

'You know,' Talan said when they were out of earshot. 'I knew it was a mistake hooking up with you two.'

'I did not ask you to,' came Brood's sharp reply.

'Now,' Talan rebuked him. 'Is that anyway to speak to a brother. What kind of brother would I be, to leave you to the wolves?'

'Are we brothers?'

'We are,' Talan smiled. 'Can you not feel it?'

Brood frowned and shook his head.

'Not of the blood,' Talan continued. 'Of the spirit. We are bonded in our hearts. Open your mind and you will feel it.'

'I feel…strange,' Brood said.

'Strange is a start,' Talan smiled again. 'And what of you Joshua, do you feel strange also?'

'Brothers,' came his whispered response seeming to charge the very air around them.

'Yes,' Brood answered, smiling back, feeling the bond open in his heart and in the air. 'I feel it now.'

'Good. For you will be our leader,' Talan's smile seemed somehow appropriate despite their circumstance. 'The first among equals.'

'I can feel that too,' Brood did not return the smile.

'I know you do,' Talan replied. 'Now, any suggestions?'

'Yes. We need water. Or we will not survive the desert. It will claim us by nightfall. We will move quickly into the dunes, and you will continue with Joshua. I will return to scavenge supplies before the guards break camp.'

'I feel something else,' Talan had a puzzled look on this face. 'You have another agenda. Anger. You are going back for Appias.'

'It is not anger,' Brood assured his brother.

'Then what?' Talan asked.

Brood did not know. What did he seek? It was not for himself. It was for his new brother.

'Vengeance,' Joshua answered for him, and the boys nodded in agreement.

*

Isela did not flinch when the man's eyes opened. She had tended many wounded men before and been injured herself. There were no whites to the eyes. They were of a red hue inset with black stones. It was a disturbing sight and she had to look away. The eyes seem to see right through her into her very soul. Daemon eyes.

'It is only a result of the fire,' Edom touched her arm gently. 'I doubt he can see anything.'

Isela nodded and, lifting the soft cloth, she applied more water to the man's forehead and cheek before setting it in place over his eyes. She took the opportunity while he was awake to pour some water into his mouth hoping that he would be able to swallow. Up to now she had been wetting the lips and letting the moisture satisfy his thirst.

'It is particularly important to keep him drinking. He must moisturise his body from the inside as well as out,' Edom added. 'If he survives another night that is. I have given him the Last Rites in case the Lord claims him in the night. You have done what you can for now Isela. Please leave me with him that I might pray for his soul.'

'His heart has stopped twice now,' Isela said.

'Yes,' Edom sighed. 'His lungs have stopped breathing more times than that. I do not know how he is holding onto this human life. He is a very strong-willed man. Stronger than I. The pain alone would be enough to cripple even the bravest of men.'

The warrior lay on a makeshift bed consisting mostly of the stretcher that Ben had transported him to the cabin on. He made incoherent noises from time to time but had not wakened fully enough to speak since his discovery.

'What happened to him, Edom?' Ben did not address the priest by his proper title. He was never a deeply religious man; wars that can bless a man with faith can also strip it from them.

Edom and Ben had served together as teenagers and through many foreign campaigns after that in the countless wars that the mercenary Ellistrin Legions had been loaned out for. Ben had remained in the army before invalidity had retired him. Edom had understood something clearly at last. Twenty years now, Ben thought to himself as he eyed his one-time friend.

'He has been exposed to a very sudden burn. Something liquid, I think. Oil perhaps? Tar? Pitch? I don't know. It is not a natural occurrence anyway. It was done to him either on purpose or by accident. He is lucky to have survived.'

'Do you think it is safe to have him here?' Isela asked, putting her arm around her husband.

'I cannot say, and I will not give you false hope. He may bring danger to your home' Edom was thoughtful. I cannot bring him north with me. I do not have the strength. The journey would kill him at this stage anyway. I could send a patrol back for him when I am met by the scouts.'

'Provided he survives the night,' Ben nodded agreement to Edom's suggestion. Priest or not, he could still think like a soldier.

'Yes. If he survives. I will pray for him tonight and prepare the way for his passing,' Edom said.

Lauren, you should be in bed asleep,' Isela scolded the child as she appeared behind them. 'What are you doing up?'

'Aw, Mama, I want to sit up and hear Father Edom tell stories to Finn.'

'Finn?' Ben asked.

'Yeah, Papa,' Lauren replied in her best *don't you know anything* voice. 'The prince who fought the dragon and was burned while rescuing the beautiful princess.'

'Oh, that Finn,' Ben recognised the bedtime tale. 'I guess it will do until he can tell us his real name.'

Edom took his seat beside the bed and set Lauren on his knee. 'What story shall we tell Finn tonight?'

'Hmmm,' Lauren thought hard, snuggling in sleepily to the priest. 'Tell him about the Messiah and how he came to look after us.'

'What a good choice,' Edom agreed, thinking of where the name came from.

Ben and Isela left them to it and went into the main cabin room for some privacy.

Edom started into the story, but Lauren was asleep within minutes. Carrying her the few feet to her bed he lay her down and pulled the sheets up around her. 'May God watch and protect you, little one.'

Edom had brought Lauren to live with Benjad and Isela when she had been orphaned four years previously. Her mother had been killed during a Puritan raid. Her father had died shortly after she was born while fighting during a Legion attack on a garrison post at Kilmessan.

Ben and Isela, their own children killed during the invasion, took her in like the Godsend she was.

Edom tenderly kissed Lauren's warm forehead and moved silently back to sit beside the man. His chest fought to rise, and each breath and his heart was beating irregularly.

'So, my son. It is to be Finn then. Very well, Finn, let us pray.'

Edom gently took Finn's scabbed hand and began to pray in the tongue of the ancients. The language was only used now in prayer and in formal ceremony. The fluid, musical tone of the words was very soothing.

As the prayers continued Finn's heartbeat steadied and the breathing became deeper, less laboured. His lips began to move slightly, following the prayer. Edom was lost in concentration. He did not notice.

*

The gift of life is not an easy one to hold on to, is it Finn?

The warrior looked around the bleak grey landscape. The daemon leaned against his rock once more, his arms folded across his chest.

'Is my name Finn?' the warrior asked.

So it seems warrior. Daemon drew his tongue along this elongated incisor. *Free will can be such fun, and my master has such a sense of good form.*

'I do not see the joke, Daemon,' Finn leaned against his own rock. Fatigue ate at him.

The child named you, and in doing so endeared you to her family, and more importantly to that foul priest. Fate is helping you along it would seem.

'How is it helping?' Finn asked, rubbing his eyes.

All in good time. These events are not of my making, but you will see.

'Why have you brought me here, Daemon? What would you have of me now?'

I did not bring you here, warrior. You have come here every night. This is the Void.

'Am I dead?' Finn did not understand. He looked around him and saw the grey land where he had first met the daemon. This time though he was wearing dull grey armour.

You are dead. Your body does not return to this road by accident. Each night you have visited this bleak land and each night you have managed to return to the realm of the living. Who knows? Tonight, you may reach the end of this road.

'Death holds no fear for me, Daemon,' Finn said, feeling the familiar edges of his breastplate.

You are tired. Tired because your spirit is holding so dearly to the realm of life. Do not tell me that you do not fear death, warrior, for I know that to be a lie.

'I do not give anything up without a fight, Daemon, especially my life. You would be well to remember that should you decide to call me a liar again,' Finn said, firmly, his steel eyes locking on the daemon.

Daemon smiled.

It is amazing how we can immediately get off on the wrong foot, warrior. I am not here to cause you any harm. I am here merely because you are on your path in the void. If you do not hold to your life, then I will need to make fresh plans.

Finn nodded. He did not trust the Daemon but what he said at least made tactical sense and that was something he understood.

'What is at the end of this path?' he asked.

I cannot tell you and you would not believe me if I did.

'That is no answer.'

Daemon shrugged.

It is an answer. At the end of this path answers are what you will find.

'To what?' Finn asked wondering where his sword might be.

To all the questions you have ever asked and those you have never thought to.

'What questions have I asked, Daemon? I do not even know who I am. I remember nothing' Finn stopped examining the featureless moonscape and focused entirely on the daemon.

Answers to the questions of life, mortal. The most important of which is 'why?'

Finn's mind raced. It was impossible to comprehend the enormity of what was happening to him.

'You look somewhat haggard yourself, Daemon,' Finn observed.

The daemon's perfect features were marred with signs of stress.

We all have masters to answer to, he answered.

'Who is it I am to save? The priest? The child?' Finn asked remembering their first conversation.

Excellent, warrior. Thinking of the battles that are to come in your life. I chose well. You will save none or all. That is not yet decided.

'The child named me,' Finn said, recalling that child's words.

Yes, Daemon laughed. *How I love the innocents. It is rewarding to see them corrupted by time, to watch them slide into decadence and war.*

'Who is Finn?' the warrior asked.

She named you Finn after a character from a story her father tells her. He is her hero and how she hopes her future husband will be. Strong brave and true. In the story, Finn must travel the lands searching for his exiled people to restore the princess to the throne. In the decisive battle against the dragon, he is horribly scarred yet still he saves the day.

'Who is the girl?' Finn asked.

Her name is Lauren, and she is five years old, Daemon held up his hand spreading his fingers as Lauren does when she is telling people her age. *She has been praying to God to save you and look after you.*

'And you show up?' Finn snorted.

I am privy to all things on the human world. It is a part of the rules. I was intrigued by her petition and answered on her behalf.

'Answered with me?' Finn quizzed.

Perhaps she needs your help in life.

'Perhaps she would be better waiting for God's help,' Finn suggested.

Perhaps God did answer her prayer through me.

'I do not think so,' Finn said.

He does move in mysterious ways, you know, Daemon said smiling.

'A good deed from you? With no ulterior motive?' Finn asked, but Daemon merely continued to smile.

I did not say there was no ulterior motive, warrior.

'What does she need protection from?' Finn asked hoping to glean as much information as possible before returning to his body.

Life. Perhaps you will be there to stop her falling. Perhaps merely by agreeing to help me, fate will choose not to claim her, and she will not need your service. Who knows how the universe works?

'You do, according to you. Why do you want the child safe? Is she a daemon?'

Revealing my motives is not a part of the agreement. They are my own affair. But to answer your question, no, she is not daemon seed. She is a beautiful, innocent child from loving parents who have done no wrong.

'I do not understand why you need her protected or me to protect her.'

I do not need her protected nor do I need your understanding for this. I merely need for you to decide that you wish to live.

'I will live,' Finn asserted. 'With or without your interference.'

Very well, return to your body.

'That is it?' Finn asked.

Yes Finn, sighed Daemon. *Were you hoping for something more elaborate? Hocus pocus perhaps? It is imperative though that you restore your body to health as soon as possible or you will not be able to sustain your spirit. Death will be inevitable then.*

'What happened to my body? To my mind?' he asked.

Both were injured in a battle. Restore your body and your mind will follow. Go and see the girl. Stay or do not stay. Do as you please. Remember warrior, free will. Daemon reached forward to touch his shoulder and…

*

…The pain from the touch lanced through his fragile body making him shudder and convulse. The priest snatched his hand back from his shoulder, startled by the reaction his touch produced. He had been using a sponge to moisten the dry and cracked skin for most of the evening. Lauren, who had been keeping the vigil with Edom, did not seem bothered in the slightest. She just smiled widely and clutched his leathery hand all the tighter, fascinated by the texture.

'Welcome back to the land of the living, my friend,' Edom said, gathering himself quickly. 'We did not think you would make it through the night. Are you able to speak with us?'

Finn opened his eyes, the scabbed skin on his eyelids breaking and flaking slightly. The sores wept through the breaks and glistened on his face.

'Father Edom, why is he crying?' Lauren asked nervously, clutching the priest's robes.

'Do not worry, child he is just happy to be alive,' Edom lied easily.

Finn turned his eyes to look at the priest and then at Lauren. Closing them again he was afraid of drifting back to sleep. A sleep he may not wake up from. Grimacing he sought the pain. It gave him life and he savoured every delicious, agonising moment.

He gritted his teeth and forced himself to sit up, the blanket of moist moss sticking to him giving the impression of a forest monster. A forest monster that Lauren told herself she was not in the least bit afraid of.

Edom was the one whose irrational fears caused goose bumps to run down his back. At least he hoped they were irrational fears.

'I thank you for your help,' Finn said, looking at Edom's robes before adding, 'Priest?'

'Yes,' Edom confirmed. 'Priest.'

The effort it took Finn to speak was apparent in his voice. Edom was worried that his patient would pass out again at any moment.

'Thank you,' Finn said again.

'You are welcome,' Edom replied, cautiously.

'Special thanks to you though, child,' Finn said to Lauren. 'You have done me a great service, one that I would make up to you.'

'And what service is that?' Edom asked, thumbing the dagger concealed beneath his robes.

'The prayers she offered up were heard,' he bowed stiltedly. Lauren beamed with delight.

'Do you have a name?' Edom asked his hand now closed on the knife. He did not like this at all.

'I do not know it, priest. Finn will have to do for now,' he said, smiling at Lauren.

'Can we do anything for you, Finn?' Edom was worried now. He did not like the way the man called him 'priest.' The strange bond that seemed to exist between the man and the child disturbed him. He was anxious to interrupt their conversation.

'I need herbs and roots to heal myself,' Finn said easing himself back in the bed and reluctantly closing his eyes. 'Can you collect them for me?'

'I can. The child's father will help me,' Edom was eager to press that there were more people, especially males, present should the stranger prove to be the threat he appeared.

'The warrior who found me in the river?'

'Yes,' Edom confirmed. 'How did you know he was a warrior?'

Finn did not answer.

'I need you to collect a flower of the slopes of the hills north of the river. The flower has a red, purple bulb centre with white petals,' Finn's voice became stilted as sleep threatened to steal him again.

'I am familiar with the flower. What is it for?'

'Later priest. I also need wort and aloe. Are you familiar with these things also?'

'I am.'

'Good. I need moss, honey and fruit. I would rest a while now. I fatigue easily.'

Finn listed more poultices and tea remedies that he would need as Lauren stroked his good hand and fawned over him.

Sleep eventually claimed him.

Edom was unsettled. He reluctantly left the child where she was and went to report his progress to Ben and Isela who were working at the rear of the cabin. Looking back in he saw Lauren giggling into her hand, but he could hear no words or see no movement from the sleeping form.

Edom subconsciously blessed himself and went into the yard.

Chapter Four

'You think the killer is one of the men from the keep?' Kastor asked, pressing his thumb and forefinger pressed against the bridge of his nose. The headaches were getting worse, and the recent spate of murders was doing nothing to help.

'Yes, sir,' the captain of the militia stood at attention. It would not be wise to relax until invited to do so. The general was known for the iron discipline with which he commanded his men. He was not the garrison commander of the capital for nothing.

'Sir,' Kastor waved him to a chair. 'Bring it over to the fire, warm yourself.'

Sevill gratefully accepted the chair and the broth as offered by the general's aide.

Sevill watched as the bodyguards subtly repositioned themselves in the room. All the better to slaughter him should he be turn out to be a threat. He did not look at them directly though, lest they take it as a challenge.

'What makes you think it is one of our soldiers?' Pogue asked. Kastor blanched at the use of 'our.' His unwelcome guest had no military experience and had bought his commission with gold and political leverage.

'Commandant Pogue,' Kastor said, addressing him politely. 'While we appreciate your frequent visits from the Plandor garrison I would prefer if you let me deal with my own men.'

'Of course, general,' Pogue relented, flashing his bodyguard a glance to see if the reproachful look was once again on his face. Roche had been one of the Imperial Guard and served as bodyguard to the senators. He was not happy to have been assigned to Pogue through political wangling and backslapping.

The bodyguard's face was stone.

'The civilian population do not engage in this manner of activity, sir,' captain Sevill replied.

'What? Of course they do,' Pogue blurted. 'They are mindless heretics. If we were not here trying to bring order, they would be butchering themselves and having sex with their sisters.'

'Indeed,' Kastor interrupted, as Pogue slurped another gulp of wine into his fat face. 'Continue, captain.'

'I believe the attacks are being carried out by one individual, the footprints where the attacks occurred, only showed one set,' Sevill tried to stop his lip curling into a snarl at the obese Pogue. He was a professional soldier and took his position seriously.

'And?' Kastor pressed.

'I believe I have seen this type of thing before. In other areas. Garrison towns where we have men stationed,' Sevill added. 'The killings did not seem just so...brutal, then.'

'Have you deduced which regiment might be involved?' the general asked, thoughtfully sipping at his own broth. He watched as his own bodyguard signalled an insult at Roche who returned the sentiment in kind.

Kastor smiled. The bodyguards had served together under his command, once upon a time. The signals were subtle, a simple repositioning of the thumb. Communication had to be disguised. At least these men were professional when the diplomats they guarded were not.

'No, general,' Sevill met the general's probing gaze. 'The killings are random. Each town is like this one in only one respect. There is a large turnover of men as regiments and sometimes entire army groups are passed through.'

'The killer picks his territory well,' Kastor observed.

'So it would seem, sir,' Sevill agreed. 'Either by plan or by chance. Perhaps he kills cleverly on instinct?'

'Perhaps,' said Kastor. 'Either way he has eluded your militia.'

'Unfortunately,' Sevill admitted.

'What effect on the townspeople?' Kastor enquired.

'They are fearful, they know it is one of our men,' Sevill advised.

'I have already said, it is not one of our men,' Pogue slammed down his cup. 'We are the civilised ones here. We do not carry out actions of this nature. Do I make myself clear?'

'With respect, Commandant Pogue, I hold rank here. If you do not shut your face, I will have one of the guards shut it for you.'

Pogue went bright red with barely controllable fury, as Kastor had one of the guards refill the fat man's cup for him.

'What can we do?' Kastor asked, his voice not having changed at all throughout the exchange.

Roche accepted the subsequent silent insult from his friend with good grace. His ward was a fat bastard after all.

'I would like to have the off-duty furloughs restricted and any coming or goings from the keep recorded, including patrol names. I would be able to narrow the field of suspects substantially.'

The general stared into the fire for a long while, stroking his trimmed beard as he often did. It was a trait he had inherited from his father, also a military man. Never rising above the rank of sub officer, Kastor's father had nevertheless made sure his sons were cared for and the money he had earned had been invested to send them all to school. Kastor's two brothers worked in the capital, one a merchant the other a banker. Kastor alone had followed in his father's footsteps and joined the army. His schooling had earned him a scholarship to the prestigious military academy of Yashtan where he had excelled as a junior officer.

Now he was just a policeman.

'I agree with you that it is important to find the beast that is carrying out these killings. It does us no good in the long term when we eventually make this a principality of the Empire,' Kastor replied sadly. 'But in the meantime, we have more pressing concerns that a soldier who takes out his…peculiar tastes on the populace. Things happen in war, captain that is a fact. People are murdered every day and I do not have the time to develop a conscience for these isolated incidents. I am sorry captain, I can afford to divert no resources to an endeavour that might have only marginal results at best, and lower morale even further at worst.'

'I understand, general.' Sevill did understand, which made his position as captain of the militia even more disturbing. The soldiers could plunder, steal and kill as they pleased but if they took any army property they would be imprisoned in the stockade or executed as an example to others.

'It does not sit well with me either, captain,' Kastor rose and poured the young officer more broth himself. 'And I appreciate your concerns. The interests of the Empire come first, until the end of the war at least.'

'Yes, sir. May I be dismissed, sir, I have other duties to attend to,' Sevill asked rising.

'Of course, captain,' Kastor said as Sevill stood and saluted. He liked the young man. He was a good officer and his men respected him. No officer is ever liked by the ranks, but as testament to Sevill they did not hate him. 'Take your broth with you. The northern winds are wicked this evening.'

'Yes, sir. Thank you,' Sevill saluted with his free hand and left.

'I do not like him,' Pogue gesticulated as the captain left the room. 'He has no stomach for this sort of business.'

'And you do?' Kastor looked at Pogue's swollen paunch under the ill-fitted armour.

'I certainly do,' Pogue missed the reference and charged on. 'I have command in my blood. The man responsible should be given a medal for killing this scum.'

'They are just people, Pogue, caught in the middle of a war,' Kastor observed solemnly.

'They are vermin and should be eradicated as such. I will not tolerate such scum in my garrison to the north.' Pogue was only missing the pulpit from which such fanatical speeches are normally made.

'Yes,' Kastor eased himself back in his comfortable chair and closed his eyes, it would do his blood pressure no good at all to let this political son of a bitch annoy him. 'North. You are heading to Plandor again tomorrow.'

'I was planning on staying for a few more days,' Pogue announced grandly.

'You are heading north tomorrow, Pogue, it was not a question,' Kastor did not open his eyes. 'You are dismissed.'

'Dismissed?' Pogue could not understand.

'Get out of my sight, man, I have work to do,' Kastor shouted.

'Of course, you are tired, I understand,' Pogue faltered and walked to the door.

'Have you forgotten how to salute, Commandant?' Kastor demanded harshly.

Pogue stopped dead at the door. Roche made no move to open it. Turning back to face the general, Pogue did as a crisp a salute as his podgy frame allowed. Kastor did not return it, instead waving him out with a flick of his hand.

'Idiot,' the general said to himself as he heard the flat footfalls disappearing down the hall. He stared into the flames seeking the face of the soldier, or officer he corrected himself, that was raping and butchering whole families at night. He thought of his own family and pulled his thick cloak tight against an already warm room.

He did not sleep well that night.

*

The long train of Osocan Cavalry moved slowly towards the Plandor plain. The lines of trees marked their route, huge silent sentinels stretching lazily to the skies.

Garrad was feeling maudlin today. He thought even the trees were conspiring against him. Why two of the Temple Knights had accompanied the regiment was beyond him. As if aware that he was thinking about them the taller of the Knights turned slightly in the saddle and fixed him an icy stare.

The general did not look away from Tobias' gaze. He thought of his days in the service of his country. At fifty-five, he was a respected warrior, leader of one of his nation's finest regiments. These fanatics did not intimidate him.

Garrad conceded that he was no longer sure if that was the confidence in his own abilities speaking or apathy brought on by age.

The Temple Knights rode to the front of his men, setting themselves apart from them by thirty yards. Their black armour was matted and dull, it absorbed light and not release it again into the normal world.

Lest it taints it, thought Garrad, finding quickly that the thought did not make him feel as light as he had intended.

The Knight turned and faced forward, not conferring with his brother. They rode high in the saddle, Garrad noticed, unaware of the arduous journey they had made to reach this point. He himself was slightly slouched, his body gently moving in time with his mount. All the fine young men he had the pleasure of leading were slumped also.

These Knights, who were men of God, made him think more of the Devil. He blessed himself subconsciously.

'The staging point is not far now,' his captain interrupted.

'Maybe ten miles,' Garrad returned. 'Not any farther.'

Duncan agreed, though he himself made it more like twelve miles. He knew that his general's understanding of the lie of the land and the movement of his troops far out matched his own immodest ability.

'You are not looking forward to reaching Plandor?' Duncan asked.

'No, captain, I am not. The thoughts of pandering to that fat fool, Pogue, are not very appealing. I would much rather march straight on, through, or over, the town and get on to the front. I do not like these delays any more than you do.'

'What are you implying, my general?' Duncan chuckled. 'I find these military courts to be the backbone of the army. We have travelled for more than fifteen hundred miles to get this far, with another three hundred to get to the front. Why we are going there I still don't know, by the way.'

'Don't start on that again,' Garrad reprimanded him.

'I'm not, I'm not,' Duncan replied, good-humouredly.

'We are going where we are ordered,' Garrad reminded him. 'The fact that imbeciles are issuing those orders have nothing to do with whether they are followed or not.'

'Precisely what I am saying. I will be glad to see the end of those boys, though,' Duncan indicated the Knights. 'They give me the creeps.'

'They do not make for pleasant company,' Garrad stated simply, not really wishing to get drawn on the subject.

'Why are they with us?' Duncan asked. He did not like it when military matters were taken out of his commander's hands. If his future was to be in the hands of another man, he much preferred it to be his general's.

'We are merely providing escort as the Holy Father himself decreed. They did not wish to ride with us either.'

'We will be well rid of them,' Duncan stared at them. 'I am just glad they are on our side.'

'Why is that?' Garrad asked.

'Because I have never been afraid of an enemy before and I do not wish to start now,' the captain confessed.

'You are afraid of them?' Garrad interest was piqued.

'Yes. I think it will help me to stay alive in their company,' Duncan admitted. 'You are not afraid?'

'No,' Garrad answered. 'But then I am old and stupid.'

'You are only two years older than me,' Duncan laughed.

'If you are saying that makes me just stupid, you will be a part of the fastest court martial in history,' Garrad laughed with is old friend. His voice was more solemn when he continued. 'We have both served on the Crusades, Duncan, we know what they are capable of. We were both there when we sacked the City of Agrafes. Forty-two thousand civilians.'

'I did not see them take part,' Duncan said.

'They gave the orders. We followed. We are all guilty.'

'I heard of their abilities in battle, but I have not witnessed it. I am sure much of it is exaggeration,' Duncan said confidently.

'I have seen them in action. There is little need to exaggerate. One of them anyway. I saw him during the push for Agrafes. It was the Temple Knight Nathan, one of the original Knights. I was a newly drafted lieutenant, young, and dumb. The Agrites ambushed our supply train as we were moving down to their far border, looking to flank one of their outposts. We fumbled a bit, startled. Nathan however was not startled. The Knight had turned his mount toward the attack and charged straight for it. I had led the lancers after him. My captain ordered regrouping at the wagons.'

'We cut straight through the Agrite ranks and the killing began. The Knight carried two swords. One long, one short. No shield. I swear I could not see them move, only the sun on the blade occasionally reminded me they were really there. The Agrites swarmed around us and on to the wagons, but we managed to contain them. We had organised in the minute that the Knight's attack had created. Even when the Knight's horse was cut from under him, he fought like a man possessed. The Agrites eventually stood back from him, refusing to engage. It would have meant certain death. Their attack broke and we routed the rest. During that skirmish we killed seventy-nine and took sixty three prisoners, for the loss of twenty men.'

'And?' Duncan had not heard this story before.

'After the battle, the Knight had us prepare for Mass. He stood on the largest wagon and gave service. We were not even allowed to put out sentries, he said we would suffer no further attack while we performed God's work that night. He said he was going to purge the land of the heretics. The prisoners were bound and held while he gouged their eyes and beheaded each one. He then impaled the head on the high pommels of each of the enemy horses. When the sixty prisoners had been executed, he galloped them away, knowing that the horses would return home to their camps. The remaining bodies he had brought with us and impaled one on a stake every half league after castrating the corpse.'

'I have heard many stories of the Agrafes campaign,' Duncan swallowed. 'I had not heard that.'

'I was ordered by Nathan himself to track the horses back to the enemy strong holds and mark their position,' Garrad reminisced.

'Smart,' Duncan agreed.

'Very. The main army group was brought in and the Agrites were found in their mountain stronghold. It did not take long to breach the inadequate defences. Nathan offered surrender at each enemy position. If they refused to surrender, they were slaughtered to a man. If they surrendered, they were spared.'

'More surrendered then?' Duncan asked. He had been a sergeant back then and had taken part in many of the main battles.

'Soon all surrendered,' Garrad confirmed. 'All but Agrafes itself.'

Duncan remained silent. He had been at Agrafes. It was a solemn day.

'The other Knight on that campaign is sitting on the horse to the right up ahead,' Garrad said watching the Knight.

'What?!' Duncan started. 'Who is he?'

'That is, the legendary, Brood. Temple Knight, warrior priest, leader of the Holy Order.'

'He was honoured by the Holy Father for his actions against the heretics and the sacking of Agrafes. He was given command of our forces in the sub-continent to do with us he pleased. He marched our army against the neighbouring nations and in one year had control of the whole peninsula.

Within five years he had marched the entire fourth and fifth army groups across most of the southern continent and civilised it.'

Duncan raised his flask to his lips and drank deeply.

'So that is Brood,' Duncan said, eyeing the dark figure.

'I read the reports, though thankfully after that day I served only with the army and never with the Knights. I have never seen anything to match that. That day I saw everything we accused the heretic enemy of doing. On that day, I did not know who the real enemy was.'

Brood's companion turned in his saddle and fixed his stare on the general, fire burning dangerously in his dark eyes. The air stopped in Duncan's lungs. Fear grew that they had been overheard, or worse that they had read his thoughts. When the Knight looked away again, he drank greedily on the fiery liquid, coughing noisily.

'Careful, my friend,' the general cautioned his aide.

'Butchers. We will be well rid of them,' Duncan said.

'They were not the only butchers on that day Duncan, and it would grieve me to have you executed as a heretic. Remember that many of our own men believe as they do and aspire to be like them in every way.'

'Yes, my general,' Duncan said, watching the Knights warily and glancing unconsciously over his shoulder at the line of lancers.

*

Tobias leaned forward in the saddle. The hatred of the minions behind them was apparent on his features. He gripped his sword, eyes glaring straight ahead focusing on the thought of gutting the man who had spoken.

'Do not concern yourself, brother Tobias,' Brood said gently. 'Calm your thoughts. A shepherd does not get angry when sheep bleat. He merely controls them that little bit tighter. If the sheep are afraid of the shepherd, then control is easier.'

'Yes, brother,' Tobias reigned in the momentary lack of control. 'It would not do for me to react in anger to the lesser men behind us.'

'They are not lesser men, brother. They are merely men. We are in their service as much as they are in ours. Just as sheep are lost without their shepherd, a shepherd is nothing without his flock.'

'Thank you, brother, you humble me with your wisdom,' Tobias bowed slightly.

'It is a question of how best to control them. Since we need them alive, mostly, fear is the best tool,' Brood explained. 'Watch, brother.'

Brood turned his horse sideways and waited for the troops to move up to his position. As the lead men approached, Brood did not move his mount to one side to allow them to pass. The lead soldier, unsure of what to do, raised his hand to stop the regiment. Two thousand men stopped, wondering what was happening.

Garrad, Duncan and several officers rode to the front.

'What in the name of God do you think you are doing?' Garrad thundered.

Brood did not look at him, his gaze was locked on Duncan. The silence grew. Duncan began to sweat openly as the seconds passed.

After what seemed like hours, Brood spoke.

'It is precisely in the name of God that I have stopped,' Brood said evenly, his voice carrying, despite the softness of his words, his eyes boring into Duncan. He continued before Garrad could react. 'I need to ascertain the loyalty of your men before I continue our quest. We are sanctioned by the Holy Father, and therefore by God, to carry our works into this land. I now hear seditious comments being used by officers of this supposedly elite regiment.'

'I would suggest that you are mistaken, Lord Knight,' Garrad countered. 'The loyalty of my men to the Holy Father is without question.'

'Perhaps, general. Perhaps I am not convinced. You would not wish me to test the loyalty of your men.' Brood watched as Duncan's face became flushed with fear. 'The tests are somewhat...demanding on a body.'

'No, Lord Knight, that will not be necessary,' Garrad pulled his mount directly across the path of the Knight and rested his hand gently on his sabre. If the Knight moved towards any of his men, he would die on the spot.

'Good,' he finally lifted his eyes off Duncan. 'I am glad we understand each other, general. It would not do for warriors in a holy war to make battle with one another.'

'No, it would not,' Garrad responded his voice and gaze steady.

Brood moved his horse close to Garrad, so they were only inches apart.

'Had you drawn that blade, old man, I would have cut you down like a dog and ordered your own beloved regiment to hack you to pieces,' Brood hissed. When Garrad did not react he added, 'You would have been lucky if your family survived the subsequent purge. Do we have an understanding?'

Garrad again thought of reaching for his sword, Brood leaned back and smiled, the coldness of it cutting him to the bone.

'Yes, we have an understanding, brother Knight,' Garrad agreed.

'Good. Now move your men on,' Brood ordered. 'We have wasted enough time.'

Garrad nodded to the captain, who, with a sweep of his arm started the men back on their path to Plandor. His teeth gritted, Garrad moved to one side of the dirt track allowing his men to pass, surrendering to Duncan's original offer of a drink.

'Sufficiently cowed now, I think,' Tobias said, smiling when Brood arrived beside him.

'There is no honour in humbling a sheep,' Brood said. 'Perhaps you should concern yourself with the wolves we are likely to meet on this journey, brother.'

Tobias was not concerned with meeting any wolves.

*

'Glad to see you are alive,' Edom said, lifting the bowl of foul-smelling broth and stirring it.

'Alive,' the man repeated as though savouring the word. His eyes were heavy, and he knew he had been unconscious for extended periods. His moments of wakefulness were not engrained on his memory though he knew he had spoken to the old man before.

'We did not think you were going to make it for a time,' Edom lifted the broth to his nose and frowned before passing it over to the injured man. 'It does not smell very good but since it is a recipe you requested, I would hope that you would drink it anyway.'

'I gave you it?'

'In one of your moments of lucidity,' Edom spooned a helping into the Finn's mouth, mopping it off his chin as it inevitably spilt.

'Who are you?' he managed after the swallowed. It tasted better than it smelled but that was no great achievement.

'I am Father Edom,' the old man shrugged, the gesture lost on his patient. Edom had introduced himself seven times now and each time been forgotten.

'I thank you, priest, for your kindness,' Finn said, making more of an effort to keep the foul broth in his mouth.

'It is not me you should thank, Finn, it is the family whose house you now share,' Edom held another spoonful poised.

'You called me Finn.'

'Yes,' Edom laughed. 'I suppose I did. You were not in a position to give us your name, so the child named you. Has your identity returned to you yet?'

Finn lay back and closed his eyes. Nothing came to him. No memories, no images. Nothing. A daemon. Grey. Landscape. Armour. Pain.

'Nothing,' he replied.

'Well then. Finn will have to do in the meantime,' Edom spooned the last of the broth into his mouth, gratified that he managed to swallow it all.

'I am in pain,' Finn stated flatly.

'Do you know what happened to you?' Edom asked.

'No,' Finn managed a slight movement of his head. A deal. Save a life. Daemon. 'I know nothing.'

'That makes two of us, my friend,' Edom smiled. 'Benjad found you in the river several miles away. You were close to death and severely burned. You had an arrow in you. It looked like you had been attacked.'

Finn did not answer.

'Have you been in a battle?' Edom set the bowl to one side.

'I do not know,' Finn replied truthfully. 'I do not remember.'

'Are you a warrior?' Edom asked.

'Why would you think that priest?' Finn asked. Armour. War.

'When I was stripping you of the burnt clothing, I noticed that your undershirt was silk. It allowed me to withdraw the arrowhead without damage.'

'The main damage from an arrow,' Finn recited aloud as though quoting a military text. 'If not instantly fatal, is when the arrowhead is pulled out. Silk would envelop the barbed head and allow it to be eased clear with minimal damage to the tissues.'

War.

Edom was silent.

Finn closed his eyes, wondering where he had learned that. He knew he was a warrior. He could feel it. Warrior was how Daemon addressed him. Armour?

'Are you a soldier?' Edom asked.

'I am a warrior,' Finn answered, opening his eyes and looking at the priest.

'For whom do you fight?' Edom asked, fearing the answer.

'I do not know. Priest. Honestly.'

The two sat looking at each other for a time.

'The Legionnaires use silk underclothing to protect against arrows,' Edom explained. 'Though the material is hard to come by these days. We do not have the resources for war that we used to. There have been no allied incursions by uniformed units. That would leave only one alternative, Finn.'

'And what is that?' he asked.

'That you are our enemy, a soldier of the Puritans,' Edom said sadly.

'I answered you honestly when I said I remember nothing. It may be as you say,' Finn admitted.

'What are we to do with you?' Edom sat back in the small chair. It was uncomfortable. Ben was a fine warrior and husband, but he was no wood smith.

'Whatever you please,' Finn said. 'I am in no position to resist you.'

'Should we turn you out into the forest? Give you over to our army or return you to your own?' Edom asked.

'I do not know, priest, but I know that you will do what is…appropriate' Finn closed his eyes against the pain.

'But not what is right?' Edom asked.

'Who is to know what is right or wrong? Certainly not I. Apparently, I am atoning for enough as it is, priest, without having to wrestle with your conscience also. You care for this young family and would see no harm come to them. I also wish them no harm. You will make the right decision.'

'Yes,' Edom was tense.

'I am no threat. I swear I will bring no harm on this house. I will be gone as soon as I am healed or as soon as is required of me.'

'That will have to do then. Sleep. I will give the family your assurances. They will help me decide.'

'Thank you, old man,' Finn said as sleep took him.

Chapter Five

The cold of the desert night had bitten deeply into the fragile bodies of the knights in training, as they huddled together for heat. The water they had collected from the sparse indigenous plants and what little food they had scavenged was gone with neither of them providing much in the way of nourishment. They had set traps in the night and cleared leaves to collect dew from the frost so the morning should bring at least some relief.

'At least there is no wind,' Nathan said, through chattering teeth.

'No wind,' Talan replied.

They had found their brother, Nathan, in the wilderness and were trying to keep themselves awake fearing the permanent sleep that closing their eyes may bring.

'It is beautiful,' Nathan looked at the cloudless sky and the myriad stars that fought to outshine one another.

'Yes,' answered Talan as he huddled closer to the others.

'Beautiful,' Joshua said. He did not want to talk. He was looking deep inside himself for the place he dared not normally go. In this place he knew he would find sanctuary. Peace. Heat.

'I did not know the desert could be so cold,' Nathan said, talking about anything that came to mind. 'At least there is no wind.'

'No wind,' Talan intoned again.

'We will not die here this night,' Joshua said, his teeth chattering.

'How can you say that?' Nathan asked. 'We are going to die. If the elements don't kill us, then we will starve or die of thirst by the end of tomorrow.'

'To quit is to die, brother,' Talan replied. 'We must keep our strength and trust in God. He did not bring us together only to have us die. We will survive this night and many more like it.'

'How can you know this?' Nathan whined, the cold becoming a pain all its own.

'God has a plan for us,' Talan tried to smile but his face muscles would not respond.

'No wind,' Joshua said again. Had the boys not been huddled together he would not have been heard. Joshua's breathing slowed, came in short gasps and then stopped entirely.

'He is gone from us,' Nathan said sadly.

'No, I can still feel him. He is close.'

Joshua let the unconsciousness wash over him, giving himself up to the darkness. The cold was still eating at him but could feel faint waves of heat coming from deep within him, from the dark abyss that hid his soul. The heat was coming from there, tugging at him with a gravity all its own.

He tried to resist at first, fearing death, then letting go of his lingering fears, he closed his eyes and let go of his conscious thought.

Talan held his dying brother as Joshua's body went limp in his arms. Tears would not come. His body did not have enough water to spare.

Joshua was anything but dead. He could feel the soft radiant heat coming from deep inside the husk that should have been a youthful body and sent his spirit plummeting towards it. He could feel the warmth of his inner spirit drawing him in. The journey was difficult though short. Joshua felt as though he was trying to squeeze through an exceedingly small hole, his fingers extended to try and reach the warm glow.

After what seemed like an eternity, he managed to reach it. Warmth. Heat. Rebirth.

Nathan and Talan felt the warmth rush into Joshua's body and after only a moment felt it pour into their own. The cold of the night was driven back, and Nathan felt at ease.

Joshua opened his eyes and smiled.

'At least there is no wind,' he said, and the brothers laughed together. The warmth brought with it a sense of peace and contentment.

'How are you doing this?' Nathan asked as Joshua let go of his brother and stood to look out over the desert.

'How are you doing it?' Joshua returned.

Nathan realised that he was now generating his own heat even though they were no longer touching.

'I do not know,' he said, shaking his head but still smiling.

'How do you feel?' Joshua asked.

'Content,' he replied. 'Whole.'

'Is this the danger point of the cold?' Talan asked. 'Hypothermia? Is this our bodies shutting down, the euphoric feeling before death?'

'It does not feel like death to me, brothers,' Nathan said. 'It feels like life.'

Talan moved his hands before his face, waggling his fingers as though they trailed light in their wake.

'I think that is what this final stage was about,' Joshua continued. 'We were to find ourselves or die. That is what Lord Saladin said. The only way for us to survive out here was to unlock the power we hold within us. I found mine on the brink of death. When your mind felt mine, it recognised it and opened in you.'

'This is the test?' Talan asked. 'To live or die?'

'God accepts no less from his followers. The Holy Father Saladin will not accept us as his chosen warriors if we are less than we can be.'

'I can feel everything,' Nathan said, his mind expanding out to explore the desert. 'I can feel all the life around me.'

'There is someone coming,' Talan cautioned. 'He is moving quickly from the east.'

The brothers separated across the clearing, creating a larger fighting area.

'It is our brother, Brood,' Talan said.

The boys gathered again as Brood crested the ridge at a jog, heading straight for his brothers.

'I see you have managed to survive the night,' he said amicably, as he sat beside them setting a larger leather satchel on the ground before them.

'Where did you get that?' Nathan asked, his eyes wide in wonder.

'I went back to the camp. Appias saw the error of his ways and gave it to our cause,' Brood explained as he unfolded the leather bindings and lifted out a large water container, fresh bread and cold meats. He also pulled a large dagger with which he carefully sliced strips of dried beef for the drooling boys.

'Easy, now,' he chided. 'Don't rush it down. We don't know how long we will have to make this last.'

'Your injuries seem to have cleared, Joshua,' Talan said. 'I cannot feel your pain.'

'My pain is still there,' Joshua replied. 'But I have hidden it deeply.'

'You have healed yourself,' Nathan observed.

'As can you. As can we all,' Joshua said. 'The same power that is giving you life at this moment, that is providing you with inner heat. It allowed me to control my body. My ribs are still broken, but they are mending. My lungs are better now though.'

Brood reached out and placed his hand gently on the injured ribs.

'I can feel it,' he said. 'We will be able to help you.'

'I know,' Joshua agreed. 'But first we must eat, our spirits still need our bodies to survive.'

The boys ate their portions, struggling to chew slowly. They could feel the energy adding to their life force and no longer feared the sun as it now cleared the horizon, its rays marching across the sand towards them. Talan pulled a large hide cover from the satchel and erected it quickly on the rods that had originally given the satchel its shape. Huddling out of the sun they sipped on the water.

'How did you get the supplies from Appias?' Nathan asked.

'He had no further need of them,' Brood shrugged as he turned on his side to sleep through the heat of the day. It would be more prudent to travel at night. 'It appears he swallowed his tongue in the night and died in a fit as he choked on his own blood and vomit.'

Nathan and Talan exchanged a look.

'It would appear,' Brood said sleepily as he poked idly at his healing ribs, 'that the powers we were chosen for are as useful for killing as they are for restoring health. I staked him out in the dunes and flayed the skin from his body while he was still alive. I want the desert predators to have a go before his body is discovered.'

Nathan smiled, surprised that he was pleased at the suffering of another. A warrior in the service of the Lord should not be beaten by anyone. That is the act of a heretic, says the Holy Father, and he should be treated as such.

Brood had acted justly, and Nathan could see no fault in his action.

Talan saw the events replayed in Brood's mind but took no satisfaction from it. He was pleased to see that Brood had taken no pleasure from the incident. It was merely an act of retribution. No more.

The brothers lay down together, still cuddling this time for comfort as much for the need of heat and survival. They began their morning prayers together and then their meditation. They focused on the brightest star as it faded from the sky and let it fill their entire consciousness, imagining the sailor navigating at night by it, finding their way home. Just as the boys were trying to do now.

'What will we do?' Joshua asked.

'We will find no more brothers,' Talan said.

'In the desert?' Nathan asked.

'No,' he replied. 'The rest of the boys are dead.'

He did not need to go on. They could all feel the absence of the recruits' life forces in the desert. None had lasted past the first day and night.

'Home, then,' Joshua said, saddened at the loss of young life. They had not really known the other boys, but they had suffered a common hardship and were bonded by it.

'Home,' Brood confirmed. 'We have much work to do. We four are the start of something beautiful. We are the apostles of the Lord God and will bring his message to the world.'

'Twelve,' Talan said.

They did not speak as the sky itself seemed to ache with the effort of holding back the dawn. The horizon glowed in warning of the imminent arrival of searing heat.

The sun, which brings life to the rest of the world, was merciless in its destruction of desert life.

'Yes,' Brood said. 'Twelve.'

*

Finn lay on the bed and for once he was not in pain. The pain was still there, he was sure, but it was manageable to the point of ignoring it. Unless, of course, he tried to move.

Ben had collected all the flowers, roots and fruits as directed. The child had helped, or so Isela had informed him. The priest had followed Finn's instruction and made tea infusions, salves, poultices and rubs. The immediate effect had been to aggravate the entire surface of the skin as though he were again on fire. Finn had made no sound when the priest had applied them though his body had spasmed. During one application Finn had grabbed the pole of his stretcher bed and snapped it in his clenched fists.

He had been upgraded to a much sturdier frame. Had his body not been in constant torment he would have found the bed tolerable.

'Is he alright?' Ben had asked when Edom came out of the cabin after applying the salves.

'Yes, I believe so. He appears to know what he is doing.'

Finn could hear them from the cabin, despite their hushed tones. He did know what he was doing but he did not where this knowledge came from. As with all things now, he was just accepting them. Even his new name seemed appropriate. A good fit.

'You still think him to be Puritan,' Ben said.

'I do not know,' Edom replied. 'He prays more often than I and his accent is of this land. I believe he is truthful when he says he does not know either.'

Ben looked to the cabin and rubbed his chin. He had cut himself shaving and wondered at his old face.

'We will have to deal with him soon,' Ben said at last.

'We cannot kill him in his sleep,' Edom said.

'"We" cannot but "I" can,' Ben corrected him.

'Then why bring him here and nurse him to health? As soon as he is well, we will send him on his way,' Edom said. 'We are not going to restore him to life just so that he is well enough to be executed by either side should we make a mistake.'

'That is not the decision of a good solider, old friend,' Ben chided.

'But it is the decision of a just man,' Edom said. 'I do not want him haunting my dreams through the injustice I cause. We must let things run their own course.'

'Not at the expense of my family,' Ben said firmly. 'You will send a patrol back when you go to the mountains.'

'I will,' Edom agreed.

'When you go soon,' Ben fixed him with a warning glare.

Edom nodded.

'And we will keep him alive until they make a decision?' Edom asked.

'We will,' Ben agreed, hefting his wood axe and heading off to vent some frustration. He would not have the wrong decision come back to haunt his family.

Finn relaxed, not for his own safety, but in the knowledge that, at least for the moment, he was not causing distress to the family. He would leave as soon as he had the strength.

*

The child had not come to see him for the two days he had been treating himself and Finn found that he missed her company. The gelatinous salve covered him from head to toe. He looked as though he had just been birthed, again. From the womb of what creature, he could not imagine but he was sure it would not have been pretty.

His eyes were covered with leaf pads containing a thick herb and fresh mud, secured in place with a cotton gauze bandage. The bandage did not permit him to see but his vision had deteriorated so badly he was effectively blind anyway. He hoped this was only temporary after being exposed to the heat that had caused the damage.

The priest had been his only constant companion.

'How is the weather today, priest?' Finn asked.

'Cold on my old bones,' Edom smiled, the expression lost on his blindfolded patient. 'But sunny. Lauren likes it.'

'The air is good in the mountains. Fresh.'

'Yes, it is.' Edom sat beside the bed and began again to mix the herbs for more tea. 'The cold winds come down off the glacier far to the north.'

'I see,' Finn replied, and smiled since he obviously could not with the bandage in place. The expression caused his face skin to crack and brought much pain with it. The humour was lost on the old man anyway.

They sat silently for a while.

'Have you dreamed of the daemon again, Finn?' Edom asked, curious as to the meaning of the dreams Finn him confided to him.

'No,' Finn replied. 'No more dreams.'

Edom peeled away the drying salves and bandages.

'You are healing very quickly, Finn,' Edom cast an expert eye over the damaged areas.

'Good,' Finn replied. 'Then the pain it causes is not for nothing.'

Edom pressed the skin and could feel moderate elasticity coming back into it.

'You are a skilled healer,' Finn offered.

'And you are a skilled patient,' Edom countered. 'Your knowledge of medicine far outweighs my own.'

'Perhaps I worked in the army hospital,' Finn suggested.

'You do not seem the hospital orderly type,' Edom smiled.

'I do not feel the orderly type,' Finn admitted.

'What do you feel?' Edom asked.

'I feel constant pain in my body, I feel pain in my mind when I try to delve into a past, I cannot see, I am tormented by daemons in my sleep and I am putting in danger the only people I know. How would you feel, priest?' Finn's tone carried no self-pity. It was merely a question.

'I would feel happy to be alive, still in the service of my God.'

'A fine answer,' Finn replied.

'Are you happy to be alive, Finn?' Edom asked.

'Happiness is not something I believe I have ever known. I am alive and that is enough.'

'Is it enough?' Edom sat back in the chair, tired after the long treatment.

'It will have to be for the moment,' Finn answered. 'You are happy to be alive because you feel you have purpose. When I have my purpose back, perhaps I will be content again.'

'But not happy?'

'I do not think I have ever sought happiness,' Finn answered, not knowing why he knew this to be true. Images of his past were lost to him, but feelings and sentiment sometimes pushed to the surface.

'Then I am sad for you,' Edom said. 'To miss out on the happiness of life and love is a waste of God's gift.'

'Perhaps God had other plans for me, priest.'

'Perhaps he did at that,' Edom replied. 'Maybe you should ask your daemon friend what he thinks of it.'

'I shall. Though I doubt he will answer. His bedside manner is not as good as yours, old man.'

'Nor is he as charming as you, invalid,' Edom laughed.

'Why are you a priest?' Finn asked.

'You say it like it is a dreadful thing, Finn. You call me it as though it were my name. Being a priest to the people that need me is the most important thing in my life. It is not a title; it is who I am.'

'Why do it?' Finn asked.

'Someone has to,' Edom smiled. 'I bring comfort and guidance. Leadership where necessary. I keep the mountain camps on the path of righteousness.'

'Pious rhetoric, priest,' Finn said.

'Really. You know my prayers as well as I, Finn. I hear you. You speak the old tongue better than I. I had thought you a holy man at first, warrior. There are not many who understand the healing arts. A warrior you may be, but you are also a scholar, healer or a priest in your previous life. I look forward to finding out which.'

'A philosopher too?'

'Many things I am sure,' Edom agreed.

'You are going to the mountain camps when you are finished here.'

'I am,' Edom admitted.

'I will go with you.'

'Why?' Edom was confused.

'I heard you speak with Ben. You do not know me. If I am an enemy, you cannot in good conscience turn me loose. The family will be named collaborator and executed. You will be exiled at best. It is better for all that I go with you, as prisoner or travelling companion until the matter is resolved.'

'It will be as you wish. I will stay until you are well enough to travel.'

'You are a good man, priest. I do not mean to be harsh with you.'

'Yes, you do,' Edom smiled, 'but then I am used to listening to children. I may put you across my knee and spank you.'

Finn smiled. More pain.

'Thank you, Father,' Finn said.

'"Father" is it now? That is an improvement.'

'Do not get used to it, priest.'

'I won't. Rest now. I will speak to you again later. You can berate me some more.'

'I look forward to it, old man,' Finn said, sleep claiming him.

'As do I,' Edom said sincerely as he stood and walked from the cabin.

*

Reyes manoeuvred the Puritan scouts cautiously up the trail. The horses were happy with the slow pace, recovering from the previous days of hard riding. Though still a little farther south for the usual raids to take place there was no point in being careless.

Reyes had kept his men alive by being wary to the point of paranoia. What did his old colonel used to say? "Just because you are paranoid does not mean they are not out to get you?" Truer words had never been spoken, especially when it came to working in the reconnaissance patrols. Reyes had been in the saddle for six full days now and his ass was sleeping soundly, moulded to the saddle. His favourite horse had been cut from under him three months before and he found his new mount, though well trained, hard to get used to despite the well-worn saddle.

He thought back fondly to the days when he and his charger had ridden in the great campaigns to secure the southern end of the Empire. At sixteen hands it was a majestic animal. Reacting to the tide of battle, sometimes before Reyes, their unspoken relationship had saved him on many occasions. He wondered briefly if it was natural for a grown man and soldier to miss a horse so. Perhaps, but he did not wish to invite ridicule by sharing it with another.

The nations he rode against had crumbled before the military might of the army. The Crusade had dwindled to skirmish action with small pockets of resistance usually in the highland areas.

Dominate the land and you dominate the battle.

The natives knew their land and would fight to the death for it. It would take longer to flush them out, but flushed they would be. It was just not interesting work for a professional soldier.

Reyes had been glad when his unit had been moved to Ellistrin. Preparation for the big push across the lines. War on a grand scale. Lies and false promises. Now his entire reconnaissance company had been broken down into small raiding groups to scout along the front line, deliver messages among the garrison towns and generally be given every scrap job the army had going.

Raiding brothels in the capital was the only raiding they got to do now and even then, the whores had to be imported. The indigenous females would likely try to kill you if molested them or commit suicide after.

Reyes leaned over and spat on the ground. He hated this. His men hated this. He had the feeling his men hated him too. They resented him for what they saw as his disfavour, which resulted in them being assigned these mundane tasks. He would not be surprised if he woke up one morning with his throat cut.

He was the first to admit that he was not an ass kisser. He would not bend over and take it like a good little non-commissioned officer.

When he had not kissed ass in Plandor, that fat bastard, Pogue, probably did this to him on purpose. With things moving slow at the front Commandant Pogue had the power to assign his troops as he saw fit. He commanded mid-country. Reyes thought lazily about getting himself assigned to Southern Command. The ports to the south were warmer and more hospitable than this wretched north with its piercing wind.

Reyes had been born at the lower end of Avalon, which meant the lower end of the eye could see. Plains extending from horizon to horizon and steppes that rose straight up from the earth as if to converse with God himself. And women. Women with flaxen hair and passion that could drive a man insane.

Reyes had married such a woman once upon a time. A beautiful woman with a fiery temper. They argued and made love. He was infatuated with her from the moment he saw her to the moment he strangled her in a fit of jealous rage when he had caught her in bed with a man from the local militia. He was absolved by the minister for killing his wife, an act that he did not regret. It was seen as lawful in the eyes of God as she had broken the holy vows for fidelity she had sworn before him.

He had been given a choice of prison or the army for castrating the militiaman though. Reyes had always considered the military and opted for that. He smiled at the thought. The army had been like a reward for the retribution he had exacted on the man. Divine intervention perhaps? Reyes doubted it.

One thing he had come to learn in all the bloody battles he had been through, was that if there was a God, He was a fickle bastard at best to allow so many young men throw away their lives in what they thought was His name.

Reyes looked round at the figures drifting along the path behind him. Young, old, new, veterans. It was the veterans that were worrying him at the moment. These were men he had served with for the last eighteen years, through campaigns in nearly every corner of the Empire. Now they sat slumped in the saddle, brows furrowed, and a look of murderous intent painted plainly on their faces. The new boys were worried by the sullen veterans. Instead of inspiring the recruits the veterans were intimidating and bullying them.

Reyes had not known fear in battle. But he felt it now. It was not his age either. At forty he had seen and done everything he could hope to do. He did not want money or glory. Merely to serve with his comrades in arms and die in battle. He did not want to die old and infirm. He did not want to die at the hands of the men behind him either. When they rode into settlements now, they invariably killed someone innocent. If there was such a thing.

One of the newer recruits had accused Vorden of raping a girl on the outskirts of one of the towns when they had stopped a month before. During their next engagement with the northern Legionnaires, the accuser had conveniently ended up with his throat cut. Reyes did not have any evidence with which to court martial and hang the offender. He knew the witness had been murdered and not died in combat, but he could not prove it. Not that anyone would have done anything about it. He knew Vorden, or one of this men, had done it.

'Time to make camp, chief,' Yasin said reigning up beside him.

'We'll settle at the next clearing. Cold camp. Give the order,' Reyes said.

Yasin was a good soldier, he thought to himself. Trustworthy at least. They had been through a lot, and he did not seem to side with the other veteran soldiers against him. Too professional for that. He would have to be rewarded for his loyalty.

As they entered the next clearing Reyes watched as the men set about making camp. Cold camp meant no fire, and no hot food or tea. With morale already low, he knew that every order of cold camp was an order closer to his own death.

He would not telegraph his position to a very competent enemy just so his men could have a brew. The last thing he wanted was an ambush from a Legionnaire patrol.

'Everything is set,' Yasin reported handing Reyes a flask of cold soup. 'Though they are not happy about it.'

'They don't have to like it…'

'…they just have to do it,' Yasin said, finishing a phrase that had been drilled into their unit. 'Vorden and his boys are complaining bitterly. Best keep an eye on him, chief.'

'I know, Yasin, but I thank you for the warning,' Reyes said as he watched the enormous form of Vorden moving easily between the trees. 'I guess we have a reckoning coming soon.'

'Could be, chief, could be. I would sleep softly tonight all the same.'

Reyes nodded. In the field, military justice was rarely a thing for the courts. It would eventually come to a clash of personalities; a blade would be drawn and difference would be resolved when someone was dead.

It was a war, after all, and these things happen.

*

Emperor Saladin looked out over his city. Time and again he was drawn to this vista.

His city.

Emperor no less. His parents would have been pleased had they lived.

Had he not killed them.

It was dusk in the city and the oil lamps were being lit. Saladin watched them expand outward from the palace like a spider's web. How appropriate he thought, and not for the first time.

Saladin closed his eyes seeking to join with the mind of the killer. He savoured the fresh kill that the murderous soldier had made only this night in the Ellistrin capital. The Emperor followed the killer's moves closely, sharing his twisted emotions with him and at time adding to them, leading him in his frenzy of insane killing.

Raw hatred, fear, anger, futility, surrender, passion, love, lust. They all flooded through the mind of the deranged man as he plunged his knife home again and again. Saladin could find no sweeter prize than to share the mind of such a human animal.

'He has killed again,' Altai said from the other side of the curtain, not wishing to intrude on his master.

'He has,' Saladin beckoned his minister onto the veranda.

'Quite an appetite,' Altai observed.

'He does,' the Emperor replied, sleepily. 'It pleases me greatly.'

'It never seems to last just long enough,' the minister said.

'No,' Saladin agreed, 'but then he does not have your years of experience.'

Altai was more than minister to the Emperor. He saw himself more as confidant. A man with similar powers and tastes. He was most trusted of the Holy Father and as such was given freedom to experience his many varied, and some would say evil, tastes.

Saladin saw him as a familiar. A pet. A foreign dog who served a useful purpose. Altai procured specimens. Human fodder that could fill his soul.

'I need nourishment,' Saladin said.

'I know,' Altai bowed. 'I am working on it. There has not been much to choose from these days. Slim pickings.'

Saladin was about to berate him for failure but understood the sensitive nature of the work.

'Let me know as soon as you have some' Saladin said of the drug that was more intoxicating than any narcotic. Human life force.

'A few days at most, my Lord,' Altai assured him. 'I can feel it.'

'Good,' Saladin said, closing his eyes and returning to the image of carnage in Ellistrin. Altai revelled in the depravity of the acts. Saladin merely watched them unfold as he would a spider and fly.

'Why does he do it?' Altai asked. Though gifted, he could not discern all that his master could.

'Because he can,' Saladin said simply and dismissed his minion.

Chapter Six

'You are recovering well,' Isela set the bowl of stew in front of Finn and mashed the vegetables to a pulp. He was still having great difficulty eating. The skin was mending but if he opened his mouth, it caused the flesh to crack setting the healing process back even further. With the eye pads still in place he had nonetheless graduated to spoon feeding himself under Isela's watchful sentry.

'I am feeling stronger, my lady,' Finn said, taking another bite.

'You never say much during these meals, yet you speak with Father Edom. Do I frighten you?' Isela asked.

'Yes,' Finn replied. 'Though I mean no disrespect. You do make me uncomfortable.'

'Really? In what way?' she asked, stirring the pungent tea infusion that now accompanied Finn's meals.

'I am sorry. I do not wish to offend. How can I talk openly with you when I am so indebted to you? You have sheltered me, fed me and openly cared for me. You took me in when I could have been an enemy or open threat to you. I may even still attract harm to your home. You accepted without question that I had no memory of my life before my accident. You have never questioned my motives. You have left your daughter with me and allowed her to play with me. You allow me free run of your home. I feel…humbled.'

Isela picked up the ladle and shovelled a huge portion of stew onto his plate.

'You need not feel humbled, Finn. I would have done the same for any man,' Isela said truthfully.

'I believe you would, my lady, and that is worse again. You did it for me despite the fear you have that I will bring trouble upon your family, harm to your daughter or send your husband off to war.'

'You see a great deal for a blind man,' Isela replied, no longer liking the conversation and wishing it could go back to the silent meals.

'I see enough to know that I owe you a great service, one that I fear I may never be able to repay,' Finn said.

'You do not need to pay us, Finn,' Isela replied, grinding the potatoes vigorously.

'Which is exactly why I must, my lady.'

Finn spooned the last of the stew into his mouth, careful not to stretch his face too far but the inevitable tearing soon needed tending.

Isela took the empty bowls and set them on the table returning with a clean over shirt and trousers.

'Father Edom said you should be able to start wearing loose clothing,' she said setting them by his hand. 'I will help you dress.'

'Thank you,' Finn said, 'but I am overwhelmed by a sudden sense of modesty. My lady, I will manage it when you have gone.'

'Such a gallant notion, Finn but I am an old woman now and there is little I have not seen,' Isela said. 'And you do not need to call me "lady".'

'I know, but it is nice to see you blush when I do,' Finn said slyly.

'Ha. You do see far too much for a blind man, and you shall call me Isela from now on.'

'As you wish,' Finn replied. 'Would you answer me a question, Isela?'

'If I can,' she said warily.

'Why do you let me stay?'

'Truly, I do not know. Father Edom is right, Finn, that you are a dangerous man, but you are not a threat to us.'

'How do you know this?'

'You are not from here, Finn. When you spoke our language at the start, you spoke with an accent. Now that accent is gone, you have learned from us in your time here. You are educated far beyond our simple measure. You know herbs and medicine and healing arts beyond the ken of even Father Edom with whom you can debate for hours on issues of politics and religion. You are a man with a past to be wary of for I do not believe you to be a holy man.'

'You think all this, yet I am not a threat to you?'

'No. Lauren likes you,' she said simply. 'And I have seen the way you are with her. You will not bring harm to her or her family.'

'You see a lot for someone who is not blind, Isela,' Finn said, the smile appearing as a grimace on his still healing face.

'I see with the eyes of a mother. I can tell when my cubs are in danger.'

'And they are not now?'

'Yes, Finn, they are always in danger, but not from you.'

*

The sun was high over Avalon, its incessant heat causing the smooth quarried stones to shimmer. The slaves had no reprieve as they sat in the open yard while they were pawed and prodded by parasol wielding merchants.

Sansha watched as the rough looking men moved up and down the lines, prodding here, squeezing there. They took particular interest in her because of her youth and her dark skin. The tall, pale skinned ones seemed so unkind. They hurt her when they touched her but at least they did not mark her or make her bleed. She was just merchandise now. Damaged goods did not fetch a fair price.

Sansha could not understand the guttural barks that seemed to make up the language of the white barbarians, but she could understand them if she relaxed and concentrated on their thoughts. Sansha had always had this fit, reading a person's thoughts.

'Are you doing it again?' her mother used to shout, scolding her for using her talents. Mother could always tell, as she too had had the gift.

'My mother had the gift, and my mother's mother. It is a gift that has been passed to me and I pass it to you,' mother had told her one day when she had found Sansha staring at a bird in a tree for hours.

'What gift, Mother?' Sansha had asked coming out of her trance.

'The gift of the Open Mind. It allows you to feel all living things, to communicate with them, to understand them.'

Sansha had turned back to the bird, but whatever she had been feeling was now beyond her.

'I felt something…' Sansha said.

'Tell me,' her mother had bid as she moved to sit down beside her tiny daughter.

'I was hungry, and oh so thirsty. I had travelled a long way and the heat of the early day had made me very tired. I needed to rest.'

'That was the bird talking to you,' her mother said, as the brightly colour bird hopped to another branch, its small head turning swiftly, watching for any sign of danger.

'I cannot understand what he was saying,' Sansha smiled at her mother. Silly notion.

'I know,' her mother returned the smile, 'but you do not need to use words to talk. I can tell you I love you by hugging you and kissing you. As a baby you knew I loved you when I rocked you in my arms and sang you to sleep at night. You know that your father loved you when he hunted and brought food for our table, when he fought against the white devils who destroyed our land. You can feel the emotions of the bird, sharing them for a time. The bird also feels yours.'

'It does?' Sansha enquired, eyes still locked on the beautiful plumage.

'Yes, when you share with an animal, it also shares with you. You understand each other. Sometimes the animal will not understand what it is feeling but it still feels it. That is why it has stayed in the tree. There are no berries but still it wishes to eat. It stays there because you have shared your happiness with it.'

Sansha and her mother sat for a time watching the bird.

'I will give it some water,' Sansha announced.

'Hmm. She would like that,' her mother said.

'She?'

'Yes. It is a little girl, just like you,' her mother kissed her head softly.

Both her mother and the bird watched as Sansha scampered off to get some water, crumbs and moist seeds they kept for grinding. Returning to her mother she sat and extended her tiny hand to the bird inviting her to eat and drink. The bird watched but did not respond.

'I think she is shy,' Sansha sounded sad when the bird watched her but made no move.

'Perhaps,' her mother tilted her head and watched as the little bird jumped from branch to branch and flitted down to land beside her daughter. The bird was not so shy when it went straight to the water dish and began to peck at it and the seeds.

'See, she likes me,' Sansha beamed.

'Yes. Did you say something to her?'

'Oh, yes. I told her that I was a friend and understood that she needed to eat and drink. I told her that I would protect her until she had her fill,' Sansha smiled warmly at the little bird and her mother could feel the wave of contentment that her daughter was radiating.

'How did you do that?' her mother asked.

'I just thought about it, and it happened,' Sansha said as she leaned forward and gently stroked the bird. 'It was easy.'

'I was not able to do that until I was much older than you are now,' her mother continued. 'It can be a dangerous gift if you are not able to control it.'

'Why?' Sansha sat up straight and focused her attention on her mother. As soon as the bond was broken the bird tensed and in a rustle of feathers flew for the safety of the tree.

'There are people who would want you for your gift, Sansha. It can be used to hurt as well as to heal.'

'I would not hurt anyone, mother,' Sansha said, her eyes wide at the horror of the thought.

'You are incredibly young, child. Things change. I want you to promise me not to use your gift for a time.'

'But?'

'No, child, listen to me. No 'buts'.'

Sansha had been good. She had been good for a long time and her mother had taught her how to be subtle, how to hide its use. Sansha had watched as her mother had helped the medicine man when he performed the rituals of healing or had visited shortly after him. She had enquired after the sick in their presence and let her mind share the pain and the sickness. She healed all she could and those she could not she helped to pass with less pain. Sansha loved her mother and knew that her mother loved her.

The day she had used to her power openly was a day still burned into Sansha's heart. Her mother was mocked and beaten as a witch. They were driven from the village and forced into the burning desert. Years had passed but they did not ease the pain of watching her mother weaken and die. Sansha had been strong enough to ease the passing. She could not forgive herself for not stopping it.

The strong slap brought her out of her trance. The man stood over her shouting at her, his hand lifted to strike until another voice shocked him to stillness.

'Forgive him my child,' the voice was kind and Sansha craned her neck to see who had spoken.

'You speak my language,' she asked the small man who had spoken.

'Yes. In a way.'

The small man was old but still fine featured and Sansha could see the kindness in his eyes. His skin was golden, touching yellow, and his eyes were as almonds.

'I have not seen anyone that looks like you before,' Sansha said quietly afraid of reprisals should she be heard to speak.

'Do not worry, Sansha,' the man stood and barked at the others and Sansha withdrew from the anger in his voice. The men moved off quickly and the other slaves were herded from the plaza.

'You know my name,' Sansha asked as they were left alone.

'Yes, but how rude of me. My name is Altai,' he said as he handed her a jug of cool water. 'I am gifted as you are, and I can see this gift in others.'

'Gifted?' Sansha was suddenly very frightened.

'Do not fear me little one,' Altai soothed. 'I mean you no harm. Come, relax your mind and you will be able to feel what I share with you.'

Sansha relaxed and let her thoughts become one with the man before her. She could feel his warmth, his kindness and his tenderness. As she swam in his thoughts, she could sense the tightness. He was holding on to something. Supressing it. Hiding it.

Altai gently nudged Sansha out of his consciousness and smiled at her. She returned the smile, but a small frown crept to her forehead as she lingered on the area he would not let her see.

'Ah, my little Sansha, do not concern yourself with everything you discover in another's thoughts. I, like you, have things I do not wish to share.'

Sansha nodded, thinking once more of her mother.

'I understand,' she said and lowered her eyes.

'I know you do. You are a bright girl,' Altai stood again and looked her over. Holding out his hand he smiled and said, 'Come with me, Sansha. I will get you something to eat and something warm to put on. Those rags do not do you justice, my little princess.'

Altai waved a hand and a guard on the other side of the plaza rushed forward to unlock the manacles that bound the girl's feet. Sansha wondered why the guard showed such fear at being near her. She realised it was not her but Altai he was afraid of when he barked at him to hurry.

Sansha could not understand how anyone could be afraid of the little old man. He was the only one who had shown her any kindness during her time in the land of the barbarians.

Altai reached down for her as the guard disappeared back to his post. He lifted her to her feet and holding her hand he headed off away from the building into which rest of the slaves had been taken, his bodyguards falling in to step behind him.

'First thing's first, my princess. Food and drink. Then we will get you cleaned up,' Altai cooed to her. 'We want you presentable when we meet the Holy Father.'

Sansha smiled as she followed the old man towards the doorway, happy for the first time since her mother died.

*

Vorden moved his men without any profound sense of urgency. It was unlikely that the fool Reyes would pull the men back to come looking for him. If anything did come of it, he was sure he could uphold a lack of confidence in Reyes' leadership and say that he had taken a more direct approach against the northern resistance.

Either that or just kill him and be done with it.

In reality he had more lustful intents at heart. The army life, especially with the raiding units, had given Vorden more than he had ever dreamed possible. Growing up in the slums of the capital he had lived each day on his wits alone, never knowing if he would survive another day. He had run with gangs, the only way of guaranteeing survival. Loners were quickly killed. In his teens he had grown large. But it was not his size that had earned him the illustrious title of 'Vorden.'

It was his way with women.

While many of the gangs went foraging and burgling, Vorden found that he liked to rifle through the woman's clothes in the fanciful houses they targeted. Discovered one night, when the owners returned unexpected, he did not run as the others had. He waited in the bedroom. As the husband entered, Vorden caved in his head with a hammer. The hammer that was normally used for shoeing horses crashed through the man's temporal lobe like it was an eggshell. The brutality that he inflicted on the wife had earned the name "Vorden." 'Beast' in the Southern tongue. He left her tied to her husband's body while he ate from their small scullery, always promising her life if she did not scream. After two hours of beatings and abuse he caved her head in also. Only finishing then because they were out of food and the smell of her husband was upsetting his appetite.

Now Vorden ran with a special gang. The army had taken him in and taught him well. He was fed and trained to kill. Skilled killing was something he had taken to surprisingly easily. Escaping to the army was his only option when the militia closed in on his gang. Under new hard-line orders from the Holy Father, they were ordered to rid the city of the vermin that infested it. Vorden had made it out just in time. His entire gang had been wiped out. The army was an easy option. Now he was being paid to kill and often congratulated on his ability to do so.

His tastes were satisfied also. For each engagement he and his friends enjoyed what he had come to know as "the spoils of war." The raping and pillaging that followed the major battles allowed him to grow and twist. If he were to be titled now it would be "Barbarian" and not "Vorden". The torture he inflicted on women and girls was too much at times even for his small band of followers. All except Hein but he had been one exceptionally crazy son of a bitch.

'Where to, big man?' Quint rode alongside Vorden.

'We'll track north a way. There are cabins to the north of the main supply route. We could go foraging there for a week or two.'

Vorden's mind wandered to the soft flesh waiting for him at the end of the journey, 'By tomorrow I want to be buried deep in soft Ellistrin flesh.'

Quint grunted acknowledgement. The six men moved north slowly.

*

Saladin was sweating. The exertion that had drained him physically had sharpened his mind and senses. He could feel himself alive with the energy he had stolen from the broken body on the table before him.

His acolytes liked to think of it as an altar, that they assisted their Holy Father in a deeply religious ceremony. Only Saladin knew that was just murder. Murder and theft. Saladin used his abilities to plunder and take the life force from his victims.

'Leave me,' he said quietly. It took all his effort to even form the words.

The acolytes shared furtive and confused glances before silently moving one by one out of the secret chamber. Only Altai remained.

'Are you alright, Holy Father?' Altai asked but did not approach. He could see the effects of the new infusion of energy bristling the hairs on Saladin's body as he leaned for support against the table. The air above him seemed to haze as though from tremendous heat. Altai had not seen the Holy Father affected in this way before.

'You were strong, weren't you, my child,' Saladin said to the corpse that decorated the table. The husk that was once a vibrant human being lay contorted, limbs in the impossible positions that only the extremes of agony can induce.

Altai remained at the peripheries of the Holy Father's vision, no longer wishing to attract his attention.

Saladin moved round the table slowly, small hands gripping the edge, his knuckles white under the strain. His pupils were dilated as though his system were racked with opium. Reaching the head, he gently drew one finger down what was once a beautiful face.

'You are so beautiful,' he leaned close to the drained body, whispering intimately. 'I appreciate the gift you have surrendered to me. I will cherish it, I really will.'

Saladin began to giggle, lifting his hand to cover his mouth as a child might. Altai moved around the table and placed a light robe around the Emperor.

'She was stronger than expected,' Altai commented, reappraising the corpse. He had underestimated her strength.

'She was strong,' Saladin agreed, 'but I have taken stronger.'

'Yes, Holy Father,' Altai agreed.

'I was distracted. There is another close by whose light burns like the sun.'

'Yes. I have found you a rare flower. Her power is immense.'

'I shall enjoy taking it from her,' Saladin smiled. 'Make her ready for me on the night of the new moon.'

'I shall have her prepared,' Altai bowed again and left Saladin alone in the dungeon.

'You fought so bravely, my child. You tried to deny me what was rightfully mine,' Saladin said as he kissed the dead maid's sweaty, blood-streaked face.

The constant influx of servants from the outlying reaches of the Empire ensured that many could disappear before one would be noticed. In the capital, if anyone did notice they would not take the time to care about the fate of a slave.

Puritan law did not allow for slavery, but a life subjugated to the service of the Holy Father, and therefore God, was not slavery in the eyes of the law.

Altai had seen the girl when she had been brought to the palace. Her skin was light and unblemished, her spirit unbroken and radiant in her eyes. Altai was blessed with the gift of discernment. The Sight. The Open Mind. He saw the raw power that had flowed through her. Unbridled and unchecked power that she merely considered to be strength of will.

Her will had been strong. Until it had been smashed against the perverse rocks that Saladin and his acolytes had erected in her mind.

'Break the body, then the will,' Saladin had instructed his followers. He reached out with his mind to touch the girl that Altai had placed in the next room and was stung by the raw force that flowed behind the strong walls of her mind.

Saladin smiled. This truly was a prize. She alone would give him great power. Not like the maid who surrendered only a trickle of energy though she did indeed have the Sight.

The maid had sometimes had premonitions of coming events. Her sweet and naïve innocence had remained unsullied by the war in her homeland and while she had certainly suffered at the hands of the Puritan soldiers, she had been able to retreat behind the walls of her mind and hide there while her body was abused.

The walls were no protection from Saladin.

He straightened as Altai returned.

'Have them get rid of the body,' he commanded and left.

*

Finn lay on the bed. His skin was softening but still did not allow him much movement as it caused the skin to break allowing the possibility of infection. He had stuck fine needles of oak into different areas of his skin. The technique he knew, even a deep understanding of the principals involved, but he still did not know where this knowledge had originated.

'I have heard of these techniques you are using but I have never seen them done. This acupuncture is fascinating,' Edom took in all that was being done, frequently asking questions.

'It is only fascinating, priest, when you are watching it being done. Not when you are crippled and trying to regain control of your body.'

'I can only suppose that that must be true. It intrigues me to know where you came by this knowledge.'

'It intrigues me also. I feel like I have been dropped on the surface of the world. The origins of these techniques are shrouded in mystery and are older than the written word. They are described in legends of the farthest nations.'

'Have you been to these far nations?' Edom asked.

'I do not know. Maybe. I still have no memory of where I might have been in my life before now. Or how I came to be here.'

'Where are you from, do you suppose?' Edom asked applying more salve to the skin of the joints.

'Heaven, perhaps. Or hell, priest. What do you think?' Finn asked, his breathing changing yet under control as he tensed and relaxed different muscle groups. Just because he could not move did not mean he could not exercise.

'Hell, most probably. I could not see the good Lord God disfiguring you in this way, unless of course it is an improvement from what you once looked like.'

'I hope not,' Finn said, laughing lightly.

'What do you think? Really, Finn.'

'I do not know what to think, priest. When I try to look back to before, I see nothing. It is a bottomless black pit that makes me dizzy. I feel sick and my head pounds. I have given up looking.'

'What of the daemon?'

'Nothing more,' Finn said. 'He was created by my fever.'

'I hope so,' Edom replied, 'for your sake, Finn, as well as my own. Now that you are getting stronger, we will be leaving soon.'

'To the mountains?'

'Yes. Back to the mountains, Finn. I have been away too long. There are many people there that need my help. I have been on the other side of the front line for six months.'

'How do you manage to move backwards and forwards across this front?'

'I am old but not without skill. I was once a canny warrior of the Legion also. All the priesthood must serve their time.'

'Are there many?' Finn asked, curious.

'Priests? Not enough,' Edom replied sadly. 'Once we were many. Before the occupation and the purges. Now we are few but there is still work to be done.'

'Tell me about your war, Edom.'

Edom stood and walked to the pot on the fire, stirring in the herbs he had collected. The rancid smell emanated up from the pot. Wrinkling his nose in disgust he was amazed that Finn could drink it, yet the remarkable improvement was testimony to his knowledge of medicine.

'There is not a lot to tell. Ellistrin was once a proud nation. We have little to offer in the way of resource. The land is mostly mountain or barren plain. Farming produces barely enough to support individual families. Our people came here centuries ago after the War of the Moons. The original settlers were all soldiers from the war that had spanned three continents. Brought here by the Messiah himself. They were a collection of many nations and bonded through the hardship that the land presented. They formed a new nation, one that would hold strong against invasion.'

'A military nation.'

'Yes. And so were born the Legions. Veterans from the wars brought with them experience and knowledge, strong leadership and discipline. They forged the refugees who came here into the finest regiments on this continent. Our borders were disputed at first, our neighbours claiming them to be unjust and illegal. Our first war lasted only nine days during which we brought our neighbours on both sides to their knees. We sued for peace on their terms and returned their land to them in return for them acknowledging our borders.'

'And so, you were strong but with no structure.'

'We had no experience of farming, and the land was unforgiving to our meagre efforts. All we knew was war. Our main export quickly became mercenary regiments. Legions would be loaned out in time of war and there is always war, Finn, though it saddens me. Every day was spent in training from we could walk until we died in battle or were retired. Children are given their first wooden sword as soon as they can hold it and their first knife as soon as they can walk. They quickly learn to respect the blade.'

'How is it then that you were invaded? Surely it must have seemed folly to any nation to declare war on you.'

'Ah yes. You must not discount the arrogance that comes with power. We were the finest warriors, the most disciplined Legions. Who would dare attack us? We were xenophobes at best. The Puritans gained our confidence through war and campaigning together. They adopted many of our Legions full time and paid handsomely for it with trade. They sent envoys. Diplomats. Their troops were invited onto our sovereign soil by our ministers, even though our generals counselled against it. Soon we were conducting joint exercises across the plains, and they moved more and more troops in. Unknown to us they also massed a huge army on our border. When we stood down in observance of our holy day, The Night of the Blood Moon, they attacked from within and without. It was a rout from the start. In one night and a day they had taken our border garrisons, the ports in the south and slain our entire government with most of the generals. Within a week they had driven the remaining Legions either into the mountains to the north or across our eastern border, where we held them forming a new front line and the coalition of eastern nations as it exists today. Close to a million men on each side they estimate. Within a month they had complete control of the country with most of the pockets of resistance in the towns effectively quelled, the mountains sealed with garrisons and three full army groups effecting a front line.'

'Why did they come?' Finn asked.

'They did not want us. We are merely the most efficient way of moving across the peninsula into the eastern continents. A doorway. It is from here that they will stage the next expanse of their Empire.'

'So it is to your Legion camps that you will go in the mountains.'

'It is. The camps continually move and are broken into many cells spread over hundreds of miles. They cannot find us. They have tried and have paid dearly for it. We have no base for them to pitch one attack against. The mountains and forests are treacherous. We train there for just that reason and so are at home. We are so few in number that if we were found they would surely overrun us.'

'Now you fight the little war. Guerrilla. Hit and run.'

'Yes, mostly running though. We ambush the supply routes, harry troop movements. Occasionally we attack a garrison in strength but not for a few years. The reprisals against those that were caught and now live in the towns is too great a price.'

'Stalemate,' Finn observed.

'For some time now.'

'Do you hope to hold out indefinitely?' Finn asked. 'What are you waiting for?'

'Inspiration,' Edom smiled. 'The Legions that were forced over the border are not strong enough to force through the lines. There are not enough of them. The coalition forces of the eastern continent are happy enough with the front lines as they are because their lands are safe at this time.'

'But the stalemate will not last.'

'No. Nothing lasts. Once the Puritan army is strong enough it will roll over the eastern border and destroy all before it as it has in the rest of its Empire. It will be the War of the Moons all over again. The death of nations.'

'They have lost the opportunity to pre-empt this.'

'Had they counter attacked to our defence in the beginning they could have pushed them back to our western border and we could have consolidated our loss, regained the Legions and fought back. Now it is too late. They would not help us because they are secretly glad to see us vanquished. We were too strong, and they did not easily forget the blood of centuries ago.'

'It is not easy to see your land torn apart,' Finn observed.

'I am a man of God, Finn. I pray every day, as do all my compatriots, for the Messiah, God's holy envoy on this earth who will come to lead the spiritual war against the invader who has perverted his name. We worship the same God and follow the same holy days. Their Emperor, Saladin, has usurped the power of their church and unites the people behind the banner of a crusade. He has labelled us heretics. Holy wars are the worst, Finn, for they stir the blood, and he has no shortage of young men seeking God's glory.'

'I do not see an easy peace in your future, priest.'

'Our nation may never stand again, Finn, perhaps we have been judged by God and found wanting. But until we are beaten to dust, I will give peace where I can and draw blood if I must.'

'And you don't mind the killing as a man of God?'

'I despise killing in any form. I wish it could be otherwise. This, however, is a land of men, with all of men's failings. We are fighting for our right to follow God. To not be exterminated in the pursuit of that right, I think, is the noblest of fights, one that I am extremely glad to play my part in. Were I a younger man I would be fighting and not preaching.'

'You are a strange man, priest.'

'That is a fine jest coming from you. I think I would forego it all to know how you came to be involved in all this. Perhaps you were a priest as I am, it is possible that we have merely not met before, the camps being so widespread. Not that I would recognise you anyway.'

'No, I suppose not,' Finn smiled again, feeling it broaden when Lauren bounced up the steps into the cabin, skipping and singing to announce her unmistakable presence.

'Hi Finn, Father Edom. How are ya feelin' today?' she chirped.

'I am feeling better for hearing you sing, little one. I am glad you are here. Father Edom's company is less than cheerful on this frigid day,' Finn gave the priest a mocking look. 'He has been telling me what a good girl you are.'

Lauren positively beamed her delight that she was being talked about. She coyly set herself on the bed beside Finn.

'I am. I have trained hard all morning and papa says he would not cross me when I have my knife. He is pleased. He will take me to the north soon so I can practice on people my own size,' Lauren glowed.

'God help them,' Edom said.

Lauren gave him a withering look that she could only have learned from Isela.

'Father Edom was just going to tell me again of the Messiah. Would you stay and listen with me?' Finn asked.

'Yeah! Go on Father Edom, tell us, tell us!' Lauren said, forgetting all thoughts of killing and fighting.

Edom settled down again and retold the story of the one who had been and the one who was to come.

Chapter Seven

Saladin's acolytes had taken Sansha on command, brutally ravaging and beating her over a day and a night. They had branded her body with irons and cut her repeatedly.

Saladin's trained mind knew when she had withdrawn fully behind the walls of her mind. She had pulled her spiritual presence with her and would have passed for dead to those without the gift. The acolytes had this gift.

Saladin had chosen them all from the ranks that had come to stand for selection to the Chosen, those from whom the Temple Knights were drawn. He had walked among them as he always did, his mind open and flowing. He could read them all, not random thoughts and images as Altai sometimes received, but with a sense of completeness. Saladin knew their heart. He chose the weak of body and the weak of mind. It took a special type of person to be bent to the will of the Holy Father.

The strong entered the ranks of the Chosen and the elite to the Temple Knights. Their ilk would never bend from the path. Saladin had tried before and had to destroy the whole order in the Night of the Long Knives when he had them executed by their brethren as unclean heretics.

That had cost him dearly. They had almost turned on him then, but he rallied them to his cause and now they were more loyal than ever with Brood as their leader.

He focused again on the child, waiting until she had withdrawn fully before calling his misguided children back from her body. It was not her flesh he wanted. Saladin had closed his eyes as if in solemn prayer.

'Hello, Sansha,' he said, as he appeared in her world.

The grey walls that were Sansha writhed in pain as Saladin stood before her. The walls had no substance but were no less impassable for it.

'Come now, is that anyway to behave?' Saladin asked. He stood before the wall and opened his arms to her. 'Come Sansha, I can make the pain stop, I can make it all go away.'

The wall stopped moving as Sansha listened to the soothing tones.

'You could make it stop?' she asked from behind the walls, her voice was faint but alive with unchanneled energy. It felt like nettles on Saladin's spirit skin.

'Did I hurt you?' she asked, the concern only a child can show when she has accidentally caused pain.

'No, my child,' Saladin replied quickly. 'I am fine, but please be careful.'

'My mother told me to be careful,' Sansha agreed. 'When I was a little girl, I hurt people by accident. It used to make my mother truly angry.'

'She did not understand the gift you had,' Saladin told her as he gently pushed forward with is mind, probing her defences. He could see no way in. 'Not like I do.'

'I hurt one of the girls in the village,' Sansha sighed. 'I did not mean to, but she was teasing me.'

'What about?' Saladin asked, amazed at the power she had put into her walls.

'I do not remember,' the voice was so slight he had to strain to hear.

He probed at the walls but did not think he could penetrate, even if he were to engage in open battle with her. She lacked the ability to fight but she had learned to defend herself well.

'Do you love your mother?' he asked as he concentrated, focusing his power.

'Yes,' Sansha replied sadly.

'Was she beautiful?' he asked. 'Like you?'

'She was wondrous.'

Saladin could feel her smile behind the wall, the warmth streaming out to envelop him. Distracted for only a moment he forced his mind against her defences.

'Then why do you spit at her you wicked child!' the venom sprang from his throat.

The walls writhed as pain tore through her sanctuary. The place that she had retreated to was no longer a haven. Here, too, she felt pain.

'I do not,' she shouted. 'I love her.'

'She does not love you,' Saladin began to bore into her walls. 'You treated her so badly. She told you to hide your power, she told you how dangerous it could be.'

Images came at Saladin of the little girl in her mother's arms as they were forced from the village, and he threw them back at her defences as mental ballistae.

'You had your mother branded as a witch. You are to blame for this!' Saladin shouted at her, the walls buckling as he used the force of his mind to give substance to his words, hate beating at the child's fortifications.

'No!'

'Yes! How she hates you, how you have tormented her, she would have been better off if you had died at birth. She had been happy then. You gave her pain then and you gave her pain all her life until she died of a broken heart. A heart you broke!'

'NO!' Sansha cried in pain as the walls were torn asunder. Erected to protect herself from the enemy without, she could not protect herself from the enemy within.

'Yes!' Saladin screamed exultant. 'You know you do not deserve to live. Give yourself up, feel the pain your mother felt. Perhaps then she will forgive you!'

The walls were destroyed as light and energy burst forth, catching Saladin in the blast of raw power, sweeping him aside and casting him back into his body.

Saladin's spirit hit his body with enough force to knock him from his feet. He opened his eyes to watch the body of the girl squirm and flail against the table restraints as her life left her. Soon the corpse was still.

Smiling and exhausted, Saladin was helped to his feet in a rush of robed acolytes. He could feel her power combining with his, could feel his aura of power changing colour and texture. His system was suffused with power and pleasure as the endorphins coursed through his veins. His skin tightened as fresh growth ran over him like a river, fresh elasticity coming into his face, wrinkles lifting. Eyes closed he could feel his arteries softening and joints loosening. Strength returned to his muscles.

'Holy Father?' Altai asked.

'Yes?' Saladin smiled through the narcotic effect of the girl's essence.

'Are you alright?' he asked.

'Oh, I am better than alright,' Saladin answered. 'I have not encountered power like that before.'

'She was strong,' the narrow eyes of the first minister watched as the decay began to set into the child already.

'If she had been trained, she would have torn me apart in her mind,' Saladin filled a cup of wine and drank deeply. 'She destroyed herself to escape the pain. The blast of her energy surprised me. Had she been able to focus it, to use it as a weapon, I would have perished. It was exhilarating'

Altai was aghast.

'Fear not Altai, God is on our side,' Saladin said, aware that his continued perversion of his position depended on the subjugation of his minions. 'Or more accurately, He is on my side.'

'Yes, Holy Father,' the acolytes intoned as one.

'She has been cleansed,' Saladin said, stretching his lithe body.

'Cleansed!'

'She has been saved,' he said, feeling the youth and vigour rip through him and restore function to his internal organs.

'Saved!'

Such power. What was the point of being Emperor if he only had to give it up some day? Mortality did not sit well with the Emperor. It was as well that he had learned how to slow it if not stop it. So far.

'Praise God,' he said finally.

'Praise God!' came the response.

'Get that cadaver out of here, it sickens me,' Saladin ordered as he left the room, swaying as though drunk.

*

Days at the Plandor camp had progressed with the usual monotony. Duncan had been careful not to repeat the loose talk about the Knights even after they had left the day before. Feeling as though a weight had been lifted from his shoulders he settled back into the military existence, which was his whole life.

'I would rather stay here and go fight this faction in the northern woods,' he said bringing the general out of his reverie. 'They are canny boys by all accounts. Excellent fighters. Clever too.'

'I'd like to be heading to the mountains also,' Garrad replied, subconsciously lifting his head and gazing north, only to be met with the impenetrable wall of trees. 'There is a challenge in that. Not heading off to the stalemate in the East. The lines have advanced or retreated no more than ten miles in the nine years since they were established. Getting sent here is wasting us. The finest regiment in the army, baby-sitting.'

'Exactly. Look at our men,' Duncan indicated the lancers slumped in the saddle, and the infantry plodding along behind. 'They look like they have just lost a battle rather than going to one.'

'They are tired from the journey.'

'It is more than that and you know it,' Duncan said, a little too abruptly.

'You would be best to keep your thoughts in check, captain,' Garrad warned. 'You would be best not to tell me what I am thinking.'

'I am sorry, my general. I forget my place.' Duncan often did.

'No, Duncan, it is your place to advise me. I will be myself again once we stop. My temper is not what it should be this day,' still aggrieved over the confrontation with the Knight.

'Still thinking about the Temple Knights,' Duncan asked. It was not a question.

'You are as perceptive as my wife,' Garrad replied. 'Are you sure you are a soldier?'

'Allegedly so,' Duncan confirmed. 'It is not too difficult to tell when you are troubled, general, you are a warrior, not a politician.'

Garrad nodded, not entirely pleased that he could not conceal his emotions well. But then Duncan had known him for twenty years and had seen more of him in that time than his own wife had.

'The Knights bother me too,' Duncan continued.

'It is not the Knights themselves,' Garrad said softly, making sure his voice did not carry. 'They are merely a symptom of a bigger problem.'

'What problem?' Duncan asked. It was unlike his general to be so outspoken. Perhaps as he was getting older, he was getting more cynical, the curse of any old soldier.

'They are a symptom of a diseased Empire. I always thought we were right in the crusades, Duncan,' Garrad admitted.

'How can we not be? The Holy Father has blessed this war.'

'What Holy Father? There is little holy about him. He is a mad Emperor who thinks he is a deity, maybe even God himself. On his word we have marched across the known world enforcing his beliefs on all nations irrespective of who they are.'

'He is the Emperor,' Duncan added. 'Our Emperor.'

'That does not make him right.'

'No, but it does not automatically make him wrong either.'

'Some of the far lands would not even stand against us because it was against their faith to take another life. Even the life of an animal never mind an invading army. They try not to step on a bug and if they do so they spend the day in prayer. Who then is right or wrong? We march in the belief that we are right, and they are so wrong. How can we be completely right following an Emperor who orders the executions of his own family and friends when they displease him? He is the head of our church. Our faith preaches forgiveness and peace, yet we march to battle and conquest in the name of God. Sanctioned by the church to purge the land of heretics. For what?'

'For the good of the Empire?' Duncan suggested.

'For the Empire yes. Why hide behind the façade of doing it for God?'

'We are a nation under God. The heretics stand against everything we believe in.'

'I…we are getting too old in the tooth for the feverish ideals that they use to motivate the troops. The people we invade show more of our beliefs than we do. Genocide cannot be justified by any rhetoric. I am loyal without question. But that does mean I have to believe without question. That is the mark of a fool.'

'You are a fine general and nobody's fool. I just wish we could return home and forget all this madness.'

'Home,' Garrad thought back to better times. 'To see my boy grow strong. To teach him not to be easily led by the masses. To teach him to be his own man.'

'Ha,' Duncan scoffed. 'I want to return to Avalon and go wenching with the young whelps of the regiment. Show them how it is done, by God. Do you remember the jungle campaign in Sumer?'

'You talk too much,' Garrad responded without reproach.

'Not that night I didn't talk! Or for the two days following. That young girl knew things that would make even Avalon's whores cringe. I don't think I could walk for those two days.'

'Fortunately for us you mastered horse-riding,' Garrad's voice was laden with sarcasm.

Duncan grinned to himself, pulling the riding cape tighter around this face, the drizzle starting to come in harder now.

Garrad watched his old friend. Taking warmth in his good humour. If they had not been soldiers, they would probably never have been friends. They were vastly different but so much the same. Garrad was feeling his age. He wanted to retire and listen to Duncan recount his stories over wine by the fire, not listen to it in the freezing Ellistrin rain.

As they rounded the crest of the hill, they were able to look down on the disarray below. The Plandor camp. Staging area for mid-country.

Garrad had his officers summoned to him.

Tents and shacks were erected at all angles without any semblance of planning. The general sat erect in the saddle letting the regiment file past him.

The junior officers were ordered to give their critique of the camp.

Cooking fires were unattended and built too close to the tents. The corral was badly arranged and the hay for the horses was not stored properly, exposing it to the elements. Sewage pits, which had been dug too close to the living areas, were overflowing in the rains surely spreading infection and disease.

Sloppy.

Negligent.

Commandant Pogue had obviously been at his work. Or lack of it. The mount that Garrad was riding probably had more flair for strategy and running a battalion than that incompetent braggart. The horse snorted in complete agreement.

The grey skies did nothing to make the scene of laziness and stupidity any more appealing. The regiment moved down along the thoroughfare, there by accident more than a planned route for troops to pass. Garrad signalled Duncan who turned his horse to give orders to the phalanx leaders. They moved through the chaos to find a clear area that they might set up camp, separate from the rest of the mess that called itself an army.

With the section commanders taking care of organisation and the disciplined troops busy with their duties, Garrad and his aides galloped off to the town to present themselves to Battalion Commandant Pogue.

*

Reyes woke in the night. As always, he did not move immediately. The hair on his neck was raised as though a cool breeze blew gently. He knew at once there was something wrong. Opening his eyes just a crack he made sure there was no one near and moved slowly to his feet, drawing his sword on the way. The camp was quiet. Normal forest sounds still echoed in the forest. There was little ambient light from the moon breaking through the dense thatch of branches above them.

Reyes remained crouched and moved forward to where he knew the sentries would be. Stealthily moving up behind the young soldier, he whispered slightly to announce his presence.

'It's ok, sir, I heard you coming,' Tariq replied from the pitch darkness.

Reyes could not see him but knew the young soldier was stifling a smile at having detected his approach.

'I knew you would Tariq, I made enough noise to wake those bastards in Plandor,' Reyes lied. 'What is happening?'

'They moved out just under half an hour ago, sir,' Tariq replied in a whisper.

'Who moved out?' Reyes demanded irritably.

'Vorden and the others, sir. They passed by me and said they were heading on down the trail to scout ahead for us. They said you ordered it, sir,' Tariq was worried now that he was about to get himself in a lot of trouble.

'How many were with Vorden?' Reyes asked of the huge ringleader.

'Five, sir. Quint among them. They headed south along our present course. Shall I get the men ready to move out?'

'No. We will move on as planned at first light. I will take the rest of the watch lad, get some sleep. Tomorrow is going to be a long day.'

'Yes, sir, thank you sir,' Tariq whispered and moved off towards his sleeping comrades.

Reyes watched the shadow that was Tariq move through the trees. Silent. The captain thought his knees made more noise bending than the young soldier made moving in the forest. The ground is wet, softens the twigs. That is all.

Getting old.

'I think we will have a reckoning Vorden,' Reyes thought to himself.

*

Battalion Commandant Pogue sat on the wide chair. The ignorance that radiated from him mixed with the foul stench of his body odour.

His armour shined magnificently.

'Pompous ass,' thought Garrad.

The general hated this official business. War was not about making lists and ordering supply chains. It was not about paying homage and asking visiting rights to the field outside.

It was about war.

The fool in the chair had bought his commission in the military through his rich politician father. Garrad wanted to be in the field commanding his troops. Leading the Empire's bravest men into battle.

Garrad's sub commanders stood to rigid attention behind him. The armour polished but dented. There were no fancy inscriptions on their breastplates and forearm guards. It was all functional. These men were warriors. Garrad let his gaze take in the rest of the room. Duncan stood completely still with his eyes closed. Garrad grimaced. The bastard was asleep on his feet.

Pogue's grubby fingers worked against the sweat on his palms. Garrad felt his brow furrowing in contempt.

As the meeting drew to a close the general approached the battalion commandant and requested, he and his men be dismissed.

'What is your hurry, general?' demanded the commandant. 'So eager to be back among the sweat and dirt?'

Pogue's question brought laughter from his lackeys.

'Yes sir,' replied Garrad curtly. His men would not move until he gave the order. The heavy armour was making them sweat openly in the heat of the log reception room. Garrad saw a dark shape detach itself from the wall and move to stand close to Pogue. His eyes narrowed as he recognised Brood.

'Yes, sir?' mulled the commandant. 'You do not seem too respectful when you say that. I would hate to think you did not respect the authority of the Holy Father, especially in the presence of one of his holy Knights. You have met Temple Knight Brood, haven't you, general?'

'Yes, Commandant,' Garrad's eyes locked on Brood. 'I had the pleasure of escorting the Lord Knight to Ellistrin.'

'Good, good. Now, perhaps you would care to explain to the Knight which particular aspect of the Holy Father's business does not seem to deserve the full attention of you and your men.'

Pogue sat back on the divan, immensely pleased at how he was manipulating events.

Brood had no interest in the direction Pogue was heading but made no move to interrupt him.

Garrad moved to the side of the divan so that he might directly face the Knight. As he moved, he was aware of Duncan and his officers subtly repositioning themselves around the room.

Pogue was of no consequence.

'How should I address you, Temple Knight?' Garrad asked formally.

The question hung in the air with no reply forthcoming.

'Very well. This is not how I would have any meeting go, but you may take disrespect as and how you see fit from my actions. I do not care to, and will make no effort to, pander to neither your ego nor the ego of this fat fool. I am a soldier, sir, first and foremost. I am a general and wish to return my men to their posts so that we can get on with our duties. I find these exercises in court theatrics tiresome and futile.'

Garrad's eyes blazed at the Knight.

Brood did not react.

Pogue jumped to his feet, bulging with rage, threatening to burst the vein in his forehead.

'You impudent wretch. Who do you think you are addressing?' Pogue frothed as he stammered at the general. 'I would advise you to tread warily in my company. I could…'

Garrad's blow landed low and hard, doubling Pogue over and bringing him to his knees. As his bodyguards stepped forward, they found Garrad's commanders had their blades already out, covering their general.

'Enough,' Garrad shouted. His men stopping in their tracks. 'You know I mean him no serious harm. Had I wished it he would be dead already. I am general of the Osocan Regiment. I know you know me. I am a man of honour. I will not be spoken to in that way by a fat, bastard son of one of Avalon's penny whores and her impotent husband. Any man who stands against me stands against the Empire.'

Garrad let the words sink into the room before nodding to Duncan. His men sheathed their swords as one and returned to attention. The bodyguards hesitated briefly before following their example. Pogue was helped to his divan by his chief bodyguard.

'I apologise for the display, Lord Knight,' Garrad bowed curtly.

Brood still had not moved. His eyes remained fixed on Garrad, betraying no emotion, though a curious smile touched his lips.

A well-built soldier stepped in front of Garrad and raised his sword.

'I am Roche, general,' the chief bodyguard said by way of introduction. 'I agree with all you have said but I cannot permit you to harm my ward. Step back from him or I shall be forced to kill you.'

'Or die trying,' replied Garrad coldly.

'Whatever. Step back,' Roche stated evenly.

Garrad stepped back creating space, which the bodyguard did not advance into.

'Kill him! Kill hiimmmmmm!' screeched Pogue. No one moved. The other attendants and officers in the hall were afraid to move less they attract attention to themselves.

Roche bowed formally to Garrad.

'It does not have to be this way,' Garrad said sadly.

'It does general,' said Roche solemnly, 'for I am a man of honour, and must obey my ward.'

'Kill him!' Pogue shrieked.

'Commandant Pogue, I follow your order for the honour of my unit and the Holy Emperor. You are a man without honour,' Roche said turning back to Garrad. 'When you are ready, general.'

Roche raised his blade in salute.

'Know that I will see your honour satisfied Roche,' Garrad said returning the gesture.

'Thank you. I would like you to know that I hold you in the highest regard, general.'

Garrad nodded. 'Begin.'

Roche powered forward with practised speed. The blade aimed straight for Garrad's chest, the deadly accuracy paying homage to the warrior and his training. Garrad deflected the blade and angled his own sabre slightly, tearing through the neck of the bodyguard. Roche stood impaled on the blade. Withdrawing, Garrad watched as Roche tumbled to the ground.

A stench rose as the bowels emptied. Wiping the blood from his sword he sheathed it and touched his hand to his heart in salute of the valiant soldier.

Pogue went to speak but was interrupted by the tip of Garrad's dagger against his cheek, hovering just below his eye.

'Do not speak. Do not utter a sound. The stench of your words sickens me. That corpse polluting the air is worth twenty of you. I would advise you to return to Avalon, lest something happen to you.'

Pogue burned with fury.

'I do not care for your idle threats, Garrad. You will die when word of what you have done reaches the Emperor. Your great military record will not save you then.'

'My threats are not idle,' the general replied, flicking his sword tip across the cheek of the commandant, drawing blood. 'Leave and live, stay and die.'

Pogue flinched at the sudden pain, tears welling.

The general bowed curtly to Brood, turned and stormed out of the hall. His long strides took him straight out of the garrison fortress and into this own camp. The slovenly attitude of the men in the garrison soon replaced by the discipline of his regiment. When he finally made it to his tent he stopped.

Taking deep breaths, he eventually sighed all his frustrations out of him in one long, controlled exhale.

Had he been a younger man he would have killed Pogue. Now, he worried about his son and who would support him.

Sitting on the stool at his makeshift desk he thought of the blond haired, blue-eyed boy who was the centre of his universe. He looked so much like his beautiful mother who had been lost to fever, three years previous.

Duncan raised one of the flaps of the tent. 'Want company?'

'Only good company.'

'Well, you will not want to see me then,' he replied pulling a small flask of fiery liquid from under his breastplate, 'for I am the worst sort of company. I hate to drink alone.'

'Thank you, friend,' Garrad replied as he took a long mouthful. 'I see you finally woke up.'

'Saving energy between battles has always been a talent of mine. I am surprised you did not kill the swine. Skewering the Battalion Commandant and roasting him in the courtyard would have made for an interesting letter home.'

'The sooner we get to the front lines the better. These soft rich farts make me want to puke. Once we are on line and the fighting starts, we will be forgotten.'

'Until the next incident,' Duncan smiled.

'Why don't you put that flask to your mouth and see if you can stop the noises coming out of it?'

'Touchy today,' Duncan observed, drinking deeply.

'Thinking of my son,' Garrad confessed.

'You will see your boy again soon.'

'Not if I do not learn to manage the politicians better.'

'It could have gone better,' Duncan allowed, setting down his helm and sitting opposite his general. Garrad rubbed a lock of his son's blond hair between his fingers.

A good luck charm.

'Every time I see him, he has changed so much. I fear that the next time I will be a stranger to him. He is eight now. He might be a man by the time I get back.'

'You'd best pray for a quick victory then.'

'Victory will suit me. I do not mind how long it takes.'

'That is alright then, because by the time it is over your boy may well be here serving under your command.'

'There are worse things I could hope for,' Garrad thought of his strong son leading a troop of cavalry.

'Hope is never a bad thing, general.'

'I have hope, Duncan,' Garrad drained the flask, 'that you have more of that drink.'

'Of course, general,' Duncan gave a mock salute and produced another flask. 'But purely for medicinal purposes. Helps against the cold don't you know?'

Garrad accepted the fresh flask and thought of the Knight's smile.

Cold.

He drank deep and thought of this next step.

DELIVERANCE

Chapter Eight

Legion General Toshak looked out over no man's land.

No man owned it or, truth be told, wanted to own it. Three miles in the distance were the enemy. At the far end of the huge plain.

The frontier.

'No action for a while, sir,' his lieutenant ventured.

'No, Ruben,' Toshak acknowledged. 'I think they will leave it for another while yet.'

'There was a battle further down the front. Ten days ago. Quite a fight. They pushed the line back fourteen miles before the coalition was able to reinforce. They were able to recover the ground they had surrendered but only after three days of bitter fighting.'

Toshak was already aware of the battle. Little escaped his attention.

'Losses?' Toshak asked.

'Our allies lost a considerable number of troops. When the lines broke, the advancing and retreating forces were intermingled. The bloodshed spread out over the forty miles. Thousands were killed or injured. We had thought at one stage that this was the last assault and that all was lost. The line seemed to collapse in on itself. We are lucky to be standing here today.'

Toshak didn't answer. He stared out towards the land that had once been his home.

'General Toshak?' the lieutenant asked. 'General?'

Was he already too old? Would he die before ever getting the chance to visit his places of childhood? The boy standing beside him would probably set foot on his native soil. Toshak was not so sure. He glanced along the lines of the soldiers. Lancers, archers, chariots, infantry. The Ellistrin Legions made up only a small amount of the coalition yet their ability on the field was second to none. They never took leave. How could they? Where would they go?

Home?

'General?' the lieutenant asked again.

'Stand the men down. Place advance scouting parties out into the field. Put the reserves up. You know the drill.'

'Yes, sir,' Ruben replied. 'Sir?'

'What is it, son?'

'Are the reports true that they are starting to receive reinforcements from their outlying territories?' the lieutenant asked.

'I believe so,' Toshak admitted. It was privileged intelligence, but he was always honest with is men. No surprises. Bad for morale. 'We are starting to see different flags among them now. New ones that we have not seen before. They are all seasoned troops. With good commanders.'

'When they have their troops together, they will attack in force.'

'Yes,' Toshak stared out over the much-disputed land again. 'And we will fight. Victory or death. There is no half measure in a warrior. When I die it will be serving faithfully.'

'There are whispers among the men that the Messiah is coming,' Ruben looked sheepishly at the general for his reaction.

'I have been a general for thirty-two years and have been on this front line for nine of those. I have heard that the Messiah is coming the entire time I have been here. I hope very much that he is coming but until he decides to grace us with his presence, I will continue to wage this war in the best way I know how. He will not find me wanting when he comes.'

'Yes, sir,' the lieutenant snapped a salute and left.

Lauren skipped rope, her long dagger flashing in the air before her as she practised her footwork drills. Ben and Isela held the rope at each end and offered gentle encouragement when the men rode up the trail to the cabin.

Lauren was aware something was wrong even before Isela scooped her up and started running.

Ben dropped the rope on the ground and walked over to the woodpile. Picking up the axe he waited to see what the unexpected visitors wanted.

Vorden and the five men ambled over to the water trough and dismounted, all of them watching Ben intently. They let their horses drink, their eyes roaming over the cabin, white smoke billowing gently into the blue grey sky.

'Welcome,' Ben said uneasily fingering his axe. The men were not acting like the soldiers that normally stopped. They were edgy.

Preparing.

'Who else is here?' Vorden asked. His impressive size intimidating. Ben gripped the axe, knowing he should put it down yet unable to bring himself to do so. Something was very wrong.

'I am alone,' he eventually answered loudly, hoping Isela would hear him.

'Alone? I would have thought a man like you would have had a little wife running around here. What is a home without a woman? Eh, lads? Quint, search the cabin.'

Ben stood in their path and lifted the axe to ready position.

'Ah. A little fight in you, farmer,' Vorden said roughly, his eyes alight.

'More than a little,' Ben stood his ground as the men inched forward.

'I do not have time for this,' Vorden said. 'Stand aside and I might let you live.'

'I will not,' Ben replied, his voice even.

'Pity,' Vorden said, as an arrow took Ben in the shoulder and spun him to the ground.

Quint and two men ran forward and began beating him with their fists and feet. Ben pulled one close to cover his own body against the beating and bit deeply into the man's neck, thrashing like a dog. A sharp blow to the temple brought him close to unconsciousness and he was forced to let go.

The soldier stood, his hand clamped to his neck, blood flowing freely.

'Bastard!' he shouted and kicked Ben viciously in the head. He pulled a knife but was ordered away by Vorden.

'Search the cabin. Then you can take your time with him,' the leader ordered.

Quint led the men inside while the wounded man tied a rag around his throat to stem the flow of blood.

Vorden nodded a 'well done' to the archers who were restringing their crossbows and providing cover in the open ground.

Quint burst from the cabin flinging Edom before him. Vorden turned to look at the prize, disappointed when it was not a woman.

'He was tending a sick man. I think he is a priest, Vorden,' Quint announced.

'Well, are you a priest?' Vorden asked.

Edom did not answer. His eyes studied Ben for a sign of life, pleased when he saw the unsteady rise and fall of his chest. The arrow would have to wait.

A sharp blow to the cheek knocked the priest on to his back.

'Well? Priest?' Vorden demanded.

'Priest,' Edom confirmed. He would never deny his faith.

'Where are the wife and child?' Vorden asked, seeing the skipping rope lying on the ground and a doll thrown to one side.

Edom was motionless.

'Do not test me, old man. Where are they?' Vorden shouted at him.

Fear was gnawing at him, but Edom refused to let it take root. There was no way out of this. He knew he was going to die as sure as the sun had been playing on his Lauren's hair only minutes before.

He knew Ben's death would quickly follow. Edom hoped they would kill him quick and not bring him back as a trophy where his death would be long and horrible.

'I can wait, priest,' Vorden seethed, 'but I don't think your friend can. You will tell me.'

Grabbing the arrow shaft, Vorden began to twist it causing Ben to writhe and scream in agony.

'Tell me!' the spittle flew from his mouth, showering Ben's face. Clutching the shaft, he lifted Ben from his feet and launched him into the centre of his men who began beating him furiously.

Edom prayed hard and asked forgiveness.

Vorden quickly became frustrated. It was not going as planned.

'Bring him here!' he bellowed. Edom watched as Ben was dragged, broken and beaten, and thrown at Vorden's feet.

'Woman!' Vorden's voice thundered across the forest 'Listen to me. If you do not show yourself by the count of five, I will begin by cutting off his bastarding feet inch by inch! I will have him skinned alive like a rabbit. When you return you will find nothing but butchered pieces of him! Is that you want? To have him feasted upon by scavengers? Come to us now and I spare you both. If you do not, we will butcher him and then hunt you down. You will see your daughter violated and slaughtered before you.'

Vorden kicked Ben full in the face again drawing a crack from his cheekbone. Using a knife, he opened the trouser leg and stood back. He raised his axe.

'One!'

Ben tried to lift his head to shout to Isela not to come but he found he found he could not control his mouth. Through his one good eye he saw Isela step from the trees into the clearing.

Vorden saw her and smiled.

'Yes, my lovely, a wise decision. Come here,' Vorden beckoned her over. Grabbing her close he brusquely fondled her breasts and kissed her hard on the lips. 'No oil painting lads and a bit on in years but she is the only sport we'll get this day.'

Isela tried not to push herself away from him. His disgusting breath and unwashed beard could not revolt her more than the thought of being with another man. Vorden leaned in to kiss her harshly just as Isela swept the gutting knife towards his throat. Vorden anticipated the move and swept the knife from her hand.

He had taken Ellistrin women before. He knew their temperament.

Punching her hard in the face he knocked her from her feet.

'Find the girl, she can't be far. Take the farmer round back and kill him. We'll take the priest back,' Vorden announced, 'after we have had our fun.'

'I do not think that would be a good idea, big man,' the hard voice cut across the clearing, dowsing Vorden's urges like a cold shower.

Vorden spun to see the cripple standing on the porch leaning against the doorframe. He laughed loud and full at the pitiful sight of Finn.

'Why, old man? What do you have to say about it? Do you want to have your sport with the wench as well before you die?' Vorden asked.

The men joined in his laughter as Finn mentally checked off their numbers and position.

'What in the name of the horned one have you done to yourself? I have never seen such a hideous sight.'

'No, but you have woken up beside a few, eh Vorden?' Quint said, licking his lips and eyeing the newcomer.

The men laughed again but still no one moved.

'Let them go, and be about your business,' Finn's voice was edged and sharp.

'Death is our business, dung breath,' Vorden spat. Pointing to one of his men he ordered, 'Kill him.'

The soldier drew his sword and advanced. Finn stepped down of the porch still holding on to the pole, his skin broken and weeping openly, the bandages around his eyes sodden with blood and puss. He allowed the soldier to continue his confident march before lunging forward and driving his stiffened fingers though his throat, obliterating the cartilage and nearly breaking his neck.

The soldier crumpled instantly, dead before he hit the ground. Finn was already back in his neutral stance as though he had merely swatted a fly.

'I think you have missed your opportunity to leave, big man. Now I will have to kill you all,' Finn said flatly, as Edom recoiled at the grimace on this face.

'What? Kill him!' Vorden screamed as he looked at the now dead soldier, 'Kill him, now! '

The patrol hesitated, unwilling to die as quickly as their friend had.

'Kill him, you sons of bitches or I will kill you,' Vorden warned and his men knew to heed his words.

'A man who leads by fear is not a man worth dying for,' Finn told the men as they spread out.

Quint and the remaining men advanced warily, ignoring his words. Quint waved his sword slightly. When Finn's head did not turn to follow it, he leapt in, stumbling into the soldier beside him who was attacking at the same time.

Finn streaked forward punching the first soldier in the face, the tremendous impact smashing his nose and caving in his cheek bones. The sickening crunch echoed dully around the clearing. The soldier fell, already choking on his own blood but thankfully unconscious. He, at least, would die in peace.

Finn stepped back suddenly disrupting the momentum of an attacking swordsman who mistimed his swing. Ben's foot lashed out striking hard into his ankle. The attacker stumbled as the edge of Finn's hand backhanded down and smashed through collarbone and ribs. As the swordsman flinched under the blow Finn lifted his knee and drove his foot down hard, fetching a satisfying scream as the swordsman's knee surrendered with a sickening crack. As he slumped forward Finn lifted the sword from the man's limp hand and twisted sharply bringing the sword to bear. Such was the ferocity of his spin, the blade crunched through the helm and skull of the soldier behind him who collapsed in a shower of his own blood.

Finn kept his eyes on the remaining men and walked casually behind the soldier whose knee was now in tatters. Without even a flicker of emotion he drew the blade across the man's neck and did not avert his eyes as the arterial blood burst forth.

All was silent as the entire clearing seemed to hold its breath. Finn stood motionless as gore ran off the edge of his blade.

He smiled then, his cracked face forming a death mask with the blood of his victims staining it.

Quint and the other soldier stalked round him. Finn made no movement until the soldier leapt in driving down with his sword. Finn sidestepped and brought his blade up, disembowelling the soldier who fell to his knees clutching his spilling intestines. Finn stepped behind him and beheaded him cleanly.

Quint could taste his own death at the back of his throat. Screaming, he jumped forward and beheaded himself as Finn sent his blade crisply through his neck. Quint's corpse fell to the side, a look of surprise and shock evident on the severed head.

Vorden's eyes were wide as the carnage unfolded before him. Five men in as many seconds. This little man had been sorely underestimated.

'Now, big man, "let my people go"?' Finn spoke the words he had heard the priest use during his long recuperating hours of sleep. He did not know what made him think of them.

The priest looked up sharply at their use.

Vorden stared at Finn. Gone was the slump, the arthritic pose. He reassessed the man before him. Standing at just over six feet the man was well built but severely malnourished. He was perfectly balanced, even when he walked, he did so in equilibrium. The sure way he used the blade to despatch his fellows. It took a lot of strength and experience to cut through someone's neck. It was too late to regret taking him so lightly.

'Five men,' Vorden said, nodding his genuine admiration.

'Soon to be six,' Finn cautioned, smiling.

Vorden considered getting the crossbow, but he had not been bested by any man and this one would be no different. He shook off his jerkin and let it fall by his feet, his belt dropping beside it. Stepping forward he crouched slightly, both hands extended before him, hefting the huge battle-axe. It moved easily in his mighty hands.

His eyes narrowed as he focused on his prey, his shoulders rippling with strength, his bulk threatening to eclipse the sun. Vorden bared his teeth and prepared to charge.

Finn stood ten feet from him.

He no longer had the power to move.

The fighting had robbed him of any strength he possessed. He knew for certain the man mountain would cut him down. He had failed the girl.

'Now what?' Vorden spat, the venom apparent in his voice.

'Now you die, big man,' Finn said calmly as Isela brought Ben's axe down hard biting deep into Vorden's skull. 'Now you die.'

Vorden fell forward, his eyes wide in shock. Dropping his sword he fell to one knee, his face contorted like a wild animal. Isela ripped the axe free and brought it down again, imbedding it in Vorden's thick boned skull. The hulking warrior toppled to one side. Dead. She ran to her husband's side checking for any sign of life, crying when she heard him sigh. She glanced at the man, known only as Finn, who stood rooted in place in front of the cabin. She nodded her thanks, the tears choking in her throat, making speech impossible.

Finn's legs failed him, and he crumpled to the ground. Lying where he fell, he instructed Edom and Isela to get rid of the bodies.

'What? I have to get Ben inside, he is hurt,' Isela panted.

'No. He will live. Get rid of…the bodies, before more men come. They . . . will surely . . . kill you.'

Finn started to lose consciousness but forced himself to his feet and staggered across to Vorden. Edom watched as Finn brought the axe down again, decapitating him.

Finn realised Edom was watching him intently.

'Don't worry, Priest,' Finn said as he passed out. 'Just making sure.'

Chapter Nine

The sunset bathed the gully a deep crimson. Corpses lay strewn along either side of the narrow path through the smaller of the Great Northern Woods. The sun gathered on the foliage high overhead like drops of blood, threatening to spill down onto the death below.

'Eli! We're ready to move out.'

The shout cut through his reverie.

Eli turned to see Aaron waving in his direction and raised his hand in acknowledgement. So much enthusiasm and energy. Aaron smiled and trotted back to his squad, pointing and issuing orders, eager to be underway. He knew the troop would be heading home now after this last battle.

Eli sat with his legs crossed under him, forearms leaning on his knees. Bowing his head, he considered pouring the remaining water from his canteen over his neck and long braided hair. The waste of water would be something he would discipline his own men over. He had to lead by example. Rinsing the rusty tang of blood from his now dry mouth he spat on the grass in front of him. A dry mouth and a full bladder. Battle had the strangest effects on the body. Nothing but distance was going to remove the stench of death hanging in the air.

The enemy had been smart. They had let it be known around the garrison town that the convoy was being postponed until the following day hoping the news would offset any attack plans. Setting out at full speed they had hoped to make it through before last light. Full speed meant that their scouts were only moments in front of the main convoy. With no opportunity to raise the alarm the convoy ploughed straight into the Legionnaire ambush. Twenty were already dead or dying before they even realised they were under attack.

The silver and grey armour of the one hundred, now dead, Puritan soldiers gleamed black-red in the last light. It was hard to tell if it was from the sun or the fresh arterial blood and gore that had drenched the scene. The bodies lay at impossible angles, as only the dead can do, in the undergrowth and on the shallow banks of the path. No survivors. There had been no one of note worth taking to extract information.

The Puritan commander had fallen in the first volley of arrows and prisoners were a pointless drain on resources for a force that depended on the need to move swiftly.

Eli shared Aaron's enthusiasm at the prospect of returning to the relative security of the mountain camps. They had been out now for a month, skirmishing as always in the endless campaign against the occupying Puritan forces. Never really seeming to accomplish anything. Always burying fresh dead. More Legionnaires who had made the ultimate sacrifice. Not that there was a Legion as such anymore. The tactics of this 'little war' did not really allow for conventional action.

But that would change.

Eli surveyed the enemy dead again briefly. All young men. Their short-cropped hair and armour making them clones in death. Mostly untested, the Puritans had fought bravely and professionally. Reacting correctly and regrouping as their training dictated. Exactly as the ambush had anticipated. Their real warriors were at the front lines four hundred miles to the East. No match for the hardened veterans Eli had under his command. He grimaced. At twenty-six he was one of the oldest veterans present. A veritable old man.

'Eli, let's go.'

Softly spoken this time, from just behind.

Eli smiled. Tori always had that effect on him. Pleased that Eli had not heard her approach she nodded curtly. As much of a salute as she ever gave him. Eli picked up his now clean sword and trotted down the knoll catching up with her.

'You are injured,' he enquired after the gash high on her arm.

'Stiffening up but not deep,' Tori replied, staring straight ahead. 'He was quick, I was quicker. I see you managed not to get as much as a scratch again. Luck is a wonderful thing.'

'It is?' Eli asked, realising he was being baited. 'Seems like the harder I train the luckier I become.'

Eli picked up speed to reach the troops before her. Tori's sharp tongue was as fierce as her ability with her longsword. Some battles he knew he just could not win.

The Legionnaires hurried about, each sure in their purpose. The dead had been carried into the trees for burial in shallow, individual graves. They loaded up with supplies from the wagons ignoring anything that might slow them down. Maps had been correctly and accurately marked to show the conflict. Any horses that were not killed were immediately rounded up and sent North with scouts.

Food rather than cavalry mounts.

'Move out! Leave the bodies. Torch the wagons!' Eli bellowed across his recuperating troop, pleased at their instant response. The high spirits of the victory still pumped in their veins.

He watched as the troop swiftly left the area, splitting into three squads for the different routes to the regrouping point fifteen leagues to the north.

Happy that the wagons were catching light he turned and vanished into the twilight after his warriors.

*

Well done, Finn, I am pleased with your progress. You saved the girl, the daemon flapped some dust off his long cape. The folds were perfectly creased, the material soft and cared for.

'When you have finished preening yourself, Daemon.' Finn said, still lying in the position he had fallen into after his fight with Vorden.

Still in front of the cabin. He pushed himself up into a sitting position his muscles strong once more. Standing he lifted the bandage from his eyes.

A nice trick, Finn, lifting out the pads like that. You could see through that gauze like it wasn't there. They could not understand how a blind man was besting them, and I thought I was the Lord of Deceit

Finn looked around the clearing, the bodies still lay where they had fallen but there was no sign of the priest or the family. A strong wind was blowing, shaking the tall trees and making a shutter bang on the side of the cabin. Smoke was pulled and buffeted flat from the small chimney. Finn could see all these things but could not hear any of the noises associated with them, his own clothes were not blowing in the wind.

'Am I really here?'

Finn, don't start into all the questions again. What is really real? There are just some things you will have to accept, Daemon answered. There was no smile on his face this time though his lips seemed to turn up menacingly when he looked at the body of the big man lying on the ground.

'You know him?' Finn enquired, still looking around.

Ah yes. Vorden. I have known Vorden for a long time, I knew it would not be long before he joined me.

'Where is the family? And the priest?' Finn asked anxiously.

They are still here, do not fret, Daemon said walking among the bodies of the slain as if welcoming new friends. *You are keeping your side of the bargain well, Finn.*

'I made no bargain with you, Daemon,' Finn stated.

What? Daemon responded absently still looking at the bodies.

'You heard,' he reaffirmed.

No, no, I guess you didn't, did you? Daemon stopped and looked at him. *Force of habit. Normally when I am talking with mortals it is because they want something from me and are willing to trade for it.*

'Since I don't want anything from you, it leads us to another interesting question.'

What am I doing here? Daemon asked rhetorically. *Just here to talk Finn. Like I said before you interest me.*

'You talk then, I'll work,' Finn said, picking up the corpse and dragging it off towards the woods.

No, that is not part of the deal, the dark man said, moving forward, his cape billowing about him.

'There is no deal. Talk or leave me alone,' Finn said, walking back for the next body. Though annoyed at the indifference he was being shown, the daemon allowed him to clear away the bodies.

'What now, Daemon? I have saved the girl as you asked,' he said coming back from dropping the last body off in the woods. Kicking earth over the blood-stained ground, he removed the weapons and set them under some leaves and undergrowth.

Not as I asked. The decision to save the family was made by you alone. You could have stood by and let nature run its course.

'There was nothing natural about it,' Finn lifted a cup of water to his mouth from the bucket, enjoying, as though for the first time, the cold feeling on his throat. He dipped his head in the barrel enjoying the new sensations.

You still have yet to save the life.

'What do you mean?' Finn rubbed his callused hands over his face, enjoying the feel of his skin.

That was not the life you were to save, Finn. That is why I am here. If you had done as you were bid, then I would have no reason to come back and see you. Your company, however interesting, is not particularly compelling.

'What are you up to, Daemon?' the irritation showed in his voice.

Nothing, he sat on the porch steps, his tailored clothes out of place against the rural back drop. *I did not ask for you to interfere in this family's business. You did that of your own accord. I could care less if they had died here. But you had to play the hero, didn't you? As I said, it is free will. Only you can decide if your mission here is complete.*

'Listen, you sanctimonious piece of horse shit, I made no bargain with you, and I am on no mission for you. I am my own man. If that is no longer the case then take me now,' Finn shouted.

No, Finn, it is not that easy, I told you. I am not allowed to interfere. Part of the rules, remember? Daemon was unruffled by the outburst.

'Rules,' Finn shook his head. Looking down he saw that he was in armour from head to toe. He had a blade now as well. A longsword. The longsword.

He did not recognise the blade but knew it was his.

Finn. You are getting better. I will restore your health, but you will have to restore your strength.

Finn nodded.

'And in return?' Finn asked.

Nothing. A gift.

'Nothing,' Finn considered. 'Very well.'

Daemon smiled.

Finn felt fire through every pore and fibre of his body. The agony erupted in his very essence, his insides feeling as though they were being torn apart. Hot needles pierced his eyes. His silent scream arched up through the clouds, threatening to wake the angels themselves.

We will speak again soon, Daemon said and vanished.

*

'I do not know what happened to the bodies. I can only presume Finn moved them,' Edom rubbed his tired eyes with his thumbs.

'But he was lying in the same place we left him when we carried Ben into the house. The wind came on strong and they were gone when we came out.

Isela gently touched the wet cloth to her husband's forehead. Ben's left eye was completely closed, and his right was puffy. His whole face was discoloured, and his jaw was black and swollen. There was a network of ugly welts and bruising coursing round his body.

'Several of his ribs are broken. And his cheek. The drink I gave him will help him sleep but the pain will return when he wakes.'

Edom placed some more herbs from his small bag into the pot.

'When did he move the bodies?' Isela pressed.

'I don't know, Isela. I really don't. There are many things about Finn that are a mystery,' Edom looked out of the small bedroom towards the camp bed where Finn slept fitfully.

'Is he a danger to us, father?' her eyes pleaded for an honest answer.

'I am not.'

Isela jumped as Finn spoke, his eyes were open, and he was looking at them from the bed.

'I mean you no harm and invite none with me. I will leave tomorrow.'

'No, you are not fit to leave. Your mind is not yet restored to you.' Isela regretted talking about him. He had saved them this day. Her daughter slept peacefully in the next room.

She was alive because of the man before her.

'Nevertheless, it is time for me to go. Ben is seriously injured. He needs to be cared for. Take him into the mountains with you. More riders will come looking for these soldiers, It would be best if you were not here' Finn eased his eyes closed again. The relief was instant. His body was drained from the day's events.

'How do you know they will come?' Edom asked.

Finn thought for a while. How did he know? What surety did he have that more would follow?

'Because I would come?' he said finally.

'What kind of man are you, Finn? You are skilled and educated in medicine and healing arts that are beyond my ken. You can debate theology objectively and obviously care for the people in this house. You have a special affinity for the little girl who for some reason is enamoured with you. Yet you can kill armed and trained soldiers. You move with a speed and grace that is impossible to follow and this is in your weakened condition. You state that you have dreams about conversing with daemons. I ask again, Finn, who are you?'

'I do not know, priest.'

Edom was puzzled. He sat back in his chair and pondered the situation as Isela moved across to sit beside him.

'I do not care why you are here, Finn,' she said softly 'but I am glad you are. You have done my family a great service this day. You said you could never repay the care we have given you. I think you have more than done so.'

'I thank you, Isela. You have given me your home. I will leave. It is not safe for you while I remain,' Finn opened his eyes to look at her. 'I have no memory of my time before my injuries. I would be grateful if you would allow me to consider myself family.'

'Of course, Finn. We are family,' Isela said, gently applying fresh salve to his skin, the cool juices easing the pain immediately.

They sat together for a while as a family, sharing a comfortable silence for the first time. There was no need to pass any words between them.

Edom interrupted the calm.

'You said you were here to protect the child that named you?' Edom said, an edge to his voice. Finn opened his eyes.

'Yes. In the waking dream the daemon I spoke to said I was here to save the child that named me. Or that's what I thought he meant. He was sufficiently vague. Today I saved Lauren from death…or worse but the daemon says that is not the life I am to save.'

'I do not fully understand all that is happening, but Lauren only called you. She did not name you as such.'

'But you told me she did,' Finn was puzzled.

'Yes, she did. After a fashion. Lauren called you Finn after her story hero.'

'So you said.'

'The story is one based on our myths, in time of heroes and legends, of dragons and monsters form the sea. When the land was being overrun by the evil king, a hero appeared, to lead the people. He led them in a colossal war of Light against Dark. Cut down in the final victorious battle of the war he lay dying on the battlefield. The children of Ellistrin gathered around and sang songs to the heavens to receive their Messiah. They gathered for miles.

Messiah. In the old tongue of the songs, they named him "Feyn'leigh", which means "the Faith of the Children". The young ones now call him Finn. They no longer learn the stories in schools.'

'I have heard the story.'

'Perhaps you are here to save the child that named you after all.'

'I was named by the children of Ellistrin?' Finn felt as though a great weight was pushing down on his chest. 'And you find this a reasonable assumption, priest? You do not find this far-fetched?'

'What do I know, Finn? I am just an old man. You are the one that makes deals with the devil.'

'I made no deal, Priest,' Finn scowled.

'No. perhaps not. But what is the purpose behind all this?' Edom was angry.

'I do not know. Maybe I am mad after all. Maybe you are looking for purpose where there is none.'

'Maybe,' Edom conceded, 'but God moves in mysterious ways, Finn. Think on it. Ask the daemon if you see him again. You saved the girl. It has not ended. Maybe the daemon had this in mind all along.'

'What am I supposed to do then? Save the children of Ellistrin? From what?' Finn tried to sit up, but his body would not obey him. 'I cannot even move, priest. Am I to vanquish the armies of the Puritan Empire from my bed? '

Finn sat up but felt no pain. His head did not spin, and his eyes were able to focus perfectly. His skin was still damaged, but it no longer broke when he moved. The daemon's gift of health.

'I do not know, Finn. I do not even know if I am right. I am just sharing a thought with you,' Edom said smiling, though a little sadly. 'Like the demon said, it is free will, it is up to you.'

'I could not lead an army . . .' Finn trailed off.

'You do not know what you are capable of Finn. Before today you only guessed that you were a warrior. What other talents do you have?'

'Apparently only ones that get me in trouble,' Finn replied.

*

Reyes and his patrol were making good time north. Vorden had made little effort to conceal his passing, obviously not concerned that he would be followed.

Reyes had expected him to be more wary of Legion patrols.

Sending the rest of the patrol south to camp, Reyes had taken ten men with him to hunt the six renegades. The men he had with him were all good men. Loyal. He had served with some for over fifteen years. He trusted them. He just hoped that trust would not falter if they had to fight against their comrades. He had picked the older ones who did not like Vorden to try and forestall that possibility.

'Do you think he will come back?' Yasin asked.

Reyes did not answer for a while. He played over the events of the past days and found himself wondering over the past few years. The time he had known the man they were now pursuing.

'No, he will not be coming back with us,' he said finally.

'Understood. I just wanted to know what to expect,' Yasin's face was grim.

'No surprises, eh, Yasin?' Reyes looked at his sergeant.

'No surprises. I just don't want you to hesitate when it comes to delivering the unwelcome news to the unfortunate Vorden. He will cut you down in a heartbeat if you give him the opportunity. He will not allow you to bring him back.'

'I am not going to bring him back, Yasin. I am going to kill him.'

'I must officially advise you not to speak any further on that matter, sir,' the sergeant cautioned. 'Unofficially, however, it is about time. He has had it coming for too long now.'

'It is my fault it has gone on this long.'

'This is a war. You did not make him the way he is. He makes his own choices.'

'That does not make this any easier. The sky is clear, there is a warm breeze and birds are singing, yet I travel through a war-torn land to kill a one-time friend. There is no logic to it.'

'Then do not seek to find logic in it. Justify it to yourself after the fact, not before. You are not going to kill a man, you are going to kill a monster. The warriors you kill in battle are men, yet you do not mourn for them. Do not mourn for the beast we are hunting. I hope we get to him in time.'

'I hope so too,' Reyes replied, his jaw set. As Yasin rode on ahead he thought much of what his sergeant had said.

'I do mourn the men I have killed,' he thought, yet he would not mourn the death that would soon come in the mountains.

*

Garrad pored over the maps and charts spread out over the table.

Ellistrin was mostly a mystery to him. The lower land, from the ports of the south to the forests in the north was well documented on the military parchments before him. The forests themselves, and the mountains they hid, were an enigma. They hid an army, not a strong one granted, but an army, nonetheless.

Was it a strong army? No one really knew and, in that assumption, lay danger. The land that hid them protected them. They dominated it totally. Scouts, assassins and patrols had been sent in. Few had returned alive. There had been no meaningful incursions since the invasion.

'Join us, general,' Duncan beckoned from the corner of the tent where he was playing a game of dice with the other officers.

'Perhaps you could give me some sport, these boys are no fun at all.'

'It is no sport to take your money, captain,' Garrad did not look up from the charts, 'unless you plan on handing over all the silver you owe me.'

'Soon, general soon, I am winning it all tonight, isn't that right lads?' The captain's comments only solicited a moan from the other officers.

Duncan was teaching his fellow officers a game that he had learned in the arid deserts to the south of the Empire years ago. Of course, he was changing the rules when appropriate to make sure he kept winning. He chuckled at the look of concentration on his fellows' faces. Throwing three dice with different marked heads dictated what action was carried out for the players. There were so many combinations that Duncan had been producing all sorts of meanings, all ensuring he remained ahead, but only just far enough that the others did not suspect his cheating.

Garrad smiled, continuing to look at the maps. He looked to the door when he heard his sentries challenge someone. The flaps were pulled back and one of them entered, flustered.

'General,' he said, snapping to attention, 'Temple Knight Brood wishes to speak with you, sir.'

'Show him in,' Garrad flashed a look at Duncan who was gently edging his dagger from its sheath and moving back from the table slightly for ease of movement should the Knight prove a threat to his general. Garrad did not rebuke him.

Brood stalked into the tent, nodding to the officers who stood around the table. His powerful frame was no longer clad in the matt black armour, but he did not look any more vulnerable. No weapons were visible, but Garrad guessed that he had at least one secreted on his person.

'Greetings, general, I hope I am not disturbing you,' his voice was melodic, even musical. Gone was the dangerous tone that was so blatant at last their last encounter.

'No. You are welcome to my tent. Do you require any refreshment?' Garrad said evenly, letting the purpose of the Knight's visit reveal itself in its own good time.

'I am fine, thank you, though I would say that I am not a threat to you this night and ask for you inform your men of the same.'

Garrad glanced at Duncan and nodded. Duncan sheathed the blade and bowed gently to the Knight.

'My men are loyal and would seek to have no harm befall me. It is a trait I like to encourage, lord Knight.'

'It is one that I like to see encouraged, general,' Brood smiled. 'Please, be about your game. I would join you, but what little coin I have I would like to keep on my person.'

Brood looked directly at Duncan who shrugged. He was eager to get back to the game and forget about the Knight. He did however reposition himself at the table so he could keep a protective eye on his general.

'So, how should I properly address a Temple Knight?' Garrad asked again, taking a drink from his mug of steaming tea.

'You can address me however you like, general,' Brood stepped up to the table his eyes roaming over the maps and charts.

'What are you studying, general?' Brood asked, picking up one of the mountain maps, such as it was.

'Forgive my abruptness, lord Knight, what do you want? This is obviously not a social visit,' Garrad set the mug down and rested his hands on the table.

'This is partly why I am here,' Brood said, indicating the maps. 'I like you, general. You have little time for pleasantries when it seeks to distract you from your task at hand.'

Brood drew his finger over the mountain ranges before him.

'If I wanted pleasant company I would go home and see my son. While I am here, I intend to give all my attention to the matters at hand.'

'Do these matters include insulting your regional commander?' Brood asked.

'They do if he is an incompetent fool. It was not my intention to insult the man and I deeply regret the death of his bodyguard. I knew Roche by reputation. He was particularly good. I will mourn his passing, but I will not bow down to that fool. He would squander men's lives if he were put in a real battle.'

'I agree, which brings me to why I am here. I believe you would be better suited to lead this battalion,' Brood looked up at Garrad.

'I am honoured that you think so, Lord Knight. But you are mistaken in this.'

'It is not often I am told I am mistaken,' Brood said, with no animosity in his voice.

'You get used to it if you continue to make statements that I do not agree with.'

'Excellent,' Brood smiled and settled himself onto the chair in the corner. The chair was purely functional, easy for transporting. The difference between Garrad's ergonomic quarters and Pogue's lavish surroundings pleased the Knight.

'Excellent? I am not suited to stagnating here, lord Knight. I am a general of a fine regiment of men. The Osocan fight well and are loyal because they know that no matter what I ask them to do, I do the same.'

'I know. I have checked. You have an illustrious record. Medals, honours and citations. You have lectured at the Capor and Yashtan Military Academies on "The reactive thinking of front-line officers." "Keeping discipline in adversity" is one of your lectures too I believe,' Brood continued, his tone conversational.

'Yes. I have lectured. Only when ordered to do so by the Chief of Staff. I would rather not waste my time talking. I would prefer to be doing.'

'Good. What are you working on here?'

'I am not. I was merely looking at the charts. I am moving the regiment on in two weeks to the front. As ordered.'

'That is not what you are working on,' Brood said icily.

'Are you calling me a liar?' Garrad demanded.

'Yes. But not to cause you offence, general. You would do to keep your troops working or better still in battle. You do not want to them stagnating at the front for the next year while the Holy Father recalls his troops from the far crusades.

'Do you have the ability to read minds, Lord Knight?' Garrad asked. 'Or are you merely adept at reading men.'

Brood smiled and stood, walking to the table. He spread his hand out to indicate the northern territories.

'This land has been passed over in haste. It is no longer considered a threat yet time and again trained soldiers come down from their mountains to harry troop movements, interrupt supply trains, intercept despatches and generally cause a lot of inconvenience. The Holy Father wants the routes to the capital purged. I want you to do it.'

Garrad did not respond.

'Come now, general. You are not looking over these maps for the sake of interest. You are not that sort of man. Your mind is processing the information needed for just such a protracted war. You are estimating enemy strengths. The file before you contains reports from all the recorded engagements with the enemy over the last nine years including the reports of the original invasion and before. There are detailed reports on enemy capabilities and fighting effectiveness. You have more reports on their culture, religion and social practices. You want to go into the mountains after them.'

Garrad said nothing. It was true.

'How do you know about the reports?'

'I know many things, general. That is my job. Your job is to fight for our nation and protect it. First, though, I want you to take over the discipline of the camp.'

'What of Pogue?'

'I will make sure Pogue sees the merits of the decision. He will think it is his idea.'

'With respect, Lord Knight, why do you not simply order him?'

'My tasks call for me to control events. Sometimes the best way to achieve results is to manipulate people from afar.'

'Are you manipulating me now?'

'I doubt you would let me, general. No, you I would order.'

Garrad did not react. He knew he would have to obey.

'You will answer to me, general, not Pogue, but you will answer to me in every way. I do not tolerate failure. Your failure is my failure, do you understand?'

'Perfectly. Do not threaten me, Brood.'

Brood smiled. The cold smile of certain death.

'Do not mistake my good intentions or our mutual understanding for a relationship, general. I will achieve my goals with or without you. Thank you for your company. You will begin work on the task tomorrow by restoring discipline to the camp. You will update me as soon as you have a suitable plan to move the army north. When sufficient troops are available, if your plan is acceptable, you will lead the campaign. Do not worry about Pogue. You will find him suitably cowed the next time you see him. Good night.'

Garrad did not reply.

Much as he did not like the company or manner of the Knight, he had just been given the power to take the army north. He watched as the tall Knight stalked across the tent and paused by the table of officers. Reaching down Brood picked up the dice and, looking directly at Garrad, he smiled and rolled them. Without waiting he left the tent.

Duncan stood and walked to the general.

'That went well, ' he said pouring Garrad another mug of fresh tea.

'Well?' the general enquired absently.

'We are still alive, aren't we?' Duncan replied smiling. 'That is usually a good thing. Any fight that you can walk away from is a victory.'

'I didn't realise we were fighting.'

'What were you doing then?' Duncan sat down in the Knight's vacated chair.

'Believe it or not we were seeing eye to eye.'

'I will take your word for it, my general. He scares me.'

'I want you to find a man for me. Commander Klein, he is commanding the Fourth Regiment of Watch,' Garrad said checking his files. 'I want you to find which part of the camp he is in. I do not want him to know I want to meet him. It must appear as happenstance.'

'Yes, general.'

'The dice?' Garrad asked. 'What did he roll?'

'Three skulls,' Duncan said nervously, showing them to Garrad. It was the highest score in the game and signalled death for the opponents.

'Figures,' Garrad observed, returning his attention to the mountains.

Chapter Ten

Reyes led his men along the path through the trees. The trail was man made and not well travelled. He had seen smoke at the top of the last rise an hour before. Vorden's trail was only two days old. Their camp had not been well concealed, and they were making no efforts to cover their tracks.

Reyes held his arm out to one side and turned his hand making a slight sign with his fingers. The soldiers lifted out their crossbows and racked them, setting a bolt in place. Reyes turned subtly to look at them. Their faces were grim and set. They were worried about confronting Vorden, but they would remain loyal to Reyes.

The cabin came into view.

The cabin that Vorden had obviously made for.

The smoke was a good sign.

Someone was alive. If it was the people of the house, then he would be pleasantly surprised. Reyes hoped that Vorden and his team had lit the fire. They would be finally able to end this. He gave the signal to dismount.

'Yasin, leave the horses here with a sentry. We will approach the cabin. You do the talking. You men, hold back. Move through the woods and take up covering position. You two cover the back. If there is fighting, come running. Remember this is not a time for being a hero.'

The men fanned out on the trail, watching the trees for an ambush. The birds chirped a friendly hello as the soldiers went about their business.

'Hello the cabin!' Yasin hailed.

There was movement behind one of the curtains.

No response.

'Again,' Reyes said softly.

'Hello the cabin! I am Sergeant Yasin of the Puritan army. I wish to speak with you. I wish you no harm. I only want to ask you a few questions. You have nothing to fear from us!'

There was no further movement in the cabin.

'Those are fine words, sergeant Yasin, I hope you will stand by them.'

Reyes and Yasin spun to see Finn standing only a few feet from them. They had not heard him approach. Finn wore a long-hooded cloak.

To conceal weapons?

Yasin eased his hand toward his sword.

'There is no need for your sword, sergeant, I am sure your men would be able to cut down an old cripple before I could harm you.'

Reyes looked to the tree line but even he could not make out his men. His eyes moved across the ground. The dust and dirt were settled though he could make out signs of a lot of activity. This was not surprising as this was a well-worked cabin.

'How can I help you?' Finn said.

Reyes looked up to see that the man had addressed him.

Yasin answered.

'We are looking for six men who may have passed this way, their leader would have been a big man with a beard.'

Reyes saw hoof prints in the dirt that had been covered over. The fresh dust had settled though it had left tell-tale ridges of shod hooves.

Vorden had been here.

'Who are these men?' Finn probed, moving himself to stand between the soldiers and the cabin.

'They are soldiers. We wish to return them to their unit,' Yasin answered.

'These men were here. We fed them and they went on their way. Ask your men to join us and we will feed them too,' Finn addressed Reyes again.

'Who is in the cabin?' Yasin asked.

'No one of consequence.'

Reyes could not make out the man properly. His face was slightly covered by the shadow from his hood. It seemed disfigured.

He could make out stained dirt that had been covered. The stain had soaked up through the covering to stain it also. Blood?

'Who is in the cabin?' Yasin forced.

Finn remained silent, staring at Reyes. He made no movement.

Reyes looked at him carefully. This was no farmer. He was not nervous, as Reyes would have expected any man to be if confronted with soldiers who did not exactly have a compassionate reputation.

He saw subtle drag marks in the dirt leading to the trees, cast by the shadows of the setting sun. Reyes tried to piece together what had happened. Vorden had obviously been here. The man was hiding something. Vorden could be in the cabin holding his family hostage forcing him to speak. The hooded man did not look like he was under duress. He stood slightly stooped, though Reyes thought it was not caused by any real hindrance to his movement. When he walked his balance was perfect. Had the man fought Vorden, surely he would be dead.

Reyes suddenly realised that there was no other path leading from the cabin, only the one they had come in by. There had been no hoof marks leaving the clearing. Whoever had come here was still here.

'I will need to look in your cabin, my friend,' Reyes spoke at last.

Finn did not step to one side to let him pass. They stood facing each other in the clearing. The rest of the soldiers came into the clearing, crossbows carried loosely over their forearms, strings still taut. Reyes raised his hand to halt them. Reaching to his buckle he undid the belt and dropped his sword and knives to the ground. He pulled out two throwing knives from his boots and dropped them also. Reyes bared his hands to Finn.

'Please. I must see in the cabin.'

Finn stepped to the side, letting the soldier pass. Reyes mounted the steps and lifted the latch for the door. Stepping inside he was met with the soft aromas and cooking. The air was rich with the smell of herbs.

Walking through the dimly lit room he saw the people huddled in one corner. Lifting a piece of wood from the fire he walked towards them holding it high to throw the light on them. A man was lying on the bed, beaten to the point of death. A woman, presumably his wife, was also badly marked about the face. Vorden had been here. An old man sat in the corner with a little girl on his knee. Fear in her eyes? No. Maybe anger?

'I am sorry little one,' Reyes threw the brand back in the fire and walked out of the cabin. Standing on the porch he watched the sun setting behind the trees. Such horrible things in this world, done in the name of God, but under the pretence of war and barbarity.

At least Vorden was dead. It came to him with such clarity. Dead. Killed here.

By whom?

Had they stumbled into an Ellistrin ambush? Unlikely. For all his problems Vorden was an excellent soldier and excelled in the raiding units. He would not have walked into the ambush. Reyes looked at the man that had greeted them. This man? Surely he could not have bested six trained soldiers. And Vorden? Reyes himself had doubted he would be able to best Vorden in fair combat. Or unfair if it came to it.

'Who are you, friend?' Reyes asked as he walked back to Finn and put his sword belt and harness back on.

'I am Finn.'

'You are from here?'

'This is my family's home,' Finn answered truthfully.

Reyes walked up to the hooded man and stopped only inches from his disfigured face. He stared into Finn's dead eyes and felt fear. This man had killed them. Reyes stepped back to clear the field of fire. He was going to order his men to loose their bolts.

'Don't you think there has been enough suffering here? Enough killing?' Finn suggested, creating a pause.

Reyes watched the man. He made no offensive movements. He did not deserve to die. Reyes himself would have killed Vorden had he found him. This man had saved him the trouble.

'Yes,' Reyes felt tired after the days of travelling. More than enough.

'Move out!' he shouted to his men.

'What? What about Vorden?' Yasin demanded, his bow still raised.

'Vorden is dead, now move out,' Reyes repeated as his horse was led to him.

'Dead? How do you know?' Yasin asked, staring at the strange man standing in the clearing. Reyes vaulted into the saddle.

'Move out, sergeant. Now!' As his men moved up the trail Reyes turned to the hooded man. 'I would not stay, Finn. Vorden was not a good man, and I am glad he is dead, but there are those of my men would slay you for killing one of their own. More soldiers will come this way. Do not be here when they come.'

Reyes kicked his horse into a gallop after his men.

'Thank you, ' Finn said and walked stiffly back to the cabin.

*

Garrad watched his men finish their morning's drilling. They had shaken off the drudging exertion of the long journey here. Glad to be able to train and exercise they launched themselves into their morning's endeavour with a zealous intensity matched only by the equally slovenly behaviour of the rest of the camp.

As the training ended the rest of the camp was only stirring.

The slouching forms of troops that should have been put out to pasture.

In a camp of one hundred thousand soldiers, it was a distressing sight. Safely removed from the fighting in the north and the eastern border, the troops had been allowed to degrade. It could be hard for a commander to keep morale high. Discipline must be uniform. Garrad wanted to move on before his own regiment became affected. Infected. Though he doubted if they would ever allow themselves to sink to the level in the main camp.

'Have the men clean down the horses and walk them,' Garrad shouted to three of his officers who huddled together and complained in hushed tones. He could not hear what they were saying but it was obvious they were not happy. Best to keep them busy.

'Yes, general,' they saluted as one, but he stopped them before they left.

'Listen lads,' Garrad said, 'don't let the men see that you are unhappy about being here. It will be hard enough to keep them motivated. You must lead by example.'

'Yes, sir,' Mothar answered. 'It is difficult though, surrounded as we are with such waste.'

'I agree, captain, what do you suggest?'

'Make these beggars work too,' Lasalle shrugged.

'As it happens, Lieutenant, I have just been given charge of improving the quality of discipline in the camp, and a bit of arduous work is the order of the day. We will have to remind these wastrels what it is like to fight against real men,' Garrad smiled to himself. 'Visit each of the troop camps and pay homage to their commanders. I want you to organise an invitation to a few boxing bouts for fourteen nights from now. No restriction. Get as many as you can. We will clear an area in the centre of the camp. Take whatever you need to organise this but do not put any of our men to it except in as far as it directly affects our camp. Report to me at the end of tonight.'

'Yes, sir,' snapped Wassel as he crisply saluted.

'If any of the commanders are less than enthusiastic,' Garrad continued, 'you will say that it is unfortunate that their regiment is a regiment of women and that all the other regiments are putting forward their champion. If they have a problem with the tone of the message tell them that the message is from me and that they are invited to air their grievances to me directly.'

'Yes, general,' Wassel could not keep the smile from his face.

'What are you up to?' enquired Duncan who had listened to the exchange as he towelled off from the training. 'I thought you had promised me you were going to keep out of trouble.'

Exempt because of their rank, Garrad still encouraged all his officers to train with the men. 'Someday, captain you are going to call me "sir",' Garrad sighed. 'It is the fastest way to unite the camp other than trying to take it by force. They will take exception to the slight I have made against them and will support each other in the bouts. The rearrangements of the camp to accommodate the fighting ring will allow us to restructure the entire camp to meet the required military standard.'

'"Cunning" always was one of your more admirable traits.'

'Have Mothar clear the centre of the camp and assign each regiment an area. I want the plans for the layout drawn up for approval by the end of the day, to be implemented by tomorrow at the latest. If there is a problem I will visit and belittle the commander into submission, making him comply. Clearing the centre will cause everyone to move. No one will be unaffected by this. We will reset the camp, clear a thoroughfare for troop movements, establish proper sanitation and communication, lift morale as they support their own fighter, and re-establish our own seniority when we beat them. It will be a good day all round.'

'And all this inside three days without confronting or challenging the battalion leadership,' Duncan accepted a fresh shirt from his orderly. 'Pogue will not be pleased.'

'By the time Pogue is even aware of it, it will be done and too late. The best victories are won without the enemy even knowing you are fighting,' Garrad smiled.

*

'I don't understand, papa. Why do we have to go?' Lauren sat with her legs up under her.

'The enemy is coming for us, little princess. We have to go north to the camps. We cannot fight them all just yet. It was time for you to go anyway to continue your training. Now is as good a time as any.'

Ben decided that honesty, as always, was best. Putting a sugar coating on it would not make it easier to swallow in the long run. It was time for his little girl to start growing up. Life was hard and actions had consequences. Where they were going there was no place for weakness. Ben felt his own eyes start to well up. He had protected her for so long and now felt that it was beyond him.

Within five years she would begin her serious graft in the Legion.

Lauren reached up and touched his still swollen face, mindful not to touch his arm, which was now in a sling. The eye was badly discoloured but at least he could see through it.

'Is it still sore, papa?' she asked, forgetting her own worries for a moment.

'Yes, it is still sore. But Finn has helped. Will you help me be brave?' Ben's throat was drying up. He felt as though his heart was trying to climb into his mouth.

'Of course, papa. We will be strong together,' Lauren said, proudly.

'Shall we find your mama? She will be ready to go.'

Isela was preparing what little they could carry for the journey north. They had cleared out the cabin during the morning. Lauren had been missing from her bed, but they knew she had run off to her secret place. Isela had suggested it would be better to leave her there until they had everything organised.

Ben had only now gone to fetch her, and the sun was at its highest point. They had to get underway soon to get away from the cabin by nightfall. It would be a long enough journey, looking after the child on the way.

Finn had wanted them to press hard. The backpacks they had put together contained only food and canteens of water, though both Ben and Finn would be able to provide for them all on the way north also.

'I hope you are a good shot with a bow,' Ben had said to Finn.

'He could not be much worse than you,' Edom had ribbed his friend.

'My arm is in a sling,' Ben protested.

'For the last fifty years?' Edom continued.

'It has been sore from carrying your weight in battle,' Ben laughed and clapped the priest on the shoulder.

And so, in high spirits, they had completed their preparations.

'Is Finn coming with us, papa?' she asked, holding his big hand as they walked home to meet the others.

'He is coming north with us, princess, but I do not think he will be staying with us,' Ben said wondering about Finn's decision not to stay. 'Why not, Papa? Doesn't he like us no more?'

To a child everything was black and white.

'Yes, he does. He was very worried when he could not find you this morning.'

Ben had seen real concern on Finn's face this morning when one of his new family was missing. Even under the scarring and scabbing on his face. In the weeks Finn had been with them they had grown as concerned for his well-being as he had for theirs.

'I was alright,' Lauren said showing them her dagger and short sword, which was not much more than a long dagger. 'I am a big girl now.'

Ben would be leading them north as he knew the terrain, but he would be depending on Finn should they run into soldiers. The going would be slower still as they were going to keep to the forest to avoid all paths and clearings. Safer but slower.

'I am looking forward to the mountains, papa. Father Edom says they are beautiful. We will be happy there.'

'We will,' Ben assured her. If I make it in one piece, he said to himself.

With his shoulder, elbow, head, ribs and knees bandaged, he finished loading his pack and took the first step on the one-hundred-mile trek into the mountains, complaining under his breath as only old soldiers can.

Edom just laughed.

Isela was sad too, but she accepted events. As with most mothers, her home was where her family was. The cabin that had been their home was now not an option if she wanted to keep her family safe. Dressed moderately she could feel the cold biting through her. Once they were underway the heat generated by the exercise would sustain her and keep her warm provided, they did not stop. Extra blankets were carried for the night and rest stops. Cold would be the main enemy on the journey. Isela watched as Edom ambled around the courtyard aimlessly but obviously lost in thought. He had seemed preoccupied with events over the past weeks and especially the day before.

'What do you think of what father Edom said, Finn?' Isela asked, as she crammed the last of the supplies into the carry sacks.

'I am trying not to think of it, Isela. I am a man without a past and the priest is trying to force an impossible future on me,' Finn was sharpening one of the swords he had retrieved from the soldiers.

He had taken the heads from the crossbow bolts and refashioned them for the long bow, which now sat at his side. Isela was disturbed by the man before her now. A warrior was now replacing the quiet thoughtful man who had played with her daughter and discussed religion with the priest.

'It does not change the fact that he may be right.'

'No, it does not,' Finn agreed without looking up, the whet stone gliding over the edge of the blade. 'But I do not know how to proceed. I will guide you north until we reach the camps then I will have to take leave of you.'

'Where will you go?' despite her reservations as to Finn's role in their future she was concerned for his well-being.

'I need some time alone. I must repair my body and mind. I am no use to anyone while I am still in this weakened state. Least of all myself.'

'God will guide you back to us, Finn,' Edom interrupted joining them. 'You cannot deny your destiny.'

'If it is to be so, then it will be so,' Finn paused and examined the weapon. 'I have been a pawn in someone's game since I have been with you. I am sure they will make their plans known to me when it suits them.'

'Lauren will miss you,' Isela added, looking out to the forest for any sign of her returning.

'I will miss Lauren too. She is very dear to me?'

'Why?' pressed the priest.

'What sort of a question is that?' Finn slid the honed sword into its sheath, withdrawing it again and making small cuts in the sheath to allow him to draw it faster should he need it in a hurry. He smiled inwardly. If a sword must be drawn, it is usually in a hurry.

'It is a simple question, Finn. You do not know this family. She is no blood kin of yours. Why do you feel this attachment to her? '

'It is simple I suppose. My memories of this life begin with her. She has shown me nothing but love in the brief time I have known her. How could I not love her back? Isela and Ben have made me welcome, and it has ultimately meant that they now must leave their home. I have no memories of other people, yet I know that this is not the norm. I know that it was an exceptional act of goodness from them to me. One which I cannot repay.'

'Enough of this talk of repayment. We are family now, Finn,' Isela spoke. 'Family does not hold family accountable. We would be dead now were you not with us. I can never repay you for that. That is how it is when people act unselfishly. It does not require any of Father Edom's high-brow explanations, nor does it require the understanding that you wish of it. It just is. Let it rest at that.'

Isela stood and walked off to greet Ben and Lauren who only now were arriving back.

'She could teach us all a thing or two, priest,' Finn commented.

'Yes, she could. I would wish you luck for your future, Finn, but I have the feeling we shall meet again.'

'I hope it is under better circumstances, priest.'

'I hope so too, though I doubt it.'

Ben marched over and picked up is pack.

'We'd best get moving. Are you ready, Edom? Do you think your frail old bones will be able to make it into the mountains?' Ben helped the priest to his feet.

'Benjad, I was walking them back when they were just hills. I think I will manage another trip so long as I do not have to endure your constant complaining,' Edom said in good humour, setting a brisk pace north and disappearing into the forest.

'Tough old buzzard. Come on Finn. We'd best be after him before he gets lost,' Ben headed after the priest and his family.

Finn loaded his pack on to his back, grimacing as the straps dug into the shin on his shoulders, the weight gouging furrows in his back. His vision blurred briefly, the pain excruciating. The blood and fluid ran down his arm staining the cotton shirt and running over his hands. There was not a lot. He was not going to bleed to death but as the pain flared again death didn't seem such a bad prospect.

Finn did not need to check that the weapons were easily accessible. He had known instinctively on packing that everything was as it should be. Looking around the clearing Finn only saw memories.

He saw his only memories.

A home rich with happiness and laughter, out of place in the bleak landscape that surrounded it. He picked up one of the abandoned dolls lying on the porch. It was not one of Lauren's favourites and so had not been deemed worthy to make the arduous journey north. Finn found himself strangely emotional at the sight of the doll. Perhaps they had something in common. Picking up the doll he turned it over in his hand looking at it closely, before putting it inside his shirt.

A strong wind blew up and black clouds gathered over the hills to the south.

Finn turned and trotted into the forest after his family.

Chapter Eleven

The centre of the Plandor camp was being cleared.

Garrad's officers had organised a map illustrating where each of the regiments was to go. Each regiment moved with renewed energy. The northern quarter of the plains of Plandor was chaos itself as the whole battalion uprooted and moved. Work details completed sanitation ditches and set up fresh water supplies. Paths for communication and supply. Exercise grounds, officers meeting areas. It began to look like an army again. They knew they were under a deadline for completion in time for the fighting. The reward was that whoever finished their tasks first got pride of place at the front of the arena.

'You have worked a small miracle here, general,' Commander Klein spoke with what seemed like regret.

'You would have done the same under less ardent circumstances. It is a pity that a man with such a mind for planning should be wasted here under Pogue. You served in the northern towns for a time.'

'I did,' Klein fell in with Garrad as he walked across the camp unaware that Garrad had orchestrated the meeting to pick his brain. 'Now that was a challenge worthy of a soldier. We would go out hunting the Ellistrins in force. They would hit us and disappear. We spent most the time chasing ghosts. We used the locals. Forced them or bribed them to reveal the positions of camps. We were always attacked. Ambushes, running battles, skirmishing for weeks. And the booby-traps. Ah, but I bore you.'

'Not at all,' Garrad replied, leading him into his meeting tent. Garrad bid him sit and poured him a glass of juice. 'I am always intrigued to hear how people have implemented tactics in the field and adapted them to deal with the enemy. You mentioned booby-traps.'

'Yes,' started Klein, enthused as any general to discuss campaigns, 'I remember about five years ago we pushed north on the information of one of the captured enemy. We tortured him for hours. Possibly even a day or two before he broke. We took in a force of ten companies. I commanded one of the light companies. General Duban led the expedition.'

'An able warrior,' Garrad observed, having served with him.

'Indeed he was. He was also leading able troops,' Klein explained. The soldiers of the northern garrisons were under constant attack or threat of attack from the mountain resistance. Under such conditions they were as battle hardened as front-line troops.

'We headed out at first light,' Klein continued. 'It was springtime, and the mountains were beautiful. We made a circuitous route to the camp. After four days of travel, we found it located high on the side of one of the smaller mountains, Donard.

'The officers gathered and Duban decided an immediate attack was better. It is hard to hide the fact that three thousand soldiers are hiding in a forest. We could not risk making camp. So, attack it was.

'We entered the camp about an hour before dusk. It was deserted but as we charged through the camp, men started dropping. We thought we were under being ambushed. Men died as they ran round corners, as they entered temporary shacks. There were cries of pain and war cries. We thought we were engaging the enemy.

'They had dug trenches and filled the pits with sharpened sticks smeared with excrement. They had tied canes back from doorframes with stakes attached to the whip end. They had erected and secreted slings that released flint pieces into our men.

'There were very few deaths as a result, but the extent of injuries was enormous.'

'I had thought this to be an ineffective method of fighting, but I quickly realised that every man injured needed another man to carry him or tend him. Sometimes two men. They had effectively injured nearly a third of our force.'

'I suggested tending to the wounded and withdrawing. Duban wanted to set off in pursuit and had already ordered the trackers to locate the direction the enemy had left in.'

'Once the direction was confirmed he took one thousand men and headed into the forest leaving me behind with a rear-guard and the wounded.'

'He was not gone long. It was maybe thirty minutes before we began to hear screaming and the sounds of battle. We heard sword on sword. I already had the rear-guard set in a defensive position and our discipline was good. There was nothing we could do.'

'The battle raged and got closer. The soldiers spilled back into the camp under pressure from the enemy.'

'It was my first time seeing them. Really seeing them. They ranged from boys to adolescents to men. They fought brilliantly. They pushed us back into the clearing. Just as we were about to regroup and push them.'

'Light started to leave us. Night was falling and we were stranded and losing in their territory. Not a comforting thought.'

'They were camouflaged too. They had covered their light fighting armour with oiled leather wraps so that they could move with less sound and without light glinting off their armour. They had blackened their blades with smoke from a fire.'

'We were bright and shiny and in trouble. We reinforced our perimeters rather than pull back at night. Duban was dead. His head was tossed into the camp later that night. We had lost half our number by this stage with many more wounded.'

'We thought that they would leave us that night and attack us, hit and run again, as we pulled out. I underestimated them again. They attacked in force at a little after four in the morning. Arrows came from everywhere, volley after volley. Our troops started going down. They were loosing from the cover of the trees. We were in open ground in their camp. As we pulled back to regroup in the centre they attacked.

'There must have been at least a thousand. That is what my report says anyway. I honestly don't know. There might only have been hundreds. It was impossible to tell.'

'We managed to hold position until first light. We pulled out along the most direct route. We did not see the enemy again. Of the three thousand soldiers that went into the mountains, one thousand men walked out. Of those four hundred would never fight again.'

Klein looked out over the busy camp. All was activity. His eyes were glazed as he looked into his past and was barely aware of the present. He downed the juice then looked into the goblet, disappointed that it was not something stronger. He smiled awkwardly at Garrad and set the goblet on the bench before them. His hands clamped the back of the chair, knuckles white.

'This is the part where you belittle me, is it not?' Klein braced.

'No, my friend, it is not. I have read your report before coming here. I have read as much about the enemy as I could. I was involved with the original invasion. We rolled straight over this country. Their soldiers are excellent. We tricked them, deceived them and fought them. We effectively destroyed the military capability of this country within a week. We killed the government, council members, regional leaders, priests and youth leaders. Men, women and children. Anything that stood even remotely in our way. Since we drove them into the mountains, we have continually underestimated their ability to wage their own protracted war. Had we pursued them into the mountains at the time we would probably have eliminated the threat completely. We were that concerned with pushing forward to the eastern border that we neglected to confirm our standing in this country. Their army was able to flourish in the northern mountain areas because of our mistake. It was not of their own making. They did however seize the advantage. They now have complete control of the north of this country, and we are so involved with the war in the east that we pay them very little attention. There are minor skirmishes every day but nothing of great import. If we go into the mountains we lose. If they come into the plains, they lose. They are annoying and nothing more to the scheme of things.'

'Yet every day our soldiers die,' Klein said, blaming himself more than his senior officer.

'That is something that is unforgivable and must change, commander. I am going to bring the battle to them on their territory. That is the challenge you are talking about.'

'That is quite a claim, general,' Klein said, accepting a stronger drink from Duncan's flask.

'It is. But I am nobody's fool. What I am interested in commander, is learning from your experience. What would you do differently if you were to lead a similar force or larger into the mountains?'

'There is much I would do differently, general,' Klein admitted.

'Humour me. What would you do?' An aide took extensive notes.

'Is this going to happen?' Klein asked.

'It is,' Garrad assured the commander.

'I would not go in blindly again for a start,' said Klein interested now.

'Scouts?' Duncan asked.

'Of course. But first I would take regional information from each of the garrison commanders stationed along the base of the mountain range. With their information on most recent enemy activity, I would then enter the mountains at the western tip with a huge force, preceded at each stage by advance patrols to engage the enemy.'

'It sounds sensible,' Garrad nodded.

'On contact,' Klein was enthusiastic now, 'I would split the force into four or five sizeable groups depending on the forces available to me. One group would head into the camp, the other four skirting around it, blockading it. The first group, protected by the blockade would initiate the attack if the camp were not deserted. They would signal which way the enemy was being driven from the camp allowing the blockade to move to cut them off. We would then butcher every one of them. If the camp were empty the soldiers would withdraw instead of testing the booby traps. An unnecessary drain on resources. The men would quickly lose heart if they started to take casualties without contact.'

'Would you withdraw from the forest?'

'Yes, unless I had more definite information on another camp location.

'Why?'

'If we were to go thrashing around the forest, we would let absolutely everyone know where we were and where we were headed. We are not expert enough in their territory to bring the battle to them currently. We could push through into the forest along a known path and build a fortress and use that as a staging point to attack out from there. I do not believe that they would be able to sack a fortress. That is not underestimating them. They may well still be able to function in that way. The dense forest would negate catapults and siege machines. I think that would be the way forward.'

'What of their numbers?'

'Impossible to guess at. My report on that campaign was generous on our part. I stated thousands of the enemy. The report was changed to indicate hundreds. It would not have been seemly to indicate that there may be a fully operational army in the northern woods beyond our control.'

'I understand.'

'Is there talk of heading back into the mountains?'

'Not yet but I do not intend to waste a year on the front waiting for our full army to mass from the other continent. I would like to lead a campaign to the north while we wait. I think that the battalion you see before you could spearhead that campaign.'

'I would be honoured if you would consider me for a role in that campaign, ' Klein stood to attention.

'I would be glad to have you. There are not enough soldiers of calibre in this outfit,' Garrad said graciously.

'How do you propose to be allowed to go north?'

'I will petition the war council for the use of this battalion for training exercises. I will then lead them north for battle.

'Vengeance at last,' Klein said, a little too loudly.

'It is the virtue of the righteous,' Garrad agreed.

*

'Well, what have you to report?' Saladin demanded.

'The troops are being recalled from the farthest colonies, Holy Father even now they are moving across the Empire. We expect them to start arriving within our own borders with the month. They will station here and begin their advance into Ellistrin an estimated five weeks after that. Regiments are arriving weekly on the Plandor plain. We are using our own border as a staging point as the land in Ellistrin is not capable of sustaining a massed army,' Suchart explained.

'What of supplying them here?'

'We have taken care of that, Holy Father,' the chief of staff replied. 'We have set the supply train up to follow the armies moving north. We have enough to sustain them should the entire army be delayed here for an additional month.'

'Delays, what delays? I do not want to hear about your logistical problems, general. I want performance,' Saladin's voice shook the paintings on the walls, making even Altai flinch.

'Yes, Holy Father,' Suchart stammered. 'I merely wished to point out that we have been preparing for any contingency. The extra supplies will be carried with the army when it marches. As I said, Ellistrin cannot sustain our forces on a long campaign. We will need to march straight to the front line and march straight over the lines by force of numbers.'

'Projected losses?' Saladin asked absently.

'Extremely high, Holy Father,' the general could feel the sweat beginning to gather at the small of his back. His eyes flicked to the Temple Knights standing just behind the Emperor's council chair. The other high council members did not meet his gaze. If blood was in the water, they did not want to get caught in the kill.

'High, general?' Saladin's tongue flicked around the inside of his mouth, touching his lips briefly.

'Yes, Holy Father. But we knew this. We are using auxiliary troops from the satrapies. We expect to lose more than half their number, possibly three-quarters. But we will effectively walk straight over their lines. The defeat that will be inflicted upon them will decimate them as a fighting coalition. We expect them to withdraw onto the huge plains behind their position where we will annihilate them with our cavalry. Those that withdraw to their own borders will not be able to stand alone against your army.'

'Good, general. Good,' Saladin's mood swung back to placid as quickly as it had erupted. He found he was more heady since he had taken the girl. 'You are dismissed.'

The general saluted and marched out of the council chamber, the door opening and closing at the hands of two guards.

Saladin looked at the twenty members of the high council. They were weak and afraid. There was a time when had had to pander to them, cajoling and coercing when necessary to maintain control.

Now his power was undisputed, as it should be. They were in constant fear of the day he decided they were an inconvenience he could do without. That day was coming. Perhaps on the day he destroyed the enemy to the east. Yes, the day his troops massed on the border waiting to advance.

'The council meeting is adjourned,' one of the Knights announced disrupting his train of thought. The council meeting would soon be over permanently.

*

Ten miles away from the fighting Eli's troop crossed some open ground on a slope. The full moon cut through the sky, illuminating the rising cloud, giving it an ethereal life of its own.

The scouts had taken their bearing from the stars and moved on again.

As always, they made no sound. Stealth was life.

The sound of horses could be heard in the distance. The lancers that were searching for the missing convoy.

Eli looked back along the line of warriors. Shadows furtively moving across the open ground. Moonlight catching the oily leather giving only an eerie semblance of a human shape. The purposeful and steady march was the only indication that the shapes were human and some animal.

The Legionnaire troopers were the only predators at work this evening.

Eli took his place in the advancing line, methodically working his way through the sparse undergrowth. He could see a warrior in hiding off to the left and knew that he was approaching the regrouping point. Sentries already taking first watch. His two-man teams were out in the forest, spread to each point of the compass. Two men would mean less chance of them sleeping despite their discipline.

There was still no talk at this time. One Legionnaire in the sentry unit advanced a further thirty yards into the night. Making sure that once daylight came, they had not inadvertently camped close to an enemy camp. They had planned the regrouping point in advance and knew that there was not likely to be anyone close but there was no excuse for breaking procedure.

It had saved lives before and would again.

The advance sentries returned directly to the camp, reporting to Eli that all was well, before retreating to their partner in the darkness. Eli lifted his hide backpack over his head and settled it onto the ground. He then signalled the troop to rest. They immediately unslung their travelling packs and set their sparse sleeping kit on the ground, trying as best they could to find a smooth area.

Eli moved to where Aaron was sitting. His white teeth cutting through the gloom as he flashed another of his smiles. If there were an enemy close, he would have no trouble aiming at night. Just whisper a joke in Aaron's direction and loose shaft at the gleaming white beacon that appears.

Eli lowered himself to the ground so that his back was to the oak. He looked up through the huge expanse of branches to try and glimpse a star but to no avail. It was as though the noblest of trees had thrown a blanket to protect his sleeping warriors. Aaron leaned close.

'Fine battle today. A good way to end our patrol. Not long until we head home now.'

'No, not long,' Eli said, taking some of the bread and dried meat from his pack. Spoils taken from the convoy. Warily, the meat was checked. On one occasion the Puritans had poisoned the supplies and set them up to be taken. Twenty Legionnaires had died.

'I can't remember the last time I had had real meat,' Aaron rubbed his stomach in feigned hunger.

'It will be good to get home,' Eli said. He preferred to be in the field.

'You are not looking forward to getting home?' Aaron asked.

'Always,' Eli lied smoothly.

'I am looking forward to seeing Elisha again,' Aaron continued.

'She is a fine girl,' Eli said drinking deeply on his water canteen.

'She is,' Aaron drifted into a daze thinking about her until Tori and Saul joined them disrupting his reverie. Saul was his usual sullen self.

'Still thinking of rutting,' Tori quipped, wiping the embarrassed smile from the young Legionnaire's face.

'Leave him be,' Eli cautioned, before starting the debrief of the day's action.

'We lost seven men,' Saul said, 'including three of the recruits we set out with. The convoy was well manned, and they held their discipline, as we would have expected from the absolute best of our own troops.'

'The ambush worked well,' Tori continued, 'although we should have had the flanking archers closer.'

'That was unavoidable given the width of the path,' Eli said bringing a nod of acknowledgement from his squad leaders.

The merits of the attack were discussed immediately so that lessons could be learned immediately, saving lives the following day. Again, protocol that existed to save lives.

'I see you were at your usual work again today,' Tori said, as the briefing ended. 'I didn't realise it was fitting for the senior officer to abandon his post and run to the aid of a Legionnaire who was wildly outnumbered and about to fall to possibly the largest axe man I have seen in my born days.'

'Any officer can have an off day,' Eli shrugged.

'I saw a young man with captain's markings running across twenty yards of open ground, killing four soldiers along the way, piling straight into the axe man and sending him into his own men, rolling to his feet in one move and continuing the fight with the three swordsmen still on their feet, killing them and running straight on into the thick of the fighting,' Tori paused for breath. The admiration for her captain was getting in the way of natural story telling ability.

'You always were prone to exaggeration,' Eli countered. 'You must be mistaken.'

'That's right, it was more like five on the way, and six when you got there, ' added Aaron.

'All the men saw it,' Saul said quietly. 'They are talking of it, even now.'

Eli listened to the listened whispers of the men in the clearing but could hear no words. He did not doubt Saul and his assessment.

'Next there will be songs,' Tori said, knowing that Eli did not relish the thought. 'Perhaps the Messiah himself will set you at his side when he leads us to victory.'

'Enough!' Eli warned. 'You would be well to ask forgiveness for blaspheming.'

Eli blessed himself for her. She smiled that she had vexed him so. There was no further sport in it, so she apologised demurely for offending him.

'So, my war captain, we were waiting for you to justify your actions,' she said flashing her piercing blue grey eyes at him.

'I do not have to justify my actions to the ranks,' Eli replied, wondering how she always managed to make him feel like a scolded infant. 'But since you might actually learn something from it, I will tell you. My run across the open ground allowed me to create an opening, permitting our troops to press their advantage. I went straight for the axe man, as he was a rallying point for their soldiers in the absence of their officer. When I removed him, the group panicked. I was able to kill them all individually, as they were no longer fighting as a unit.'

'So, really it was a clearly thought-out military decision in response to the rapidly changing needs of the situation?' Tori was at her most sarcastic. 'Thank you for that lesson. I thought you had rushed blindly to the aid of a young warrior who, only two days ago, you had promised you would see safely home from his first campaign. But what do I know, I am only one of the ranks?'

Eli frowned at her. Aaron stifled a laugh as Tori waited expectantly, eyes wide and innocent, denying culpability for her words. Eli's frown eased and he relaxed back against the tree eyes scanning the great expanse of the oak for sky or stars but more specifically for salvation from the daemon woman sent to torment him.

'I think you are too bloody clever for your own good,' Eli rebuked her and then continued seriously. 'But I would prefer that to stay with us. It would not be seemly for the troop to think they could act as they pleased and not follow orders.'

Saul nodded his agreement in the darkness and took his leave of them, joining one of the sentries on stag. Aaron followed him into the darkness and joined his own partner.

'It is seemly that the Legion knows its captain cares for them,' she said, removing her armour so Eli could tend the wound from the day's fighting. 'But I will not talk of it.'

'Thank you.'

'They have eyes enough to see it for themselves without my assistance.' The last word as always.

'I am surprised they had time to notice me. How were they not besotted with your beauty and form as you glided through the battle with the deadly grace of a lioness?' Eli's voice became husky as Tori got closer.

'I am sure that they did notice me. How could they not? I think the glamour that I put on the enemy with my beauty was enough. Stunning them into indecision so that a statue would have been able to walk up and slay them.'

'How I ever ended up with the most modest Legionnaire under my command I don't know. I think I will request to be reassigned on return to camp.'

'And have to deal with all the requests for transfer to your troop from everyone here? Is it really worth your while?'

With the bandages and comfrey poultice freshly applied Tori nodded her thanks and lay down.

'Perhaps you are right, Tori, I think you have been sent by God to torture my existence for some great wrong I have done in a previous life.'

'Do you really think that, my love?' Tori gave him a soft kiss on the cheek before lying down to sleep.

'Perhaps not. Perhaps you were sent by the devil himself.'

*

Curate Pile sat on the floor. The back of his hand pressed to his bleeding lip. The flash of pain had been momentary. He was used to it. Pile looked up at the centurion. Apathy had long replaced the fear and hate in his eyes.

He knew they could not kill him.

They needed him to log all the riches and artefacts they had sacked from the temples and museum. He would probably live long enough to finish selling out his nation's history then he would be put down like the dog he considered himself to be. He had never been a brave man in his youth. Never a fighter as his two-year service in the militia had shown.

He had been capable, as all Legionnaires proved to be, but he had had no love for it as his comrades had. A military society still needed its thinkers he had argued. His father had beaten him for that comment.

Looking after the legacy of his nation was a position he had treasured. Until the invasion.

Nine years.

Four had been spent in the prison camps, watching his countrymen die of starvation and mistreatment. The last five had been spent documenting the artefacts for the Puritan invaders.

He had been weak. Identifying himself to save his life but disguising it as saving the life of others whose lives he had received as payment for agreeing to work for the Empire.

Collaborator. His father's words from his childhood still stung him. "There is no greater sin against God than to betray your country, unit and friends".

His knowledge of the looted items had kept him alive while those around him perished. He had done whatever it took to live. Was survival so wrong?

The centurion picked him up and threw him against the wall.

'Soon you will be leaving, little man,' the centurion snarled, 'but until you do you had best remember that you are alive only through my good grace. If you offer any further back lip, I will have your lips removed. Are we clear on this?'

Pile nodded but lay where he was. He knew from experience that rising without permission would only get him a further beating.

'To where am I being moved?' he asked.

'You are going to Avalon to serve the Emperor. He apparently has need of knowledge such as yours,' the centurion said, striking him once more in the face and marching out the room.

Pile nodded his comprehension. From the work he was doing he knew the Emperor was interested in holy relics. Many of the historical weapons and charts were disregarded out of hand. Only those associated with healing and religion were kept. Why? He did not know.

Pile eventually stood and walked out of his unguarded cell. They did not even think that much of the now old prisoner. He walked round the fortress looking out at the full battalion camped in the plain to the north of the town.

Thinking back to the time before the invasion when he had lived in the capital working in the temple, he remembered happy times. Innocent days. Had it truly been as rosy as he remembered? He doubted it, though it could not have been worse than this.

The latest news did not bode well. It was bad enough that he was collaborating with the enemy through his work on the charts but now he would be moved to Avalon, the enemy capital.

Pile knew he would pay for his sins. He just hoped it would be soon. Before they discovered the sword.

*

'Did you mean what you said about marching north?' Duncan asked.

'There is nothing for us on the front,' Garrad explained. 'It may have been challenging at the start but now force of numbers will win the day. It is just a matter of time. Soon all our troops will mass and attack. Within the year I would guess. We will spearhead through at the top of the line and collapse in on it from north to south. We will slaughter the coalition forces. The war of attrition has no appeal to me.'

'Victory?' Duncan suggested.

'A victory that is inevitable is no true victory for a soldier. I want to go north and clear the mountains while it is still a challenge.'

'What is wrong, general?' Duncan was concerned.

'I will be retiring after this campaign. I have no longer the stomach for it,' Garrad rested back in his chair and poured some chilled juice.

'You have more than the stomach for it. You are the finest general I have ever served under,' Duncan was not pleased. 'What has changed?'

'Perhaps I have changed,' Garrad drank deeply and set the cup to one side. 'Perhaps I am just getting old.'

'Everyone gets old.'

'Yes, but not useless. I am not needed on the front. Our Imperial army will march across the lines and expand the crusade whether I am there or not.'

'Good,' Duncan replied. 'That means there is less for us to do and more chance of our men surviving.'

'I am obsolete. At times I would prefer to be on the side of the enemy. The coalition or the Ellistrins in the north. There is a real challenge in that. Fighting against all odds. They have won nothing but even in not losing there is victory. Each day that passes that they are still alive is a victory. I feel like I am stagnating here.'

'Do not let the Emperor's spies hear of such sedition,' Duncan cautioned. 'You would be flogged and tortured publicly.'

'I know. That is what I mean,' Garrad was only honest with his close friend. 'We are at the disposal of a man that is possibly mad. A petty dictator with big dreams.'

'For a petty dictator he has achieved a lot, ' Duncan checked his flask. A gift from his general. 'He rules two thirds of the known world.'

'He has had good people to help him achieve his dreams,' the general explained. 'He tells a convincing tale and promised them reward. He always keeps his promises for services rendered. This, he knows, encourages others to rally to him. Resistance he punishes immediately, lest it fester.'

'I remember. General Aulus. What a man he was. He knew his men inside out and always got even more from them in battle.'

'A brilliant campaigner,' Garrad knew the man and his exploits. Many of his strategies were now standard reading at Yashtan Academy. 'His aide told me that his reports were actually understated.'

'One night he spoke freely about what he thought of the Empire,' Duncan recalled the circumstances of his death. 'On the morning after the feasts of the New Year he was found with his throat cut. They blamed the local militia for assassination. Thirty-five "unworthy" people died that night at the hands of assassins. The Emperor's assassins no doubt. I have no wish to join that number.'

'Nor I,' Garrad agreed.

'Then, that is enough of this foolish talk.'

'It is. That is why I plan to resign my commission. I am no longer doing the right thing in this army.'

'Not thinking of joining the enemy, are you?' Duncan asked.

'I am thinking of my boy and how I can explain to him the things I have done,' thinking again of Agrafes. 'Would he understand?'

'Perhaps not, so do not tell him,' Duncan offered.

'If I am doing things for my God and country,' Garrad asked, 'why should I feel the need to cover myself in lies? I should feel proud about what I do.'

'Now you are being morbid for you know the answer and have told it to me and countless others over the years.'

'I know. The noble ideal is for the politicians and the public at home. War is an ugly business with many faces. I have done all that was necessary but still I feel shame at some of the things I have seen. I think my son will look into my eyes and see my shame. I do not want it.'

'This foolishness does not make for pleasant conversation,' Duncan downed his watered wine and reached behind his breastplate for his flask.

'The sooner we get into action the sooner you will get over these moods of yours. Get your mind on something else. Come on and we will go to the boxing.'

'To see Hamza win,' Garrad referred to their own regimental champion.

'To see Hamza beat the shit out of someone don't you mean?' Duncan passed the flask to the general. Hamza was one of the meanest fighters they had seen. At only twenty-three he still had a few years to mature as well.

'You are that sure of Hamza?' Garrad took the flask and drank deeply.

'If you would like to wager, I am your man,' Duncan smiled.

'One piece of silver says Hamza will not win.'

'I think my luck has just changed,' Duncan took a long drink from his flask and smacked his lips. 'It will be a pleasure taking your coin.'

'I have seen the others. There is some talent out there, captain.'

'You can up the wager at any time, my general. I will take silver and gold from anyone no matter what their rank.'

'Thank you,' Garrad toasted his friend and touched the flask to his lips and downed half of it, wincing briefly at the end. 'We will go to the fight. The men should have their general there to support them.' 'Even if he bets against them,' Duncan countered.

'I have already wagered on him with the other regimental staff. When Hamza wins, giving you a piece of silver will be no big deal.'

'I thought you were giving in too easily.'

'I know all the old soldiers' tricks, captain. If you are good, perhaps one day I will share them with you.'

'Perhaps one day I will let you, my general,' Duncan laughed.

Chapter Twelve

Young Caleb was not sure he agreed with alcohol. The sergeant had said that it had been created by God himself to reward the virtuous soldiers for their deeds of bravery in his name.

The Legionnaires did not, as a rule, partake of spirits or ale, except after a battle when it was taken in abundance. Perhaps that was why it felt so strange to be taking it now. He had had no battle.

Caleb squinted against the sun as it cleared the peaks to the east. What would normally have been a beautiful sight only made the young warrior wince as through slapped in the face.

At the sergeant and lieutenant's bidding he had drank half a flask of what they assured him was the best quality spirit to be found in the mountains. The fact that it was named 'Daemon's piss' by his fellow warriors had given him pause.

'Drink, laddie,' the bull of a sergeant roared at him. 'Drink! You deserve it! '

The sergeant stalked off in search of another soldier to berate, smiling insanely despite himself.

'Sir, yes sir,' Caleb toasted the air in front of him as there was no one else about worthy of the gesture.

Concentrating, he made his blurry eyes focus on the rest of his unit as they fought back and forth across the clearing with wooden swords. Erika was training on. She was not looking in his direction.

As usual.

Women.

What would it take to impress her?

'Training is the steppingstone to combat,' he heard the sergeant bellow, 'not a substitute for it. Keep those hands up. Look at Caleb. See how he is rewarded. Match him and you can all rest.'

Erika still did not look over even at the mention of his name though some of the others cast sly glances.

Caleb shrugged to himself.

Her loss.

He did not see what the difficulty was. This morning it had all seemed so easy. Perhaps this was just his day. Every dog may indeed have one, as his foster father had once said.

Caleb was an average soldier in many ways. His stamina and endurance were certainly average. He came in from the long morning runs in the middle of the field. Never first but never last. His pride would never allow that. In feats of strength his athletic, but still adolescent, frame showed immense potential but could not match the older Legionnaires whose musculature had matured beyond him.

Caleb leaned back and took another long draw. Strangely the more he drank the more he could drink. The bitter bites of the first drops seemed to have lost their edge. He could no longer see why he had avoided spirit alcohol for so long. The prospects of a debilitating hangover seemed like myth or legend.

Speech uttered forth from him but only seemed to be important to Caleb as passing Legionnaires gave him quizzical looks when he barked forth incomprehensible utterances.

His hearing only made him seem like a fool when the lieutenant finally sat with him.

'You fought magnificently today, Legionnaire,' Maelan said.

'Yes sir,' Caleb slurred. He did not really care for his officer. A man should know the names of the men he leads. This man did not, which was uncommon for a man of the Legion.

'I have rarely seen such swordsmanship. Especially among one so young,' Maelan continued. 'Why today? The sergeant says he has never seen you fight so well, and he has seen you fight nearly every day of your life.'

'I don't know,' Caleb admitted, setting the redundant flask to one side and wondering where the hell the nearest water was. 'It was easy.'

'I doubt it was easy,' Maelan probed. 'You bested veterans of many battles.'

'I concentrated,' Caleb managed. 'I practiced and I prayed. Today, they seemed to be moving in slow motion. At first, I thought they were not well or were humouring me. I do not understand it myself. They were going so slow. I could see not only what they were doing, but also what they were planning. Their feints and postures were as clear as a sunny day.'

'You showed no sign of this before today,' Maelan observed.

'Perhaps you were not looking hard enough,' Caleb said brusquely, drink loosening his tongue. 'If you spent more time with your men than licking the arse of every senior officer that walked past then maybe you would understand the nature of your troopers.'

'You would be best not to speak to me like that, Legionnaire,' Maelan said, his voice raised.

'Legionnaire?' Caleb asked. 'You do not even know my name.'

Maelan looked into the boy warrior's eyes and saw only stupor.

'I will forget this, Caleb,' the lieutenant said. 'I suggest you do too. You have done yourself proud today as a warrior, you should now focus on being a man worthy of that ability.'

Caleb did not look up as Maelan stood and left.

'So what if you know my name?' Caleb said to himself as he picked up the water flask the lieutenant had left behind. Caleb thought back over the fights of the morning. He could no longer see the training that was happening only yards away from him. The sounds of false battle drifted to him as though through thick fog.

The morning had paired him with Whelan, a thick set and scarred warrior, who had fought and been decorated across the continents. He was revered as a warrior of note within Ellistrin and without. Caleb had expected the beating to be brutal and brief. He was not disappointed.

Whelan was known for his efficiency but not for his patience with lesser warriors. The practice had begun as expected, Whelan disarmed Caleb with the first stroke and brought the heavy wooden blade crashing down on his helm with devastating force. Thankful that he was not unconscious, Caleb had struggled to stand, fixed his helm, and wondered why he had not simply stood back out of the way.

The blow had not come very quickly. Perhaps it was just nerves. It was not every day that he was set against a legend.

After the second set to, Caleb once again found himself on his back and looking at the clear blue sky. It was much easier down here. The fear in his belly left him while he lay here. The sergeant bullied him to his feet with a cacophony of abuse and belittlement.

Caleb had stood, briefly considering having a swing at the sergeant and thinking better of it.

Whelan did not smile as they faced off again. He took no pleasure from the contest, such as it was. Caleb watched as the well-muscled warrior slowly raised his arm and brought the wooden blade down in a lazy arc towards his skull. Thinking he was being mocked he simply stepped back and watched as Whelan overextended and hit the ground in front of him. Seeing an easy opening Caleb jabbed the tip of the blade into the armour opening where the neck became shoulder. 'Kill,' he said simply as he took up his position again.

Whelan glared at him in a manner Caleb could not understand. How could he be angry? Surely he had let him take the kill.

Whelan lunged forward making Caleb step to the side. The younger warrior backhanded him smartly to the side of the head before dragging the would-be blade neatly across his throat.

'Kill,' Caleb said again, this attracting the attention of the bull sergeant and the Legionnaires closest to him.

'Again!' Whelan demanded taking position and making a half-hearted and clumsy attack, his blade aimed at Caleb's throat.

The young warrior stepped into the attack and slammed his elbow into Whelan's temple and drawing his wooden blade up sharply against his thigh, simulating a mortal cut to his femoral artery.

'Kill,' he said again.

'What are you doing?' the sergeant demanded, glaring at him.

'Fighting, sir,' he replied in the ready position.

'You, you and you,' the sergeant ordered the three nearest Legionnaires. 'Take him!'

It did not take much encouragement as they attacked at once. The first falling with a gash opened on his forehead while the remaining two followed suit despite their more coordinated effort.

'Kill,' Caleb said, still in the ready position. Today he felt powerful.

Today he felt like he was becoming the warrior he wanted to be.

'Next,' the sergeant bellowed, pointing at the closest Legionnaires.

This time Caleb did not wait. At the speed they were moving, the attack would have taken all day. He powered into the next set of opponents and dropped them with ease, thankfully without severe injury. Well, nothing they wouldn't recover from in a day or two. Maybe a week.

'Excellent!' the sergeant triumphed, waving the lieutenant over and telling him how there came to be nine men lying nursing their bruises at the feet of the youngest member of the troop.

Caleb could not understand how it had happened. It had all seemed so clear to him. The attack, the counterattack. It was all one.

'I am not every dog,' Caleb said to himself.

'No, you are not,' the sergeant said arriving back over.

'No, I am not,' Caleb hung his head.

'Tomorrow you will do the same again. And again, the next day,' the sergeant warned. 'If today was a fluke I will have you lashed and beaten.

The sergeant pointed to the "losers" of today's mock battles as they received their lashes with heavy canes to the backs of the legs. Today was the first day, in his whole life, that Caleb had never received a punishment beating.

Discipline was everything.

'I will do it again,' Caleb slurred angrily.

'Good,' the sergeant patted him on the shoulder. 'Today you became a man and lost the gangliness of your youth. You have been improving for months now, you just could not feel it. Today was the day that it all came together for you. No more, no less. Continue to train hard and I see in you the potential to be one of the finest swordsmen the Legion has ever seen.

'Yes, sergeant,' Caleb managed.

The finest swordsman the Legion had ever seen. Every dog has its day.

'Big dog,' he thought. 'Woof.'

Caleb leaned to one side and threw up.

Erika was watching when he did that.

*

Pile moved slowly through the town, his arthritic limbs making prolonged movement, like walking, excruciating. Dusk had arrived and with it the cold, night winds. Bowing his head, he stood to one side to let the patrol pass in the narrow street. Glancing up furtively he saw that a couple of the guards had barely concealed contempt on their faces, but they were indifferent to his very existence.

Pulling his cloak tighter he hastened down the cobbled street, looking behind him to see if the guards were out of sight, he did not see the young boy until he was already on top of him. The boy's eyes widened with surprise as the old man tumbled into him sending them both sprawling into the street.

'I'm sorry, I'm sorry, are you alright?' Pile climbed to his feet, his hands chaffed and raw. He knew his knees were bleeding under his cloak. He was more concerned for the well-being of the boy who was crying now. The boy did not reply until Pile touched his shoulder.

'I am fine, curator Pile,' Ammiel replied simply, pleased that his deceit had worked.

'What?' Pile moved away slightly, fearing that he was the victim in a staged robbery.

'Easy, sir,' Ammiel reassured him. 'You have nothing to fear from me. Randall sent me.'

'Randall,' Pile repeated. Pile had sent out word through known men that he had information to pass on.

'I need you to follow me. Do not worry if you cannot keep up. I will not let you get lost,' Ammiel flashed him a smile and jumped to his feet scurrying off into the twilight.

Pile followed him, turning up alleyways and side streets but he felt that he was running blind. Soon he realised he was lost. The streets sloped up to the keep so he knew he was down beside the docks. Other than that, he doubted he would be able to find his way home unaided. He had not seen that damn boy for about half an hour.

Pile sighed, suspecting he had just been led a merry dance when a gruff voice spoke to him from the shadows.

'Seem to have lost our way, old man,' the voice was unfriendly.

'I have not,' Pile felt the hairs on the back of his neck rise. 'I am merely passing through.'

'You are somewhat off the beaten track, old man,' the voice put emphasis on the 'old.'

Pile was reminded that he was not capable of defending himself. He was always the scholar, never the soldier. This source of ridicule from his youth would soon be the death of him.

'I am...' Pile stopped in the middle of his lame excuse. He had none. 'Please, I have no coin. Let me live.'

A door opened further up the street throwing light into the alley illuminating the still smiling face of the boy.

'Follow Ammiel, Pile,' the voice continued. 'I will make sure you have not been followed and join you there.' Pile bowed gratefully, letting out a huge gasp of air that he realised he must have been holding for a long time. He could feel the blood flowing and was lightheaded as he shuffled off after the boy.

The light in the room came from a large fire that threw dangerous shadows against the walls of the long deserted and cobwebbed house. Thick curtains and shutters prevented the light from making the house a target for the militia.

Ammiel appeared carrying a pot of steaming tea.

'This will make you feel better,' Ammiel said lifting the heavy pot onto the functional table while Pile warmed himself before the fire. The heat worked into his skinny frame, easing the pain in his joints and muscles.

His cloak was quickly discarded.

'This is good. Thank you,' Pile sipped at the tea, the steam rising and filling his nostrils. 'Just the right amount of honey too.' Ammiel did not answer but smiled back.

'I am sorry for the long walk, Pile,' Randall said as he entered the room, 'but you must realise these measures are necessary.'

'I do,' Pile answered, watching as the boy went to sit in the corner of the room, a bowl of broth clutched tightly in his small hands.

'You thought it necessary that we meet?' Randall poured himself a mug of tea, without the honey.

'I am not as versed in these surreptitious ways as you, Randall, but I try to keep myself as right as I can. I am getting old, and my life no longer has the value it once had, but I would like to hold on to what little I have left for a while longer,' Pile's old face had little warmth in it when he smiled yet he was sincere.

'I do not know what "surreptitious" means, Pile, but I can guess. I am one of the resistance with whom you asked to meet. I can offer no proof of my credentials to set your mind at ease,' Randall looked directly at Pile.

'Some things will have to be taken on faith then,' Pile said. 'I have information that could be important.'

'Could be?' Randall refilled both cups and spooned in honey to sweeten Pile's.

'Yes. As you know I am responsible for detailing artefacts for the Puritans.'

'I am. You have been doing this since before the invasion and are still doing it. Under protest I know. What of it?' Randall threw more wood on the fire.

Pile was more than a little perturbed that the resistance leader knew of him.

'Their Holy Father wants artefacts of religious importance especially.'

'I am aware of this also,' Randall interrupted. 'Get to the point.'

'Recently I have been holding back on items,' Pile explained in hush tones. 'One in particular.'

'And that is?' Randall was interested.

'About two months ago an item was delivered for cataloguing. A weapon. The Ban'chakot. The Sword of the Messiah,' Pile watched for a reaction and was gratified to see Randall's pupils dilate at the name.

'The Sword?' Randall asked. 'You are certain?'

'I am incredibly good at what I do, Randall. It is not easy to ignore something like this. It has been on display in the palace for many years. I had thought it lost during the initial stages of the invasion. Looted by a soldier or stolen during the evacuation such as it was. I would know the Sword blindfolded, which is not far from the truth given my failing eyesight and poor lighting in which I work.'

'Can you get it out of the keep?' Randall paced in front of the fire.

'With respect, Randall, were I able to manage that feat we would not be having this conversation,' Pile stared into the fire. 'I am here out of necessity.'

'It is imperative we retrieve the Sword,' he said.

'On that, at least, we are agreed,' Pile looked at the young warrior. 'The Sword is going to be moved from the keep and sent west to their capital.'

'Can you not continue to hide it?' Randall asked.

'Not anymore,' Pile explained. 'Ordinarily I could keep it hidden indefinitely, but now they are taking everything, and I am being sent with it.'

'Is it the Sword you wish to save or yourself?' Randall eyed his guest.

'Both, if possible,' Pile said flatly. 'But I am not a fool, and I am a patriot no matter how you would judge me. I will do whatever it takes to aide you in the recovery of the Sword.'

'We cannot storm the keep. Taking the convoy without the numbers needed would be very risky.'

'Risk?' Pile asked, angry. 'The risk should not be taken into consideration. The Sword is the only thing that is important.'

'With respect, Pile, my men are worth a lot to me. I will not throw their lives away on a futile attack. I need to know how many men are going to be guarding the convoy, what route it will be taking.'

'I do not know. They do not yet know the significance of the Sword. I have catalogued it under 'other weapons' so it will receive no special treatment. I can delay it being moved but moved it will be. That is inevitable.'

'The caravan will travel to Plandor first,' Randall thought aloud, 'then continue west. We would not be able to match them in numbers on the road north to Plandor. They take a large army contingent with them before they break into their assigned areas.'

'And?' Pile pushed.

'And we will not be able to get it,' Randall said sadly, Ammiel looked up at his father.

'What?' Pile was amazed. 'You realise its significance?'

'Of course I do,' Randall replied. 'The Sword was held in the palace foyer where any could look at it. It was wielded by the Messiah, or reputedly so, when he fought in the Great War more than a thousand years ago to free us from tyranny.'

'Exactly. I am a historian. I deal in facts. I do not know if it is truly the Sword, but I do know it is from that period. It is said that if we lose that Sword, then the Messiah will never walk among us again.'

'That is just legend and myth, old man,' Randall did not sneer, he believed it as much as any Ellistrin.

'It may be, that is true,' Pile conceded. 'But I'll tell you this much, I do not want to be the one responsible for finding out that it is not.'

'Nor do I,' Randall agreed.

'I have done my part. If I try to remove the Sword, ask for it, or bring any attention to it they will never let it go.'

Randall stared into the fire, thinking through the logistics of a successful raid on the caravan. They would be able to mount an operation, possibly steal one item from the convoy. He would lose most if not all of his men in the attack, crippling the resistance in the capital. They could not be sure of finding the Sword in all the carriages and wagons, certainly not before the reinforcements arrive from the keep. No, an attack was folly.

'I will send word north. A few Legion troops should be able to mount an offensive against the convoy after it leaves Plandor,' Randall told the curator.

'Very well. It is out of my hands,' Pile said, standing to leave.

'I thank you for the information, but ask you never to contact me directly again,' Randall poured the tea into the fire to dowse it.

Ammiel opened the door to the street, the bracing wind threatening to quell the last flames in an already dying fire. Pile snatched up his cloak and moved out without speaking further.

'You will send me word when the Sword is being moved,' Randall said. Pile paused momentarily in the doorway before continuing into the night.

'Follow him, Ammiel, do not reveal yourself but try to make sure he gets home safely.'

Cupping the small bowl in his hands Ammiel drained the last of the broth and ran out after the curator.

*

Finn sat on the large flat-topped rock with his eyes closed. He had said his goodbyes to the family and the priest a week before and struck northeast. He was now close enough to the glacier that it threatened to blot out the sky. The winds seemed to carry ice, such were the freezing gusts.

Finn opened his eyes and watched as a deer tread warily from the forest and approached the stream. It remained motionless for long periods smelling the air for threats. Finn was downwind of the beautiful creature and did not startle it. Concentrating he could smell its sweat. It had been running hard for part of the morning, most likely being chased by a predator. Wolf or mountain lion. It was no longer close, whatever it was. Thirst at the exertion had drawn the deer to water.

'Easy, child,' Finn said to himself. 'You are safe.'

The deer seemed to relax and moved to the water's edge bending its neck to the water and drinking deeply.

The stream ran through a gorge giving natural defence on both sides from large-scale attack but that was not a realistic threat to him here. Finn was more concerned with the elements. The trees and shrubs were deep rooted and old with both deciduous and evergreen covering the landscape. There was no sign that flash floods had ever tried to claim the gorge and it seemed line.

The bend just beyond where he sat seemed to be the best place for camp since even in flood the stream would flow past and away from it. Even water could not move against gravity.

The gorge, while sloped, was not so steep as to stop the sun from shining there most of the day.

There were many hoof and paw prints at the river, more prey than predator. No shortage of game.

Having travelled for a week with little rest Finn had had to avoid many Legionnaire patrols. For the last three days and had not come across any sign of their passing, recent or old. This region of the country was as isolated as he was likely to find.

Thunder peeled to the north as a face of the glacier broke free and fell to the earth. The glacier was a mile high. Finn could feel the vibration of the impact shake his bones.

He found himself nodding. It was a fine place for him to seek solitude, to rebuild his body and mind. To face the madness that was within him in the shape of the daemon. Finn wanted to face his past, alone and uninterrupted in a place where he would be no threat to anyone.

This seemed as good a place as any to call home.

Home.

Pulling his hood close against the wind he climbed down and headed for the area he decided would be his camp.

The deer did not look up at his passing.

*

A powerful, teenage Brood had found the nights the worst. Had it not been for the close companionship of his newfound brothers he had thought he would perish.

That night in the desert was now two years behind them and things had changed. If it was for the better, Brood did not know. The squalor and constant hunger of their lives before then been replaced with regular meals and clean conditions. He was now healthy with wiry muscles and sinews.

'Small meals, more often,' their new drill master said,' provides more accessible energy for the warrior.'

They were no longer beaten savagely although the varied punishments all carried the same theme. Physical pain.

This, the brothers found, they could soon control.

Brood still did not like the nights. He found that he could not sleep. He did not need to, not like his brothers. Talan, Nathan and Joshua slept soundly in the bunks next to him, as were the fifteen other young boys who had passed similar tests.

Although also united to them, Brood did not feel the same bond as he did with his original brothers from the desert.

The day had been exhausting but obviously not so much as to put Talan off his midnight walk. This time, Brood eased himself from his bunk to follow him.

Getting by the guards was easy, vigilant though they were. The boys were now endowed with methods of stealth far beyond the understanding of the guards.

Brood followed Talan as he weaved his way through the mountain fortress and over the battlements onto the mountain itself. Sure as a mountain goat, Talan raced up the steep slope. Brood followed quickly not needing what little light the moon cast to guide him. His training had seen to that.

Rounding a large boulder Brood found Talan kneeling in prayer. Brood did not speak for an hour until his brother had finished.

'Sneaking out of the fortress is a disciplinary offence, Talan,' Brood chided. 'The punishments, I believe, are severe.'

'Then we had best not get caught, brother,' Talan smiled, touching Brood with his mind and reassuring him.

'Why do you sneak out?' Brood asked.

'Why do you follow?' Talan pulled his legs up under him and looked at the clear night sky.

'Curious,' Brood answered truthfully.

'About what? '

'About everything.'

'Good. That is as it should be. It is only through asking questions that we continue to grow. We must always ask questions, of ourselves and the motives of others,' Talan said, watching the shooting stars streak across the skies.

'You sound like teacher,' Brood said of their instructor in philosophy.

'He speaks of theory, brother, not of reality. Philosophy is only useful in as far as it relates to our own existence.'

'What of God?' Brood asked.

'That is not a matter of philosophy. That is a matter of faith. Of belief. There are those poor souls who debate for decades whether God exists and, if he does, in which form. They are the unfortunates.'

'They are,' Brood agreed. 'For with the simple act of acceptance of a fact, that cannot be disproved, they are missing out on a fuller life.'

'A soundly based answer, Brood,' Talan looked at him, 'but one that you feel less clinically in your heart.'

'I am in the service of the Lord. It is not a lie I would choose to live.'

'Nor I, brother.'

The boys sat for a while under the open sky, content merely to be away from the confines of the fortress.

'Do you think the Lord Saladin approves of us talking in such a fashion?' Talan asked.

'Of course,' Brood replied, 'otherwise we would not be schooled in the philosophies and theologies as well as the martial ways.'

'Perhaps it is a test,' Talan offered.

'Perhaps,' Brood conceded. 'But then he may be testing us to see if we will accept the teachings. I do not think we will win a game of trying to outguess him.'

'We will not,' Talan agreed. 'Have you tried to read him?'

'He ordered that we did not,' Brood said.

'That he did,' Talan replied watching Brood's face.

'I could feel nothing,' Brood admitted softly.

'Nor I.'

'He has power. It is an easy matter for him to block us.'

'Yet he encourages us to be open amongst ourselves.'

'That is so that we can truly be warriors of God, for the righteous have nothing to fear in their hearts. It is to keep us pure, brother.'

Talan said nothing.

Dawn, though still hours away, was beginning to set the horizon on fire. It was a beautiful sight, full of the Lord's majesty. Brood now understood why Talan came here to pray.

'It will be light soon,' Brood said, stating the obvious.

'Light will always triumph over the dark,' Talan replied.

'I wish it were so, brother, but light and dark follow each other in a cycle. One is not greater than the other,' Brood said, watching the light crest the mountains individually.

'A disturbing thought and one I shall think on.'

'Do not think on it too much, Talan, for this is another riddle without an answer. Merely accept it as a fact of God's kingdom and move on in His love.'

'You give wise counsel, my young brother,' Talan smiled, rising. 'We had best be quick. Lord Saladin will not be forgiving if we are late for battle drill.'

They would need to clear the battlements before light was upon them. The punishments for being caught were severe.

As the brothers vanished into the night a shadow detached itself from the boulder. Saladin stretched and smiled. He was pleased with their progress.

Things were going to plan.

Chapter Thirteen

Edom sat and watched the other priests pored over the manuscripts.

'Surely you are not saying that this man, Finn, is the Messiah?' Jeremiah asked, unable to mask the incredulity in his voice.

'No, great father, I am not,' Edom said for the umpteenth time that evening. 'I have never stated that. I presented the facts of my time with Finn to you over two weeks ago. Since then, I have been summoned to your council by a gradually increasing hierarchy of religious scholars and subjected to ever more repetitive questions.'

Jeremiah raised a finger in chastisement.

Edom sighed and looked out the window of the council chamber. The large fire was at the other end of the long hall and was doing little to warm his old frame. At least the log and mortar walls stopped the piercing wind.

'I am sorry you find this tedious, Father Edom. It is not our intention to unnecessarily detain you,' Jeremiah apologised though his voice lacked any sincerity.

'I did not realise I was being held prisoner,' Edom said abruptly.

'A poor choice of words. You are free of course, I merely thought you would have wanted to help us get to the root of this.'

'Of course,' Edom allowed. He could not appear to be less than helpful to the leader of the church. Jeremiah was nobody's fool. He manipulated the church council like a skilled politician, which until the invasion, he was.

Edom took another drink of the tea that a young priest had thankfully brought him and ignored his leader with practiced indifference. He fought the rising rush of envy because he knew that was not the case. He did not want to be the leader, he just did not think Jeremiah was capable of fulfilling the role. He was not a good man in Edom's eyes, yet he was a capable leader. Edom made another mental note to pray for forgiveness for the sin of pride. Who was he to judge the merit of another?

'I apologise,' Bryant interrupted. 'I am to blame for the continued questions on this occasion.'

'Not at all, Father Bryant,' Edom bowed slightly. Bryant was also a canny politician, but his heart at least seemed true. 'Please, ask your questions.'

Edom got as comfortable as he could in the old wooden chair and closed his eyes to gather his thoughts. He could hear the rustle of pages as the young scribes prepared to take notes.

'Thank you, old friend,' Bryant began. 'Please, could you tell me, what are your impressions of this man, Finn?'

'As I have stated, I do not truly know what to make of the man.'

'How can this be?' another of the council priests asked. 'Surely you are used to reading another man.'

'I am, Father Misha,' Edom replied, 'as are we all. I have much experience in counselling people, young and old and am as versed as any here at discerning their intentions. When I was with Finn, my opinion of him changed daily. I have no lasting impression of him, other than that he is a good man.'

'You have stated that he is intelligent. Perhaps more so than you.'

'He is intelligent,' Edom thought back to their conversation. 'We were able to converse in the language of the ancients, using dialects that are reserved for only our ceremonies and never as a spoken language. His knowledge surpassed even my own and I had been a scholar in that area for a time before the war. He could match conversationally any of the languages I spoke with him, without accent. We spoke at length on many of the great mysteries of faith. He could argue his point objectively, and on occasion even argued my own point better than I. His knowledge of medicine and the healing arts goes far beyond what I have learned in all my years of study. I was like a wet nurse under his supervision and still I do not know what to make of him.'

'He was able to give no indication where he had received this schooling?' Bryant asked.

'He was either unable to do so or refused to do so. Either way, I have no information,' Edom explained.

'Is it possible that he purposely withheld the information?' Misha probed.

'Anything is possible,' Edom allowed, 'although I think in this instance, he truly had no memory. I have witnessed the loss of memory through trauma before. His symptoms were consistent with those I had seen.'

'But is he was schooled in the ways of the healing arts, it is possible that he was able to fake these symptoms to remove any suspicion from him,' Bryant stated.

'Anything is possible,' Edom offered.

Jeremiah did not speak through the encounter. He was content to let his very able aides do the questioning for him.

'You suggest though, that despite all his apparent schooling, he is not a holy man.'

'At first I thought, or hoped, he was a priest, merely someone I did not recognise because of the extent of his scarring,' Edom replied. 'Yet deep down I knew he could not be one of us. I would have known of someone of his abilities years before.'

'He could be a priest, though?' Misha asked again, not satisfied.

'He could be a priest. He certainly has the knowledge of one. Had I not seen him fight I would have believed him still to be a holy man or scholar.'

'And this changed your view of him.'

'Yes. Completely. We have all served in our Legions. We are surrounded every day by our warriors, more so now than before the invasion. I have seen men of great prowess with arms, yet I have never seen the like of this man's ability.'

'There are many capable warriors among the Legions, Father Edom,' Misha pointed out. 'Many of whom are now in the priesthood.'

'The world around Finn seemed of no consequence as he fought. When he moved it was as though he was in a vacuum. His enemies fell around him, without effort. He was in such a weakened state moments before that he could barely walk or eat, yet when his family was threatened, he had the power to fight like a warrior elite. I doubt even a man of the Legion could have stood against him in his weakened state never mind if he had been in full control of his body.'

'I find that hard to believe,' Jeremiah said.

'I merely say it as I see it, great father, you asked me for my opinion.'

'How do you explain his ability to fight?' Bryant asked.

'I do not. I asked him about his martial ability. He has no more memory of being a warrior that he does of being a priest or a scholar.'

'His amnesia is a convenient scapegoat,' Misha pointed out.

'It is frustrating,' Bryant agreed.

'It was frustrating to be with him,' Edom confirmed.

There was a pause in the questioning as Misha had the scribes read out the details so far, to ensure their accuracy and to see if there was a line of questioning they had missed.

Finn had been right not to come to the camps, despite Edom's assurances that he would be fairly, if not well, treated. The journey north had been tiring since the pace was one of urgency. When they had finally met one of the Legion patrols there was no sign of Finn, although the priest had been talking with him only moments before.

The rumours had already been started by the patrol when they had returned.

There had been footprints where the man, Finn, had been. Both for where he had been in the group and when he had sighted the patrol. From that point, however, they had vanished. It was as though he had been plucked from the earth.

Edom hoped he had found peace in the mountains.

'What of his visions? His meetings with the daemon?' Jeremiah asked, bringing the questioning back on line.

'I heard him talk in his sleep. He told me of the daemon he spoke with. I do not know if it was the ramblings of a deranged mind or a true holy vision.'

'You think him dangerous then?' Jeremiah was eager to get to the end of the interrogation. Edom guessed that he was merely seeking justification to hunt down and kill the stranger.

'I think he is dangerous to his enemies, I would not like to count myself among them. After the fight with the soldiers, he was able to console the child and show her tenderness and love. It was as if the horror of moments before had never happened.'

'He is a danger to us then?' Jeremiah pressed.

'Are we his enemy?' Edom countered.

'If he consorts with daemons, or is in league with the Puritans, then yes, we are his enemy,' Bryant confirmed.

'He is a good man,' Edom said.

'But he is no Messiah,' Jeremiah thundered.

'He made no claim to be so.'

'Then who made this claim for him,' Misha asked.

'That was a suggestion I made,' Edom admitted, 'after one of his "meetings" with the daemon. There was a veiled suggestion that he was here to save the children of this land.'

'A suggestion that was ambiguous at best. Your judgement was outlandish and fanciful,' Jeremiah remarked.

'Or at best, ill considered,' Bryant offered.

'That is why I brought the information directly to you on my arrival,' Edom pointed out. 'I do not want to be the one responsible for hiding information that may be crucial to our people. That is a decision for the council.'

'I think it is too late to hide much,' Misha said. 'Talk of the mysterious stranger is already the new gossip of the mountains. There is even whisper of several ballads, some proclaiming him to be the Messiah. It is dangerous talk.'

'It is only dangerous if it is not true,' Bryant said guardedly.

'We are at war,' Jeremiah said, 'and we cannot take the risk.'

'What will you do?' Edom asked.

'Only the council can decide that, Father Edom, and we thank you for you testimony,' Bryant said.

'We will not call upon you again,' Misha added.

Edom stood and bowed to Jeremiah, giving a small blessing to those in the room. Closing the door behind him he paused briefly and listened.

'What will we do?' he heard Misha ask.

'We will have the delusional madman hunted down and executed before he can harm us,' Jeremiah replied. Edom's heart sank.

*

Curiosity nagged at Caleb.

He had been excused lessons after four days when he could vanquish all within his training troop. He was free to walk and do as he wished.

No matter where he went, he was met with talk of the stranger.

The best type of gossip was that which provided very little information to begin with. With each telling a little more was added, and a little more and a little more. When he had heard the story of the Scarred Warrior the first time, he had heard tell of him killing ten men.

The most recent story had him summoning lightning from the clear skies and scattering an entire company.

While still young, Caleb was far from a child. He had decided that he would have to find out for himself. He had confirmed that the man's name was Finn, there had been a fight and that he had vanished when the patrol had met the priest on their journey north. That was the only consistent piece of the story.

Benjad had been reluctant to discuss any aspects of the Scarred Warrior and Caleb was sure it was because he had been constantly harassed for answers.

He refused to discuss it any further when he was pressed as to how he had managed such a rapid recovery from his arrow wound and why even his knee was less bothersome.

Perhaps there was truth to the rumour that he had been ordered to remain silent by the council.

The church council had issued a proclamation that the man should be found.

Captured if possible.

Killed if necessary.

Patrols had gone out immediately, grouping at the last point Finn had been seen. They had fanned out looking for signs and found none. Even the dogs, bred for hunting and war, had been able to detect nothing.

By then it had been a week.

The patrols headed further south retracing the route the priest had said they used to come north. There was no sign that he had returned to Ben's cabin. They had then scoured the countryside, visiting settlements and homesteads, villages and garrisoned towns. The risk had been in vain as they had encountered the enemy and sustained casualties, several of the patrols being pursued back into the mountains.

Finn, however, had remained elusive.

Caleb did not consider himself anymore skilled than any of the patrol scouts, but he was curious, and it was this curiosity that had sent him to the southern marker and to the point where Finn disappeared. He had spent some time rummaging around but as expected he had found nothing but Legionnaire tracks. If there had been anything it was well walked over now.

Caleb had made cold camp there for three days pondering the problem. It was unlikely that he had simply vanished, so he was therefore merely a skilled woodsman. That means he left the area on foot, disguising his passing. He did not want to be followed which was prudent since that is exactly what was now happening.

Caleb let his mind drift over all the information he had and, as he had been taught, tried to put himself in the mind of the quarry. What would he do? The patrols had moved to the settlements and south. It was a reasonable assumption since there was nothing to the north.

'North,' Caleb said aloud.

North was a good place to go for a man that was not seeking company. He was unlikely to meet anyone there if he went far enough. The Legion trained constantly in the mountains, but operational requirements kept them from travelling too far. All attention was directed south towards the enemy.

'If I wanted to lose myself for a while, I would go north too,' Caleb smiled. But where? There was a lot of north out there, Caleb had thought. The priest and the family had been travelling northwest to the camps when they met the patrol. Northeast then. Away from the camps.

It had taken him four weeks of searching to find the stranger. The Scarred Warrior had moved high into the mountains, much further than Caleb would normally have gone. He did not know what had driven him to look here. 'Seek and ye shall find'. That's what the priests said anyway.

Perhaps he was just meant to find the man.

Caleb had visited the scene twice now, always remaining carefully hidden. He had not shared his find with his fellows though he knew he should have told his commander. He could not explain this breach of protocol to himself, but he knew that the lone figure below him was not a threat to him or his people. If he were a threat, he would not have gone to such lengths to hide himself away from them.

The man was exercising each time he came. Using sword, staff, sticks, stones, knives, boulders and tree trunks. He was obviously a warrior as the priest had said. Or rather as the rumours had said. He whirled the weapons in a blur before him. Caleb was in a daze whenever he watched him. He had seen nothing like it before.

It took three days to get there each time he had visited, so now he had brought enough supplies to last him a few days. He did not want to miss anything interesting.

Youths were encouraged to live off the land as a part of their training. His commander had offered no resistance to his departure, but he was to report back every ten days in case he was needed.

Living off the land provided no great hardship for him. He was used to it. His training had been hard and life on the mountains, as a part of the Legion, was all he had ever known.

At fourteen he had already been involved in many skirmishes with the Puritan troops. Blooded when he was twelve, he had fought well. The uncompromising fear had evaporated when he had killed his first soldier. The irrational fear that the soldiers were invincible. His father had died years before in a battle similar to Caleb's first. The old man who had raised him and his orphan brothers in arms had explained that their first battle was the decisive step from childhood into the world of men. The world of warriors.

'Do you remember your dreams when you could fly like the hawks of the northern peaks?' he would ask. 'It is only as you grew older and learned that such things were not possible that you stopped dreaming of the ability to fly. So it is with fighting. If you have never plunged your blade into another body your mind cannot create the sensation of the tremendous resistance to the press of the blade, the way a body seems to hold onto it once it is in them. The effort that it takes to pull it out. The anguish in their eyes. The spray of blood and taste of death. In your dreams your battles are like your mock battles with wooden swords where the enemy is vanquished only to get up. Once you have killed your first enemy soldier, your dreams will never be the same again.'

'How do you know of my dreams?' Caleb had asked, worried.

'Do not worry, little man, I cannot read your thoughts. I too had these dreams when I was younger as I am sure did most of the fine warriors you see around you every day. It does not set you apart, it is just so you know that these little fears are real and shared by all. These little fears can be conquered. Since we are all going to die anyway, fear itself is our only enemy. We can overcome any enemy for we are Ellistrin and do not know defeat.'

Seventeen now, Caleb had conquered his fear and was still conquering it daily. It always seemed to come back to haunt him writhing in his stomach and making him want to run. Yet always he stayed. Just as he stayed now to watch the man in the small clearing. The man was naked and sitting in the icy waters of the stream, his hands before him in prayer. Caleb was fascinated.

Stretching out to get comfortable he watched as the man pulled on his light trousers and began to exercise. The movements were slow and steady but built to a crescendo of speed and power.

Caleb stared, enthralled.

He considered making himself known but no sooner had the thought entered his mind then he dismissed it. No, watching was good enough for the moment. Pulling the blanket close against him to block out the cold he settled down on the hard earth and watched Finn perform his bizarre war dance.

*

Saladin had stood alone in the centre of the dark room when young Brood opened his spirit eyes.

'Welcome,' the Emperor to be had said, simply.

'I am yours to command, my Lord,' Brood had bowed.

'You have done very well, my boy. You are the first to make it to this place, Saladin was pleased, and Brood could feel it in waves emanating from him.

'I do not fully understand what is happening,' Brood admitted.

'I know. That is all a part of it. It will get easier each time you come here,' Saladin assured the young Knight in training.

'Where is here?' Brood asked.

'This is nowhere and everywhere. It is a place created outside of the material world and exists only in spirit form. No mortal man can ever visit this chamber for it exists only within your own mind,' Saladin explained.

'How is it that you are here?' Brood asked. Looking around the room he could see nothing. The light from the fire, in the middle of what he assumed to be a large chamber, did not illuminate any walls.

'We are joined in spirit, Brood. You have been in a trance for a week trying to get to this chamber.'

'A week?' Brood repeated.

'Yes. You are close to physical death. You will return soon. Now that you have been here once, you will be able to return here more readily in future. It will get to the point where a mere thought will be able to bring you here.'

'Why?' Brood questioned. 'To what purpose?'

'It is a special place,' Talan had answered, his form appearing on the other side of the fire. 'It is for us alone.'

'Welcome, Talan,' Saladin smiled. 'Thank you. Your brother is right, Brood. This chamber exists as a place where you can meet. No matter what distance separates you, your spirits will be able to meet here and communicate. Speech, emotions and strength all exist within this realm.'

'It is warm,' Talan said. 'I feel contentment.'

'What you are feeling is the emotion of those around you. This chamber is created by your presence. It does not exist when you are not here.'

'How do you know?' Talan asked.

'Ever the philosopher, brother,' Joshua had said, as he and Nathan appeared. 'If a tree falls in the forest and no one is there to hear it, does it make a sound?'

'Quite,' replied Talan.

'The room does not exist,' Saladin explained. 'It is merely one of the laws by which it was created.'

'Who created it?' Tobias asked as his form arrived.

'Brood did,' Saladin said.

The brothers sat in silence and watched Brood waiting for the Holy Father to explain. It was Brood who spoke.

'I created this room because it was my test. This room did not exist for we have never visited before. My mind created it to have somewhere to go. Your minds were able to follow me here once I had somewhere to lead you.'

'I remember being lost,' Nathan added, 'then I just knew where you were and how to get here.'

'As did we all,' Joshua confirmed as more Knights in training arrived and were welcome by Saladin.

'Are you our leader?' Talan asked.

'I am merely the first among equals,' Brood bowed his head in reverence to his brothers.

'I am the leader,' Saladin said, 'make no mistake. You are the sword and Brood is the tip of the blade. I did not choose him for this honour. It was the test that chose him. Each of you had it within you to find this room first. Only Brood had the strength to do so.'

Saladin let his eyes wander around the room. There were twelve boys present completing a circle around the fire.

'Twelve,' Brood said.

'No more no less,' Saladin said. 'You twelve are my apostles of the Lord. Your brothers of the Chosen will continue to train with you and will fill your numbers when you lay down your life in the service of the Lord.'

'Glory be his name,' Brood said.

'Amen,' his brothers intoned.

'Return to your bodies,' Saladin ordered. 'Rest and rebuild your strength. Your training will get harder from here in.'

Only Brood and Saladin remained.

'Be strong for them, Brood. You shall be my strongest Knight.'

'I will serve you well, my Lord, unto death,' Brood bowed and disappeared,

'Of that, you can be sure,' Saladin smiled.

*

Caleb woke with a start and stifled a yelp when he saw the Scarred Warrior sitting opposite him. Rolling to the side he came up with his sword extended, ready to defend himself. Caught off balance he was unsure of how to proceed in the absence of action.

'You are very quick, young one,' Finn spoke slowly and evenly, that he would not startle the boy more. 'I am Finn, and you are welcome at my camp.

Caleb did not move, his eyes scanned the area confirming that there was no one else. Settling his attention back on the man he saw no weapon. He was sitting with his legs crossed under him, hands resting on his knees. The longer he sat there without moving the more foolish Caleb felt.

'I am Caleb,' he said, sword still pointed at Finn's head.

'Well met, young Legionnaire,' Finn said. 'Perhaps you would like to point that somewhere else.'

'Perhaps not,' Caleb did not move the sword.

'A warrior then?' Finn asked softly, looking the boy up and down.

'Yes,' Caleb replied with no confidence in his voice.

'Good. Then you have no need of your weapon against an unarmed man. If it makes you feel better you may keep it while we walk to the camp,' Finn stood and walked away from the young soldier.

Caleb paused for just a moment before heading tentatively after the tall man. He could not get over the impression that the man was gliding between the trees instead of walking. Caleb walked silently but the man did not even seem to disturb the air. Arriving in the clearing he felt his heart begin to race again. The stranger was nowhere to be seen.

'Do not worry,' Finn said.

Caleb jumped as the voice sounded from behind him making him spin.

'I mean you no harm. Had I wanted to hurt you I would not have allowed you to wake up. Lower your sword.'

Caleb made no move to obey the command. He fought the urge to run, the fear once again in his belly. He would show no cowardice to the enemy.

'Lower your sword, Caleb,' Finn sat on a log at the edge of the clearing, his tunic was open despite the cold exposing the top of his still scarred chest.

'What happened to you?' Caleb asked, looking at the damaged skin on Finn's face and body. Hair had not grown back properly on his head, and he had shaved what little there was. The scarring was no longer severe. The man had obviously recovered well.

'I do not know what happened, truly. Would you care for some hot tea? You look like you could use some.'

'I have never tried it before,' he said looking at the steaming liquid in the makeshift bark lined pot Finn was stirring.

'Then this will be a new experience for you. Sit,' Finn indicated a place opposite him at the fire he was now encouraging into life.

'You are Finn, the man that travelled north with the priest.'

'I am. I did not realise I was famous,' Finn looked at the boy, curiously.

'They say you killed twenty soldiers, the first ten with your bare hands, and the rest with a sword you took from one of them. They say you were in such a weakened state you could barely walk, yet you could fight,' Caleb fidgeted, not knowing if he should have blabbed the information.

'And what do you think, Caleb, about what 'they' say?' Finn stopped stirring the brew and sat back to look at him.

'I think you were in a fight, and you came back north with the priest, Father Edom.'

'What of the twenty men?' Finn handed him a simply carved bowl of tea, the strong herb rising and tickling the inside of his nose.

'I think you fought better than an injured man should have, but I do not believe there to have been twenty. One or two maybe but not twenty.'

'Why not twenty?'

'Twenty makes for a better story and I believe that is what your tale has turned into.'

'You are a clever boy, Caleb.'

'I am not a boy, sir, I am a man and a warrior in the service of my nation,' Caleb's hand tightened on his weapon. 'You would be wise to remember it.'

'I meant no disrespect, although I see this is something that we are going to have to resolve,' Finn set down the tea and moved into the clearing itself. 'Come then, boy, we will see what you can do with that weapon of yours.'

'What?' Caleb asked, as Finn stood unarmed before him.

'I have extended you the courtesy of my home, yet you enter it as an enemy and do not sheath your sword. I am tired of your empty threats, boy. Use your blade.'

'I do not understand,' Caleb said. 'You want me to strike you?'

'Are you mentally, as well as physically, retarded? Strike me, boy, or I shall surely kill you.'

Caleb leapt and drove the sword forward in one fluid movement, the tip racing through the point where Finn's chest should have been. Momentarily puzzled when he did not make contact, he spun on his heel whipping the blade in an arc to behead the enemy who must surely be behind him.

'You cut air like a true warrior, boy, how is it that you cannot manage to cut down an unarmed man?' Finn's face was as stone.

Caleb stormed in again, slashing low for the groin and turning the blade high to open the throat. Finn stepped in and batted the blade to one side before hammering his open hand into Caleb's armoured chest and knocking him onto his back.

Caleb landed hard, winded but unhurt. Spinning on his back he rose to his feet lunging twice at Finn's gut. Again, Finn moved in trapping Caleb wrist and backhanding him in the face spinning him from his feet. Another heavy blow to the chest knocked him on to his back for a second time.

Caleb got up slower this time, warily moving around his opponent, the sheen of sweat glistening in his face.

'Do not strike in anger, Caleb, you will leave yourself open to a counter,' Finn stood square-on to the boy, completely at ease and untroubled by the pathetic attempts he was making.

Infuriated by this, Caleb attacked again sweeping the sword in an arc that would cleave the tall man in two. His eyes opened wide when his sword dug into the earth instead of the man before him. Finn had stepped to one side and moved in quickly, hitting Caleb in the kidneys with an open hand. Even through the armour the blow was immense and drove Caleb to his knees. The young warrior landing heavily at the feet of the tall man.

He struggled to his feet, pain and anger the only resource left to fuelling his fighting spirit. This time, however, he was unable to continue. He stood shakily and tried to lift his hands to the ready position but found that he could not. He could feel tears of futility well in his eyes when the tall man approached him with his sword in his hand. He had wanted to die on the field serving his nation, not on some foolish boy's quest at the hands of a stranger. Not by his own sword.

'A fine sword. A keen blade,' Finn observed.

Caleb's eyes widened when the scarred warrior turned the blade and returned it to him hilt first.

'Now,' Finn said, returning to the fire, 'perhaps you will have some of that tea I mentioned.

Caleb sheathed the sword clumsily and moved to the log opposite Finn.

'Perhaps there were twenty soldiers,' Caleb said, accepting the offered cup. 'Maybe more.'

'No,' Finn laughed, 'if there had been I would be dead. I barely survived against the few that there were.'

'I apologise for my actions, sir, I was merely unsure of your intentions.'

Finn rested back and eyed the young warrior for a time.

'I apologise, Caleb,' Finn sighed. 'I needed to test myself, to see if my body was recovering at the rate I had hoped. I should not have treated you in this fashion. Please forgive me.'

'There is nothing to forgive.'

Finn lowered his head. 'With ability comes humility, and I have not treated you with respect.'

Caleb nodded, his breath was only now coming back to him.

Finn did not seem to be out of breath.

'How did you know I was there?' Caleb asked once his voice had returned to normal.

'I knew you were watching me from your first visit. You have your own particular scent. This was the first time you had stayed so I thought it was time to introduce myself,' Finn did not add that he could feel the young warrior's curiosity emanating from the forest. He handed him the tea again. 'Drink it. It tastes better than it smells.'

'What is it?' Caleb looked at it dubiously.

'It is tea. A herbal infusion to invigorate the body. It is good for you.' Seeing his reluctance, Finn put his own to his lips first and drank.

'You knew I had been watching you?' Caleb sipped his tea the heat threatening to peel the skin off his lips.

'Yes.'

'I do not understand. Why did you not speak to me the first time?'

'You made no move against me. You did not let your people know you were here. I was as curious of you as you were of me.'

'How do you know I did not tell?' Caleb asked.

'They are not here. Had they known where this strange man was, they would have come looking for themselves just as you did.'

'That was a risk you took,' Caleb noted.

'Yet still you are here, alone,' Finn shrugged.

'Why are you speaking to me now?' he asked.

'You would not make much of a student if I did not speak to you?'

'Student?' Caleb was surprised.

'Yes,' Finn replied. 'That is why you are here isn't it? To learn.'

'I don't know why I am here,' Caleb replied honestly. 'I was merely curious.'

'You are here because I have something you want,' Finn finished off his tea and set the mug on the ground.

'What is that?' Caleb asked, completely at a loss.

'You came looking for me because of my ability to fight. Twenty men or not, you thought I might be a skilled warrior. You want this skill from me.'

Caleb sat back and sipped at his still roasting tea. He truly did not know why he had continually made the journey to spy on the man. The things he said seemed true enough.

'I think you possess great skill,' Caleb agreed. He doubted there were many within the Legion that could have disarmed him as easily. Certainly not in his present form. None of his own troop could even get close to him.

'What is it you want most?' Finn asked.

'I want to be one of the finest Legion warriors our nation has ever seen,' Caleb said, staring into his tea. 'I want to lead them in battle.'

And what of you, Finn, what do you want?

Finn turned sharply at the sound of the daemon's voice. Caleb was startled by the sudden movement.

'What is it?' Caleb asked, his hand on his sword.

'Nothing,' Finn was on edge. 'I am not fully healed, my mind and body still play tricks on me.'

Tricks, Finn? Tell the boy that you commune with daemons. See how curious he is about your company then.

'Leave me alone,' Finn said sharply. Stunned, Caleb stood to leave.

Scaring the boy now, are we? Get on with it Finn, kill him! You cannot let him give your position to his people. They will surely come and kill you. You know what you must do.

'I am sorry, Caleb. I am tired and I must rest. You are welcome to stay. I will begin your training in the afternoon if you are willing. You may finish your tea and leave if you are not,' Finn walked towards his shelter, camouflaged among the trees.

'You have not asked me not to tell my commander where you are.'

'No, I have not,' Finn spoke as he walked and did not look round. 'That is your decision. You will do as you feel you must. I have no control over your actions, Caleb. Someone once said that everything must be 'free will'. I trust you will make the right decision for yourself.'

Finn entered his shelter and sat down pulling his ankles up close to his body. Lighting a small bowl of red herbs, he closed his eyes in meditation as the acrid smoke billowed up around his face.

Chapter Fourteen

Hein towered above the body of the young girl. Her blood still dripped from the knife in his hand, mingling with that of her mother's. The child reminded him of his own one-time daughter, they were about the same age. Nine was such a good age to die, uncorrupted by the ravages of life.

Hein moved through the small dwelling, putrefying on the outskirts of the city. The smell of decay was clinging to his skin. He had no idea that the spirit of the Emperor Saladin himself walked with him. He would not have cared.

Hein had seen the woman that day in the marketplace. Her long red locks catching his attention, even though the teasing bitch had tried to disguise it under the dowdy headscarf. She had spurned his advances, in front of the other men.

The lieutenant, a snot nosed whelp from a 'good family', had ordered him restrained when he grabbed her. The usual speech on how to treat the civilians had followed, straight out of the whelp's Officer Academy, he was sure.

What did they know about war? Mass army movement, Legions, squads and companies. What did they know about the man in the middle of it all? Nothing. Take that town! Storm that wall!

Hein knew all about war. As had his friend, Vorden. What a pair they had been.

The woman lay on the makeshift mattress moaning through smashed teeth. Her eyes were swollen and closed though she moved her head slowly from side to side, trying to find some bearing of what was her life mere hours before.

'Please,' the pitiful plea was weak and full of despair.

Hein moved back across to the bed and stood looking at the woman he had debased brutally in front of her daughter while her husband's corpse released its stinking bowels in the corner by the door where Hein had killed him.

He thought back to the first that time he had taken a woman by force. The feeling of power. She had thought she was someone special too until Hein had stopped her on the way home one night, inviting her to join him in the bushes with the irresistible power of a gleaming blade. He had been caught for that and punished. The Puritan system of justice was swift, and he had been sent to the penal islands. She was the daughter of a well-thought of merchant. He was lucky that he had not been sentenced to death.

Then came the war and with it the chance to get out of that human cesspool. Hein was so much better than the rest of the human trash they had incarcerated him with.

'You will be given the chance to atone for your crimes by fighting in the holy war against the heretics. May God look kindly on your souls,' the magistrate had announced before letting the warden speak. He advised, in less inspiring tones, that any man who did not deem his life worthy of the Holy Father's challenge could consider that life forfeit.

Hein had helped dig the mass graves into which were tossed the bodies of the old and infirm, those that could not fight in the holy war.

He had fought in many battles and in all the compass points of the Empire. He had been ordained by God and absolved of his many sins. Therefore, in his own mind, he could not be guilty of the crime.

Of any crime.

Hein had murdered his way across continents. He had learned quickly that while God might be on his side, the mortals who ruled the armies did not share his proclivities. He learned to hide his handiwork. Hunting alone at night, Hein took his victims mercilessly, sating his overwhelming appetite for power through the debasing of women.

He sensed movement out of the corner of his eye and turned on it, knife raised. It was not the husband making a bold attempt to avenge his daughter. He was well and truly dead. The movement was rats as they began their feast.

'Please,' she whimpered again, tears flowed down her face. When her daughter's sobbing had ended abruptly, she knew she was dead. Her soul felt like it had been torn from her.

Hein mounted her again, annoyed that she did not react. She was beyond pain. Hein found that he could not climax. Withdrawing he tied his trousers again. Plunging his dagger deep into her neck ending her moaning. It was starting to grate on his nerves.

Feeling unfulfilled Hein wiped his blade on the blanket that he tossed over the woman. The sight of her disgusted him.

The drizzle felt good against his face as he left the hovel. The smell of the sea lifted his spirits, reminding him of the prison life he had been pardoned from, so many years before.

Hein moved slowly up the back street, slipping momentarily on the slime that covered everything in this damn city. Cursing he began to walk more rapidly, less cautious, heading back to the barracks where he could endure another night among petty men, unaware of the splendid work he did in the name of the Lord.

'I do not know what you expect me to be able to do with a blindfold on,' Caleb protested.

'I expect you to stop whining and get with it,' Finn said harshly. 'And I expect you to stop relying on your eyes. Relax.'

Caleb was anything but relaxed. Finn had been punishing him hard all week and this morning had been particularly gruelling. He was fit to lie down and not much else. They had run, lifted, sparred, fenced, fought with spear and shield, knife and club.

Caleb had a few gashes on his arms and scrapes on his brow. One particular cut to his face and scalp had bled profusely and would undoubtedly make an appealing scar. Any area that did not bear a cut was purple from a fresh or receding bruise.

'You train hard so that you can fight easy, Caleb,' Finn had said. 'Though there is really no such thing as fighting easy. When you have been swinging your sword for thirty-six hours, your shield has been a dead weight on your arm and you are fighting to keep your body weight up, never mind the weight of your armour, you will know what an easy fight is.'

Caleb nodded, though his tired head merely bobbed up and down on his shoulders.

'An easy fight is one that you have walked away from alive, no matter what it takes. The hard fight is the one that cripples or kills you.'

Again, Caleb nodded, poking idly at the cut on his face.

Caleb had thought Finn was joking when he had suggested the blindfold.

'The blindfold will eliminate the sense you rely most on. It provides you with a secure feeling. Safety in that you can see the enemy coming from a great distance and give yourself time to react. That same security is removed when you are at close range as the enemy will use your sight to deceive you,' Finn said as he walked around the blindfolded Caleb.

'How am I supposed to fight without my sight?' Caleb asked, worried, as Finn stalked around him.

'You already do, to a degree and do not realise you are doing it,' Finn continued to circle the boy.

'How?' Caleb tried to relax.

'How do you know to deflect a sword blade to the left or the right?'

'It presses against my blade,' Caleb replied, after pondering the question.

'Yes. You cannot see the way the sword is pressing yet you know the direction of the force and respond to it without thinking. I want to train you so that is not a thing that happens by accident, but one that you have honed to an effective tool.'

'I understand,' Caleb said honestly.

'Good. This ability will give you more vision in a battle. You will be able to see more of what is happening around you while still combating the enemy you are engaged with.'

'I understand.'

'Now. Where am I?' Finn stopped circling. 'You are behind me to the left?' Caleb said.

'How far away? '

'Three feet,' Caleb replied, confident.

'Good,' Finn started circling again. 'Your hearing is working. 'That is something at least. What else can you hear?'

'I can hear a few birds in the trees behind the cabin. I can hear you circling me, the stream frothing over the rocks, the wind passing through the branches,' Caleb said.

'Listen. Relax,' Finn tried to guide him. 'What can you smell?'

'I can smell the cut wood at the corner of the cabin, the left-over rabbit, the sap from the fir tree, and smoke from the fire....'

'What do you feel?'

'Cold, sore muscles, the wind against my face, sweat down my back.'

'Good. Let us begin,' Finn stepped in and took Caleb to the ground hard. Straddling him, Finn threw strikes at his face and head, not enough to hurt, but enough that he would know he was there. Caleb covered his face against the blows.

'Think, Caleb,' Finn spoke calmly. 'This is nothing new to you. What would you normally do?'

Caleb bunched his muscles and rose into a bridge lifting Finn high on his waist. Turning as he did so he grabbed Finn's wrist and spun him off onto his back.

'Excellent,' Finn smiled but the expression was lost on the blindfolded Caleb. 'It is the same. Now, how did you know where my hand was to grab my wrist?'

'I don't know,' Caleb answered, sitting where he was.

'You must know, or you would not have been able to grab it,' Finn said quietly.

'Truly, I do not,' Caleb replied. 'I just did it, I did not think, I knew it was there.' could tell from the position of the rest of my body as it touched.

'I do not understand,' Caleb finally conceded.

'That will do for now. One thing, when you throw me off do not let me roll away, stay with me, always touching.'

Caleb had just managed to nod acceptance when Finn powered him onto his back again.

FALLEN ANGEL

Chapter Fifteen

Kannon sat at the corner table of the tavern. Smoke hung low from the ceiling, the smell of fish and spiced meat fighting for supremacy over the stench of urine.

'My, how the mighty have fallen,' Kannon thought of himself. Clutching his ale, he did not drink. A film of grease thinly layered the surface. He did not roll his eyes or sigh. Such were the cards he had been dealt.

The tavern was full. Sailors from the Puritan and merchant navies, soldiers from the keep and soldiers from the companies that were passing through the capital on the way to the front, lined the dank bar swilling the foul brew.

'Much as pigs do,' Kannon thought.

While waiting for his food, which he was now sorry he had ordered, there had already been four fights. God's army for the holy war. Kannon was only too familiar with their kind, he had been among them for centuries. Scum, all.

You could always go back to the old ways, Melchior.

'My name is Kannon, now,' he replied without looking up.

Very well . . . Kannon, the word rolled off Daemon's tongue, savouring the sound. Already sitting opposite Kannon, he asked, *Do you mind if I join you?*

'Not at all,' Kannon looked up, pushing his drink across. 'Care for a drink?'

Ha! It is good to see you . . . Kannon, no I don't think I will.

'A fine decision,' Kannon eyed the brew suspiciously once more before setting it aside completely. 'How can I help you?'

I think I should be asking you how I can help. Hardly the auspicious surroundings you are used to. Daemon's dark eyes flicked around the room. *I expect I will see many of these fine souls before long. I thank you for the dark souls you send me. Have you singled out one of these to join them?*

'No,' Kannon was watching several men over Daemon's shoulder bragging at the bar. 'It is none of these for now.'

Come my friend, tell me why you are here, Daemon smiled treasuring the moment. *Is it out of penance to your God for the many evils you have committed?*

Kannon looked directly into the black-on-black eyes of the dark Lord. Daemon was a mirror of his own form, the sleek hair, hard body and chiselled features recreated but more pleasing on the eye.

'I see you still like to preen yourself.'

Of course, Daemon smiled, opening his hands. *I am vain. Would you have me any other way?*

'I would have you many other ways, Daemon. Most of them putting some distance between us.'

Ha! Come back to me Kannon, end this charade. You are not for this life of drudgery. You are special. You are not mortal like these soiled pieces of flesh around you. You are a creature of the millennia, misunderstood by the masses.

'Misunderstood?' Kannon raised an eyebrow. He quickly waved away the serving girl who brought the steaming bowl of . . . whatever it was. Her eyes lingered too long on Daemon whose wicked smile charmed her more than his wealthy apparel.

'It would not please her mother to arrive home with you,' Kannon smiled tightly.

Then I would take her mother too, he said, licking his lips.

One of the soldiers was becoming animated about his bravery, his voice carrying across the bar.

'I swear, there were thirty of the bastards,' he shouted as only a drunk can, believing everyone within earshot to be deaf. 'Black as night and bones in their noses, squealing away like good heathens. I stared them down alone when all the others had turned and ran. I swear I would have spat in the eye of the devil if he had raised his ugly head.'

The speaker made a brief gasping noise and clutched his chest. Dropping his brew, he pitched forward onto the floor. It took moments to recover but he did so absent his verve.

I don't mind the spitting part, but ugly? Daemon turned back to face the unsmiling Kannon. *Don't tell me the holy one has robbed you of your sense of humour as well as your vocation.*

'My vocation?' Kannon was getting less agreeable at this unwelcome intrusion.

You are not mortal, Kannon. You are a killer. You need to kill to survive. God made you that way. It goes against Him when you go against your nature.

'I feel no need to explain myself,' Kannon was stony faced.

You still serve me, Kannon, in all that you do. To go against nature and God is to serve me. Surely you see that. Do you think you have reconsidered? Wrong? The only thing that has changed is who you think you are. You will find no salvation, Kannon, there is none for the likes of you.

'I am not the monster I once was,' Kannon hung his head, seeking inside himself for justification.

You were never a monster, Kannon, set aside the turmoil that is burning you up. You once led Empires like the one you hide within now to hunt your prey. You could have armies kneel before you. Instead, you seek out the individual, taking only enough to sustain your miserable existence.

'I am leaving the humans alone to find their own path to the light,' Kannon said.

No! No! Daemon was out of his seat. *They are sheep! Cattle! They need to be led! What does it matter if we slaughter them by the thousand when they try to kill each other by the million?*

'That is no longer my concern,' Kannon was rigid in his seat.

It is, Kannon, you long to taste the innocent blood again. Youth untainted by life.

'No. Now I serve the greater good.'

There is no greater good than I, Kannon. God does not love you as I do. He finds you abhorrent. He wishes to uncreate you. I love you, Kannon, for your simplicity. You are a killer. You keep my halls filled with fresh souls.

'No. Now I return your misguided children to you.'

Who are you to judge? Who are you to judge the worth of a man's soul? Do you think yourself to be the equal of me? Of God? Is your conceit that colossal? Your very blasphemy will seal your fate. I will feast on you for eternity. Daemon's eyes blazed.

'I hope you choke,' Kannon said calmly.

You amuse me, Kannon, but never mock me.

'I do not mock you, Daemon, and if you ever fancy your chances, you know where to find me,' Kannon locked his eyes on the daemon.

Good. I like that. Still some of the old killer left. There is hope for you yet, Kannon.

Daemon stood and instead of simply disappearing he moved to the door of the tavern, bodies dropping on either side of him as he passed. Opening the door to let in the strong afternoon sun, he smiled.

'He knows how to make an exit,' Kannon said to no one in particular.

*

'Did I tell you to stop?' Finn roared across the clearing, leaving his axe imbedded in the tree he was cutting down.

'No, sir. I am tired. I cannot continue,' Caleb let the branches drop his shoulders aching from the continuous drills and exercises.

'Then you are dead, boy. You cannot stop. Stopping is death. You will keep going until you pass out or until I tell you can stop. Do you understand?' Finn glared across the clearing at the boy.

'Yes, sir.'

Caleb raised the heavy branches, continuing with the drills Finn had been showing him over the past weeks. Each time he left he thought he would never return to the high peak where the strange man punished his body. Standing, he shuffled his body forward and back, side to side, jumping and spinning as dictated by the fighting forms he was learning.

The weighted stones, tied to his ankles with rope and leather, restricted his mobility while the stones on his wrists made even holding his hands up an impossibility. The backpack of boulders threatened to topple him at every opportunity. His muscles burned with fatigue and the pain now lanced through his head. Lunge, counter, twist, kill, counter, slash, kill. The drills burned through his head.

Finn continued to cut at the trees, felling and dividing each to prepare the walls for his cabin. The foundation has been dug out and the timber laid. It was a fine sturdy foundation. Finn smiled. Wasn't that how foundations were supposed to be?

He looked at Caleb again. The boy's balance was failing him. It would not be long now.

Red spots swam in front of Caleb's eyes. The clearing seemed to be moving around him.

Lunge, counter, twist, kill, counter, slash, kill. The world went black.

*

Caleb woke beside the fire. He had been stripped and his clothing was washed and drying beside him. His armour was oiled, and his sword sharpened and within reach. He sat up to see Finn stirring more of that goddamned tea over the fire. Caleb shook his head and was rewarded with a tremendous sense of nausea.

'Rest. You have done very well today,' Finn took the tea off the fire and began to stir at the pot of stew.

'I passed out,' Caleb rested his head back on the pillow pulling the blanket up tight to his neck.

'Are you cold?' Finn asked passing a bowl of stew.

'Yes. I feel drained. No tea?' he asked, smiling.

'Later,' Finn returned the smile, aware that it still looked menacing even with the scabbing gone from his face. The skin had a taut leathery look to it. 'Your body and mind are exhausted, you will feel the cold more acutely.'

'What happened?'

'You worked hard. Harder than your body ever has before. It is something to be proud of.'

'Proud? I have seen people pass out from exhaustion before. It is nothing to be proud of.'

'That depends on your perspective, as do many of the things you believe. You knew you could not continue, that you would pass out. Yet you continued. Most men would rest or sit down. They would slack and rest at the expense of others' labour. You kept going, through pain and fatigue and the nagging voice in your head telling you to quit. That is something to be proud of.'

'I do not feel proud,' Caleb admitted. 'I feel like I have failed.'

'That is how you should feel. You came here full of the vigour of youth. Strong and invincible. Even when I bested you it did not matter because you merely accepted that I was superior in that respect. I needed you to fail before we could continue with your training.'

'I do not understand,' Caleb closed his eyes.

'Your understanding is not important, merely the training. You have now given up your ego. You realise your limits. A man who does not accepts his limits will never make a great warrior. A warrior who accepts his limits learns that those limits can always be exceeded. You are reborn, Caleb. Rest. Sleep. Tomorrow we will begin your proper training.'

Caleb was already snoring soundly.

Finn watched the young boy sleep for a while. He was making fine progress and his strength had increased. It was time to begin working on his skill. Resisting the urge to tousle Caleb's hair he headed for the freezing waters of the stream for his prayers.

Sitting in the icy waters he closed his eyes and slowed his heart. His breathing became barely perceptible.

'Daemon,' he said.

*

Do you think you summoned me, Finn? Is that it? Daemon stood staring over the cliff waiting for Finn to join him.

The cliff was an impossible height above what he could only assume was water below. He could not see the bottom of the cliff, but he could hear the thunderous crash of the sea, muffled by the mist. The mist spread to the horizon and beyond, stretching for eternity. Twin suns were setting over the land behind them, the landscape was flat and without feature.

Daemon's face was illuminated with a red hue, which still did not lend any warmth to his presence.

'Summoned or not, Daemon, you are here,' Finn replied.

Daemon merely snorted.

'It is beautiful here,' Finn said arriving at the daemon's side.

This land is desolate under the radiation of the twin suns' rays. All life on this planet is predatory, seeking to feed off those that would pass through it. The sea is like acid providing no solace for those that would test the waters. The creatures that live there are like nothing your mind can conceive of, with claws that can shear a man in half. Yes, it is beautiful.

'It is simply nature, Daemon. Appreciate the unimportant things for what they are, no matter how fleeting. I do not know how you can tolerate eternity with such an attitude.'

You do entertain me so, Finn, Daemon turned to him smiling, *there are not many who would speak to me such.*

'Then you should get out more,' Finn said looking over the cliff face. 'You must get very bored, why don't you kill yourself and do us all a favour?'

Not possible I am afraid, Daemon watched the little man.

'Against the rules?'

No, Daemon smiled, *if I die, so does God. How can good exist without evil? If one died the other would cease to exist.*

Finn said nothing, contemplating the philosophy of the statement but doubting that the practicalities were as simple as the daemon had stated.

'What do you want, Daemon? I am tired of these interruptions.'

I just wanted to see how you were getting on. You seem fond of the boy.

'Leave the boy alone, he has nothing to do with this.'

He has everything to do with this, Finn. A lot depends on him. More than he knows.

'He will not leave.'

Good. That pleases me, Daemon's face split into a huge smile, his incisors momentarily seeming too long in the last rays of the sun.

'A day is coming when I will grow weary of your manipulation of my life. When that day comes you and I will have our own reckoning.'

I know, Finn. I am looking forward to it.

The twin suns sank below the horizon plunging the alien world into darkness.

*

Caleb tripped while going up the slope, his thighs burning from the climb. The log they were carrying between them crashed off his shoulder as he hit the ground. Catching the log before it landed, he wondered if he had broken a rib or two under the impact.

'Up! Move!' Finn said simply still holding the back of the log. The sweat running freely down his body was the only indication that he was under any sort of pressure.

Caleb picked up the log with effort, hoisting it back on his shoulder he headed off again along the tree line at the top of the slope. His lungs were on fire. As they turned down the slope Caleb was glad to be heading back to the cabin. The thin frosty air was impossible to breathe yet he understood Finn's reasoning. If he could function as a warrior in thin air, then he could fight better for longer in the lower valleys. Careful of their footing, the two men propelled themselves down the steep slope.

Caleb knew the punishment for dropping the log. It was a test of endurance and teamwork. One man could not negotiate a log this size, it was hard enough for the two of them. The four miles down hill was, in many ways, harder than the arduous climb. As well as the weight he had to have maximum co-ordination. Trying to keep alert he burst through the tree line into the cabin clearing not stopping running until he reached the stream at the far end.

They dropped the log together. Caleb started to strip off his top to wash as they normally did. He turned to find Finn's double-edged dagger brushing the skin on his throat.

'Come Caleb, defend yourself,' Finn's voice was cold as death.

Caleb's hand whipped up swatting the blade aside, only a fraction but enough to duck under it. Ducking and rolling in toward Finn he drew his own dagger and lashed out towards the femoral artery only to have his wrist crack against the edge of Finn's boot. Dropping the dagger, he rolled to his feet and ran to the cabin. Hand on his weapon, Caleb drew his sword he tossed the scabbard back on to the porch. He wheeled to face the tall warrior bearing down on him. When Finn got within five feet Caleb lashed his foot forward kicking dirt high towards his teacher's face, at the same time throwing the piece of firewood his hand rested on. Keeping the initiative, he streaked forward to disembowel his enemy.

As his blade was parried, he dropped it and batted the dagger from Finn's hand disarming him and throwing a left hook to his head. Finn drove his forearm into Caleb's bicep killing the blow and brought his open hand back sharply onto his ear stunning him momentarily.

Caleb stumbled back throwing a kick to Finn's groin on the way. Finn's foot shot forwards catching Caleb's kick above the knee and stepped in with two rapid punches to the head opening Caleb's lips and brow.

Caleb leapt to the side, but Finn's kick tore his legs out from under him.

He landed with a grunt as the air was forced from his lungs.

'Get up, Caleb. Don't be the little boy you have always been. Fight.'

Caleb burst forward with a flurry of punches before leaping back suddenly and dropping to pick up his sword.

'Control is all-important. Controlled aggression. Controlled fury. Unleash the beast only when you need to. Do not let it guide you.'

Caleb crouched and waited for Finn to move first. He was exhausted and did not want to expose the weakness to him. The blow to Caleb's face had open an old cut above his left eye from which blood was now flowing freely.

Finn tossed him a dagger he had concealed in his tunic.

'Here. Disarming me was a good move when you had overextended your lunge,' Finn moved forward slowly. 'But you did not allow for a concealed weapon. Show me what you can do, boy.'

Caleb sped forward both blades arcing towards Finn's head and body. Finn moved to the outside of the sword arm and pushed in, trapping both Caleb's arms against his own body.

'Do you see how the weapons are only an extension of the fighting drills we practice unarmed?' Finn punched, rewarded with a crunch as the nose broke. Caleb staggered back blood gushing down over his mouth. With his vision swimming, Caleb lifted his hands for the next onslaught.

'Excellent, Caleb. Rest.' Finn lowered his hands just as Caleb powered in with a trio of punches. Finn stepped forward and to the side allowing Caleb to move past before striking sharply to his carotid artery collapsing him to the ground.

'Enough,' Finn said softly as he brought the boy around and moved away from him.

Caleb sat up slowly before rising unsteadily to his feet to join Finn by the stream. Kneeling in the freezing water he inhaled involuntarily before closing his eyes in solemn prayer.

The end of another day.

*

Hein moved carefully through the streets. There was no direct order given but he knew the guards were to be more vigilant about who left the keep. That bastard Sevill was devious, but Hein had the predatory cunning that had kept him alive this long.

The extra security was easy to negotiate if you knew how.

They were using the excuse of increased number of attacks on soldiers, but there was no increase. There had always been attacks on soldiers. The attacks had diminished, of course, as any established resistance was rooted out and exterminated.

Hein had slipped out in the last patrol change. His body was charged and ready for the night's entertainment. Standing in the shadows he waited for his prey, his sign from God that there was someone to be purged. His mind began to wander to the acts he would make the women perform before he sent them to be judged by their maker.

Snapping out of his reverie, Hein could hear laughter and light music from the path behind him. The night was clear, and the sound could have travelled far yet he knew, as only a predator can, that his quarry was close at hand.

Blending with the shadows he followed the line of shacks to the source of the noise, a gathering of sorts. Neighbours congregated to keep each other's spirits up.

Hein waited out of sight. The moon was in its descent before the opportunity presented itself. A young girl, about sixteen, came out of the hut alone, laughing over her shoulder at some farewell remark from a deep voiced man. Waving, she started to walk home.

Hein let her get a head start, making sure some amorous suitor would not join her. He had made that mistake before and had his night interrupted by a young well-wisher. He had made the young man pay for that error.

With thoughts of castration making him smile, Hein detached himself from the shadows and took off in pursuit of his victim.

*

Clara was aware something was wrong, though it took a lot longer than usual to realise she was being followed.

Pausing at the next turn she listened intently. All she could hear was the pounding of her heart in her ears and the wind through the loose boards on the houses around her. A shoe scuffed stone. She was being followed.

Clara's initial thought was that it was her younger brother, come to walk her home. Suspicion and danger reasserted themselves as thoughts of the killings over the past weeks came to her mind unbidden. Fearful for her life she did not continue on the route home, lest the killer be lured to her mother and sister.

She decided to hide in one of the deserted huts.

If it was her brother, he would get a surprise. If it was the killer, she thought idly as she thumbed the small dagger in her skirt, perhaps he would get a shock.

Clara remained in the hut for what seemed like an eternity. She was about to enter the street again when she became aware of a figure in the shadows across from her. He was sniffing the air. The moonlight tried in vain to reveal his features to her but could not defeat the skulking shadows.

The man seemed to have been there forever and she did not know how she had not been aware of him until now. As though attracted to her by her new awareness, the man locked his cruel eyes on her and raced across the small entry shattering the small door of the hut with his broad shoulder.

Clara leapt to the attack, but her knife was knocked from her hand and a hard slap sent her tumbling to the floor with a yelp of pain. Spinning on to her back she scuttled away from the menacing figure who stalked towards her, his intent apparent in his every movement. He was going to kill her, painfully.

'Where are you going, whore?' Hein stared down at the girl. 'You are only going to make this harder for yourself.'

Clara tried to scream but her throat was swollen with tears and fear, a barely audible croak was all she could manage. Clara had pushed herself back into the corner. There was nowhere left to go.

'Nowhere to run, child, for the Lord can seek out the sinner in us all.'

Hein's face contorted in barely camouflaged rage. Lowering himself to his knees he began to pray frantically for her, spittle frothing at his lips.

Clara's eye was swollen from the slap, the heat of it strangely throbbing on her face. The figure before her rose to blot out what little moonlight illuminated the inside of the hut.

Hein never felt the blow that rendered him unconscious.

Clara managed a scream as the limp form fell across her.

'Quiet, child,' a strange voice spoke to her now, reassuring her. 'Go home now, you are alive and well.'

'Who are you?' she asked, as she scrambled to the door, carefully avoiding the large man who struck her attacker once more in the side of the head.

'You may call me Kannon,' he replied from the near total darkness.

'Thank you, Kannon,' she choked back tears. 'Is he the killer?'

'He is the only killer you need worry about this night, Clara,' the silhouette revealed nothing of his features, but his eyes shone brightly in the night.

'You know me?' Fear once more clutched at her throat.

'Go home, Clara,' the rich voice commanded as he lifted the attacker with impossible ease and slung him over his shoulder.

Clara stepped backwards into the street, as the man moved to the doorway. Turning, she fled into the night.

*

'Use the sword and dagger together. If you use a shield you are part attack and part defence. You must be wholly attack.'

'The shield is a valuable weapon,' Caleb countered, performing one of the many drills with dagger and sword, this time against Finn.

'It is only a weapon if you use it as a club. Other than that it is a defensive tool that most soldiers rely too heavily upon, especially when they are tired or afraid. The small shield you use is for confined fighting in forested terrain. Larger shields are used in company sized engagements in open ground to hold off weight of numbers. These fighting principles are for open combat. After the initial clash of shields.' Caleb followed the drill closely, the light clash of their blades singing softly in the morning air.

'I will have to return home again soon. We are due to go active again shortly. Our skirmishing parties will be heading south to harry the supply routes. They are considering an attack on one of the garrison towns.'

'I wish you well, young warrior. It has been a pleasure to train with you.'

'I have learned a lot from you,' Caleb stepped back lowering his weapons Finn stepped in swiftly and drove his blades forward disarming him.

'Do not lower your guard, Caleb, ever. If you get used to doing it now you will do it in combat and die as a result.'

'I know, sir. I merely wished to say goodbye.'

'We will meet again,' Finn said.

'You say that like it is a sure thing,' Caleb walked over to the cabin the pair had built. Lifting a large bundle he returned to where Finn stood, bending to untie it.

'Nothing is for certain, Caleb. Except death, and I have found that even that has its own laws.'

'I would like you to accept this as a gift from me,' Caleb gestured to the cabin.

'I was wondering what was in the strange bundle you brought with you.'

Finn stepped forward to see his gift. Caleb lifted a freshly made set of leathered armour. The same as his own, it was a dull leather overlay with splits to insert the steel exo-skeleton. It offered protection to the upper body, arms and forearms, the groin and the outside if the thighs with full greaves on the shins.

'I like the design of this armour,' Finn tried the suit on, not surprised to find that it was a good fit.

'I . . . acquired it from our supplies. It looked like your size. The adjustments are easy since the steel plates are the same for all. You only have to adjust the leather strapping.'

'Thank you,' Finn bowed slightly. 'I wish there was something I could give you in return.'

'You have already given me more than you know.'

'Take care in the coming battles, Caleb, I expect you to return and share the lessons you have learned with me.'

'Will you not come and fight with us?'

'I would not be so readily accepted by your people as you accept me, Caleb. I will consider visiting with them though, but only if you promise to visit with me on your return. Bring the girl. We will have dinner.'

'I will see you again Finn,' and with that he turned and headed out of camp.

*

Hein slowly opened his eyes, the haze settled, and his vision cleared though his head pounded. It took some time for him to realise he was bound to a chair and his mouth was gagged.

Angry, Hein struggled for a few seconds, but the bonds did not give or slacken at all. He tried to spit the gag of smelly cloth from his mouth but felt himself wretch and choke.

'Careful now, Hein,' the voice said from behind him. 'I do not want you to choke on your own bile.'

Hein tried in vain to turn his head towards the voice but was bound in such a way that he could not move.

'If I remove the gag, do you promise to scream?' the voice asked, interested.

Hein tried to move his head, sweat forming on his brow with the frustrated effort. The tall man came into view. He was smooth shaven, and his hair was hanging loose about his shoulders. Hein saw a tie band at his wrist for fastening it in place. The clothes were not a rich, but they showed no sign of wear and tear.

'Do you, Hein? Do you promise?' Kannon asked, his tone friendly and bright.

Hein moved his head slowly up and down to show assent. Kannon smiled and reached forward to remove the cloth.

'Who the hell are you?' Hein snarled.

'Now, my friend, do you forget your promises so quickly? You promised to scream for me,' Kannon walked out of Hein's line of vision, arriving back with a stool in his hand which he placed in front of him and sat down.

'I think a man should keep his promises,' Kannon said as he reached forward and took hold of Hein's left knee and began to squeeze. Hein glared at the man defiantly, until the pain began to rise in his knee.

'Uncomfortable, isn't it,' there was no strain in his voice and the hand continued its crushing with little effort or resistance.

Hein's eyes bulged in momentary disbelief as his knee snapped, the kneecap coming off under the skin, the ligaments and tendons shearing from the bone. A scream tore forth from his body. Grinding noises and a dull pop sounded from the knee as Kannon kept the pressure on, his knuckles were not even white. No exertion showed on his face.

Hein started to pass out from the pain, so Kannon let go.

'Not a very impressive pain threshold, Hein. I would have though a man with your tastes would have been more used to the thing that gives him most delight.'

'Who . . . are . . . you?' Hein's eyes were bright with fear and colour had drained from his face.

'You may call me Kannon,' he answered.

'Kannon,' Hein mulled the word over in his mind, finally coming up with nothing better than, 'I do not know you.'

'No, I suppose you do not,' Kannon offered him a strange, pungent leaf. 'Here, this will take away the pain. Place it under your tongue.'

Hein hesitated for a moment, dismissed the possibility of poison, and greedily lapped it from Kannon's fingers. The release was immediate. Hein let out a sigh as high muscles relaxed.

'What do you want?' his eyes were glazing over as the drug took effect, the vision becoming sharper, sounds and smells were crisper. Hein became aware that he had soiled himself. 'I want you, Hein.'

'How do you know me?' Hein smiled, such a strange conversation.

'I know all about you. When I sniff the night air, I can taste your essence. You are a vile creature, Hein, and it excites me,' Kannon's eyes glistened darkly.

'How did you find me?' Hein thought for a moment that he must be dreaming.

'You found me, my friend, your vile deeds cried out to me from afar summoning me to your side. We are meant to be together,' Kannon stroked his face like an old friend, yet there was nothing intimate in the touch.

'I feel strange,' Hein said.

'The leaf is a very powerful drug. I have seen it taken to heighten the sexual experience. It makes all sensation that much sharper. Soon, each touch will bring pain, and each pain will bring its own fresh agony.'

The veins began to throb on Hein's forehead as the pain from his crushed knee revisited him, stronger than before.

'It hurts,' Hein managed, through gritted teeth.

'It will do more than hurt in a minute,' Kannon said looking into his eyes. 'Soon it will have you crying out for me to take your miserable life. Soon you will see me peel one of your eyeballs.'

'Who are you?' Hein focused on the strange eyes before him.

'I am many things, Hein. I am vampire, demon, devil and king,' Kannon smiled. 'I am everything that your puny mind could never understand.'

Hein shook his head.

'What do you want with me?' he murmured through the searing pain as Kannon crushed his other knee.

'I hunger, Hein. I need your heart. It gives me life.' Hein was very conscious of the beating in his chest.

'No,' he said, weakly.

'Your dark heart will sustain me, and I thank you for the gift.'

'No! Take someone else!'

'There is no one else,' Kannon cooed.

Hein struggled frantically in the chair.

'Listen, Hein, can you hear the skin tearing?' Kannon tied back his hair and dragged one long finger along Hein's chest, the nail slicing through skin and muscle.

Hein could smell the blood, so sweet and cloy. The sound of the fingernail across his sternum threatened to deafen him. He began to scream, gasping in huge gulps of air and screaming it back out. He could feel everything.

Kannon flashed his nails across Hein's scalp, cutting him to the bone. With the skull exposed he gripped the flesh at the hairline and peeled the skin down from his face.

There was much blood.

Kannon systemically tore the bonds and peeled the skin from Hein's body. Having to tug slightly at the joints was the only problem. The skin came off in one careful, well-practised piece. Hein's back was contorted in a silent scream.

There was no glamour in death. It came to all. Perhaps he was deluding himself. Perhaps he was an unredeemable killer. God had not answered his prayers, had never given him a sign. The priest who had sought him out for seventy years had found him and had it within his power to kill him. The priest instead had given him the opportunity to save his own soul.

He had given up his name of Melchior and assumed the mantle of Kannon. Forsaking the pursuit of flesh and riches he had kept his word to the priest, to God, for over four hundred years now. Seeking out the wrong doer and sending them to their maker.

Kannon did not have to feed often, but he did have to feed.

'Perhaps I am just a monster,' he said to the now screaming Hein, 'and for that I apologise.'

Kannon stood over the writhing man and with a swift movement punched through his chest to seize his heart.

Hein shuddered violently as Kannon pulled it, still beating, from his body. His eyes were wide, the life fading as Kannon began to devour it.

'A monster,' he thought again as the blood spilled over his chin.

Finn worked his body hard, the palms of his hands slamming into the twenty-year-old tree. The hard bark threatened to tear at his skin and pull the flesh from his fingers, but the callused hands caused the bark to break under the impact. The incessant hammering of the percussion blows was like a low drumming in the midmorning quiet. A number of birds had stopped to watch the bizarre ritual which had been going on since sun up. Increasing the tempo to an impossible rate, the strikes became one constant noise with no discernible pattern or beat. Finn suddenly stepped forward and to one side, snapping his arm up through one of the lower branches snapping it easily and cleanly. Without hesitation, several other branches quickly followed suit.

Finn stopped, his body bathed in sweat. A good sign since it meant that his skin had healed well enough to pass the body fluids. Stretching he felt the knotted muscles release their tension. He was on fire after the

'Good of you to join us, Caleb,' Finn walked towards the young warrior but his gaze settled on the young woman he had brought with him.

'You knew we were here?' Caleb asked of his teacher, throwing a sideways smile at his beautiful companion.

'How could I not know, my young friend, when you move with the grace of a dying hog,' Finn stooped before the pair and took the girl's hand in his own. The hand, though small, was hard and muscular, the knuckles callused, the skin rough.

'You must be the Lady Erika,' Finn bowed gently to kiss her hand, bringing a blush to her face and neck. 'Caleb's stories of your beauty do not do you justice.'

Caleb blushed even more.

'Why are you still sitting there, Caleb? Does the presence of beauty make you unable to train?' Finn fixed him with steely eyes.

'No, sir,' was all he could manage.

'Good. The tree. Do not stop until you have stripped it of its bark.'

'Yes, sir,' Caleb smiled at Erika once before running to the tree. Stripping to his waist he began thundering in heavy blows. The tempo increased as he blanked out the pain in his hands, bloody patches were already forming on the tree.

Satisfied, Finn offered Erika his arm, which she declined and walked by his side to the cabin. Sitting on the porch for a while in silence they watched the young man as he and tree fought to see who would quit first.

'Why are you making him do that?' Erika asked. Finn knew that she asked, not out of concern for her betrothed, but out of interest for the training technique.

'As well as conditioning his body for combat, it will condition his mind as well,' Finn said, his tone conversational instead of instructional.

'How?' she watched as the hardened muscles on Caleb's back and arms pumped in fluid rhythm.

'He is in pain. The bark is rough and jagged and is cutting his skin. Soon it will begin to tear at the muscles in his hands. His arms and back are beginning to cramp. He is in physical pain, yet his mind is blanking it out. He refuses to accept that his body must stop.

'The pain must be terrible,' she observed.

'It is enough to break even the strongest of men, but not the strongest of minds. He will be able to fight on in battle, even with the pain of injury. It is a matter of training. That is all.' Finn watched his student, pleased at his efforts.

'How long must he do this?'

'Until I tell him to stop,' Finn said. 'Until I feel he is close to breaking or doing his hands and wrists serious damage.'

'He speaks highly of you,' she said, turning her attention at last to the mysterious warrior.

'A student should speak highly of his teacher,' Finn met her gaze.

'He would not tell me anything about you,' she said.

'There is nothing to tell, Erika.'

'You are a warrior?'

'Of sorts.'

'What does that mean?' she certainly was direct.

'It means that I do not choose to tell you, girl,' Finn scolded. 'Do not seek to come into my camp and act the spoiled child with me, or you shall find yourself over my knee for what I suspect is a long overdue spanking.'

The words bit through her, and she fought to control her anger. Her eyes blazed with silent fury.

'If you would like to put that anger to a more constructive use, you can fence or fist fight,' Finn suggested, turning away from her to complete her chastisement.

'Fighting would suit me fine,' the young warrior's muscles were bunched and taught, seeking release.

'Good,' Finn said. 'Caleb!'

Caleb stepped forward, his strikes smashing through the branches.

As he stepped back his hands were shaking and blood was running freely. Much of the bark had indeed been stripped away and the whole trunk was a mess of blood.

Finn set a bucket of fresh, icy water from the stream at his feet and bid him put his swollen hands in. Undoing a wrap of medicines Finn began to tend the wounds.

'These salves and ointments will clot the blood and ease any pain. There will be little bruising. By tomorrow only the cuts will remain and they will heal soon.'

'What are they?' Erika asked, forgetting her anger momentarily.

'They are gathered from different flowering plants and roots growing on the northern slopes. There are better ones but they do not grow in these climes.'

'And you are versed in these?'

'It is no good to have a warrior who cannot fight because he is training too hard for the battle.'

Finn applied generous amounts of the salve to Caleb's palms, causing him to wince at the sting they produced.

'So you can strip the bark from a tree and render your hands to a pulp, but one sting from ointment and you surrender,' Finn provoked the boy who only smiled at the situation.

'Now. The two of you will box,' Finn said bandaging his hands tightly to keep the salve in place.

'Come then, Caleb,' Erika flexed and stripped her leathered amour. 'It has been a while since we have fought. I hope you have not forgotten the last time.'

'I have not,' he replied, thinking back to the black eye she had given him. Like all the warriors, she was a capable fighter, able to use her leverage and speed in the absence of the strength her male counterparts possessed.

'Good,' she said darting forward with a low kick to his knee, which he stopped easily by lazily extending his foot. She followed with a snapping left jab to his head, which he slipped under, and to the side. A short sweeping motion with his right foot lifted Erika into the air, only to fall heavily and awkwardly. Rolling to her front she pushed on to her feet and circled Caleb more cautiously.

'I do not want a sparring session, children. I expect you to fight, not dance around each other,' Finn barked, not watching the fracas but focusing his attention on the rabbit he was skinning.

Erika feinted with a low kick before skipping forward with a hard punch to Caleb's face. His hand shot forward deflecting the blow and his fingers brushed her eyelashes causing her to blink. Stepping in he hammered his elbow into the side of her head causing her to hit the ground hard.

'Not the boy you remember,' Caleb suggested.

'No,' she replied rising slowly stepping in abruptly with a head butt that missed as Caleb slipped to the side and dropped her with a short uppercut to the chin. Erika slid to the ground and this time did not move.

Checking that she was breathing and moving her tongue to one side of her mouth to prevent her gagging he walked over to Finn to help him prepare dinner.

'So that is the love in your life?' Finn asked.

'She was,' he acknowledged, 'but I am not sure how we are after that.'

'You will be fine. She will forgive you,' Finn reassured him.

'She will not thank me for it,' he looked at her resting form.

'I think you will find that she has a new found respect for you. Caleb no matter what she might say to the contrary. You had best move her to the cabin. Let her sleep.'

'She has a scathing tongue, and a wicked temper,' Caleb laid her down, placing a blanket under her head and brushing back the hair from her face.

'She is a strong young woman, and fast. I do not judge her harshly. She uses her temper to mask her fears.'

'What fears?' Caleb asked.

'Like you, she feels that she is not adequate to the job of warrior for her people.'

'I no longer feel that way,' Caleb corrected.

'You did when you came here. If you remember that is why you came to me months ago. You have trained hard and you have fought hard. You survived your latest battle.'

'I did,' Caleb smiled.

'And your new found abilities were noticed were they not?'

'They were,' he grinned. 'I fought very well. When we were pushed back I rallied the troop and formed an attacking wedge that won the day. My captain was pleased.'

'Did you kill many?'

'I killed as many as I could,' Caleb answered.

'A fact of which you are proud.'

'Of course, is that not the purpose of battle with the enemy?'

'At this time, perhaps' Finn continued. 'A better victory would have been to make them withdraw without joining battle.'

'A better victory would have been to kill them all without losing a man,' Caleb replied.

'To make an enemy surrender without the loss of life on either side is a better victory.'

'Victory is victory,' Caleb said simply.

'You should pray on this tonight, my young warrior,' Finn replied. 'Each man must find his own path.'

Caleb lapsed into silence at the rebuke from his teacher.

'Do not worry too much, Caleb, the path of life is long. You will learn in time. Your more immediate problem is lying unconscious on the cabin porch.'

'Are you ever short of an insight into my troubles?' Caleb asked, not unkindly.

'Rarely,' Finn gutted the rabbit, tossing its viscera into a bucket. 'Work on your weapon forms.'

Caleb nodded curtly and moved to the heavy undergrowth where the trees were packed tightly, poles in the ground making the area even more cramped. The dense training area recreated the need for flow even when the environment was hindered. You could not clear space around you in a battle to fight to your optimum performance.

Finn watched him move. His understanding was accelerating as well as his physical ability. He understood without questioning that weapons were mere extensions of the body, able to be practised with or without. Finn set the rabbit on the spit, turning to look at the girl.

She would make a fine partner for the young man, as soon as he was strong enough to deal with her and hold her in check while still allowing her to bloom.

'Good luck to you,' Finn smiled to himself.

Chapter Sixteen

Plandor seemed to writhe upon itself during the day such was the magnitude of the reorganisation. The new boxing ring was just that, a raised circle in the centre of the rapidly reforming camp. A layer of sand covered it so that blood would be quickly soaked in or shovelled out for the next match.

'He moves well for a big man,' Tobias said idly.

Brood nodded in return. He did not know which of the two fighters Tobias was indicating since they were both tall and well-muscled. The Dance of the Sands had lasted for three hours and had built up to an eagerly anticipated final.

Brood had never developed a taste for combat as a sport.

He watched as Hamza rolled his head on his thickly corded neck and had his back arms and legs rubbed feverishly by his corner men. Hamza sported a puffy eye and cut lip but the greatest cause for concern was a nasty gash on his forehead that his first opponent of the night had opened with a head butt. His corner man applied some more congealed cow fat to seal it.

'Who do you think will clinch it, brother?' Tobias asked.

'I have no interest in these matches,' Brood answered.

'Come now,' Tobias said. 'Two men pitting it all for the honour of their regiment and Empire. It is a great spectacle. This is Hamza's second fight this week.'

Brood watched as Hamza's opponent, Priebke, received his warm up massage. He bore no marks to his face though his ribs were purple for some vicious body blows.

Brood touched the mind of both fighters.

Anticipation, fear, anxiety, children, the regiment, women, gold, sex, victory, death, women, glory, property, honour, reward.

Brood saw only the pursuit of self-gain. The men wanted to raise their own standing in the army. A promotion and gold to take home. Maybe to be honoured with a gift of land.

They knew Pogue was in attendance and would like to make a generous gift to the winner.

Pogue saw it as a way to take the credit for the fights and reorganisation of the camp. Word of his generosity would be talked about in court at Avalon.

'Wheels within wheels,' Brood said aloud.

'What, brother?' Tobias asked.

'I think Hamza will take it,' Brood said. 'He wants it more.'

'Don't you think it is cheating to read the fighters,' Tobias laughed and drank deeply on the chilled water. 'I do not think the gambling would benefit from your opinion. I still think Priebke will win. Care to wager?'

Brood did not answer, even though he knew Tobias was jesting. The Knights did not gamble. It was a base human need. One that they were above.

'You will be heading north,' Brood said, watching as the fighters met in the centre of the ring. They bent and picked up some dirt and rubbed it on their hands, drying the sweat.

'I will leave in the morning for the garrison towns,' Tobias nodded, not taking his eyes from the fighters as they refused to shake hands bringing wild cheering and shouting from the assembled soldiers.

'Everything is prepared?' Brood asked as a formality. He knew Tobias was thorough.

'I have one hundred picked men and will take the rest from the garrisons as and when I need them,' Tobias smiled as the first low blow was landed by Priebke. 'It will be hit and run as you have said, my brother. We will use the enemy tactics against them. Ambush and withdraw. Wound and not kill. Drain their resources. Public executions for any that we do capture.'

'You have scouts?' Brood.

'Four trained trackers,' Tobias confirmed. 'Mountain men from the Outlands. Very skilled. They will track any retreating men to the mountain camps and return immediately.

'From the Outlands?' Brood asked. 'Can they map read?'

'No,' Tobias confirmed, 'but do not worry. I will explore their minds for the information when they return.'

'That will kill them,' Brood stated, his tone flat.

'That it will,' Tobias said and grinned as Hamza tackled Priebke's legs from under him and they now wrestled for superior position in the dirt.

Brood remembered the Lord Saladin.

'This is a holy war,' he had said. 'The ends must always justify the means.'

Brood had agreed then.

But now? Why was now different? Perhaps now was not. Perhaps he had changed.

'He is light on his feet,' Tobias continued. 'Must do a lot of speed work.'

Brood eyed his brother Knight and wondered at the strangely dark motivations of the Knight. Tobias was ever present at the gladiatorial contests in Avalon and accompanied the Lord Saladin whenever he attended the jousts.

Feeding criminals and prisoners of war to wild beasts was not something Brood thought a warrior of the Lord should take delight in. He had prayed for the souls of the prisoners and for his brother Knight.

The Lord Saladin had chastised him for his weakness. Brood was supposed to be the strongest of the Knights and an example to the Empire. Brood had expressed his apologies but still, try as he might, could not commit to the sacrifice.

He watched the blood-lust running high in the assembly of soldiers. The week's preparation had allowed for the ring to be situated in a natural depression, accentuated by raised seating. Brood's expert eye estimated eight thousand soldiers now watched and cheered their regimental champions.

'Ohhh's and 'Ahhh's filled the night as did many expletives.

Hamza stepped back casually as Priebke advanced with a low kick and quick jab to his face. Hamza countered with a thunderous right hand splitting the well-built fighter above his right eye. Priebke did not finch, instead his stiffened fingers shot forward grazing Hamza's eyes and causing him to blink. The blink allowed Priebke to follow up with a rapid succession of blows to the gut and body with an uppercut that all but knocked Hamza from his feet. The entire arena was on its feet.

Ohhhh!' they said as one.

Hamza was far from done, however.

Brood sought out the general, Garrad, and soon found him with his officers on the other side of the ring. They were close enough to the ring for his men to see him but far enough away that he could still have discussion with his officers. He was not watching the fight. Perhaps he was sure that his fighter would win? Perhaps he did not care?

Brood opted for the latter. Garrad was a warrior.

'Ohh,' Tobias gushed, distracting him for a second.

Hamza had swung a wild kick and Priebke had capitalised on his mistake, taking him in close for a choke hold. Hamza managed to sink his teeth into Priebke's arm and tore flesh, releasing the hold and head butting the stockier man. Priebke staggered back, blinded, and Hamza kicked him hard in the testicles. An uppercut to the face and elbow to the temple drew blood in a spurt along with a sickening thud from the impact.

Priebke went down and Hamza's arms went up. The whole arena rose with him and cheered as one. Priebke was forgotten for a moment as all adulation went to Hamza. He did not notice when Priebke was dragged from the ring. Still alive thankfully.

Tobias clapped loudly.

'I would not like to have missed that,' he said, and smiled broadly.

'I would just as rather not have seen it at all,' Brood did not return the smile. He could smell the blood lust in the air.

'May God watch over you and guide you on your mission, brother,' Brood said rising, frowning as a shadow seemed to pass over his fellow Knight.

'I shall return within the month, Tobias said, though Brood suspected that he would not see him alive again. It did not bode well.

He would pray on it.

*

Finn was deep in prayer when he heard the young warriors coming. Caleb moved more gracefully now than Erika but they still sounded like stampeding elephants to Finn's heightened senses.

Finishing his morning prayer he stayed in the water and allowed his mind to wander to elephants. He could create the image of them in his mind but could not remember where he had seen them.

'Good morning, sir,' Caleb saluted him.

'Sir,' Erika said, copying the salute.

'I am not your officer,' Finn said rising form the water and dressing himself in loose clothing.

'You seem distracted,' Caleb said, eyeing his teacher.

'I was thinking of elephants,' Finn replied absently.

'I have heard of them and seen paintings and drawings,' Erika added as she boiled the water for tea.

'Have you seen elephants?' Caleb asked.

'I have. Huge beasts that ran in the wild but were also bred for war. I have seen beasts three times the height of a man with chambers on their backs that could carry warriors or archers into battle,' Finn described the scene in his mind. 'They are ferocious and impossible to stop. They can charge, their tusks sharpened to points or fixed with armour. They are draped in mail for their own protection.'

'You have seen them in battle?' Caleb asked, eyes wide.

'I see,' Finn tried to clear the picture in his mind, 'a charging line of more than one hundred battle elephants. The destruction they left in their wake was terrible.'

'Where did you see this?' Caleb asked.

'I do not remember. A battle. War. There have been many,' Finn said slowly. 'It seems so clear yet I cannot recall the details.'

Erika began to chop vegetables with her dagger setting them to one side for the soup they would make as soon as the tea had been cleared from the pot. Sending Caleb to draw fresh water from the stream she passed the now silent Finn a steaming cup of the foul-smelling brew and poured both for herself and Caleb.

'Your memory is not as it should be,' she ventured.

'No,' he answered.

'Caleb will not tell me about you,' she said as the young man arrived back with the water, 'He says if I have a question I should ask you directly.'

'That is wise counsel,' Finn agreed, nodding at Caleb.

'You do not know if you are friend or foe,' Erika added.

'I am friend,' Finn replied.

'But you do not know if you were an enemy soldier before you lost your memory,' she corrected herself.

'No,' Finn drank deeply.

'The patrols have given up looking for you. The council thinks you have headed far to the south.'

'That is good,' Finn replied. 'Perhaps they will leave me in peace.'

'Will you teach me the ways of the warrior that you are teaching Caleb?'

'Why do you wish to know them?' Finn asked.

'So that I might return the favour,' she smiled, rubbing at the bruises Caleb had left her with the day before.

'Then I will teach you,' Finn matched her smile. 'But on this occasion I will ask that you keep my existence a secret. For the time being.'

'I will,' Erika bowed.

'Very well. Let us begin.'

Erika's eyes gleamed at the prospect.

'First you must learn patience and control, Erika,' Finn said, the tea and soup forgotten. 'Let us pray.'

*

Toshak watched as his Legions formed battle lines quickly and professionally. He would have expected no less but it always lifted his spirits.

'The men are ready, general,' the lieutenant said from his left as the final banner was raised into place.

'Hold the lancers back,' Toshak said scratching at his chin. 'Present the infantry. Surging formation, advance. See if you can draw the enemy close for a bit of a barney. Hold the lancers back but let the enemy see their pennants.'

'Yes, general,' Ruben replied and shouted an order. Banners were raised and bugles blared. The lines moved forward as one, the sun gleaming off their polished armour and spear heads. As they marched slowly forward the front lines would suddenly run forward for a step or two with the rest of the lines following suit. It gave the impression to the enemy that the line was surging and alive. It distracted them at the very least and put fear into them at best.

Only the Legion lines did this. It was a reminder to the enemy that they were facing Ellistrin soldiers. Legionnaires. They had best be prepared.

'Seems like a lot of them,' the lieutenant said looking across the plain.

'Plenty of party invitations have been sent out for this one,' the general said brightly.

'Yes, sir,' Ruben replied, not sharing his superior's good humour.

Across the divide, Toshak watched as the enemy rapidly formed up. From the look of it they were disciplined but not prepared to attack. They certainly were not prepared to receive an attack from the Ellistrin Legions.

'Do you suppose they know what they are doing?' the lieutenant asked.

'Must do,' Toshak said. 'They have been doing it long enough.'

'Before an attack they must reinforce the point of thrust because the lines are so long. They must know that it is obvious to us that they intend to attack.'

'They do,' Toshak scratched his chin again. His "tell" as it had been called by a gambler. He scratched it when he was mulling complex decisions. Unprepared for the attack as the enemy must be, there were still a lot of them.

'Hold the line,' he said. The order was relayed and obeyed immediately. Legion discipline was second to none. 'Withdraw.

'Yes, sir.'

'Double rations for the next three days,' the general said. 'Rest three to one.'

For every man on guard three would be sleeping.

'They aren't going to come soon. A week, maybe,' Toshak offered.

'How do you know, sir?' Ruben asked, though he did not dispute the information.

'They are just auxiliary troops. Their Puritan masters have not yet arrived to direct them,' Toshak indicated the lack of a Puritan Imperial banner. 'They like to be there to sacrifice their pawns.'

'Next week, then?' the lieutenant asked. 'Shall I ask for reinforcements from our allies?

'Ask,' the general frowned deeply, 'though I doubt it will do much good. Observe their protocols. Play their game. Make them feel important. We will have to take our land back in our own good time. I fear they are happy to hold this status quo.'

'Yes, sir,' Ruben acknowledged. He was extremely aware that on the last two occasions that the enemy probed their lines in force, the Ellistrins had been left to fend for themselves. Not that they had need of help in the battle but reinforcements would have meant less Legion casualties.

'They will come,' Ruben said, glancing at the enemy.

'They will find us waiting,' the general said, and clapped the young soldier on the shoulder, laughing loud so that all those near would hear.

*

Finn was awake first, as always.

Caleb wondered idly if the man ever slept.

The wind swept through the clearing threatening to suck the very air from his lungs. Pulling his woollen cloak a little tighter he headed to the stream. Stripping completely, he washed quickly, thankful for the renewed heat the clothes provided. Finn had warm broth prepared on the porch of the cabin, which Caleb spooned greedily into his mouth.

'I have seen lions gorge themselves with more grace than you eat,' he remarked.

'Possibly, but then you don't make lions clean their plates. I am enjoying it while I can,' Caleb grinned back. The mood was warm if not the weather. The sun was still trying to climb past the far peaks bringing the much sought heat to the air.

'I notice your manners are better whenever Erika is here.'

'I notice yours are too,' Caleb smiled.

'Manners cost nothing, boy.'

'I think she is special too,' Caleb laughed making Finn smile.

Erika had left the day before to return to the camps. She was due to move south with her troop for a raid along the garrison supply routes. The four days she had spent at the cabin had won Finn over.

'She will make a fine warrior,' Finn acknowledged. 'Perhaps even a fine wife if you ever become worthy of such a treasure.'

Caleb blushed and stammered a response but Finn had already had his fun. He was busy sorting supplies and weapons for the journey east. It was time for the boy to see the border.

'We will cut north a ways first. I do not want to have to fight any patrols.'

'Fine,' Caleb nodded. 'It is about five days away over the mountains.'

'We will be there in four,' Finn said, placing the last of the supplies into his pack. 'And we are bringing a friend.'

'A friend?' Caleb asked.

'Yes,' Finn pointed to the hateful log.

'Yes, sir,' Caleb said picking up the plates and headed to the stream. It was not going to be an easy trip.

Finn did not regret their talk the previous evening when they had talked of war. He could not remember the battles he had been in but he could recall the sense of futility, of utter despair. Caleb's experience to date was limited to a few protracted skirmishes when patrols had pushed north or when his own troop had tried to penetrate south. The hit and run did not come close to the sheer numbers Finn had talked about.

It had been decided that they should travel east, to the main front to see the real face of war. As a part of his training Caleb was also to map out the region as he went. It was important for a warrior to know the terrain as it may be the deciding point in a battle. 'Ready?' Finn asked.

'Always,' Caleb hoisted the log high onto his shoulder.

'Then let us begin.'

The two men trotted off gently, heading northeast.

*

Ammiel sat tossing pebbles at carefully placed targets across the path. At eight years old he was already on his way to being a man. Gratified as another imaginary soldier fell under his wicked aim he shielded his eyes from the sun and looked down the street to where the other sentry sat. Cohn was nine, but it was Ammiel who was always chosen for the watch at the front door. Cohn subtly signalled that all was clear.

At Ammiel's back was the door to just another insignificant rundown house that families shared across the outskirts of the city. Inside was something a lot more precious.

Five men sat in a rough circle on the floor, their names were all known to the young boy, but the most important one was undoubtedly his own father, Randall.

Ammiel looked forward to the day when he would be big enough to fight by his father's side and drive the Puritans from the land. He thought briefly of his mother who had her throat cut when he was four. Ammiel's childhood was a blur of hardship and half memories but that image would burn in his mind until he died.

Or had his revenge on the murdering soldiers that had done it. His mother had been murdered during a raid on his house in the middle of the night. They had been looking for his father.

'Tell your father we will find him, runt,' the leader of the patrol had said to him, his stinking breath inches from his face. Ammiel's eyes had locked on the gruesome sight of his beautiful mother, leaking blood over the floor. 'Tell him we will find him and all his murderous scum soon.'

Ammiel threw another stone hard at the targets, a tight grin of satisfaction as another soldier died.

'Perhaps your time might be better spent if you bought some food for yourself?'

Ammiel started at the voice.

'It might take your mind off pick-pocketing those rich Puritan merchants,' the dark man suggested.

Rooted to the spot he did not know whether to run or raise the alarm. He could see Cohn in his peripheral vision but he was looking the other way.

'Don't worry, Ammiel,' Kannon said softly, his eyes not leaving the boy's face. 'I have no interest in what goes on behind that door.'

Ammiel made a tiny fist and turned to rap quickly on the door. When he turned back the man was gone. Several copper coins littered the ground. There were no footprints where he had stood, the dried dirt remained undisturbed.

Cohn merely gave a puzzled shrug when Ammiel signalled to ask him where the stranger was.

The door opened and Barton looked out.

'What is it?' he demanded his eyes flashing up and down the street.

'There was a man here,' Ammiel said realising how stupid he sounded. He knew Barton did not like him anyway.

'Where is he now?' Barton fixed his steely eyes on the boy.

'I do not know. He disappeared,' Ammiel ventured, lifting his chin a mite higher, he would not be cowed by a bully when he was in the right.

Barton pushed his head out the door and looked about. Cohn was on his feet facing them, curious as to what was going on.

'What is happening, Barton?' Randall's strong voice asked as he came to the door.

'That boy of yours is imagining things,' he said, fixing his withering gaze on the now defiant boy.

'What did you see?' Randall asked his son. There was no affection or favour in the voice. These were serious matters.

'There was a man. He knew my name. He suggested I should get something to eat. I knocked the door and when I turned back he was gone,' Ammiel reported.

Randall looked up and down the deserted street and settled his eyes on his son.

'What do you think, Ammiel?' he asked.

'I do not like it. He meant me no harm but it makes me uneasy. I not happy with this anymore.'

'Do you think we should move?' Randall asked, again looking down to the now agitated sentries. The boys were restless.

'Move?' Barton asked. 'On the hunch of a boy? You cannot be serious.'

'I am always serious, Barton,' Randall held his eye, though only for a moment before looking at his son again.

'Yes, I think we should move. Now,' with the words said, a sense of urgency came to Ammiel. They had to get out of here.

'Clear out!' Randall shouted over his shoulder into the house. He was rewarded with a scuffing of feet from inside. One man came out past them, nodded curtly and walked briskly up the street. The others left by the back door.

Ammiel let out a short, sharp whistle and the other lookouts vanished in a swirl of kicked up dust.

'We will meet later, Barton. I will contact you,' Randall ruffled his son's hair and walked up the street.

Barton stared after him for a moment before turning and walking in the other direction.

Randall stopped at the top of the avenue and checked the coast was clear. Grabbing Ammiel he pulled him into one of the houses where he could have a clear but safe view of their meeting house.

'This man you saw, describe him. Was he local?' Randall was peering out from behind shutters.

'No. I have never seen his kind before,' Ammiel sat with his back to the wall. His small fist clutched the copper coins tightly.

'Is he a soldier?' Randall sat down beside his son, pondering the words "his kind".

'No,' Ammiel tipped the coins into his father's huge hand, smiling like a boy his age should but so rarely does in these times.

'Where did you get this?' Randall was pleased with his son's find, it meant he would not have to risk scavenging at the market and thieving from the stalls.

'The man left it,' Ammiel said.

'Did he indeed?' Randall was concerned. 'And you do not know how he knew your name?'

'No,' Ammiel was thinking that he must have been exceptionally good to follow them and to get past the lookouts without the alarm being raised.

Half an hour had passed before they heard the troops moving through the streets. The gentle clang of sword and armour of men moving in formation through streets that were too narrow.

Randall eased himself up to look out the window. Forty men converged on the door of the now deserted meeting house, smashing it to splinters as the huge lead man charged in. Randall could hear more men smash in from the rear of the house.

'Come on, Ammiel, time we were not here' Randall moved quickly out the rear of the house and into the alleyway. His mind was working hard to understand all that had happened today.

'They went straight to the house,' Ammiel said, running alongside his father, trying to match his strides. 'We are betrayed.'

Randall did not answer.

Chapter Seventeen

Caleb sat perfectly still, taking his lead as always from Finn. Across the clearing, no more than one hundred yards away, two young wolf cubs were playing roughly. Finn shook his head gently as Caleb slowly moved his hand towards the bow.

'What if they are not alone? They can't have been left unattended.'

'They are not alone,' Finn replied quietly pointing to a spot beyond the cubs. 'Just back in the trees yonder. Watching us.'

Caleb tried to make out the shape of the wolf but could not. The hairs on the back of his neck were standing up. He had the impression that the wolf, wherever it was, was looking right at him. Hopefully, it had eaten recently.

They had been four days into the journey when Finn had changed course, seeming to home in on this position.

'I don't see it,' Caleb said trying to relax, his muscles aching from the constant pace. The log seemed to weigh on his soul now, as well as his body.

'"It" is a she,' Finn took a deep breath and turned his face up to the sun. The treetops around the clearing swung in the wind but created a sanctuary from its undiscriminating harshness. The sun felt good against his face, as did the cool air filling his lungs. Finn smiled gently as he turned his gaze back to the young cubs, mimicking in fun the skills they would need to bring down prey, or defend territory, in later life. Finn turned and grinned at his own wolf cub.

'You seem happy,' Caleb said, looking at the older warrior.

'You must take these simple moments of pleasure. I despair for the man who goes through life only seeing the hardships around him. God has created so much beauty it should be a sin to let it pass us by.'

'Even when we are in the middle of a war?' Caleb asked.

'Especially in the middle of a war. When times are at their toughest, moments like this become all the more beautiful. A man realises he loves his wife after years of neglect when he realises he may lose her or savours the trivial things when he is about to die. It is the way of the world, and one of God's little ironies. A reminder that we should not have waited until it was too late to appreciate the simple things.'

Caleb eased himself down to lean against the log and watched the cubs.

'They have no worries,' he remarked.

'Not yet,' Finn replied. 'They are cubs with someone to watch over them. They do not realise that we are men, and by the very nature of being men we are the most dangerous predator they will ever meet.'

'That is why the mother is watching us,' Caleb realised.

'She does all their worrying for them. It is the way of mothers. She knows of the danger. She does not wish to antagonise us by revealing herself in case we hurt her babes.'

'As any mother would.'

'Yes,' Finn closed his eyes and relaxed, his breathing slowing, the heart rate undetectable.

'She will watch us, gauge our intent.' Caleb was speaking but Finn only heard him as an echo.

Focusing his whole being Finn could hear the heartbeat of the wolf, feel its anxiety and its bond with the cubs. The wolf was tense, ready to bound across the clearing to tear the throats out of the human intruders. It could not smell them as they had approached upwind. This was unsettling, as she could not tell from the scent if they were afraid or a threat.

Finn could not communicate with the wolf, but he tried to stimulate the senses that would reassure the protective mother. Finn thought of the scent of family, of safety and began to growl extremely low in his throat.

Friends. Allies. Pack.

The hairs on the back of the wolf lowered. Feeling the wolf relax, Finn withdrew once more to himself.

'Look!' he heard Caleb say as he came out of his trance. 'The mother wolf is coming into the clearing.'

'She means us no harm,' Finn watched as the cubs began to attack their mother. Hunting as a unit one cub distracted her as the other leapt at her neck. The wolf pawed them playfully aside and stretched in the afternoon sun, her huge tongue lapping contentedly around her lips.

Occasionally, she glanced at the two humans, just to confirm they were still there.

'How did you do that?' Caleb gazed in awe at Finn.

'I do not know that I did,' Finn replied.

'One second you are in a trance and growling, then the wolf comes into the clearing like nothing is wrong. How did you do it?' the young warrior persisted.

'I do not really know. I am changing. I feel a . . . bond with things around me. I feel at one with the forest. I just reassured the mother that we were no danger to her or her cubs.'

'And she believes you?' Caleb could not understand.

'I did not tell her or have to convince her. I just let her feel my intentions and she accepted.'

'You can talk to the animals?' Caleb sounded like he was on the verge of hysteria.

'No, I shared a feeling with her. That is all,' Finn said.

'That is all?' Caleb watched the cubs hunt butterflies. 'Can I do it?'

'In a way you do, with your scent and movement. I think I was born with the ability to see beyond,' Finn picked his words carefully so not to scare the boy.

'I cannot believe it. Yet I saw it.'

'Not all things carry an answer, Caleb, some things just have to be accepted,' Finn said.

*

'You have done a fine job, general,' Temple Knight Brood said loudly.

'Thank you, Lord Knight,' Garrad bowed stiffly at the waist.

'I take it that everything has been completed to your satisfaction,' Brood said, addressing Pogue who slouched on his divan. The bodyguards were strategically placed to give him maximum protection although Garrad had no intention of getting anywhere near the fat fool ever again.

'It is adequate,' Pogue allowed, nonchalantly eyeing one of the serving maids.

The camp was now functioning well after the restructuring that Garrad had carefully implemented over the last weeks. The boxing had proven a superb motivator. The champion's regiment did not have to take part in the work details and since, to date, Hamza had outfought all comers, the general's regiment had been able to concentrate on their own tasks and logistics.

'It is more than adequate,' Brood scolded him, causing the fat man to sit upright in his chair. As upright as his frame would allow.

'Yes, Lord Knight,' Pogue corrected himself. 'I merely meant that I had not really noticed. By looking after the menial work, the general allowed me to look after the more important matters involved in running a garrison town.'

'Quite,' Brood said turning his attention back to Garrad.

'Indeed, lord Knight,' Pogue continued, 'the sheer scale of the work load is sometimes overwhelming. I am of course from a family of politicians and am more than capable for the task.'

'See that you remain as useful,' Brood frowned at him causing his mouth to slap shut. 'General, if I could speak with you further?'

'Of course,' Garrad replied following the Knight from the courtroom, his own officers in tow.

'You have indeed done well, general. Better than I had imagined.' Garrad did not thank him again, merely waited for him to continue.

'The fighter, Hamza. He is your man,' it was not a question.

'He is.'

'He fights well. It would be better if he did not win his next fight,' Brood suggested.

'I will not order one of my men to fight to lose,' Garrad said boldly.

'I do not want you to. Have him pull out from injury before the next final. Allow one of the other regiments to have their champion for a while. It will be good for the morale of the camp.'

'Yes, Lord Knight,' Garrad conceded to the merits of the suggestion.

'Hamza will not like it but he is a good soldier.'

'Good, he will need to be when you take the army north,' Brood said.

Garrad stared at the Knight for a moment.

'Am I to be given the command?' Garrad asked.

'That has not been confirmed yet and the final decision will be mine,' Brood advised. 'You will draw up provisional plans for the cleansing of the northern mountains. I want everything detailed and considered.'

'How many men will I be given?' Garrad asked.

'As many as are available,' Brood replied, 'so long as it does not take men from the front line.'

'Good,' Garrad said. 'Good. When will we be likely to undertake this campaign?'

'When do you suggest?' Brood gave the question back to him.

'Spring is not far away. I would say the start of the summer to allow for the first thaws and the river levels to settle. The glacier can be very unpredictable.'

'Have your plans drawn up by then, and ready to be implemented, should I give you the order,' Brood said.

'Yes, Lord Knight,' Garrad replied, his mind already turning over logistical questions that he had been asking himself for weeks anyway. He was already familiar with the terrain along the garrison towns but not the mountains themselves. That is something he would have to fix.

'I am returning to Avalon tonight. Knight Tobias will remain. He will be returning from the garrison towns on completion of his tasks. He has consented to meet with you and update you to the situation there,' Brood held Garrad's gaze. 'I trust this meets with your approval.'

Garrad nodded, although the prospect of meeting the volatile Knight did not appeal to him at all.

'Very well, general,' Brood strode off. 'May God smile on your endeavours.'

'And yours,' Garrad replied.

The general watched as the Knight marched off into the camp, his bodyguards falling in behind him.

'That was some meeting,' Duncan said arriving by his side.

'Eavesdropping, captain?'

'One of my better qualities I assure you,' he replied.

'Some meeting,' Garrad confirmed. 'I think this is what the Knight had in store for us all along.'

'How so?' Duncan asked, not doubting his general's insight.

'I think that is why he travelled with us from Avalon and gave me the task of restructuring the camp here. It was his plan all along to have the Plandor garrison prepared for the invasion of the north. He wanted to see if I was the man for the job.'

'He seems to have answered that question,' Duncan observed.

'I think so,' Garrad agreed.

'He does not seem to have much time for Pogue,' Duncan offered.

'He is a good judge of character then,' the general replied, refusing Duncan's flask. 'I would guess that Brood was ordered not to have him killed.'

'By whom?' Duncan wondered who could order a Knight to do anything.

'The Holy Father himself. Presumably, he has his own problems with the politicians at home without rocking the boat,' Garrad suggested.

'To hell with all this intrigue and infighting. At least we will get to play soldier again for a while,' Duncan drank deep and passed the flask on to one of the younger officers, smiling as the lieutenant winced at the taste.

'This is to be kept between us for the moment,' Garrad ordered his junior officers.

*

Ammiel sat on a low pillar and watched the bustle of the market. In the shadow of the keep, life tried to go on. There was no laughter, trading was a matter of survival for the local population. The only smiles came from the faces of the merchants who had docked days before at the huge port. The huge ships that did not belong to the Puritan navy had been pressed into service to transport goods and troops. Everyone worked for the greater good of the Empire.

Some of the captains, of course, worked for a higher power. Themselves. Once the holds had been cleared of men and supplies, less a small handling fee of course, the merchants unloaded their own produce, some of it illegal in the pacified territories but overlooked in the occupied zones.

Before the invasion markets were not about profit. Most food goods had to be imported into the barren land. The markets and ports were about survival. Survival that was now controlled by depriving the Ellistrins of food and clothing. They were only ever one step away from starvation.

Ammiel hated the Puritans. They soiled his land, polluted his people. He could smell the spice and perfumes emanating from the people as they passed. He knew who worked up a sweat and who gave the orders. He liked to think he could smell the soft leather that made up the purses.

There was a talent to pick pocketing.

Looking across the market he could see some of the other boys communicating silently with one another. They had made a strike and been successful. The militia tried to police the market but it was impossible. Thousands of people filled the streets. They could not watch everyone.

It was for this reason that the resistance groups chose market day to pass notes and information. Knowledge was the most important commodity in the market. Troop movements were passed from runner to runner. Group commanders rarely met, it was too dangerous.

Ammiel had already carried out his running for the day and was now set to do a little thieving. All the young warriors were encouraged to thieve and scavenge. Even before the invasion thieving was encouraged as it taught them how to survive. Capture was treated severely.

Money bought food and bribed guards but it also bought information from the merchants on the state of the war. Ammiel saw a lean merchant threading his way through the crowd. He had the eyes of a hawk, and the nose to match. His left hand hung slightly by his side as he walked.

Ammiel and his friends had arranged signs strategically around the market. They warned of pickpockets. Contrary to helping the merchants, they subconsciously touched the place they hid their purse checking it is still there and in one piece. It was a beacon to a ship. The pickpocket did not have to risk exposure by looking for the booty. Finding where it was, was half the battle.

Ammiel shifted his weight to drop from the pillar and a vice closed on his small forearm making him jump. Ammiel spun to see the stranger sitting beside him, his impossibly strong grip gave no impression that Ammiel would be able to wriggle free.

'That mark is not for you, Ammiel,' Kannon said gently, to reassure him, pointing one long slender finger towards the merchant 'you might be best to find another.'

Ammiel followed the finger to watch as moments later the merchant spun on his heel grasping the wrist of an urchin whose hand had located and tried to separate the merchant from his loot. Seconds later the militia had the wide-eyed boy in custody and were dragging him away.

Ammiel slowly relaxed the pull on his arm and turned to look at the strange man his eyes were wide.

'Do I frighten you, Ammiel?' Kannon asked to be rewarded with a nod. 'You have no reason to fear me, boy, I mean you no harm.'

'Who are you?' Ammiel asked nervously.

'I am Kannon,' he replied.

'You are not . . . a man,' Ammiel phrased the words carefully.

'No, I am not,' Kannon smiled at the rare insight only children seemed to have. 'Do you know what I am?'

'An angel?' Ammiel volunteered after a long pause.

'Angel?' Kannon was slightly taken aback by the statement. For all the things he had ever considered himself to be, an angel was not one of them. All the monstrous things he had ever been called did not prepare him for this.

'Why an angel?' Kannon asked. 'Because I gave you money?'

'Because you saved my father,' Ammiel looked him straight in the eyes. No light seemed to reflect from them.

'Ahh,' Kannon nodded.

'You came to warn me,' Ammiel offered.

'Yes, I suppose I did,' Kannon said. 'I do not like betrayal.'

'How did you know we were to be betrayed?' Ammiel tried to glean this piece of information for his father.

'How does an angel know anything?' Kannon asked, amused. 'I can smell it in the air.'

Ammiel sniffed as though sampling a fine wine from the southern countries, wrinkling his nose as the smells of the fish and spice market suffused his senses. Kannon laughed.

'Betrayal and wickedness smell unimaginably worse, Ammiel,' he said smiling.

'How do I smell?' Ammiel asked, afraid to know the answer.

'You? You smell like a warm summer's breeze, with just enough pollen to tickle the inside of your nose,' Kannon remarked honestly on how the love the boy had for his father and his natural sense of justice permeated from him.

Ammiel smiled and began to kick his legs once more against the pillar. The comment obviously pleased him.

'Do you kill the bad men, Kannon?' Ammiel watched the market flow around him, the sounds and excitement now dulled in comparison to his new secret.

'Why do you ask?' Kannon watched his little friend with interest.

'You are not a good angel, the ones that kiss babies to sleep at night. Are you the angel that punishes the bad men? Are you the angel that saved the girl, Clara, from the killer many nights ago?'

'I am,' Kannon said sadly. It both hurt him and pleased him that the boy saw his killing as a good act.

'Good. I like that,' Ammiel looked up. 'Does that make you sad?'

Kannon had walked the earth for millennia and fought both daemon and spirit, human and monster. He had been faced with death at the hands of his own kind and had to atone now for a God who did not answer his prayers and a devil who plagued his waking life. Now he found his soul being bared by the inquisitive eyes of a young boy.

'It makes me sad, Ammiel,' Kannon admitted.

'That proves you are an angel,' Ammiel said as though Kannon had measured up to the yardstick of rules that only Ammiel knew existed.

'It does?' Kannon asked distantly.

'Of course. If you were a devil you would feel no remorse,' Ammiel added as though everyone should know this.

'Where did you learn to be so wise, young Ammiel?' Kannon smiled, the sun seemed strangely warmer against his skin, the air slightly lighter.

'My father teaches me not to hate the men we are at war with. They are not at fault he says, many of them are brave men fighting for their country, just as we are. We should feel remorse for those souls that we send to God,' Ammiel stopped beating his feet against the pillar.

'But you do not totally agree with him,' Kannon asked.

'No,' Ammiel said guiltily. 'I do hate them. They took my mother from me. I want to see them dead.'

'All of them?' Kannon felt the sadness return to his heart.

'No. Just the ones that killed my mother. The rest may leave in peace.'

'There is a difference?' Kannon asked.

'The ones who killed my mother were not soldiers, they were murderers. There is a difference.'

'Yes, I suppose there is,' Kannon flexed the sinewy muscles in his jaw. Reaching out his flawless hand Kannon touched Ammiel's head gently, bracing himself as the raw emotions and images of that night flooded through him.

'It would ease your pain if the man that killed your mother was dead.'

'No. It would ease my pain if she were avenged,' Ammiel felt tears rise that had not been there for many years, he and his father did not discuss such things.

'You have given me a great gift this day, Ammiel, you have let me see the world through the eyes of a child. I will ease your pain.'

'You will find him? Kill him?' Ammiel asked.

'I will make his death more agonising than any that have gone before.'

Strangely, Ammiel smiled.

'If only God would listen to my prayers also,' the dark man said.

'He did, Kannon, he sent you to me,' Ammiel smiled warmly, before jumping down and running into the crowd.

Kannon closed his eyes fixing the image of the murderous patrol leader in his mind.

'Perhaps he did send me to you after all,' Kannon smiled and walked from the market. The stench of corruption was too much.

*

The last day and night had been spent evading patrols. Caleb was at least thankful that they were no longer carrying the log. There was no spring in his step but he felt a foot taller.

'The front lines will be visible when we crest the next slope,' Finn said.

This was as far south as they dare travel. Any further would invite certain discovery by the enemy. It was only Finn's uncanny awareness of when a patrol was close that had kept them alive.

It was now dusk and the sky was painted with rich hues of purple and blue as would normally only be found on the velvets of royalty. The darkness provided a false sense of security, as night vision was as effective in humans as it was in animals. Movement attracted attention but the greatest danger was the breath that they released into the chill of the night air.

Finn rotated his hand slowly at the wrist, signalling Caleb to join him. He slowly moved up the slope, crawling methodically for much of the twenty yards separating them. A rest followed each limb movement, face into the dirt so the breath was spreading along the ground and dispersed before it could be detected. The twenty yards seemed to last forever.

'Welcome to the war, Caleb,' Finn did not move to speak to him, his voice was barely above a whisper.

Pulling himself above the natural ledge they had climbed to, he looked down on the huge plain below stretching far into the night. Unable to see the ground as night swallowed everything, Caleb could see the camp and cooking fires, the watch fires, sentry fires and pyres for the dead. They blanketed the ground like stars spreading to the horizon in all directions. The stars were separated in the middle by a yawning vacuum.

'That is no man's land. The two lines fight over that piece of bloodied ground. Sometimes weeks can pass without a battle then, in one day, thousands die as one army marches across to meet the other. There is a river running down the centre that traces out the border. It is up to that mark that the Empire has extended its reach. It has not managed to go further.'

'Do you remember this place?' Caleb asked, looking at what must have been hundreds of thousands of men below him.

'I do not have specific memories of this place, or of this war, but I know I have been here,' Finn struggled, at the point of retrieving a full memory. The feeling was only fleeting and soon Finn was unable to concentrate on what had suddenly been so close.

'That smell. It smells like rotting bodies.'

'It is. The smell lingers in the air, it stains the soil and the trees. That smell will be here long after the fighting has finished.'

The moon began its ascent, its crescent a bright slice in the blue night sky. The light glistened off tent tops and spears in a gentle flowing sparkle.

'It is beautiful, is it not?' Finn asked.

'It is,' Caleb replied, taking in the huge expanse of lights. It had a narcotic effect on him as he was so used to the closed environment of the forest and mountains. When he had been on the war parties to the south they had still had to remain close to the forests so they could retreat quickly when the enemy arrived in numbers.

Finn pulled himself under the tough gorse and heather, waiting as the young warrior followed him. It would be an uncomfortable night but it guaranteed cover in the morning.

'You will not think it so beautiful come first light,' Finn closed his eyes in simulation of sleep, letting the boy take the first watch.

I love the smell of decay in the night air, Finn, don't you?

'What do you want?'

To see how things are going, Finn, that is all, the daemon strode out along the crest of the hill staring down over the huge battle lines below. Finn followed his gaze and found that he could make out every soldier, even as far as the horizon.

'Things?' Finn watched as a soldier took a bowl of broth back to his seat, joining in the laughter of his comrades. They were due to attack at dawn and were filling their bellies beforehand. The man was more than two miles away.

Yes, things. Surely you do not think you were brought back just to instruct the whelp in the ways of war, Daemon was a part of the night.

'I told you before, I do not care what your reasons were. I saved the girl, now that crazy priest things I am the messiah.'

Perhaps you are, Feyn'leigh.

'Am I? Is that the role you would have me play?' Finn demanded.

You may play the role if and how you see fit, Finn. That is your concern.

'Why did you come here? To torture me with riddles and half-truths again?'

Yes, Daemon said simply.

Finn scanned the mountainside and back into the forest but could detect no sign of a patrol.

Fear not, Finn. There is no one near your position. They are cold camped in the far gully. They will not make their way here until late evening tomorrow. I suggest you be gone by then.

'We will be.'

Good, Daemon clapped Finn on the shoulder. *I would hate to think something might happen to you. Well, something that I was not solely responsible for.*

Finn woke Caleb from his sleep as the first traces of orange broke through the dawn sky. He watched as God was turning his canvas into a beautiful tapestry that no man could ever hope to match. Hues of purple faded to reds and orange, tinting with blue as dawn broke for real.

Caleb did not move, but merely opened his eyes inspecting for danger. Slowly he orientated himself and lifted his head.

'Look,' Finn directed, 'they are preparing to attack.'

Suddenly awake, Caleb watched as the plain below him became a frenzy of activity. The soldiers rushed to formation, cavalry was brought to bear.

'About five thousand cavalry, one thousand archers and fourteen thousand foot soldiers,' Finn cast his eye over the advancing formations.

'So many,' Caleb replied.

Some miles distant he could see the opposing troops rally into position. The cavalry advanced slowly, the infantry behind, bowmen had their arrows in place. The cavalry crossed the river without recourse, advancing unhindered on the enemy.

'Those flags,' he pointed to the coalition army, 'they are Ellistrin.'

'They are,' Finn agreed.

'The Legion,' Caleb said in wonderment. Gone was the leather over armour and camouflage. These Legionnaires wore polished armour and bright banners. 'They are the Legion armies that were caught outside the border when the invasion happened.'

'It would appear so,' Finn replied, concentrating on the drama unfolding before them.

'Why isn't the Legion doing anything?' Caleb asked the tension rising in his voice. He was excited.

'They are,' Finn said. 'Watch.'

The enemy and Ellistrin lines formed and reformed, grouped and regrouped. Setting the pieces on a chess board.

'Why aren't they attacking?' Caleb said as minutes drifted past.

'Because this is war Caleb, not a hit and run. The general will try and break the attack before it reaches him. If he can turn it he will have saved the lives of his men.

'Are they afraid to die?' Caleb was shocked.

'On the contrary, they are probably as headstrong as you. If they fall there is no one to replace them. This is war, Caleb. If the line falls, the enemy will overrun their position. It could be the beginning of the end for the allies.'

Caleb was silent as the Puritan army drew closer.

As the enemy cavalry passed some imaginary demarcation line the air became thick with death as the Ellistrin released huge static ballistae of fist sized rocks at the enemy.

The Ellistrin lancers let out a huge scream and charged as one causing the Puritans to falter slightly. The hesitation caused them to remain in the range of the ballistae too long.

Volleys of rocks smashed riders from their feet.

When they rallied enough to force their mounts through the barrage they were met with the raised Ellistrin lances ploughing into their lines.

The effect on the battle was immediate and conclusive. The Puritan cavalry was too far ahead of the infantry for them to help. Out manoeuvred, they tried to pull back. The Ellistrin lancers wheeled in formation and split into two wings closing on the flanks of the cavalry. Thinking they were penetrating the lancers' defence the Puritan cavalry bore down on the infantry only to find their numbers cut down by arrows as they approached.

Forced to turn back on themselves the cavalry was decimated as they tried to retreat through the Ellistrin lancers. In full retreat the Puritan cavalry lines were mixed with the advancing lancers. They tore into the lines of Puritan infantry leaving carnage in their wake.

Pushing through, the lancers headed straight for the reserve troop still camped to the rear. Forming a wedge they charged for the assembling troops and cut into them.

The two masses of infantry were now engaged in thick battle on the Puritan side of the river. After the brief contact with the reserves the Legionnaire Lancers wheeled and tore into the back of the Puritan infantry.

The fighting was dwindling as the entire Puritan force was in full retreat.

'Why are they not pushing on?' Caleb was exasperated. He was breathing as hard as if he had just fought the battle.

'Where would they go? Their allies did not advance with them. They are now isolated. They have no choice but to retreat.'

Caleb looked further down the border lines and saw that the armies on both sides had remained in place. Only the Ellistrin army had been attacked.

'They achieved nothing.'

'The enemy will not attack this point again. Not for a while anyway. This frontier will fall, Caleb. That is a statement of fact.'

'But it is so . . .' Caleb was at a loss.

'Futile? Did we not already discuss this? When the line falls no one will care that some poor soul lost his life defending his faith in God.'

'The Ellistrins have no fixed defences erected like the rest of the coalition,' he noticed.

'They do not want to be fortified in one place. It is their land that they are trying to get back to. The other coalition armies merely wish to hold the Puritans in place, away from their lands.'

'Damn it,' Caleb said.

'The lines will surely fall,' Finn instructed.

'Why?' Caleb asked. 'They have held for ten years.'

'Lines of defence exist merely to slow advance, not stop it entirely. The Puritans are putting in unseasoned troops or dissidents and criminals they want to kill off. They sacrifice their conquered allies. For each attack they lose nothing. The coalition forces lose everything.'

'It is such a waste.'

Finn merely nodded, watching as the Legionnaires pulled back in tactical formation to their own lines.

'Why do we bother? With any of it?'

'Because we are human, and born to err,' Finn said. The plain was carpeted with the dead from both sides though the Puritans had come off substantially worse.

Finn crawled back from the ledge and began to move back to the dense cover of the trees. Caleb remained rooted to the spot, watching as wounded were collected or finished off by their own side.

'Come, Caleb. Let's go home,' Finn said, feeling the sadness emanating from his ward.

'Home,' Caleb repeated the word as though savouring it.

Finn felt the young warrior's fresh resolve as he moved down the slope past him. The youth he had met months ago was being replaced by a strong young man.

'I will see that all my kinsmen come home,' Caleb said, 'or die trying.'

'I know,' Finn said, hoping it was not to be the latter.

Chapter Eighteen

Tobias had led his men straight to the nearest garrison town and resupplied. Taking a force of over a hundred infantry and cavalry he had prowled the lower rim of the great forest and engaged the enemy on two occasions when they had attacked a supply convoy. The battles had been brief and decisive, as all battles should be, the Knight thought to himself.

'Behead the corpses,' Tobias ordered the captain of the guard, pleased when the officer did not wince. The Knight had no time for the fainthearted. 'Let the bodies lie were they fell.'

'What would you like done with the heads, sir?' the captain asked.

'Collect them. I will bring them to Avalon as a gift to the Holy Father. It will show him what a superb job you are doing in his name when I present the heads of the Ellistrin heretics,' Tobias smiled.

'Yes, sir,' the captain saluted and went about his business.

That was how to gain favour and make a name for himself. If he was the talk of Avalon then he might be made the leader of the Temple Knights. Brood was going soft. Humility? Respect? These were the ways of the old Knights, not the new order. Tobias knew the path that the Holy Father intended for them and he was up to the task.

The purging of Ellistrin was only the first step.

'Send word to the garrison,' Tobias spoke to one of the lieutenants. He would not waste messaging services on one of the six Chosen that were with him. 'Tell that idiot commander that the threat in the lower forests has been eliminated. He can expect the main supply convoy within a week.'

The lieutenant saluted and left, pleased to be away from the Knight's company.

The Chosen looked at him, never questioning his decision but wondering at his breach of protocols.

'Do not worry,' Tobias reassured them, 'The commander will claim that he is responsible for the clearing of the lower forests, which are far from cleared. The convoy will be sent and attacked in force by the Ellistrins once the commander's loose lips send word straight to them.'

'And we will have them,' one of the Chosen said, smiling.

'And we will most certainly have them,' Tobias smiled and strode off to make sure that the decapitations were being carried out as ordered.

The Chosen looked at each other. It had been a brief but hard fought skirmish. Thirty of the Ellistrin scum were dead for fifteen Puritans, and that had been with the benefits of a careful ambush. It was now time to pray and thank God for delivering them through it.

Tobias had declined to lead them in prayer as was the custom after battle.

The Chosen were not pleased but then they could only take their lead from the Knight. They would ask the holy council for guidance when they returned to Avalon in the spring, but not before.

'Let us pray,' they began, and the Chosen lowered their head and sank to one knee, their swords before them.

Tobias watched the circle of the Chosen.

Frowning he wondered briefly if he should have led them and dismissed the idea. He would pray at the right hand of the Holy Father when the killing was complete in Ellistrin.

He would be exalted on his return and placed most high.

First the convoy. Bait. A lure for a sizeable attack. They would surely come in force for a wagon of food supplies. Perhaps they would not need them but they would surely try to keep them from the garrisons. Morale. Break that and you break the enemy. That is what the Ellistrins would be thinking.

Tobias would settle for merely breaking them.

*

Edom watched the young warriors busy themselves for the long haul south. Small rations load. They would have to travel fast. Edom had no doubt that he would be able to match them. Years in the mountains had given him an endurance that these young bucks could only hope to match.

'Pride cometh before the fall,' he warned himself.

The priest did not move when Ben sat beside him.

'I hear wind of an old priest who is travelling south with the war party,' Ben said at last.

'I hear word of an old warrior who wanted to go south with them, Edom replied.

'At least they are letting you go,' Ben sighed, watching the boys and young men who were preparing to go in his stead. 'I fear I am too old to be a warrior.'

Edom turned to see his friend's face. The lines of age were etched there but the eyes were still bright.

'I do not think you will ever be too old, you galoot,' Edom smiled and slapped his friend on the back.

'Where are you going?' Ben asked.

'I am to head south with the troop,' Edom said, he did not use the term war party. It was an archaic term from half a century ago when he and Ben had served as young warriors. Battle was anything but a party. 'After the ambush on the supply convoy I will head south, right to the capital. The townsmen have need of support from the north. They need guidance and strength.'

'And you can give it to them?' Ben asked.

'I can try,' Edom shrugged.

It was Ben's turn to appraise his friend. Edom was not the soldier he had once been, the athletic musculature was still there if worn on an old frame. He would not be fit for war now but he still had the burning strength of spirit that Ben had always admired.

'See that you keep safe, Edom,' Ben watched as Eli shouted rapid bursts of instructions to his men. 'He seems like a capable officer. Listen to him and stay close to him.'

'I shall,' Edom said as a young warrior approached and saluted.

'Well met, Father Edom, Benjad Ashoud,' Caleb said formally, touching his hand to his heart and bowing his head slightly out of respect.

'Do I know you?' Ben asked.

'This is Caleb,' Edom said smiling. 'I have not seen you for some time my boy, barely since I have returned to the mountains.'

'I have been busy training, father,' Caleb admitted. 'You can never train enough.'

'That is true,' Ben said looking the boy over. His hands were callused and strong. He was strong but there was a strange glint in his eye, like he knew something that others did not. Confidence that knew few bounds. 'I believe you have grown to be an excellent warrior of the Legion,' Edom said, pleased when he saw Caleb's chest swell with pride.

'I am now a warrior,' Caleb said. 'A man to make my father proud.'

Edom nodded. He had first met the boy on the night that his father had died in battle. The gangly youth had been replaced by the man he now saw before him.

'You are the talk of the day,' Edom added.

'That is not important,' Caleb said, 'I am ready to make my father, you and the Legion proud.'

'That is a noble thought,' Ben said still eyeing the youth carefully. The way he moved reminded him of someone.

'I made a promise a long time ago that I would be the greatest warrior the Legion has ever seen and lead them to victory. I plan on living up to that promise.

Edom nodded. He had been there when the promise had been made in the form of a prayer to his father.

'You remind me of someone,' Ben said at last. 'Though I cannot think who.

'A warrior I hope,' Caleb said smiling.

The two men eyed the boy curiously.

'You seem different,' Edom ventured.

'I am not the boy I was,' Caleb admitted. 'My training has taken me beyond that.'

'So I believe,' Edom said. 'You were selected for this mission because of your startling improvement. Captain Eli himself asked for you to join his troop.'

'I will not let him down,' Caleb replied.

'I do not believe that you will,' Edom said.

A strange silence followed.

'Do you have something else to tell us?' Ben asked, when Caleb did not move away. Even when the captain gave the order to muster.

'I bring word of a mutual friend,' Caleb said softly.

'Which friend is this, boy, for I have few?' Ben asked directly.

'A scarred man, friend to us all,' Caleb explained in hushed tones.

The men exchanged furtive glances.

'Is he well?' Edom asked.

'He is,' Caleb assured them. 'He teaches me in the ways of combat and strategy. He is very gifted, as you know.'

'That he is, boy, but do not get yourself too far into things that you do not understand,' Ben's voice was that of the sergeant he used to be.

'Your loyalty is to the Legion, not a stranger.'

'He is no threat to us, sir, as well you know,' Caleb stood firm. 'He merely wished me to impart to those that he trusted that he is well.'

'We thank you,' Edom replied. 'Give him our love and tell him he is in our thoughts.'

'I shall, Father,' Caleb nodded, looking over his shoulder to see that his troop was ready to go.

'Has he ever spoken of the prophecies? The Messiah prophecies?' Edom asked hopefully.

'I have heard the stories,' Caleb answered, 'before I went looking for him. He is a warrior. He prays every day and I with him. I do not know if he is the Messiah, but I would follow him should he choose to lead us.'

'Beware of blasphemy, Caleb,' Ben said, lacking sincerity.

'I did not say I would follow him because he claims to be the Messiah, merely because I think he would be an able general.'

'Your sergeant is looking for you,' Ben replied.

Caleb turned to see Pol shouting and bellowing at the lines of men. Seventy Legionnaires would be making haste for the supply routes to attack and retrieve wagon supplies, burning what was left. The garrisons would not get its much needed stores.

Pol saw the young warrior and shouted, the veins standing out on his neck and forehead.

'Yes, Sergeant,' Caleb replied, 'I am coming.'

Pol saw that he was talking with Edom and waved his indifference letting them continue.

'We will talk more of this on the way south,' Edom said to the young warrior.

'Perhaps,' Caleb said, 'but I think our hands are going to be busy with battle, Father, perhaps you could spare a prayer for him instead.'

'I shall,' Edom agreed.

'As shall I,' Ben added punching Caleb slightly on the shoulder guard. 'Perhaps even one for you, little man.'

Caleb smiled and he blushed as he saw Erika.

'Why are you wasting your time with us old folk, when you could be saying good bye to that doe eyed female?' Ben asked.

'It is not for your good looks and charm anyway,' Edom countered, receiving a withering look for his trouble.

Caleb did not go to the arms of his love, if his love she was. They had never spoken of making their relationship one of courtship, though Caleb guessed that she might now accept him. Something he would have to remedy when he returned.

'Come on, son,' Edom whispered, 'before Pol makes an example of you.'

Caleb waved and smiled when Erika returned it, blushing at the cat calls it raised from the other gathered warriors.

Ben smiled. It was always so when the young went off to battle. And the old, he corrected himself, remembering that Isela would have been here seeing him off had he been accepting by General Corbin for the mission.

Isela would have understood. She always had.

*

Weeks passed and Finn felt health return daily.

He had plenty of time to hunt and train in the time that Caleb had been gone. He had grown increasingly fond of the boy and knew it was not a bond he had shared with many others in his life. He found that he missed him. Finn's legs burned with exertion as he drove himself harder every day.

While vitality eluded him strength and power flowed.

As he breached the final slope his thoughts drifted again to his missing companion.

He hoped that the smell of burning was not an omen for the boy.

Finn had smelled the smoke long before he was in sight of the cabin. Moving quickly, but with added caution, he stalked toward the clearing. He had encountered no sign of a patrol as he completed one full circuit of the area.

Caleb would not have lit the fire though he was due to return from his skirmishing soon. Any day now in fact. Finn knew, however, that it was not Caleb.

Whomever had lit the heart fire had not tried to burn the cabin down which was promising, he thought. Easing himself forward he studied the surrounding trees and the dirt in front of the steps to the rough porch. Only one set of prints. Small. A woman?

Loosening his sword and dagger under the cloak he strode to the front of the cabin, stopping short of the door.

'Show yourself ' he said loudly enough to be heard within.

'Finn!' Erika's voice called as she ran from the cabin.

'Erika? What's wrong? Where is Caleb?' Finn demanded, knowing everything was not well.

'Caleb has been taken, Finn,' she ushered him inside where she had been preparing rabbit stew. 'His troop had been ordered south to attack a convoy. They were to ambush it and burn it but it was they who were ambushed. Most died but some were taken alive. A couple escaped.'

'Caleb?' Finn stared out the door, no emotion registering in his voice or on his face.

'I do not know,' Erika searched Finn's face.

'Where are they?'

'They have been taken to the garrison town of Lanyon,' Erika explained.

'How many men in the garrison?' Finn asked.

'I do not know. Hundreds?' Erika half guessed. 'But that is not all. The ones that made it back say that it was one of the Temple Knights that led the ambush.'

Finn still did not react. He had guessed that the daemon intended for him to fight one of the Knights.

'How many were taken?' he asked.

'Twenty they think,' Erika replied 'Legionnaires. And the priest. Father Edom.'

Finn winced when Edom's name was mentioned.

What trouble had the old fool gotten himself into now?

'Damn him,' Finn seethed before asking a question to which he already knew the answer. 'No rescue?'

'No,' Erika explained. 'We cannot commit enough men to the action without compromising them. The generals have advised the council that it would be foolhardy as all the garrisons are probably on alert for just that reaction.'

'Wise counsel,' Finn agreed, 'they are right. Still, we cannot leave your young buck to die, now can we?'

He stormed across to the makeshift table bringing the lantern Erika had left lit on the stove. Rummaging through the prepared papers and cloth maps, Finn took bearing on how to get to the garrison. Throwing some dried meat and roots into his pack Finn gathered up his weapons and brushed past Erika. His long strides were already carrying him across the clearing as Erika ran out onto the porch after him.

'Finn. You can't do anything,' she shouted after the rapidly departing figure. Finn did not turn but seemed to quicken his pace. Erika ran after him.

'Finn, you do not know if he is alive,' she pleaded. 'You cannot do anything.'

'He is alive. That is enough,' Finn kept his eyes on the path before him, Erika was running to keep up.

'How do you know?' Erika asked.

'I would know if he were dead' was all Finn said.

'They would not send men from the camps, you cannot save him on your own, Finn,' Erika pleaded.

'Then I will die trying,' Finn spat the words. 'Return home. Tell your commanders that you have seen me. Tell them I have gone to do what they would not. Tell them to send troops south with medical supplies and rations. Enough for twenty men.'

Erika stopped and watched as the warrior strode through the forest.

The trees themselves seemed to ease out of the way of his angry steps.

Messiah

Chapter Nineteen

Finn avoided both the Ellistrin and Puritan patrols easily as he pressed south from his mountain sanctuary. His journey was made more difficult as he did not have the luxury of being able to move only at night.

If he were too late, his young friend and the priest would not survive the week. Dressed in the armour Caleb had given him, he was fully laden with as many implements of death as he could secrete about his person. The only thing he had not managed to bring was the long bow as it would be too difficult to hide.

The trees thinned and the air became noticeably warmer the further Finn travelled from his home at the edge of the glacier. He knew it was relative and that it was still dangerously cold. Only the heat generated by his constant marching created enough heat to prevent the onset of hypothermia. Eating on the march Finn had maintained a fast pace although he knew he was tiring.

Fatigue could kill him as surely as an enemy but he had no choice.

His progress had been slower over the last few hours as Puritan activity had increased. He was in the heavily patrolled garrison line now.

In the distance he could make out a patrol of some thirty cavalry as they herded cartloads of civilians towards what was presumably one of the garrison towns.

Lanyon, by his estimation.

For the public executions?

Finn changed course to intercept the throng as it broke the tree line onto the plain. The patrol did not notice him as he joined the mob of bodies and few of the crowd raised their eyes to acknowledge his presence. Those that did quickly averted their gaze.

Finn quickly adopted their submissive behaviour lest he attract unwarranted attention. He welcomed the opportunity to rest, or at least move at a more energy conserving pace. He hungrily ate at his remaining rations and listened to the murmurs around him.

'I hear they are going to execute twenty of our lads,' he heard one gruff voice whisper.

'I heard it was to be a hanging,' another replied.

Finn looked up to see who had spoken and saw only the old and infirm. Faces that were leathered by years in the mountains under extreme conditions. The young and able were all in the mountain camps. These were all that patrols could find.

'What do you think?' the gruff voice asked him.

Finn quickly lowered his face again, realising that he had invited the question.

'I try not to,' Finn answered softly.

'Do you think they will hang them?' the man asked.

'No,' Finn replied.

'Beheading then?' the man asked again.

'No,' Finn answered, unable to move away from the man in the tight crowd.

'What do you think will happen?'

'I think they will be rescued.'

'Rescued?' he heard a few around him snort.

'I would like to see that, stranger,' the gruff voice said. 'Who are you?'

'A friend,' Finn answered.

'A friend who sneaks into captivity from the forest when the rest of us would gladly escape the way you had come.'

Finn did not answer but his hand moved to his sword.

'Do not worry, stranger, we mean you no harm. I am Gault and I am sure that the blades you have concealed under your cloak are for a good use.'

'A good use?' Finn asked.

'This rescue you speak of,' Gault suggested in a whisper.

Finn quickly decided. Trust or flee. Fleeing would mean fighting now and no rescue attempt.

'I am Finn,' he answered, turning to look at the old man.

Gault might have been old but he looked like a hunter. His strong face and hands were not strangers to hardship. Finn remembered that each man of Ellistrin was a warrior or had been at some stage. Gault must have been good to have lived into his retirement unlike so many of his countrymen.

'Well met, Finn,' he said. 'Now, you mentioned a rescue.'

Finn looked out across the plain as they left the last of the trees behind them. This was the point of no return. Without the cover of the forest the cavalry would cut them down should they try to run. About a mile away he could see the large wooden and stone structure of staked battlements. The design was the same for all the garrison forts along the northern frontier. It would not withstand a prolonged siege and would not last a half day against any form of ballistae, but then it was not supposed to.

The Ellistrin did not have the capability to move siege machines unnoticed through the heavily forested mountains and did not have the manpower to hold the fort once it was taken. The secret of the garrison line was that reinforcements could easily be sent from the other garrisons only ten miles away. A full regiment could be on hand within a day. Hit and run was a much safer tactic. Prudence was keeping the battle alive and tying up much needed resources in the mountains and towns that would otherwise be in the front lines.

'A rescue would be a much happier end to the day than the execution of some young men, don't you think?' Finn asked as he took in the details of the surrounding countryside and the fort itself.

'It would,' Gault agreed. 'It is good to think of better times and happier outcomes. Do you think it might happen? Do you think the Legion will try to save them?'

'I do not know,' Finn replied honestly, 'but the battlements are well manned. They are prepared against such an eventuality. I think they hope it will happen, as it is doubtful a Legion force would be able to storm the fort.'

'It was too much to hope for,' Gault said sadly.

'That is why I am going to have to do it myself,' Finn said.

'Yourself?' Gault said aloud and received a withering look from one of the cavalry guards. 'How do you propose to do that?'

'Ah. That is the easy part,' Finn smiled at the old man. 'I am going to walk in and kill everyone I see.'

'Ha! That is good. I like a simple plan,' Gault said clapping Finn on the shoulder and showing him a sheath knife he had concealed under his own over cloak. 'Perhaps when the Messiah comes we will fight back to back and free all our people.'

'Perhaps, Gault. But for today, let us just concentrate on the killing.'

*

Eli tried to roll onto his side but the ropes held him in an impossible position. Blood gathered in his throat threatening to choke him and it was an effort to clear it. Several times he had gagged.

'Be strong,' he told himself. 'Never give the enemy the satisfaction of knowing he has broken your spirit.'

He repeated the sentiment to his men who lay close and asked them to pass it on. It was carved into the Wall of Counsel in the capital or had been before the invasion.

He wondered if the wall was still there.

Eli managed to open one eye. They would just have to be content that they had broken his body. The other eye was still sealed closed with dried blood. The beatings had been severe and he knew he was concussed. He saw the remains of his troop lying about him on the platform. Beaten men, awaiting execution. He had failed them all.

'I am sorry,' he managed to whisper. It still felt strange to speak. Eli had not uttered a word under the interrogation.

Tori, who had been beside him all along, managed to move closer to his face. Eli felt an incredible sadness settle on him when he saw the battered features of the only woman he had ever loved. He could not imagine the pain and indignity she must have suffered. The soldiers had surely taken her, the prize awaiting any of the female Legionnaires should they be captured. That was why they were renowned for their ferocity in battle.

'I am sorry,' Eli managed again.

'You have nothing to be sorry for,' Tori replied.

'Except for not giving me the money you owe me,' Saul said from behind him. Eli did not make the effort to turn and his only reply was to spit blood onto the deck of the platform.

'Rest easy, sir,' Saul said before rolling on to his back away from the couple. His breathing was ragged but at least he was still alive.

Eli closed his eyes and saw only the battle that had cost him nearly his entire troop. The ambush had been carefully set and while his men had reacted well they were cut down in a hail of crossbow bolts. The cavalry charge led by the Temple Knight had split the force in two and the sudden advance of the infantry had crippled their ability to react as a fighting unit. Eli had forced a rapid retreat but was cut off. He watched as the other section of his men were rallied by Caleb who saved the priest they were escorting south. The boy fought with venom and Eli was briefly transfixed on the carnage the boy was wreaking before him.

Eli had watched as the boy had cleaved a man clean in two.

Eli felt a sense of terrible loss when he remembered seeing Aaron fall. The young warrior was being pressed back by a couple of the Puritans. Aaron parried and thrust but his blade was turned aside. Eli grimaced as he watched the blade disembowel his young friend.

The sadness hung around him like a shroud. Soon they would all be dead. Eli could see the priest, Edom. He wondered what the priest was thinking. Was he afraid?

Eli doubted it. He was a brave old man. In his time as a warrior, Edom had developed something of a reputation. He now had a different reputation as a priest, though not any less deserving. Eli did not see the mantle of a terrible butcher resting easily on the old man's shoulders. Death would bring the release it so often promised.

Eli felt Tori tense when one of the guards stopped by her. Looking up he could just make out the markings of a commander. What must be the garrison commandant stood over her bound form and looked at her without speaking. Tori tried to roll into a protective ball away from him.

Eli focused on the man's sharp features. This must have been the bastard that gave Tori 'extra special attention.' Even the rage that burned in his belly could not give Eli the strength to break his bounds no matter how much his muscles bunched against them.

'Not so strong now?' the commander said, spitting on her before turning and strutting off.

'He is gone, my love,' Eli said, seeing her relax. He could not even protect her when she needed him. 'Soon he will not be able to hurt you anymore.'

Eli moved over beside her and lay there with his body touching hers.

Tori's breathing slowed as she passed out.

'Sleep, my love,' Eli cooed. 'We will be together again soon.'

He could not turn his face to see but he could hear the murmurs of the crowd. What were they thinking? Were they outraged at having to watch their countrymen slain? Did they want to rise up and sweep the Puritans from the garrison and begin the battle that would liberate the land? Eli guessed that they probably did. The strength of the Ellistrin spirit was never to be underestimated even in, what Eli knew from experience, would be an old crowd. Old, in Ellistrin, merely meant that you had survived your battles and were to be honoured.

Eli did honour them. He would not shame them by being weak and cowering before the Puritan scum. Eli took a deep breath and forced himself, through gritted teeth, onto his knees. A soldier kicked him in the chest, knocking him over. When Eli struggled to right himself the soldier was ordered away before he could kick him again.

'Come on lads!' Eli's voice was strong. 'Let's not give the bastards the satisfaction.'

The Legionnaires that could, and even some of those that did not think they were able, righted themselves and sat as proudly as they could on the stage. Eli watched as Tori struggled, and failed, to rise.

'Rest easy, my love. It will all be over soon,' Eli reassured her softly.

*

Yasin watched the civilians being herded in past him as he loitered inside the main gate.

'Hardly the job for a soldier,' he said aloud.

'No,' Reyes agreed as he cast his eyes over the people. There were now a few hundred gathered in the main compound. With only four hundred men garrisoned there it was not wise to invite so many potential enemies inside, despite their apparent age and disabilities.

'I have never liked executions,' Yasin said, his eyes straying to the large, raised platform at the far end of the compound.

'Nor I,' Reyes admitted. 'I do not think they are a useful tool in wartime.'

'Or in peace,' Yasin added.

'I think criminals should be executed,' Reyes said, now looking at the small figures on the platform. Even at this distance he could tell that they had obviously suffered during their captivity. 'In war it serves no purpose. They are being publicly killed as an example to the civilian population. It demonstrates what will happen if they give aid to the enemy.'

'You think it doesn't work?' Yasin asked.

'Would it work on you?' Reyes returned.

'Maybe,' Yasin was not sure.

'I doubt it my friend. These spectacles merely display our weakness. It says that we still fear the enemy. That they are still a threat. It shows our ability to torture and our lack of compassion for the population. They will never tolerate our presence while we massacre their kinsmen in cold blood. Every time we kill one like this we rally more men to their ranks. We harden their resolve that little bit more and lengthen the war.'

'What is wrong with you today?' Yasin asked. 'You are rarely this morose.'

'It has been a long month,' Reyes admitted, removing his helm and running his fingers roughly through his hair. 'I am tired.'

'Why didn't you say so?' Yasin smiled. 'I have just the thing.'

Reyes watched as his sergeant produced a spirit flask with a discrete flourish, lest the other officers take offence.

'Not appropriate,' Reyes said, accepting the offered drink, 'but appreciated nonetheless.'

'Good health.'

'Long life,' Reyes smacked his lips as the fiery liquid burned his throat and warmed his chest. He croaked.

Yasin laughed.

Reyes passed the flask back and watched as the Temple Knight Tobias strode across the platform, his black form seeming without shape in the overcast day. Reyes watched the way he moved, fluidly and with purpose. He moved with the grace of a shadow.

'I do not like to be around the Temple Knights,' Yasin said, following the lieutenant's gaze.

'They have their purpose,' Reyes said guardedly.

'What is that?' Yasin asked, touching the flask to his lips again. 'To strike fear into the heart of poor sergeants?'

'Among other things.'

'The lads who were at the ambush said they had never seen the like of the way he fought. From horse and on foot they said he just reached out and men died. They said he ran from corpse to corpse after the battle and beheaded them. Puritan and Ellistrin alike.'

'I heard this also,' Reyes said, shaking his head. 'It is disturbing.'

'That is an understatement,' Yasin put the flask away. 'I will be glad to get away from this place.'

'As will I, but we have been ordered to wait until after the executions.

'When will we leave?' Yasin asked. It would be up to him to make sure the men were supplied and ready to go.

'Tomorrow. Let the men rest and get the loss of Vorden out of their system.'

'They have been drunk since they got here,' Yasin mentioned. 'They work hard.'

'They are taking the piss,' Reyes observed. 'They want to see the executions. They could prove difficult on the journey south.'

'It would certainly not do to depend on their good favour.'

'Perhaps not,' Reyes replied.

'The boy,' Yasin pointed at the execution platform, 'He is said to have killed fifteen of our men in the ambush.'

'I heard,' Reyes replied. 'Exaggerated?'

'Most likely,' Yasin admitted. 'But then something sparked the story.'

'The longer they have them on display the longer the story survives,' Reyes said. 'Soon it will be taken as the truth but the number will have risen to twenty. I am tired of this.'

'We will be leaving soon,' Yasin reassured him.

'Beheading. Public executions,' Reyes tasted bile. 'It makes me sick. I will see about getting reassigned to home when we reach Plandor. Even the front line is better than this.'

'I hope you have room for another,' Yasin said, meaning himself.

'I always have need of a good sergeant,' Reyes smiled. 'And you will do until one comes along.'

Yasin laughed and jumped down from his perch, heading off in search of the men to give them their orders to be ready to move in the morning.

Reyes watched as his sergeant moved through the arriving crowd of civilian 'guests'. He watched as they marched in past him, their heads bowed in submission lest they be asked to join their comrades on the execution platform.

Reyes noticed one head in particular among the bob and heave of crowd but as quickly as he saw him he was gone. It was hard to tell from the stoop but Reyes was sure he recognised the man, Finn.

Reyes considered speaking to him, asking him in private what really happened to Vorden but thought better of it.

Vorden was gone, and best forgotten.

'Let the stranger live in peace,' he thought to himself and headed off to see about the horses.

*

The guards at the gate paid little attention to the rabble that was being marched into the fort. Those manning the ramparts leaned against their spears and chatted lazily. The peasants were no threat to them. The Puritans believed they had been sufficiently cowed through years of starvation and killing.

Finn ambled along with the crowd happier that Gault was no longer at his side. The old man was off spreading good cheer with those men he knew. Old comrades in arms. As they moved through the gate he ducked his head when he saw the man, Yasin, who had been to the cabin. Pulling his hood slightly tighter he slouched and hid his face as the sergeant passed him without recognition. He could not risk discovery at this stage.

And the other man. Reyes. Neither men reacted but he had felt the spark of recognition from Reyes. He would have to move quickly now.

Once inside the settlement Finn slipped quietly away from the milling crowd. He attracted no attention as he surreptitiously moved in the shadows seeking an entrance to the fort itself.

A soldier sat on a chair outside what looked like a doorway. He died quickly, his crumpled body landing in a heap before the stew he was eating landed on the soft earth beside him. Finn looked around quickly and eased inside.

Putting his back to the timber walls he let his eyes become accustomed to the dim light. Lamps lined the walls at intervals providing light but the air smelled stale and unhealthy, especially after his time in the fresh mountain air.

Finn breathed deeply and relaxed.

He could smell the sweat of unclean soldiers, the fiery nip of peppers that the soldiers used to spice their food and grease for weapons and saddles. Sounds drifted to him. Sounds of the crowd outside, of soldiers walking the ramparts above his head and footsteps coming from deeper inside the poorly lit corridors. Pressing his hands against the walls he could feel the top layers of the wood flake away. Much of the building was rotting timber and typical of the temporary way the garrisoned soldiers looked upon their mission here. At least it was dry. The pitiful construction was going to work to Finn's advantage in any case.

Picking a direction he was sure would bring him to the heart of the fort Finn moved off quickly hearing his feet squelch slightly on floors that were damp from poor drainage and lack of care. With his senses heightened through training and adrenaline he was prepared for the two unsuspecting guards as he rounded a corner. They were not so fortunate. Blinking in surprise one opened his mouth to challenge him. Finn palmed his face viciously, obliterating his nose and cheek bone. Both palms slammed into the guard's chest powering him into his companion. The second guard was thrown against the wall, the sword impotent in its sheath. Finn did not break stride, his knife flashed up under his enemy's chin, driving it in to the hilt and penetrating the brain. Placing his hand against the guard's forehead Finn pushed back and twisted the blade, dislodging it from the bone. There was a dull scrape from the knife and a thud as the corpse crumpled to the floor.

The guard with the smashed nose lay slumped against the wall. Conscious but fading. Finn slapped him in the face and jerked him upright by his mail shirt so they were eye to eye.

'The oil store. Where is it?' he demanded.

'Oil?' the guard replied, dazed and on the brink of passing out.

'For the lanterns, the defence pits. Where is the store?' Finn pressed, his voice low, the tone hard. Finn pinned the terrified guard to the wall by the throat, careful not to restrict the breathing or blood flow in case he passed out. The guard's vision cleared as he saw the tip of Finn blade hovering before his left eye. Blood gushed down his face and over his mouth, covering Finn's hand.

'D . . . down the hall. The bolted door,' the man's eyes were wide in anticipation of his death.

Finn did not disappoint him. The hand clamped shut on his throat bringing unconsciousness immediately and death moments later.

Dumping the bodies in the nearest alcove he headed for the store.

*

Edom sat at the back of the platform, his frail body emaciated and He looked around at the crowd that was gathering for the spectacle. His eyes moved in and out of focus giving the world pleasantly unreal feel. Edom's eyes were puffed and swollen from the beatings and he had lost a number of teeth. Looking at the younger men beside him he did not seem to have fared too badly.

'How are you, young Caleb?' he managed with some effort.

Caleb lifted his head slightly and had to turn it fully to see the priest. The priest blanched. One of the boy's eyes was completely closed from the punishment that he and the rest of the raiding party had endured. The face was swollen and black from the impact of fists and clubs, the imprints from knuckles adorned the forehead and cheeks of the young warrior. Caleb's lips cracked and fresh blood oozed out as the young man forced a smile. Edom was reminded briefly of Finn and wondered how the enigmatic man was faring. He hoped he had found the peace he was looking for.

'I am well, father. As well as can be expected,' Caleb hung his head back down like a puppet that had just had its strings cut.

'I don't suppose it will matter much longer,' Edom looked at the blocks before them to which the fifteen survivors would soon be bound and publicly beheaded.

Twenty had been taken. Five had died under interrogation. None had talked.

'No, father, I suppose it won't,' he did not look up this time.

'I would prefer if you called me 'Edom', Caleb. I came into this world a man and I guess that is the way I am going to leave it.'

'Was it all worth it, Edom?' Caleb was having trouble speaking through the pain and restriction of the broken ribs. He was determined to speak, to make the most of his last moments alive.

'Who is to say? I have enjoyed my life, tried to have influence with my people. I have touched and been touched by a lot of them, both good and bad. I will know if it was worth it when I meet my maker.'

Edom watched the Puritan soldiers patrol the crowd. They were the enemies of his homeland yet he could not hate them. They were boys, much like the young warrior he was soon to die beside. They were merely misguided. Was that the word he was looking for? Edom watched their young faces as they moved with purpose about their tasks. Proud soldiers in the service of their Emperor. Had he been born there Edom supposed he would have been as proud as they to serve their Emperor. Misguided.

No, he could not bring himself to hate them but he would just as readily have them all suddenly drop dead so that the Legionnaires could return home once more.

'Do you really think there is a God?' Caleb looked up again.

'I truly hope so. I need to believe in something Caleb. We all do. I am not afraid of the hardships of life, I am afraid of finding out I am wrong at the end of it all.'

'It is a matter of faith,' Caleb said simply.

'Ha!' Edom smiled, wincing at the pain that shot through his mouth. 'It is I who should be counselling you for the salvation of your soul, but they are welcome words nonetheless.'

'If the words hold merit then surely it does not matter who utters them.'

'You have a wisdom beyond your years young Caleb, or perhaps it is that I am too old now to tell.'

'Finn has been demanding in his education,' Caleb explained.

'I should like to have met him again, one last time, before I died,' Edom said sadly.

'I too,' Caleb said, coughing blood. 'It would mean that I would not be listening to you.'

'Nor I you, whelp,' Edom replied, smiling.

'It has been good to know you.'

'You too, young warrior,' Edom said softly.

'I do not know if I ever thanked you for your care after my father passed. I did not accept it as a warrior should. You made it bearable. I thank you for your time and words.'

Edom did not answer. He reached across, hands bound as they were, and touched Caleb's head. The boy was unconscious again.

Edom looked around him at the bound Legionnaires. They had all fought magnificently. The trap had been sprung with precision and audacity, something that even the seasoned garrison troops were not known for. Half the Legionnaires had fallen in the first minutes of the ambush at the river with more dying as the Temple Knight had ridden in with his cavalry. Edom shuddered at the thought. The Knight had looked like death itself as his black armour and cape had charged into the Legionnaire patrol.

The captain, Eli, had responded superbly as a veteran Legionnaire was expected to but Caleb had been the biggest surprise of the day. The young warrior had deftly beat a retreat and regrouped the surviving members of the patrol. Together they had fought a retreating line back into the trees and held fast, constantly reforming as Caleb bellowed instructions. Edom had been grabbed by the young man and pulled to safety, his body shielded by the now impressive warrior.

They had nearly managed to escape before the Temple Knight had engaged the line and pushed through, his whirling blades killing and hacking all before him. The objective had been to take them alive for information. They had not talked and five had died in the interrogation. They must have decided that more would be gained from an execution than revealed under further torture.

Edom closed his eyes. His own torture had been terrible. Had they not stopped, Edom knew he would have given them something if not everything they asked of him. He felt a deep guilt that he was not a stronger man.

'Let us pray, my friends,' he said aloud to the battered remnants of the patrol.

'What shall we pray for, Father?' Saul asked.

'Forgiveness?' Tori offered.

Edom pondered the question for a moment. Forgiveness was appropriate. Mercy perhaps. Enlightenment even.

'No,' he said at last. 'We pray for Deliverance.'

Chapter Twenty

Finn quickly found what he had come for. Ten large vats of oil for the lanterns and tar pits, which acted as the defensive perimeter, were stacked in one corner.

Picking up an axe from one of the racks he smashed holes in the vats allowing the oil to burst out and pool in the soft earth. Taking a staff, Finn dragged a furrow in the dirt to the far side of the storeroom, some twenty five feet away. Here, he set the flame in one of the lanterns and, breaking the protective glass, moved to the door. Glancing back he made sure the oil was moving along the furrow.

The hall was empty as he moved quickly up and into the main square again. He entered the courtyard without being challenged. Most of the guard detail was out of the building, either on patrol, on the battlements or guarding the gathering crowd.

At the far side of the square he could see the raised dais with the bound prisoners. He could make out Caleb and the priest just in from the end of the line. He was in time, they were still alive. Finn glanced about, checking the positioning of the soldiers. On the platform itself there were a couple of guards and the executioner. The sight of the dark Knight did not disparage him. Thoughts of the Knight caused memory to flicker but he could not focus on it now.

Frowning he stormed forward, pushing through the crowd. As he came through the line at the front he found himself ringed by soldiers.

None of them took any interest in the shabby, stooped, old man. The need to attack was on him but he quelled it. Surprise, speed and aggression. The three elements of a good attack. It would do no good.

He might kill some of the guards on the way to the dais but numbers would soon prove insurmountable. He had to distract the soldiers. The oil would do part of that but he needed the attention of the crowd. Surprise would have to be omitted from this plan.

He cleared the crowd and stepped to the front of the dais. No one paid any heed.

Just another pitiful local.

'Release the prisoners!' Finn bellowed at the top of his voice and rising to his full height.

The soldiers, momentarily caught off guard, recovered and raised their crossbows. The crowd gasped as one and moved back, unintentionally making Finn an easier target for the bowmen.

Gault stared wide eyed at the tall stranger and eased his knife from his sheath. Today really was a good day to die.

Finn held his ground and ignored the Knight. Instead he focused his attention on the garrison commander.

Tobias tilted his head slightly, curious at the stupidity of some people.

He made no move towards the man but signalled for the bowmen not to loose their bolts.

"And who are you?' the commander asked, his eyes moving left and right to ensure his men were moving to take up position. Secure that he was safe, his natural bullying came to the fore.

'Who I am is not important,' Finn replied, his voice as steel.

'I am Wendall, commander of this garrison. You are either very brave or very stupid to be making demands of me. Identify yourself?'

'Know this, Wendall, if you give the word for those men to die, I will see that you die first,' Finn said, and the crowd held its breath.

The commander blanched at the cold remark. There was no malice in the words, only the certainty of death. Aware of his men watching him he shrank from the decision.

'You expect us just to release these traitors?' Wendall stammered hoping for one second that they would all just get up and leave. He did not like the eyes of this stranger.

'You will release these men. I will take them with me when I go,' Finn said simply, his posture and voice calm and relaxed.

'Go? Go?' spluttered the commander, indignation being replaced by fear of what the Knight would do to him. 'You will not be going anywhere!'

'Shut up, fool,' Tobias said stepping to the front of the dais. 'Who are you?'

'I am merely a messenger,' Finn replied, feeling his heart beat quicken. At least it had not stopped. Tobias smiled.

'A messenger for whom?' Tobias asked.

'For God,' Finn replied. The Daemon had suggested he might be doing God's works. Was he now compounding his stupidity with blasphemy?

'Really,' the Knight's smile was pure menace. 'And what does the Almighty have to say.'

'Let my people go,' Finn smiled.

'Your people?' Tobias asked, looking the man up and down. Finn's thick full length cloak reached to his ankles. Tobias had no doubt Finn was armed under it but it did not concern him. 'Your people will be going nowhere, except hell. Release one and arm him.'

The Knight motioned to one of the guards who cut the binds on the nearest prisoner and handed him a sword. Unsure of himself at first the

Legionnaire dropped from the stage and prepared himself to meet whoever was sent against him.

Finn watched as the man moved his fingers subtly against the hilt of the sword, testing the balance. He was a seasoned warrior and did not want to reveal anything of his ability in the simple test swing of the blade. He knew everything he needed to know about the weapon, the only test remained to see how much he had left in his body.

The Knight himself stepped down from the stage and the Legionnaire smiled at the prospect of killing him. Die he might, but he would not die easy. Tobias did not draw his own sword and stood instead with his thumbs tucked in his belt.

The soldiers ringed Finn but allowed him a clear view of the spectacle.

'I have left it too late,' Finn thought. 'I have given them time to prepare. I should have attacked, not talked.'

Another voice calmed him, 'No, this is how it was meant to be. These words are important.'

Tobias watched the Legionnaire prepare himself and smiled widely. He was worried for a moment that he might actually laugh aloud, but that would not be seemly.

Tobias settled his mind and felt the power grow, railing against the confines of the disciplined mind, eager to be set free.

'Come then, little one, meet your fate at the hands of the faithful,' Tobias said as his hatred spilled out.

Flashing into deadly movement the Legionnaire launched himself through the air at the Knight only to collapse on the ground in agony as the power of the Knight's mind hit with deadly force.

Clutching his hands to his head, the Legionnaire tried to stop the pain that was threatening to cave his skull. Blood began to ooze from his eyes and ears finally spurting from his nose. The crowd watched as the horror unfolded before them. Even the Puritan soldiers began to move back when the screaming started.

'This is how God treats the unworthy. He has stood in judgement this day and demands the blood of the heretics,' Tobias prowled around the writhing form at his feet. 'You were not brought here today to witness the execution of your countrymen. You were brought here today to witness the hand of God. Judge for yourselves.'

Murmurs carried through the crowd, they were on the edge of panic. Tobias' rich voice reached the back of the assembled peasants.

'Executioner! Carry out the Word of the Lord!' Tobias spread his arms and bowed his head in a solemn gesture, his eyes mocking Finn. The Legionnaire slumped forward onto the ground.

The hooded axe man raised his huge double blade, hesitating for effect. Bunching his huge shoulder muscles he breathed out sharply to slice the razor blade through the deceptively tough necks. He was not even aware as the bolt punched through his skull under his ear killing him instantly.

Finn dropped the bow and was moving before it hit the ground. He threw a steel spike at the Temple Knight but Tobias drew his sword and swatted it aside easily. The soldiers moved for Finn but too late, he was already gone from their side.

Pandemonium erupted as did the oil vats and a large section of the compound, exploding in a shower of splinters and debris. The wooden structure was a huge torch billowing smoke into the sky. The fire engulfed the guards on the ramparts while splinters and burning oil alike brought down those close to it in the courtyard.

The crack from the explosion was still resounding in the square as Finn spun on his heel. A sword whipped from under his cloak and through the neck of the nearest soldier and, stepping back quickly, he slammed his dagger into the groin of the man next to him, severing his femoral artery. As the bodies collapsed, Finn raced forward through the confusion and leapt high, rolling onto the dais.

A bowman was ready to lose his bolt but Gault dissuaded him plunging his knife repeatedly into his neck and pulling him to the ground. Taking the bow, Gault fired at the nearest soldier hitting him in the stomach. Laughing aloud as he flushed with memories of his warrior youth, he pulled the sword from the dead man's scabbard and rushed to the battle. Seeing his example, others in the crowd screamed and made a rush for the nearest guards. Some died quickly but the sudden press quickly overpowered those soldiers closest to them. Soon the soldiers and Ellistrins were locked in battle.

The guards were not prepared for the ferocity of the old men they had only moments before thought to be sheep.

Rolling to his feet Finn's blade sliced up through the groin of another guard and punched through the throat of yet another. He hacked the hand off a soldier who made a lunge with a spear and beheaded him with one backhand swipe. Dropping quickly to one knee he severed the bonds holding Caleb to the block and pressed the hilt of the dagger into his hand.

'Come, boy, time we were going,' Finn said and was gone again his elbow crashing into the face of a burly soldier.

Without acknowledgement or thanks, Caleb took the dagger and moved purposefully to the next prisoner releasing him. Leaving the dagger with Saul he picked up a sword and launched his frail body into the fray.

'I am with you, my brother,' Caleb shouted as he parried a thrust and drove his own blade under the belly armour of the last guard.

'It is good to see you Caleb, you have not been eating,' Finn did not glance at his friend.

'No, sir,' Caleb replied, smiling at the ludicrous conversation. With Saul and another Legionnaire beside him, Caleb ran to engage the soldiers coming up the steps of the dais.

Wendall was forced back by the ferocity of Finn's attack. Pushing a guard in front of him Wendall was spared for another valuable second as Finn cut the soldier down in a flurry of steel. He continued to back away, straight into the arms of Tori.

'I told you I would kill you,' she whispered in his ear and drew her knife back across his windpipe causing bright red blood to froth from the opening. Wendall tried to struggle but she held him fast stabbing him repeatedly in the back. Tori continued to stab the corpse long after all life had fled. Exhausted, she fell back onto the platform, watching as Finn moved over the top of her, his blades cutting a swathe before him. She smiled at the image of death.

The Puritans were trying in vain to control the panicked crowd. They were trying to flee the flame engulfed fort but as many were now embroiled in the fierce hand to hand fighting beside the platform.

Eli rallied the Legionnaires and, though exhausted, began a retreating battle from the dais. Reinforcements were rushing to meet them.

Order was impossible to restore now as the fire spread rapidly to the surrounding buildings and the soldiers fought for their lives. The fort could always be rebuilt. Only their stone foundations would remain after being ravaged by the fire.

Black and grey smoke hung thickly in the square, it was difficult to see more than a few feet.

'People of Ellistrin! Listen!' Finn's voice cut through the smoke like a strong wind. 'Choose to live or die this day! You can live as a people or perish. The choice is yours and yours alone! Join us! Fight for your freedom! '

Eli and his men screamed a battle cry in response, which was taken up by Gault and his comrades and soon the whole square.

The crowd moved with purpose now, trying to get to the gates, which were still barred. Through the smoke they looked like a sea in a storm. A storm that soon became uncontrollable.

The soldiers, outnumbered and outclassed, could not contain the substantial numbers they had brought into their midst and opened the already burning gates. The crowd were more afraid of burning and fled the fort as did many of the soldiers. The fighting followed them but the poorly armed civilians did not fare so well in the open ground against the better equipped garrison troops. They still died hard though and many of the enemy would follow them into the afterlife.

Finn dropped his cloak and jumped from the stage. Spinning in the air he dropped behind two soldiers, his short sword cleaving down behind collar bone, piercing lung and heart. Rushing into the smoke he headed for the Knight who was ringed with corpses of both Legionnaire and civilian. Blood was splattered across his face and helm giving him a demonic expression against the backdrop of the flames.

'Come heretic. Time to die,' Tobias shrieked, stalking to meet the scarred man that dared challenge the power of God. Feeling the rage grow he uncoiled the power that nestled deep within him. It sprang forth with a will of its own, seeking to kill and destroy anything before it. The rage reached out to touch the mind of the heretic and withdrew as if stung.

Finn smiled.

'How?' Tobias' mind whirled. It was inconceivable that any man might stand against the power of the Knights. Incredulity was quickly replaced by fear. 'Who are you?'

'I am Death,' Finn's sword thrust through the neck of the momentarily paralysed Knight. Finn stared at Tobias for a moment wondering what he saw in the dying man's eyes. Fear? Sorrow? Recognition?

The slight squeal sounded very loud as the steel of the honed blade scraped bone when Finn withdrew it from the Knight's neck. The arterial spurt lanced high and hit the ground, mixing with the already stained soil. Time seemed to move slowly as the he watched the body topple to the side and bounce slightly on the soft ground.

Finn raised the blade once more and decapitated the corpse.

'Misguided,' Finn said, as Edom arrived at his shoulder.

'Lost,' the priest confirmed, staring at the impossibility of a slain knight.

Edom's legs gave way and Finn caught him gingerly.

The sound of the cracking timbers came slowly back to him. The smoke was overwhelming and his lungs worked hard to function as the thick cloud billowed up into the sky. He could hear coughing close by and turned to see that the fighting had stopped. Most of the assembly had seen him defeat the Knight with apparent ease. The uneasy calm was not certain, the soldiers still had not dropped their weapons, merely paused. Finn had to act now before they regrouped. The civilians would be no match for the soldiers if they organised. The benefit of surprise was now over.

'Listen to me! Listen to the words of your own Temple Knight!' Finn shouted. 'God has indeed stood in judgement this day! '

Caleb and Eli rallied the remaining Legionnaires and prepared to move out. Only ten remained alive.

'Soldiers of Saladin, your fort is destroyed,' Finn continued when he saw that the soldiers had made no move. He had to keep the momentum going. 'Leave this place now, let no more blood be shed here today. If you choose to fight, you will join this wretched Knight in death.'

Finn hoisted Tobias' head up by the hair and threw it towards the soldiers. With the commander dead and no one to lead, the soldiers were torn between the blood lust and the desire to flee the field of battle. The head of the Knight made the decision for them.

*

Reyes was the only officer to react.

'Sheath arms. Prepare for withdrawal. Yasin! Take some men and fill as many canteens and barrels of water as you can' Reyes started barking out orders.

When the men did not jump to, he grabbed one of them and shoved him into action.

'Sergeants to me! Take the ram and clear the gate, get any wagons that did not go up in the blaze, see if you can salvage any rations from the store, get patrols out and round up those damn horses. Have the fallen checked and any wounded stretchered to the southern field. Move! Double time it! Regroup at the southern field. I want every man present and correct and ready to travel. Get as much supplies as you can from the fort before we go.'

Yasin took up the shouting and soon the soldiers were moving, casting fearful glances over their shoulders at the tall warrior.

Reyes turned and met Finn's gaze. Walking the short distance between them he stopped and took stock of the man who single handed had reduced the garrison to rubble.

'It is good to see you again, Finn, you are looking well.'

'I have seen better times,' Finn replied.

'As have I,' Reyes looked at the headless corpse of the Knight. 'I did not think they could be bested in battle.'

'He was just a man and any man can be bested,' Finn replied without moving. The Legionnaires were already pulling out, though through injury, their pace was not prodigious.

'Perhaps. I was unsure how you managed to kill Vorden and his men,' Reyes gazed at the fallen Knight. 'I guess now I know.'

'That was unavoidable, as was this,' Finn replied.

'Unavoidable?' Reyes asked.

'Yes,' Finn confirmed. 'I offered them a peaceful way out. They did not take it. They brought me into their war. I wanted no part of it.'

Reyes searched the steel grey eyes of the tall warrior for any sign of mockery but found nothing. Nothing at all. Finn sheathed his sword and Reyes followed suit.

'You saved many lives today,' Finn said.

'I saved your life today, had we regrouped, you would all have been slain.'

'But you did not regroup,' Finn reminded him, daring him to reverse his decision.

'No,' Reyes stroked his chin musing the situation.

'Perhaps it was God's will,' Finn offered.

'I doubt it, Finn. It is the actions of men that concern me. I do not try to understand the way of God.'

'He certainly moves in mysterious ways,' Finns hands rested easily on his hilts. He looked completely composed.

'Yes, I suppose he does,' Reyes still had a perplexed look on his face.

'Is there something I can help you with?' Finn asked checking that most of the crowd had dispersed. Soon they would be alone.

'Who are you?' Reyes asked.

'I am no one of consequence,' Finn turned to walk towards the gate.

Reyes stood in place and watched the warrior leave the fort.

'Who in the name of God is he?' Yasin asked.

'Who, in the name of God, is right,' Reyes replied.

*

Brood was the last to appear in the spiritual chamber. The remaining seven Temple Knights sat around the fire awaiting their leader. The room seemed strangely cold and Brood wondered why. The chamber merely reflected the emotions of the Knights who were present.

Did they feel fear?

'Tobias is dead,' Nathan began, when Brood indicated for the meeting to begin.

'I know,' Brood said, flatly.

'How did it happen?' Brace asked.

'We do not know. As with you, we felt his fear, then nothing. He vanished.'

'So we are not sure if he was killed or not? He could still be alive!' Brace exclaimed.

'Settle yourself, brother. He is dead,' Brood assured them.

'He was killed in battle,' Nathan said.

'He was in the northern garrison towns. The Lord Saladin requested that we reconnoitre the northern forest region before we press into the mountains to deal with the surviving Ellistrin Legions.'

'So he was killed in a skirmish with the heretics?' Brace asked. 'I find that hard to believe.'

'Hard to believe or not it happens. We are merely mortal, my brothers, and our Lord God can claim us at any time. I look forward to the day when he claims my soul to stand at his side.'

'As do we all, brother,' Nathan said, bringing nods from the rest of the Knights.

'Good. I am not concerned that Tobias is dead, I am more concerned with what caused him to feel fear.'

'Are you sure it was fear?' Madre asked.

'Do not seek solace in false answers, my brothers. We all know he felt fear and was then killed,' Brood said. 'We must embrace this and set ourselves to face this enemy, not hide from it.'

Brood watched as the others muttered among themselves. Only four remained of the six Knights that had been despatched to Ellistrin. Himself included. There were only ever twelve Knights at any time. Talan's suicide, then Joshua and now Tobias, with no indication as to what had happened to either of them. Both lost in this land of no consequence. The sooner their mission was completed here, the land vanquished and the army rolled across it wiping out everything in its path, the sooner he would be able to return to quiet contemplation in the Temple.

The sin of greed.

Banishing such selfish thoughts from his mind Brood tried to get back to the task at hand. He was a tool of the Lord and his whole existence was to serve His Word, in battle or in prayer. It was not his choice.

'Perhaps he was not as prepared for death as a Temple Knight should be,' Madre suggested.

'That is a possibility,' Brood said, accepting the argument. Tobias was certainly less disciplined than his brothers.

'What shall we do, brother?' Nathan asked.

'I am on my way north to the garrison towns. I will find where our brother was slain and see for myself what came of him. I will call to you when I have found something.'

'In the meantime?' Brace asked.

'I believe something is happening to the north. Lord Saladin has directed our attention there and it is most probably for a good reason. One that he does not wish to share with us as yet. We shall prepare for battle, in the name of our Lord God. If he is willing, we will live to fight for him again another day. If we do well enough he may let us die, and claim us as his own, to fight at his side in the next life.'

'Amen,' the Knights replied as their spirit forms faded from the room.

*

Finn pressed his party steadily through the now dense forest, eager to outdistance any pursuit. On foot and with so many gravely injured people it would be an effort at best. If they were pursued and caught it would likely be a massacre and a short one at that.

'His party,' Finn thought, shaking his head. He did not know at which point he had accepted responsibility for the band that now made its way north.

Finn had ordered as many civilians as could make the journey gathered up and brought with them. The reprisals after the sacking of the garrison would be terrible. The pace was slow but once they had made it deeper into the forest the likelihood of attack diminished.

Many of the Legionnaires were being stretchered by the now beleaguered refugees and rest stops, though unavoidable, were frequent.

Saul was up ahead as scout. Finn could sometimes make out his form moving through a break in the trees. He was a capable woodsman and scout who had fought well back at the fort. Now, however, his wounds were severe and his movement somewhat disjointed and slow. He would not accept a rest that the others did not take and would not be carried.

'Pride is a terrible sin but a formidable ally,' Finn thought, the words as spoken by an old man hidden in his memory. He tried to concentrate but the whole image would not surface. Frustrated, he gave up trying.

Finn glanced back down the line of about one hundred men and women. The only children were infants and were being carried by the mothers. He could see the strange looks they were giving him. A look that appeared to be generated by awe. The Legionnaires who could still walk were at the back of the column forming a rear guard should the enemy track them.

Finn saw that Gault was with them, as were many of the old warriors. Gone was the stoop and the years of oppression. Gault looked about twenty years younger and smiled to prove it.

'How is the priest?' Finn asked Caleb as the young warrior made his way past.

'He is alive,' he replied through gritted teeth, 'as are we all, thanks to you.'

Edom was being stretchered and had not woken since passing out at the fort that morning. It was uncertain if he would make the journey north alive.

'You are in pain,' Finn observed.

'It is nothing,' Caleb replied.

Finn stopped him and pressed his ribs through the armour they had stolen from the bodies at the fort. Caleb winced.

'Nothing,' Finn confirmed. 'It will be dusk soon. We will make camp and I will tend to you.'

'There are others who need attention more,' Caleb said.

'Then I will tend to them also,' Finn said as he moved to where Edom was being carried past. Taking the unconscious priest by the hand he whispered a small prayer to him as he walked along beside him.

'You are fond of the priest,' Caleb said.

'I am,' Finn replied. 'He is a kind and wise old man.'

'He is,' Caleb agreed.

Finn let the priest go and continued walking alongside the advancing column. He opened a small sack and began to pluck at flowers and pieces of bark as they picked their way slowly up the slope.

'For medicine,' Finn answered Caleb's quizzical look.

'How did you know to come for us?' he asked.

'Erika came to the cabin looking for me. I came as quickly as I could,' Finn said, setting some berries into the pouch.

'Erika,' Caleb said, savouring the name as though he had not heard it before. 'I did not think I would ever see her again.'

'Nor she you,' Finn said. 'I am sure she will be pleased, though I do not know why. I find you bothersome at best.'

Caleb was offended until he realised he was being baited.

'I try,' he said simply.

'Try harder,' Finn replied.

Finn carried out the logistics of their forced march in his head. They had no provisions, no shelter, no weapons fit for hunting and no time to set snares. They had no time to cook any game anyway in case they were being pursued. It had taken three days to get to the garrison from the mountains. It would take Erika two days to get to the camp. If they believed her they could expect help by tomorrow or the day after. They had to keep pushing north.

'What will you do when we get to the mountains?' Caleb asked.

'I will bid you farewell,' Finn said, sadly.

'Where will you go?' Caleb asked. 'I doubt you can disappear back into the mountains. The council will send out patrols until they find you. You sacked a garrison single handed and saved Legionnaires who were to be executed. They will not stop until they find you.'

'They will not find me,' Finn said confidently.

'What of the Puritans? You are now a marked man in their Empire. I would be surprised if there is not already a full company on our trail. West is definitely out of the question. As for east, it would mean travelling across the border, which is now one big front line. We send scouts across with intelligence. Many of them die. Even if you made it, it is probably only a matter of time before the lines collapse and the Imperial army rolls across the whole continent.'

'I go where I please, Caleb,' Finn said simply, closing his now full pouch.

'I know that you do. Surely there are other options.'

'What would you suggest, Caleb?' Finn asked idly, knowing what was coming.

'No matter where you go you are going to end up fighting,' Caleb offered. 'Why don't you stay with us? Fight with us against our common enemy.'

'You have all the guile of a diplomat, boy,' Finn said sarcastically and regretted it, not wishing to hurt his already injured friend.

'I did not profess to be, nor wish to be, a politician,' Caleb said. 'I am a Legionnaire. A warrior of Ellistrin. I want what is best for my people.'

'As do we all,' Eli said as he joined the two men.

'Forgive me, sir,' Caleb said, 'I was just saying….'

'I know what you were saying,' Eli replied. 'Pray continue.'

'I was saying to Finn that we have need of warriors such as he.'

'That is true,' Eli agreed leaning heavily on a staff. His injuries were such that he needed it to support him.

'It was just luck in the fort, boys, don't kid yourselves that it was anything different,' Finn said, sternly.

'Luck that we could be doing with,' Eli remarked. 'But you must make your own decision, warrior. I am beholden to you for saving my life and that of my men. I will respect your decision whatever it may be.'

'Come north with us to the camps, sir,' Caleb asked again. 'We can face our enemy together.'

'They are not my enemy, Caleb.'

'They will hunt you down and kill you. How does that not make them your enemy?' Caleb asked.

'They are soldiers obeying orders. I do not hate them. They are not my enemy. It is the orders that are wrong, the people issuing the orders, not the soldiers.'

'Then help us stop the people issuing the orders,' Caleb demanded.

'How would you suggest I do that?' Finn wiped a hand across his brow. His skin felt as though it was under attack from insects. The pores were not allowing him to sweat properly.

'Fight with us, Finn. Lead us. Help us rid our land of the oppressors,' Caleb pleaded.

'Fight the good fight. Die standing and not on your knees,' Finn glanced back, checking the group was still together. 'I have heard many such call to arms. Do you believe in what you are fighting for Caleb?'

'Of course!' he answered indignantly, drawing glances from the rest of the party.

'So do the young men we fought this morning. These Puritans. They are young impressionable boys, much like you. Much, I think, like I might have been. They would consider you to be in the wrong, and they in the right. You both believe the one true God is on your side, when in reality, he is on neither. He is a voyeur in this great drama we faithfully create for him. He does not care who is right and who is wrong.'

'And you, sir, do you care?' Eli asked.

'No, I suppose I don't,' Finn replied.

'Then join us in the mountains,' Eli suggested. 'At least for a while. The men you saved today will wish to show their gratitude.'

'I do not need their thanks for doing the right thing,' Finn said.

'Maybe not, but it is our way,' Eli smiled. 'We will drink and sing songs and eat. It will be a feast. Eh, Pol?'

Pol heard the mention of feasting but still could not manage a smile. He had received a cracked jaw while being beaten. Touching his hand to his heart he nodded his agreement.

Finn walked in silence for a while and the others followed each lost in thought. Edom would want to see him. It would be good to see Lauren and her family again.

'I will journey with you to the mountains and meet with your people,' Finn said at last. 'I will offer to fight with you and accept their judgement.'

Caleb smiled broadly.

'They would welcome you, Finn, as I have,' Eli said.

'We shall see,' Finn replied, aware that if Daemon were here, he would no doubt be smiling.

Coming in

REVELATIONS

The Finn Chronicles

Book II

The priest is not going to make it. You saved that brat boy, but you could not save the crippled old man.

'Leave me alone,' Finn snapped. It was long after dark and he was tired. He had not slept now for over four days and was drained, emotionally, physically and now spiritually. Days since he had risked all to save Caleb from execution. Days since he had surrendered to whatever the fates had in store for him. His path was marked out before him.

Pain.

Atonement.

Redemption?

Anger is one of my very favourite emotions, Finn. So much good work is done in my name, during . . . anger.

'I am tired, Daemon. Leave me be,' Finn replied.

Come now, you do not still think you control your own destiny. You are merely a tool of my choosing. You serve me. That is your whole purpose of being.

'Then be on your way and let me get on with it.'

Now, that is not being nice.

Finn ignored the daemon and looked around the clearing. He had ordered fires to be lit and broth made. Eli had protested but Finn had insisted, stating that many would die in the frosty night if they did not. Eli had relented but was not happy. Finn, and a few civilians on sentry duty, were now the only ones who remained awake.

Finn had made a foul smelling broth from the medicines he had collected on the journey and everyone had taken some. Most, however, had been given to the more severely injured Legionnaires. They all slept now in a tight circle around the main fire. Finn sat cross legged at the centre of that circle oblivious to the heat from the fire.

Before the daemon had interrupted him, Finn had relaxed and, during meditation, had let his spirit flow out from him. He touched the minds and bodies of those around him in much the same manner as he had with the wolf.

Finn's touch did not hurt. Nor did it kill. Instead he healed. He could feel the pain coming to him in waves at the centre of the circle and he accepted it, welcoming it into his own body. He nurtured the pain and let it stay with him. Slowly, and only when he could take no more, he began to break down the pain inside himself, healing his own body of the pain.

Exhausted from the effort he was depleted when the daemon came calling.

'They will all live, Daemon, there is no one for you here this night,' Finn said.

I know when souls are crying out for me to feed on them, do not seek to warn me. Count yourself lucky I am in a good mood.

'Your moods are fickle at best,' Finn replied.

They are, Finn, so watch your tongue or I will direct the pursuing troops to your position or have a rabid bear pay a visit.

'What do you want?' Fin asked.

To be a pest, isn't that right, priest?

'Finn,' Edom said weakly without opening his eyes.

'I am here, old man,' Finn said softly.

Kill him, Finn. If you love him that much, end his suffering.

'Who is with you?' the priest asked.

'I am alone,' Finn answered.

'You are not alone. Is that the daemon with which you speak?' asked.

'It is,' Finn acknowledged and watched the priest make a subtle, protective blessing.

That will not protect you, Father, the daemon spoke, hissing at the priest, making the heart spasm in his chest. *You are mine as are all here I can claim you at any time.*

'But not now,' Finn's voice was as iron.

No, Daemon replied, letting go his grip on the old priest. *Not now.*

'You are not welcome at this fire, daemon,' Edom said as he fought for breath against the pain in his chest.

I am not welcome in many places, Daemon laughed, *yet I go where I please.*

'What is your business here?' Edom demanded.

I merely wish to see my champion and thank him for all the fresh souls he sent me this day.

'He is not your champion,' Edom corrected.

Any man who sends me fresh souls is my champion, father.

'Finn is on the side of good, ' the priest said.

So sayeth the faithful, Daemon said smiling. *You see Finn? You see why they tire me so? They can justify anything to themselves. How I love the little talking monkeys.*

'Leave us be, Daemon,' Finn said, as he lay down to rest.

I will because it suits me. You are doing well, Finn, I will see you again soon.

The priest sat with his jaw agape as the daemon vanished.

'You were not hallucinating,' Edom said. 'The daemon is real.'

'He is,' Finn confirmed, exhausted, 'or we are both sharing the illusion.'

'Are you his champion?' Edom asked.

'I think not. I do not deliberately serve his needs.'

'Maybe he is using you to satisfy his own agenda,' Edom suggested.

'Then he is using us both, Priest,' Finn slurred, fatigue claiming him.

'What? How?'

'I do not know. But you did not see him through some great gift you have, Edom, he allowed you to see him. It serves his purpose in some way. He wants you to know that I am not mad and that I do not serve him.'

'He seeks to validate you beyond any doubt in my mind.'

'Perhaps. I do not try to outthink him, priest, I try not to think of him at all,' Finn said.

Edom felt a strange comfort from the daemon's visit and was now fully awake as though his soul had been charged in his sleep. The daemon was real. It was proof of at least some form of heaven and hell. His life and his faith had not been misplaced all these years. It was a strange epiphany but a welcome one, nonetheless.

'Sleep, Finn,' Edom said quietly. 'I will pray to the Lord God for guidance. Perhaps he will help us in our time of need.'

'It would take someone to, priest, for I am exhausted,' Finn replied and promptly fell asleep.

Printed in Great Britain
by Amazon